OVERTURE

1

Bacon and egg. Streaky bacon cut very thin and cooked not too crisp, leaving a bit of succulence in the meat. The eggs still wobbly on top – lifted out of the pan at the precise moment when the white is neither liquid nor solid, but melting. The Barlow family's morning ritual since time immemorial.

Except that this morning, Monday June the nineteenth, the ritual was compromised because Carly had a cold. My only daughter, ten years old going on fifteen, had a runny nose and a sore throat, and was standing in the kitchen, still wearing her pyjamas and asking for a day off school.

This was out of the question. I had to go to work, at Opera London, where I was casting director. And my wife the Diva, known professionally as Lindsey Templeton, was still in bed. She had a première that night and couldn't have her routine disrupted, even by an ill daughter. The nanny had been sacked the previous month for thieving, and we were desperate to avoid getting another. And Mum wasn't free until pick-up time, or so she said. Carly simply had to pull herself together and get to school.

"You're not really ill, Carly," I said. "You're just tired. Now get dressed, then come and eat your breakfast." She stomped upstairs without a word, and reappeared two minutes later, miraculously clad in her hideous maroon and black school uniform.

In my usual state of suppressed panic I'd overcooked the bacon, and the eggs were hard as nails. Carly pushed away her plate in disgust and began to bawl her head off.

"Keep quiet, for God's sake," I hissed, "or you'll wake your mother."

No way was she going to eat another morsel, so I picked up her school bag and helped her with her coat. Then I bundled her into the back of the car and made sure she was strapped in.

"Daddy, why can't I have the day off school?" she whined, as I pulled away. "My head hurts. And so does my throat."

"You said that last week, Carly, and you were fine when you got there. I asked Mrs Bodley."

"Mrs Bodley's really harsh."

"See how it goes. Perhaps Granny can come and get you if you're still feeling poorly at break time."

"Why can't Mummy come? Emma Anstruther-Fawcett's mother always comes to get her when she's ill."

"Because Mummy's got a show tonight, darling. She needs to rest."

When we arrived at school two little cherry-red spots in the middle of each cheek told me she was heading for a swift return home, and as she tottered towards the main building she looked as if she was about to faint. But she saw Emma what's-her-name on the way in, and began an animated conversation. Maybe we'd get away with it.

No such luck. At 11.15, when I emerged from my casting meeting, there was a message from the school. They'd tried home, but the Diva hadn't answered. Probably out at Lucio's having her coffee and croissants, oh, and freshly-squeezed orange juice.

The message was not good news. The school secretary, Mrs Billington, sounded concerned. *"Oh, Mr Barlow, I'm sorry to bother you, but Charlotte is not well. I think it would be a good idea if you took her home. Please ring us when you get this – I can't raise Mrs Barlow."*

I rang the school. Mrs Billington answered promptly. "Mr Barlow, thank goodness. It's some time since I rang. Charlotte has a temperature of 102."

So I rang Mum. The usual delicate negotiation.

"Oh that poor girl," Mum said. "I suppose that wife of yours is cosseting herself in some massage parlour, or whatever opera singers do when they're preparing for one of their great performances. And you are at work, leaving Charlotte to Derek and me. She sees more of us than she does of her own parents."

"I'm really sorry Mum. I know you said you weren't free. But please, we have a serious problem, which is not of our own making. It sounds as if Carly's quite bad."

2

"Very well, James," she sighed. "I'll ask your father."

I heard a thud at the other end of the line, followed by a muffled, but obviously bad-tempered conversation. I looked up from my desk. Grace, my exceptionally beautiful assistant, smirked at me.

"It's decided, James," said Mum. "Your father will pick Charlotte up from school now, and I will leave a can of soup for their lunch. Then I can still have my early afternoon bridge at Cecilia's. Or do you begrudge me my few precious hours of freedom?"

"Does Dad mind? He sounded a bit grumpy."

"Leaving aside the fact that you have not asked whether *I* mind, James dear, I'm sure the outing will do him good. He says The Ashes are on the television. But there always seems to be cricket, he doesn't need to watch it all."

"Mum, one more thing. If Carly's really bad, would you help us out for a few days? Lindsey's off to Salzburg tomorrow, and I've got a busy time at work. That Russian billionaire, Sergei Rebroff, is in town."

"I thought he was in charge of a football club."

"No mother, that's Roman Abramovitch. They're friends, apparently. Anyway, Rebroff wants to chuck a huge sum of money at one of the European opera companies. We've got to schmooze him, and I'm going to be pretty tied up."

"You don't give me much choice, do you James? What does schmooze mean?"

"It means we have to be nice to him. To try and get some of his money."

I put the phone down. Grace got up from her chair, and bent over the photocopier, pretending to check something. The gold tooling on her Dolce & Gabbana jeans stood out, pointing up the jellies-on-springs perfection of her buttocks. I might have given up my singing career, but office work had its consolations.

2

I first set eyes on Lindsey Templeton in the canteen at the Royal London Academy of Music. All the other singers, including me, were sitting at the singers' table, where traditionally the sopranos on the opera course would dismantle each other's egos behind brittle smiles and health-giving vitamin drinks. Lindsey had arrived late for her first term, having undergone some gynaecological procedure which cast doubt, as I was later to discover, on her chances of bearing children. She sat alone at the next table, looking pale, frightened, and irresistible.

"Lindsey isn't it?" I said. Please come and sit with us. I'll shift along."

"No, no, please don't worry. I don't want to interrupt."

"Then I'll come and sit with you. Do you mind?"

"No, of course not."

Cora, my Dutch girlfriend of the time, snorted, but I didn't care. I took my half-finished fish and chips and manoeuvred myself into position opposite the most beautiful creature I had ever seen.

She had jet-black hair, which hung for miles down her beautifully straight back and brushed the waistband of her tight-fitting jeans. From the front, if you could for a moment stop yourself being dragged into the depths of her huge brown eyes, you couldn't fail to appreciate either the peaches-and-cream perfection of her skin, or the pout of her tempting lips. When she smiled, which was often, these parted to reveal a row of bright white teeth which made you want to run your tongue along them to confirm there were no imperfections.

The idea that this vision of beauty might ever be mine was absurd, but I had the arrogance of youth on my side, and I was, at that time anyway, one of the stars of the Opera Course. This did not stop me from making a complete arse of myself.

"You're not eating fish and chips, then?" I ventured. "Very wise. Have you noticed all the bits of fish are exactly the same size and shape?"

"No, I hadn't noticed that. You haven't told me your name."

"Jamie Barlow. Known to everyone here as Jamie baaaah low, owing to the persistent nature of my vibrato."

"Oh God, don't talk about vibrato. My *bête noire*."

"You can't mean that that swan-like neck of yours can produce anything other than a sound of liquid perfection? "

"Well, I can't really say, can I?"

"I have no doubt, Lindsey Templeton, that you are the finest singer ever to cross the threshold of the RLAM. It must be so. One only has to look at you. Whereas I have an ageing face that only a mother could love, and a wobble to match. Your mother, I take it, has no such problems, since her offspring is the most gorgeous person I have ever set eyes on."

"My mother died when I was two. A road accident. I don't remember her at all".

"God I'm so sorry." I blushed to the roots of my receding hairline. "I'm a tithead, aren't I?"

"You weren't to know."

She smiled, without much conviction. Then she picked up her untouched salad, stacked her plate on the trolley and walked sadly out of the room. Cora gave a nasty laugh behind my back. So I sloped off for a long, self-indulgent walk in the park, convinced I'd blown it with the woman with whom I had already fallen hopelessly in love.

But, amazingly enough, she liked me too. I was rapidly turning what had been a considerable talent into a wasted opportunity, and I was lecherous to the point of absurdity. But even so it seemed I had struck a chord with her. She took me to Rutland, to her Dad's farm where she was brought up. We rode horses, fed lambs, and milked cows. Well, Lindsey did. I was hopeless at the Great Outdoors, and spent the evenings being entertained by Lindsey's father Albert, who teased me mercilessly for being a Townie.

Lindsey's singing, meanwhile, was going from strength to strength. Her teacher was gradually ironing out her voice's slightly intrusive wobble and replacing it with a thread of spun gold, which Lindsey was learning to control at will.

My singing, however, was lurching from crisis to crisis. Whatever ability I had was being methodically dismantled by an octogenarian singing professor called Hubert Gordon-Farquharson. He used to take me through a series of vocal exercises at the beginning of each lesson.

"Did that HURT?" The important bits of every sentence barked out like a Rottweiler.

"Yes, Hubert, it did a bit".

"Good. It was AWful. Whoever taught you to sing like THAT? If you wish to sing like THAT you had better take up invisible mending in CLAPham."

The lessons were almost wholly counter-productive, but at least they were entertaining. That's probably why I never left him. And probably why I never had much success in a career whose unimpressive pinnacle came a couple of years later.

Lindsey and I had both spent the summer singing in the chorus at Glyndebourne. A more hedonistic first job it would be hard to imagine. Enormous quantities of alcohol were consumed. A huge amount of sex was had. Thank God she and I were there together, because it's almost impossible to emerge from a season at the Glyndebourne Festival without having shagged someone, and we were very happy to stick to each other.

In the autumn of that same year, we both sang on the Glyndebourne Tour. Several performances in the theatre at Glyndebourne itself were followed by shows in Manchester, Norwich, Southampton, Oxford and Plymouth. Lindsey was singing Fiordiligi in *Cosi fan Tutte*, a fiendish role, but one which turned into a huge success for her. Suddenly everyone was talking about her. She agreed terms with one of the biggest agencies in London, and was discussing plans with Paris, Amsterdam, and Salzburg.

I, on the other hand, was still in the chorus. But I had been allowed, despite my by now threadbare vocal technique, to understudy the role of Eisenstein in Johann Strauss's *Die Fledermaus*, a role written for a tenor but often sung by clapped-out baritones like me.

My big chance came in Manchester, at the Palace Theatre, where the tenor whom I was understudying fell ill. He was also ill the following week in Plymouth. I had a ball. And, more importantly, earned four extra performance fees, with which I bought Lindsey a sensational sapphire-and-diamond-cluster engagement ring.

She had agreed to tie the knot while we lay in a post-coital glow one night after a particularly debauched Glyndebourne party.

"Look, Linds, there's no doubt that you are the most beautiful creature on God's earth. I know I'm a raddled old tosser with a crap voice and no career prospects, but just now you gave the impression of liking me rather a lot. Is there any chance that you might hitch that gorgeous voice, not to mention those no-less-gorgeous breasts, to yours truly, till death us do part?"

"Jamie, do you think you could say something without trying to be funny? Just for once? This is quite important, that is if I catch your meaning right."

"Yes, yes of course. Okay, here we go. I love you with every fibre of my being. Please will you marry me?"

"Yes darling, I will. I will love you for ever."

Which, perhaps rather surprisingly, considering our recent exertions and especially considering the amount of Valpolicella I'd consumed, caused me to experience erection, as my old pederast of an English teacher used to say. So Lindsey obligingly arranged herself on top of me and we enjoyed a night of the utmost pre-marital bliss.

We were impossibly happy. But there was one cloud on the horizon. Since before College Lindsey had been fighting a battle between her singing and her gynaecological problems. Something called endometriosis kept poking its snout into her extraordinary talent. The silvery quality of her voice fought a constant battle with her fearsome abdominal pain.

Often it seemed that the more uncomfortable she was, the more breathtakingly she sang. I particularly remember one February concert in the RLAM's Great Hall. Those of us who had made it to the building had braved icy pavements and bitter winds. Lindsey, with the Academy's Period Instrument Orchestra (rather new and exciting in those days), was singing Handel's heart-rendingly beautiful *Lascia ch'io pianga*, from his opera *Rinaldo*. Her face was pale as death itself. She seemed to be pulling the emotion of the aria out of the core of her being. "Let me weep over my cruel fate", she sang, while only I in the audience knew that she was being tormented by stabbing pains in her womb, right next to her diaphragm, the engine-room of the singer's body.

You never knew when Lindsey was going to be absent for a few days, as she went for yet another scrape, or whatever other vile thing they were doing to her insides. And as I got to know her better, I started to understand that nobody should be born female in this world. Periods, smear tests, stirrups. Nancy Mitford is supposed to have said that having a baby was like trying to force an orange through your nostril. Thank God I'm a man. Give me the chore of shaving and an overactive sex drive any day.

It was just after our engagement that we met John Standish, an opera-mad gynaecologist with a hilarious sense of humour. Well, I thought it was hilarious. "John Standish at your cervix, Madam" he would say, as his gloved hand made its well-lubricated way into Lindsey's most intimate parts. He was the first one to break the news to me.

"Miss Templeton, you are, I'm afraid, well aware that you have endometriosis. This tricky disease is gradually reducing the capacity of your womb. We can do an annual spring clean for a few more years yet, since you are so young, and otherwise very fit." (I'm afraid he did wink at me when he said this. He'll be struck off one day.) "However, the one thing more or less guaranteed to give you some relief from your discomfort is for you to fall pregnant. It may put the disease on hold, so to speak. Without wishing to prescribe the terms and conditions of your private life, you and Mr Barlow should consider putting a bun in the oven as soon as possible. Eventually you will almost certainly have to have a hysterectomy, but you may be able to have several kiddies in the meantime. Always assuming James isn't short of swimmers, of course. And if you are planning to marry, I shall, as the only person in the world who knows your fallopian tubes as well as your unrivalled vocal cords, expect an invitation to the wedding."

"Thank you, Mr Standish. Of course we'll invite you", whispered Lindsey. She didn't look too good.

"Now don't upset yourself, my dear," said Standish. "The disease itself may not be a bundle of laughs, but you knew about that already. This bit is good news, surely. Go forth and multiply. James, how often do you think you can point Percy at the pudenda?"

"Er, well, er, er, a lot. Percy's very keen on Miss Templeton's pudenda. Well, I mean, he would be if he'd seen them, or it, or whatever, which of course he hasn't, ha ha ha, us not being hitched yet, and everything."

"Shut up, Jamie", said Lindsey. "You are a buffoon." She wiped away a tear which was leaving a trail of mascara behind it on its journey down her cheek. We left in a welter of mumbled thanks and goodbyes, and on the way out I walked backwards into the door frame, semi-concussing myself in the process. Lindsey picked me up and marched me out into a wonderful world of sex, sex and more sex.

We married in the spring of 1996. Lindsey's Dad, who had remained a widower, made a memorable speech, full of humour and love, and regret about Lindsey's Mum, Lottie. I replied, droning on for hours about how it was terrific to be marrying a star, and how Albert might be losing a daughter, but was gaining an overdraft (well I'd never heard it before. And it was true). And then Angus Lennox, my Best Man, made a superb speech. He was about to become the hottest young conductor in Britain – "the new Simon Rattle", they kept calling him. With just one well-chosen story about the scatological consequences of my eating seventy-eight pickled chillies at a sitting in a Taverna in Cambridge when we were undergraduates, and a lovely bit about how Lindsey and I clearly adored each other, he gave the performance of his life. It was a wonderful day, only slightly marred by Standish putting his hand on Cora, my ex-girlfriend's arse. He had had a phenomenal amount to drink. But she loved that kind of thing really, and after an appropriate amount of loud complaining she took him outside, reappearing half an hour later with a radiant smile on her face and what looked suspiciously like grass stains on her Dries van Noten dress.

Lindsey proved the excellence of Standish's advice by getting pregnant almost immediately and feeling better than she had done for years. Charlotte Anne, named after her maternal grandmother, was born on September the sixteenth, 1996, a bouncing, healthy baby of 7lb 12oz. Her mother was the beneficiary of an excellent epidural injection administered by Mr John Standish, who had insisted on managing Lindsey's pregnancy himself. She had as painless a delivery as anyone had a right to expect.

And miraculously the endometriosis seemed, as Standish had suggested it might, to have been put on hold. Lindsey went back to her career within six weeks of Charlotte's birth, and carried her round everywhere, dutifully followed by yours truly, who by now had given up singing and turned into a house husband. As a sideline I managed Lindsey's career – travel, hotels, rehearsal schedules. My dog-like devotion to my increasingly starry wife was only occasionally impaired by the dawning realisation that I needed a career of my own if I wasn't going to go mad.

On her second birthday, Charlotte walked into our bedroom at 4.30am, ready to open her presents. She took a huge breath, and announced to her sleepy parents: "I'm Carly". Carly, for God's sake. She had picked it up from a ghastly American sitcom involving a precocious eight-year-old, who lived in San Francisco with her lesbian parents. They kept meeting famous people from the world of television, which gave little Carly the excuse to say cute things. However, despite my best efforts, the name stuck, and from then on Carly Barlow would answer to nothing else.

The opportunity I needed to drag me out of this domestic suffocation came suddenly, a couple of years later. Out of the blue, Angus Lennox called me.

"Jamie, it's Angus. Look, old chap, you know I'm conducting *Rigoletto* next year at Opera London. I've just been for a meeting with Lord Dunwich, the General Administrator. Great excitement. We can't cast the bloody thing because the casting director – you know, that old poof Sturgis – has just been sacked. He was having an affair with one of the baritones on the Young Singers' programme, apparently. Chap called Pogson. Not considered appropriate behaviour for a man in his position, etc. etc. Asked to clear his desk. They're trying to keep it out of the papers."

"Bugger me, Angus."

"No need for that, darling, you can leave that to Pogson. Now the thing is, they need someone new, fast. It seems to me you'd be the ideal candidate, and I told his Lordship so in no uncertain terms. Remembers your singing. Wasn't very complimentary, I'm afraid. But when I told him who you were hitched to he came up like a lily. Said he'd heard from everyone that Lindsey Templeton's hubby-manager was a sound chap, very wise about singers, and with an encyclopaedic knowledge of the repertoire. Ideal candidate, he said. You're a shoo-in, Jamie old thing. Do you want it?"

"Angus, it's a golden opportunity. Lindsey's agent can do her management – they've been wanting to take it off my hands for ages. But what in God's name am I going to do about Carly?"

"Get a nanny. Or an au pair. Seems to be quite a common solution."

"Lindsey won't like it."

"Why not? Is she worried you're going to shaft the new arrival? I say, why don't you get a bloke instead, Jamie? Apparently male au pairs are all the rage. I don't imagine Lindsey will be worried about you shafting a bloke. Anyway you can't turn this down. It's one of those blink-and-you'll-miss-it chances that can change your life. And I want you in place so that when Dunwich and the current Music Director leave, you and I can take over. The Dream Team. No harm in a bit of forward planning, is there?"

"No, quite. But I do have to run it past Linds."

"She's at ENO, isn't she? *Eugene Onegin*, if I'm not mistaken."

"Absolutely. I can ask her tonight, when she gets back from rehearsals. She'll hate the idea."

"*Coraggio*, old thing. Show the Deev who's boss. Time you stood up for yourself, Jamie."

But Lindsey, unbelievably, thought it was a fantastic idea. She made me ring him back there and then.

"Angus, it's Jamie. The Deev says yes."

"Terrific, Jamie. See you in the corridors of power."

And I became casting director of Opera London, and rushed around the world to view the up-and-comings, and the stars we just had to engage. And at home we started to employ a succession of dippy nannies. And even though we had ignored Angus's advice, and gone for girls every time, I managed not to have an affair with any of them, because my exquisite wife, still blessedly free from the plague of endometriosis, continued to provide me, when she was in Town, with the most blissful sex. And all was well in the Barlow/Templeton household, except that, despite Percy's best efforts, Lindsey just didn't get pregnant, and Carly remained an only child. But we had plenty of time. Didn't we?

ACT 1: THE MARRIAGE OF FIGARO

3

Lindsey turned up at the theatre at her usual time, about 3.30. She looked, as she always did on the day of a show, relaxed and gorgeous. But she was acting. It was the first night of Opera London's brand new production of *Figaro*, and Lindsey, the brightest star in Britain's operatic firmament, was singing her first Countess in London. The world and its wife would be there. Underneath that display of self-belief she was in turmoil.

Three years previously she had chosen to be represented worldwide by a woman of impeccable operatic connections, based in Zurich. Lindsey was now part of a stable of twelve of the most sought-after singers in the world. Her former agent, a stick-thin, balding man named Stephen Gibson, was not pleased.

"My dear, you will regret this," he had said when she told him of her plans to leave him. "I will fuck up your career. You will never work again in this country, or anywhere else, if I can help it."

Thank God the opera world was small enough for most people to realise exactly what was going on when this choice individual started playing his game. "Lindsey Templeton's voice is not big enough for American opera houses", or "have you heard her recently? That wobble is becoming a real problem", he would say to managers and impresarios around the world. But what really upset Lindsey, and caused her to approach every British press night in a lather of apprehension, was that Janet Hopkirk, the opera critic of The Statesman, was having an affair with him, and every review this woman wrote followed an anything-but-hidden agenda.

Lindsey had phoned me at twelve o'clock.

"Jamie, is that Hopkirk woman in tonight?"

"'Fraid so, sweetheart. Don't worry. No-one takes the slightest notice of her."

We'd arranged to get a plate of pasta together at Giorgio's in Vauxhall Bridge Road, just a few doors down from the theatre. They often stayed on after lunch just to accommodate Lindsey, who was their favourite customer and always ate at four on the day of a show.

She didn't speak more than a few words the entire time we were there. They knew what she wanted – spaghetti napoletana without too much garlic. I had carbonara. The difference was I finished mine. I had never seen her this nervous.

"Don't worry Linds. The rehearsals have been fabulous. Angus says it's the best Countess he's ever heard. And he's conducting the thing."

She played with her spaghetti for a bit and ate two mouthfuls. Then without a word she got up and left the restaurant. Old Giorgio himself was watching.

"Do not worry, *meester* Jamie. She weel be very great. Tell 'er *in bocca al lupo* from Giorgio."

No fool, Old Giorgio. The show was fantastic, unbelievable. Angus coaxed wonderful performances out of the whole cast, but none more so than Lindsey's Countess. It was a combination of robustness, beauty of tone and scintillating technique. *Porgi Amor*, her opening number, a masterpiece of control.

It's one of the most difficult things Mozart ever wrote, and comes from nowhere at the beginning of Act Two. She's been sweating it out in her dressing-room, scared to death, since the start of the show. The curtain goes up to reveal her lying in bed in her negligée. She has been worn down by years of the Count's neglect, and with quiet dignity bemoans the loss of his love. And Lindsey spins the most exquisite, rapt thread of floated tone I have ever heard. The house is silent afterwards, holding its breath.

So it goes on. Her difficult scale upwards to a *pianissimo* top C in the Act Two trio with Susanna and the Count, is thrown off as if she were singing *Baa Baa Black Sheep*. When she sings her great aria *Dove Sono* in Act Three she wrings your soul with her terrible sadness at his behaviour.

Then she comes on for her final entrance. Her revolting and absurd husband has spent the day trying to get her maid into bed, while at the same time carpeting her for supposed indiscretions with his valet Figaro, and with the page Cherubino. Yet at the end, when the game is up, she forgives him in some of the most beautiful music ever written. *Contessa, perdono*, he sings, grovelling in front of the whole household, and she, full of composure even in her desperate sadness, replies: *piu docile io sono, e dico di si – yes I forgive you, because I am kinder than you are.* Lindsey's rendition is unbearably moving. The release of tension and celebration of beauty that only opera, at its very best, is capable of. And it makes me, Jamie Barlow, feel exceptionally proud of my wife the Diva.

There was a particularly excellent performance from Julian Pogson – the English baritone who as a young man had put paid to my predecessor Sturgis's career. He was the ultimate Company Artist. He'd come up through the ranks (he'd slept with most of them – the male ones that is). He might have been a pompous arse, but that was rather a good qualification for playing the Count.

But the other star of the evening was Angus Lennox. The wind playing was exquisite, and the strings sounded like the Vienna Philharmonic. Ensemble with the stage was flawless, and everyone agreed that his pacing was superb – the music working together with the drama, never getting in its way. *Opera London's Saviour?* one of the papers had queried a few days before. Everyone knew he wanted the now vacant Music Directorship, and there were many who thought it should be his.

Artistically the evening had been a triumph. Even Janet Hopkirk , whom I spotted sitting just behind me, was looking happy. But there was another factor, which everyone in the Company knew was crucial for its future. Sergei Rebroff, the Russian billionaire with a mysterious past and more money than God, was in the audience. What did he think? We all trooped upstairs to the post-show party to find out.

Gregory Knipe, pillar of society, Tory MP for East Penge, and Chairman of Opera London, stood at the door of the Telenorth Bar, his broadest smile releasing a cloud of halitosis which cowed all but the hardiest of his interviewees into instant submission. Fat, and sweating copiously into a striped caftan, he looked nauseatingly pleased with himself.

Beside him stood his idiotic wife Angela, who looked (and probably smelled) a bit mousy next to her flamboyant husband. They would normally have been flanked by Lord Dunwich, in his capacity as General Administrator, and Lady Dunwich, who had a reputation for getting a bit

15

tipsy on these occasions. However, Dunwich was retiring very shortly, and becoming lax in observing the niceties. Also it was no secret that His Lordship loathed the idea of "selling out to some Russian arriviste crook", so it was no surprise that they had absented themselves for the evening. Rumour had it that he had spent the day at Lord's.

But Lord and Lady Dunwich would in any case have been eclipsed by the other people in Knipe's little group. Dominating the semicircle were two very bulky bald heavies with what I am sure were guns under their jackets. I thought guns weren't allowed in London theatres, but I soon saw why in this case an exception had been made. Flanked by these two distinguished-looking gentlemen, charming to a fault and dressed in a Savile Row suit and Church's brogues, was Sergei Ivanevitch Rebroff. His picture had been on the front page of every newspaper in the country during the past week, since he had arrived in Britain. Everyone at the party knew that he had been seen at every opera house that mattered. Not only was he mad keen on opera, but he was also, at the last count, worth £3.5bn, having left all over Russia a trail of share dilution schemes and displaced employees in his perfumed wake.

The Chairman extended a pudgy little damp hand towards Lindsey, who flinched as if under attack. "Lindsey, my dear, you were sensational", he oozed. "May I present Sergei Ivanevitch Rebroff? Sergei, meet Lindsey Templeton, Opera London's most valuable asset."

Sergei Rebroff. No-one at Opera London had spoken of anything else for weeks. He was absurdly rich. Dear God in heaven, why did he have to be handsome, too? He looked Lindsey up and down in a way I didn't like one bit.

"My God, *Contessa*. Your singing was captivating. And you are so beautiful."

"Mr Rebroff, what a pleasure to meet you. You are even more good-looking than your pictures in the newspapers."

She fancied him. Cow.

"You must not flatter me, Miss Templeton. It is I who am in awe of you."

His English was exceptionally good, and he affected every accessory of the perfectly-dressed English gentleman. This Anglophilia was what gave everyone hope that he would settle his millions somewhere in Britain.

The Royal Opera was interested, so it was said, but not at the expense of losing its independence. Glyndebourne had shown him the door - the Christie family had had much the same reaction to him as Lord Dunwich

16

had. They liked the sound of his money, naturally, but weren't willing to kowtow to his every demand, and didn't want East Sussex to stink of Russian scandal. So now he was being assiduously wooed by the rest, who, Dunwich apart, had no such scruples. The front-runners among the British companies were English National Opera and Opera London.

But my thoughts were not on the money. They had been hijacked by Rebroff's eyes, which were glued to Lindsey's cleavage. He had turned his back on Knipe, and appeared to be speaking sweet nothings to my wife. She was pink-cheeked – the same spots of high colour I had seen on Carly's face this morning.

I nudged her arm. "Lindsey, no-one's introduced me".

"Oh, Jamie, sorry. This is Sergei Rebroff. Sergei, this is my husband Jamie Barlow. He is the casting director here."

"The performance was great compliment to your work, Mr Barlow," he said. "And your wife is great compliment to your taste, both in artists and in women".

Lindsey gave a high-pitched giggle.

"Thank you Mr Rebroff," I said.

"Call me Sergei, please."

"Yes, of course, Sergei. And you must call me Jamie. Lindsey is a wonderful singer, don't you think?"

"The finest *Contessa* I have ever heard. When I was boy I heard all great singers at Bolshoi. I never cared for Schwarzkopf – too *innig*."

"Yes, quite." What the bloody hell did *innig* mean?

"My favourite *Contessa* till now was Kiri Te Kanawa. But Lindsey, this is something different. Tonight she changed my life."

He touched one of the heavies gently on the shoulder, and said something to him. The bald head nodded, and its owner moved off to fetch two glasses of wine from a nearby waiter, who blanched visibly. The wine was duly brought to Lindsey and Sergei, who clinked glasses, and she smiled one of her most gorgeous smiles. The green-eyed monster rose like a hot lump in my throat. I had been seamlessly excluded from the conversation, and had no alternative but to look elsewhere in the room, both for a drink and for someone to talk to.

Gregory Knipe, who had clearly been equally put out when Rebroff turned his back on him, had struck up a conversation with Janet Hopkirk. This encounter was to be avoided at all costs, so I wandered over towards Angus, who was propping up the bar. He had his arm draped round the neck of Gloria Forrest, the pretty redhead who had sung Susanna in the show. His hand was hovering perilously close to her all-but-completely-exposed bosom.

"Aye-aye, Jamie. What's going on over there then? Lindsey seems to be very taken with Sergei Rebroff. Is she negotiating on behalf of the Company?"

"Very funny, Gussie."

"Who the hell are Mutt and Jeff? The two baldies."

"Mutt and Jeff are presumably the bodyguards," I said. "You'd need them, wouldn't you, if you were worth 3.5 billion?"

"Absolutely. It's an eye-catching sum of money."

"I think Lindsey thinks so, too." I looked over my shoulder at her little group. Lindsey was smiling broadly, and clearly enjoying herself

"Anyway Gussie," I said, "you don't deserve me to say so, but you were sensational tonight. So were you, Gloria. Well done."

Gloria smiled, and wiggled in a bit closer to Angus. He said: "Thanks old boy. Listen. I need to talk to you urgently. Any chance of lunch tomorrow? I want you on your own. Without the Deev."

"She's off to Salzburg tomorrow. She's commuting back here for the performances. You agreed."

"Yes of course I did. *Bacchus* at one o'clock?

"Better make it twelve. We've both got an audition at 1.30."

"Oh yes, you're quite right. That American blonde with the nice bottom." Gloria licked Angus's index finger like a lolly. "Twelve o'clock then. You needn't come, little Gloria. I need to talk to your boss alone."

Gloria giggled. I don't think she cared as much about what was happening at lunch tomorrow, or even about the American blonde, as she did about the next couple of hours. She fastened her mouth onto Angus's, and he waved me away, winking at me in mid-snog.

Sergei was still deep in conversation with Lindsey. I walked over in what I hoped was a purposeful, John-Wayne-sort-of-way. Sergei smiled at me and put his arm round my shoulder.

"Hallo again, Jimmy", he said. "I am talking to Lindsey about her trip to Salzburg. Fiordiligi, I gather. *Cosi fan Tutte* is my favourite opera. Except for Russian repertoire. When you go, Lindsey?"

"Tomorrow."

"You come in my private jet. I come with you."

Lindsey glanced at me, and than looked at the floor.

"I'm so sorry, Sergei, I really can't. You see I must go home and pack, then I have to catch the flight that the Festival have booked for me. If I don't take that flight they might not be very happy."

The 6.40 Freshair to Salzburg was the only direct flight available from London, and all singers hated it with a passion. But all the Salzburg Festival cared about was that she should arrive on time. Bet she'd have said yes if I hadn't been there.

"I come anyway," said Rebroff. "I will see Göstl-Saurau tomorrow. Tatyana, please ring Graf von Göstl-Saurau first thing to arrange appointment. He is head of Salzburg Festival. He will see me, I'm sure."

A small, exquisitely dressed woman, whom I had taken for a Board wife, but who, it now became clear, was Rebroff's secretary, said "Yes, Sergei", and gave Lindsey an appraising glance. Then she wrote something down in a little book which she took from her handbag. As she put it back, she caught my eye. She wasn't wholly unattractive, I noticed. But in those bright blue eyes I was sure I detected a trace of pity.

I took Lindsey's arm and said, "Darling, you've got a terribly early start. I think we should go."

"Oh, Jamie, not yet. We've only just arrived."

"Lindsey, you need a decent night's sleep. So do I. Carly's ill – I'm worried she's got flu, by the way. You've had a great evening, but we really have to go. I'm sure Mr Rebroff will forgive us."

Sergei looked quizzically at me. Then he transferred his gaze back to Lindsey, and his face softened.

"It has been my great pleasure, Lindsey. You must do as your husband says." He bowed. Buggered if Lindsey didn't almost curtsey.

"Goodbye, Sergei," she said. "See you in Salzburg, then."

I frog-marched her crossly through the throng, ignoring their smiles and calls of "Bravo, Lindsey". Knipe was standing by the door, still deep in conversation with Janet Hopkirk.

"Forgive me for interrupting, Gregory," I said. "Lindsey and I are going. I just wanted to thank you for the party."

"So soon, Lindsey?" he said.

"Yes, I'm sorry Mr Knipe, but Jamie thinks I should get home. I have an early flight tomorrow morning."

"I quite understand, my dear. Thank you for a wonderful performance." He turned back to Janet Hopkirk, and they resumed their conversation.

Lindsey and I made our way downstairs and into a taxi. She spoke not one word all the way home.

4

Lindsey bumped her huge suitcase downstairs and into a taxi at the absurdly early hour of 4.30. I managed only the bleariest and most perfunctory of goodbyes before rolling over for another couple of hours' sleep.

When my alarm went off at 7 she had already taken off, savouring the early morning delights of Freshair. Even with the hour's difference, she would land in plenty of time to make the 1030 model showing and production talk which presaged all opera rehearsal periods.

I went straight round to Mum and Dad's to find out how Carly was. Mum said she'd not got out of bed since she got back from school, except to go to the loo. She'd been so dizzy she'd had to be helped.

I went up to see her.

"Where's Mummy?" she asked. She looked terrible – sweaty and pale.

"She's gone to Salzburg, sweetheart."

"How was the show?"

"Mummy was fantastic, darling. How are you feeling?"

"My head really hurts. Can I come home?"

"Better to stay here with Granny and Grandpa. Granny will molly-coddle you."

"I don't want to be molly-coddled. I want to watch DVDs."

"Well I think you'd better stay here in bed while your head hurts so badly. You'll be better by tomorrow or the next day, and then you can come home and watch *The Sound of Music*. It's all about Salzburg, where Mummy is."

"*The Sound of Music* is a load of crap. I want to watch *Bridget Jones*. Emma says they say fuck in it."

21

"Carly, you mustn't use that kind of language. Do you want any breakfast?"

"No."

"Well, in that case try to sleep. I'll come back and see you this evening."

I offered today's portion of grovelling thanks to my mother, and sloped off to Queens Park Tube.

Lindsey rang while I was waiting for the Tube.

"Hi Jamie, I'm in the rehearsal room in Salzburg."

"Blimey, that was quick. Good journey, obviously?"

"Fine. Julian Pogson was on the plane. I hadn't realised he's doing Antonio in the *Figaro* here. He'll get awfully confused, flying back to do the Count in London. At least I'm in a different opera. We shared a cab – it only took ten minutes. How's Carly?"

"Not great. But she asked how the show had gone. Will you ring her later?"

"I'll try. But there's a note from Göstl-Saurau saying we're all invited out to dinner. Sergei Rebroff's going to be there."

"He doesn't waste any time, does he? Make sure you tell him to give his money to Opera London. We don't want Graf Heinrich von Göstl-Saurau getting his hands on it."

The Bacchus Taverna was trendy twenty years ago. Not any more. Same paper tablecloths, same fishing nets on the wall, probably the same bits of candle in the same wine bottles. But not an opera singer, or manager, or agent in sight. Just a die-hard clientele of women of a certain age, and a smattering of suited businessmen with their mistresses. Very discreet. And in Eccleston Square, just down the road from Opera London's theatre.

"Angus, this is all bloody mysterious," I said. "What's going on?"

"Well, Jamie, where to start? No, don't order any wine. I want you clear-headed."

"Let's assume for the moment you're not a bit woozy this morning, then. How was Gloria?"

"Shut up and listen, you old pervert. We all know who was the real star last night. Not Lindsey, although she was wonderful. Not me, although I was too. The real star yesterday was Rebroff. Everyone wants to get their hands on the dosh. What I am about to suggest to you is that the folks who need it the most are you and me. Jamie Barlow and Angus Lennox. So are you sitting comfortably? Then I'll begin.

"I told you four years ago that you and I were the Dream Team, right? And we still are. My career's going swimmingly, and you've done a great job casting. Okay, there was the unfortunate incident when you had to sack that Slovenian mezzo with hairs on her chest because she couldn't learn Geschwitz in *Lulu*, but broadly speaking you've got a good track record."

"Get to the point."

"Quite right, old thing. I have the germ of an idea about a Palace Coup."

A spotty, sullen boy took our order. Two moussakas and two glasses of mineral water. Yum.

"Angus, we don't need a Palace Coup. Dunwich is retiring next month, and the Music Directorship's vacant. All we have to do is apply for the jobs. We must have a good chance, surely?"

"Well, not really old chap. You see there's a spanner in the woodpile, or whatever you're allowed to say nowadays. His name is Gregory Knipe. He wants to install some fall guy as General Administrator, so he can run the Company himself, and he has his own candidate for MD."

"Who?"

"Leclerc. Stop jumping the gun."

"Okay, get on with it. You're saying we have to get rid of Knipe?"

"Exactly. And if we were to succeed I can't think it would be an entirely unpopular move within the Company, can you? He's got rid of half the staff. This is nominally to save money, a very laudable object I'm sure you'll agree. Whether it works is a moot point, especially since the same staff are mostly hired back in as freelancers, but what it certainly does is make Greg the Dreg a very unpopular chap. So perhaps it's worth asking at this stage why he's had to go down this road.

"We all know that Opera, like crime, doesn't pay. Therefore, in addition to the box office, every opera company needs further funding to make it viable. In Opera London's case, as with most of the major arts organisations in the UK, the bulk of this funding comes from the Arts Council, without which noble institution the company would cease to exist.

"We also know that the Arts Council loves Greg, precisely because he is the first Chairman in living memory to have an eye on the balance sheet. For years successive managements have run the Company as they believe an international opera company should be run, constantly striving for artistic excellence and not caring a great deal about how much it costs. So all of Opera London's best work has been achieved by allowing brilliant directors and designers to have their head when constructing shows. This is a high-risk strategy, because when you push the boundaries of Art, so to speak, you are bound to come up with a few stinkers as well as some productions of genuine brilliance. But you persist, because the good stuff is what gives a company its reputation.

"The unwelcome corollary of this is that when the punters don't like something, they don't come. Result: a dynamic, thrusting company full of self-confidence and artistic excellence. But with no money in the bank.

"The Powers That Were didn't worry too much about this, because they knew that either the Government or some philanthropist with a high artistic conscience would stump up when the chips were down. The Chairman, or the Music Director, or some other high-profile figure would tell the press that Armageddon was just round the corner, and that their precious Opera London was on borrowed time. Then someone would find the money from somewhere to bail them out. Hey presto: the bank account would look all black and lovely, and they could start the process all over again.

"But suddenly the goalposts have been moved. The Arts Council of England has announced that next time – well, what the mandarins have said is that there won't be a next time. Opera London is a valuable National Asset, etc. etc., but next time they venture up shit creek they will be left totally paddle-less."

The spotty boy brought our water. Angus waited till he had gone.

"So we come to my own favoured solution. You find a source of alternative income to keep the Company on the straight and narrow, and avoid the need for another bailout. Which is where Sergei Ivanevitch Rebroff comes in. He actually wants to endow a European company with untold millions, so he can have his name all over everything, and impress his influential chums.

"This approach is not without its disadvantages. Even assuming Opera London gets its hands on the loot, we don't know to what extent our pet Russian oligarch will demand artistic control. We may be stuck with fat Divas from Murmansk, who can't act for toffee. However, if you and I can convince him that we are the right chaps in the right company to mastermind his munificence, we can tackle that problem later.

24

"Greg the Dreg has tumbled this already, by the way, so don't get too excited yet. He thinks his best chance of keeping the job is to dispense with the Rebroff factor altogether. He is secretly building an impressive syndicate of donors. If he can put together enough dosh, he will be more attractive to the Arts Council chappies than poor old Sergei, with his barely legal billions."

The boy brought us each a sad-looking portion of moussaka, with a desultory salad and some limp chips. Angus completely ignored his.

"So to summarise, we have two tasks. First: we have to get rid of Knipe, so the mandarins are presented with only one viable option for the survival of the Company. And second: we have to persuade Sergei to donate his money to Opera London, with us as his management team. This task also involves persuading him that his plans have to be Arts-Council-friendly – unless that is, he has enough money to endow the Company for ever and ever Amen, thus enabling us to kiss goodbye to public funding altogether. This seems a tad unlikely, even for Sergei. What dost thou think, o fount of all knowledge and wisdom?"

I spat out a bit of aubergine which somehow managed to be both undercooked and watery.

"Okay, Angus, for starters, how in God's name do you propose to ditch Knipe? People have been trying to do it for years. And what's all this about Leclerc? You still haven't told me why we can't just get the jobs in the normal way."

A mirthless smile flitted across Angus's face. "This is the really juicy bit, Jamie. Olivier Leclerc is, as you know, a highly talented young French conductor, and, not to put too fine a point on it, a poisonous little queen. He is also revoltingly ambitious – not at all like me, you understand. What you almost certainly don't know is that he's making the beast with two backs with none other than our Chairman Gregory Knipe, Tory MP, who is hoping to become Arts Minister in the next Government, once the inconvenient matter of the General Election is out of the way."

"Olivier Leclerc is sleeping with Gregory Knipe? Don't be ridiculous. Knipe's a married man."

Angus took a demure sip of his fizzy water.

"Since when did that make the slightest difference? Pogson told me. Saw them in a restaurant last week. Went over for a chat. Knipe went puce and tried to bury his face in his moules marinière. But Leclerc was full of it. Introduced Knipe as his new boyfriend, and got up and kissed him full on the lips. To establish ownership, so to speak. Greg the Dreg didn't know where to put himself."

"So we assume that the reason bitchy little, Armani-clad Olivier is prepared to pursue this nauseating liaison is to secure the Music Directorship of Opera London?"

"Who knows? Maybe he finds the lovely Gregory exactly to his taste. What is certain is that, at the last Board meeting, Knipe announced that the way forward was to foster the *entente cordiale*. Some crap about artistic collaboration with the Théâtre du Châtelet. Suggested that Leclerc would make an ideal candidate for Music Director of both."

"Well, that ballses everything up, then."

"Quite. Unless we can dump Knipe. And at the moment I can only think of one potential powerful ally in that battle, and that is Sergei Rebroff."

Angus had picked up his fork, and started playing with his nasty-looking salad. He speared a bit of feta cheese and poked it into his mouth. He grimaced, and then spat it out.

"Jamie, this could be life-changing if we get it right. We need to get Sergei on side, and convince him that he has to get rid of Knipe. God alone knows how we achieve part two. But part one is to establish communication with Sergei. Which is where you come in."

"Now you've totally lost me."

"This is a bit delicate." He put down his fork with elaborate care. "It didn't escape anyone's notice last night that Sergei Ivanevitch Rebroff was rather taken with your good lady wife. I'm perfectly certain it didn't escape yours. Did you have a row about it afterwards?"

"No we didn't, actually. What the fuck's it got to do with you?"

"Bit delicate, as I said. Sorry. But very good news that you didn't cut up rough, because I think Lindsey, God bless her, may be the one to persuade His Russian Highness to divert the money our way. Is she going to see him again, by any magnificent chance?"

"You sly bugger, Angus. You know don't you? That he's flown to Salzburg this morning."

Angus made a visible effort not to look smug.

"A little bird told me. Is he chasing her?"

"Well, nominally he's gone to see Göstl-Saurau. But yes, frankly I'm perfectly certain he's chasing her. He's taking the cast out to dinner tonight."

"God, it's better than I thought. Can she sit next to him?"

"Angus, what precisely did you have in mind for my wife to do with Sergei Rebroff?"

"Let's stop pussyfooting around. We need Lindsey to get chummy with Sergei – okay, not too chummy, she's a sound girl, after all. But she needs to tell him to chuck his roubles our way. End of."

"Fuck." I drank the rest of my water. "What happens if she has an affair with him?"

"Will she?"

"God Angus, I don't think so, but she's been a bit out of sorts recently. You see, she's still not pregnant. We've been trying for another baby ever since Carly was born, and there's no sign. Lindsey's getting more and more snappy with me. And she was vilely flattered by that arsehole's attention last night, and I just wonder, well, I wonder whether she might succumb to temptation, if the temptation were strong enough."

There was silence while Angus tried to take in my outburst.

"Oh dear, Jamie," he said eventually, "that all came out in a bit of a rush. I know this baby thing can do funny things to people." He thought for a minute. "But look, whatever the state of her emotions, it's not going to do her any harm just to suggest Sergei puts his money our way, is it? I mean it'll mean a huge boost to your career, she must be pleased by that?"

"Maybe, maybe not. Christ, I don't know. Anyway, this morning I did actually suggest in a half-hearted sort of way that she might tell him to give his money to Opera London. She'll probably say something to him tonight."

Angus smiled. "Excellent news."

"Let's just hope that's as far as it goes."

"Quite, old boy. Oh, by the way, Sergei has a wife and two kids at home in Mother Russia, and he's all over *The Sun* saying whatever happens he'll never leave them, so don't fret too much." He looked much more cheerful. "Presumably she'll be home tomorrow night – we've got the second *Figaro* on Thursday."

"She's on the late Freshair. Home about midnight, with any luck."

"Can you bring the subject up?"

"Well, she won't talk about it on the day of a show, and I'm buggered if I'm tackling something this tricky over the phone, so I suppose I'll have to launch straight into it when she gets back. That'll go down well." I drank the last of my water, and looked at my watch.

27

"Oh my God, look at the time", I said. "It's twenty-five past. That American blonde will be waiting."

We hadn't eaten much. I for one wasn't particularly hungry.

5

The following day Carly, thank God, was much better, and I picked her up from Mum and Dad's at 6 o'clock and took her home, where she ate an encouraging amount of spag bol before going to bed at 9.00.

But at work all I'd been able to think of was the unwelcome image of Linsdey and Sergei going back to his hotel after dinner for a nightcap, or worse. And Angus was actually suggesting I encourage her.

What was I asking her to do? Go beyond the call of duty with Sergei so I could become General Manager of Opera London. Don't worry about anything so pitifully unimportant as screwing up our marriage, my darling, because my career's on the line here, and you can do what you like with Sergei Rebroff as long as we get his cash.

But I didn't hear from her until just after Carly had gone to bed, when she sent me a text to say her flight home was on time, and that she'd be getting a cab from Stansted, as she was exhausted. Could I pay the driver? She only had euros.

She walked through the front door at a quarter past midnight. Pausing only to leave her enormous bag in the hall, she walked straight up the stairs into Carly's room.

I went out to the waiting taxi. A very large driver with a number one haircut and a serious quantity of metal in his nose looked at me as if I was something the cat had dragged in. Or out, I suppose. It was pouring with rain.

"Eighty-three pounds."

I gave him seven tenners, two fivers, one pound coin and four fifty pees, plus a paper clip and assorted bits of paper from my pocket. He returned the paper and clip with a look of disgust, and then roared off into the night like Michael Schumacher, splashing my trousers with muddy water. I'd forgotten to get a receipt for Lindsey's accountant. I locked the house, and picked up her bag on my way upstairs.

Somehow she'd already had time to see Carly, then throw off her clothes and climb onto the bed. She lay there, totally naked, her skin shining like silver in the moonlight.

She watched me while I undressed, and then she pulled me towards her. Her lips closed around mine, and she kissed me, her tongue probing deep into my mouth. When I came up for air I said:

"Jesus, Linds. I wasn't expecting that. You've made Percy go all hard."

"Is it so surprising that I want to make love to my husband? Give Percy to me."

Pausing only for a moment to wonder whether she was fantasising about me being Sergei, I surrendered to her astonishing passion. We made the most complete, fabulous love, and we came together with moans and grunts loud enough to wake the whole street. We heard Carly's bedroom door open, and eased ourselves apart, rearranging the sheets demurely. The loo flushed, then Carly walked in.

"Hallo Mummy. You didn't say goodnight."

"I did, but you were fast asleep. Come and give me a kiss. Are you feeling better?"

"No. Daddy's making me go to school tomorrow. I want to stay here with you."

"Well you look better." They hugged each other.

"Can I sleep with you two?"

"Not tonight," said Lindsey. "I've got a show tomorrow, and I need a really good night's sleep. So do you, especially if you're going to school. Sorry if we woke you, darling, but now you must go back to bed."

"Come and tuck me in then."

"All right I'll be there in a moment. Carly dragged her slippered feet back to her room, and Lindsey put on a dressing gown. When she got back I said:

"Look, Linds, the sex was fantastic, but I've really got to talk to you. I had lunch with Angus yesterday, and he wants me to be *Intendant* of Opera London if he gets the Music Director's job. But it only works if we get Sergei's money. I have to know what happened at dinner yesterday. How did you get on with him?"

30

I suppose it wasn't a very bright thing to say after such intense passion, but the vehemence of her reply shook the hell out of me.

"We've just made the most wonderful love of my life, and all you can talk about is Sergei bloody Rebroff. You are an insensitive bastard, Jamie Barlow."

"Sorry, Linds, I didn't mean to..."

"Shut up and listen. If you want the lowdown on my Russian billionaire friend, here it is. I am flattered by his attention, and sometimes in the last couple of days I have caught myself thinking it would be nice to fuck him, as he clearly wants to fuck me. He stuck his tongue a long way down my throat after dinner last night, and yes, I enjoyed it. I had a hell of a struggle with myself to turn him down when he suggested coming back to his hotel for a drink. But I managed to say no, and he very gallantly put me into a taxi and told it to take me home. When I got back to my horrid little flat I cried for two hours because I wanted you there beside me, to protect me from Sergei and his millions. But all I could think of was you telling me on the phone to 'make him give his money to Opera London'. Money and opera, that's all you care about. Our daughter is next door, happy because her mother has made it home for a few hours, not to see her or even you, you bastard, but because tomorrow night she's got to sing more opera for more money. Until two minutes ago I was happy too, because I thought at least you and I can still have a bloody good time in the sack, and that might just provide the incentive for me to say no, the next time Sergei wants to jump on me. But here you go again, asking whether he's giving you his money. Well, Jamie, the simple answer is I don't know. I never had a chance to mention the fucking money. It didn't seem an appropriate question to ask, when what I was really concerned about was his hand on my knee. I don't know whether I'm coming or going, and I scarcely know who I've just made love to. I've got to sing the Countess tomorrow night, and it's got to be perfect, just like always. In fact if you'll excuse me I think I'll just totter off to the spare room, where you can leave me in peace, please. When you get Carly up in the morning, keep quiet, the two of you."

When she opened the door Carly was standing the other side of it, looking worried. "Why are you shouting, Mummy? Who's Sergei bloody Rebroff?"

"Just a friend, darling. Mummy's going to sleep in the spare room, so she can stay in bed when Daddy gets you up. Come on, I'll give you another goodnight kiss, then we can all settle down."

She didn't bother looking at me as she shut the door behind her. I cursed Angus, and Rebroff, and everybody I could think of, and turned out the light. I didn't sleep much.

6

Carly was furious when I woke her the next morning.

"Why do you and Mummy have to shout so much? You woke me up, and I didn't get back to sleep for ages. When you're ill you need lots of sleep. Granny told me. So I can't go back to school because I'm too tired, and I'm ill. Mrs Billington will be cross, and she'll make you come and get me."

But she eventually stopped grumbling, and ate her bacon and egg. It was me who couldn't face food. I threw my breakfast into the bin, and took Carly, bellyaching, to school.

Mrs Billington was surprisingly pleasant.

"Oh she looks much better, Mr Barlow. I expect all will be well."

"If by any chance she takes a turn for the worse, would you mind ringing my mobile, rather than Lindsey's? She has a performance tonight, and I'd rather she weren't disturbed."

"Yes of course. We mustn't disturb Mrs Barlow, must we? It must be quite difficult for you at home – I don't know how you do it."

A look of pity crossed her face. It was not unlike the one Sergei's secretary Tatyana had flashed at me during that ghastly first night party.

Lindsey called me at work at about eleven.

"Jamie, I'm sorry. I was wound up last night and you lit the blue touch paper. Don't worry, for God's sake. And I must say although you chose a bloody insensitive moment to tell me, I'm quite excited about the idea of you getting the top job at Opera London. You might start earning a decent amount of money. Take some of the pressure off me."

"It's ok, Linds. You had every right to be angry. Look, I don't suppose you'd have one of your pre-performance late lunches with me?"

"As long as it doesn't take too long," said Lindsey. "Maybe I'll be able to eat something this time. I've just read Hopkirk's review, by the way. She loves it. And me. Perhaps she's finally fallen out with that bastard Stephen Gibson."

"Yes, I've seen three reviews altogether. They're all fantastic. Well done."

"Thanks, Jamie. See you later."

Grace's phone was ringing. She picked up the receiver and listened for a while. She looked rather excited. "Oh, yes of course, I'll put you straight onto him. Just a moment."

She put the call on hold, and then said "it's Sergei Rebroff's secretary. Tatyana something. He wants four tickets for *Figaro* tonight. He's flying back from Salzburg specially."

The contents of my bowels headed rapidly southwards, but I managed to exert some control, and picked up the phone.

"Tatyana, how splendid to hear from you so soon. Of course Mr Rebroff can have four tickets. No, I'm sure we can find him some complimentaries" (why, Jamie? The bugger's got enough money to buy every seat in the house). "It will be a pleasure to have him. Mr Knipe is in again tonight, and I'm sure he would be delighted to play host. Shall I get him to call you?"

"Ah, thank you, Misterr Barlow, but please could you not call Knipe?" She had a very sexy Slavic drawl. "Sergei has asked me to make sure he is left alone to enjoy performance uninterrupted. Is there possibility he could have private box?"

"I'll contact the box office and ring you back in two minutes."

"Thank you Misterr Barlow."

I rang Carol, the box office manager.

"Carol, get this. Rebroff wants a private box with four seats for tonight."

"Bloody hell, he's back already. Are we going to get the money?"

"Well, I think a free box can only improve our chances. Bit irregular, I know, but what do you think?"

"In the circumstances, I think I should release the Chairman's Box. Mr Knipe will be in the stalls. He prefers it there. He gets a better the view of the stage."

"Carol, you're a brick. By the way, Rebroff wants to keep a low profile, so don't mention him to Knipe."

"Right, Jamie. I'll sort it out."

I rang Tatyana straight back.

"There will be a box set aside for Mr Rebroff – he can slip in through the stage door, if that will help."

"That would be excellent, thank you. I will pick up tickets. Where should I go, and whom should I ask for?"

Lovely grammar, Tatyana.

"Please could you be at the box office at seven o'clock, half an hour before the start? Carol, the box office manager, will hand them over personally."

"Thank you so much Misterr Barlow. May I please say I am very much looking forward to hearing your wife again?"

"Thank you, I will tell Lindsey. I hope you all have a marvellous evening."

Lindsey and I met at Giorgio's at four. She looked gorgeous. But, rather alarmingly, she air-kissed me on both cheeks.

"Sorry darling, but I don't want to get pink lipstick all over you."

"Did you know Rebroff was in tonight?" I asked.

"Yes I did, as a matter of fact. He phoned me at about midday. He was just about to get on his plane."

"Don't you think it's a bit odd that he's following you around like this?"

"Yes, I suppose I do. But honestly, Jamie, it's not just me he's interested in. He said it was the most satisfying *Figaro* he'd ever seen."

I tried to grin at her.

"Jamie, for God's sake relax. I can handle this, I really can. I just need to exploit my new-found friendship with Sergei by getting his money for the Company. Then I need to tell him I'm happily married, and spend the next few days talking endlessly about you and Carly. Remember those classes of Isobel's?"

I remembered them extremely well. A deceptively scatty woman at College called Isobel Allwood had given lessons to the final year opera course students on how to repel the sexual advances of predatory conductors and directors. The trick, said Isobel, was to keep them sweet so they booked you again, without actually ending up in the sack with them, and the best way to do this was to talk with great enthusiasm about your home life, and in particular your boyfriend/girlfriend/spouse.

The classes were occasionally followed by hilarious sessions with Isobel in the pub, where she would give chapter and verse (strictly off-the-record, of course) on certain very famous and powerful people who had a reputation for That Sort Of Thing. Male and female students alike would attend these sessions – some of the prettier boys would, as their careers progressed, have as much trouble as the girls from gents (and ladies) of a certain persuasion. And some of the students of both sexes would, as time went on, fail to follow Isobel's advice, and have ding-dong affairs which seldom did any harm to their employment prospects.

"Isobel Allwood has saved more operatic marriages than anyone else alive," I said. "And you've got it exactly right with Sergei. Just get us the money, Linds. Only no more tongues down throats. Please."

She laughed. "Oh Jamie, I can't stand that hangdog face of yours. Cheer up, for God's sake. Tell me about Angus's plan."

So I told her. The whole, unexpurgated scheme, and why Sergei's millions had to be recruited to counter Knipe's syndicate. She laughed herself silly when I told her Pogson had seen Knipe kissing Leclerc in a posh restaurant.

By the time I had finished she had almost polished off her spaghetti napoletana. "Would the Arts Council wear it?" she said.

"That's the sixty-four thousand dollar question. I guess Knipe's syndicate might be more attractive to them in one way, because it preserves the status quo. But surely they would be relieved if Opera London's financial future were guaranteed."

Lindsey delicately sucked up the last of her spaghetti. "There's only one way to find out. Leave it to me. If anyone can get Sergei's money for Opera London I can." She got up from the table. "I was right, it's very exciting. You'd be the big boss. With a fat pay packet, and lots of street cred. I'd be able to take my foot off the pedal sometimes, and maybe even stay at home and get to know our daughter properly, because I wouldn't need to make such a huge amount of money. It's a great idea. Do you mind paying the bill, darling?"

She called me, as she often did, during the interval. I was about to go and get Carly out of bed – she had been dying to talk to her mother but was still exhausted after her illness – when Lindsey stopped me dead in my tracks by telling me Sergei had invited the whole cast to his suite at the Savoy for dinner after the show. Angus and Gloria were going, apparently, as was Julian Pogson. She knew she should be going home to bed, with a plane to catch early in the morning, but was damned if she was missing this one, so "sorry, Jamie, but I'm going", she said, just as I heard the stage manager calling beginners for Act Three.

I made my way morosely upstairs and opened Carly's door. She was fast asleep on her back, the bedclothes in a heap around her, looking angelic. It tore my heart out, because all I could think of was how many more times will I see you like this, my gorgeous little girl, before you're whisked off to live with Sergei Ivanevitch Rebroff, your new Daddy?

7

I didn't wake up when Lindsey got in. The first thing I knew was when her alarm went off at four a.m. She can only have had three hours' sleep at most.

"Do you mind if I put the light on?" she asked.

"No, no, of course not. How was it last night?"

"Wonderful. We had Sevruga caviar, and the best lobster I've ever tasted, and the most unbelievable wine, which was flowing like water."

"But nothing happened with Sergei?"

There was a short pause. "No, Jamie." She said it a touch over-emphatically, as if I were a rather stupid child.

"Oh, good," I said. "You'll have to tell me all about it on the phone later. Carly wants you to wake her up before you go."

"Are you sure, Jamie? Shouldn't I leave her asleep?"

"Well, she was very insistent. Just try."

She came back in a couple of minutes later, with tears on her cheeks. "This is mad," she said. "She woke up as soon as I went in, and gave me the biggest hug of my life. Then she said 'Mummy, I love you. Please don't go', and I burst into tears. So did she. I just… hugged her again. She smelt like toast. Like she did when she was a baby. I can't walk out and leave her again, I really can't."

It was four twenty-five. The taxi was due in five minutes.

"You're right, darling, it's mad, but what can we do? Look, it's not so bad. You'll be back tomorrow evening for the Sunday matinee of *Figaro*.

"I know, I know, I've got to go."

She hovered uncertainly in the doorway, and for a moment I thought I might get a hug. But then her mobile went.

"Is that the taxi? Yes, thanks, I'm just coming." She rushed down the stairs without looking round.

Angus called me at about midday. He'd been to Sergei's little soirée at the Savoy, and he'd taken Gloria Forrest.

"Fantastic evening, old boy. Shame you weren't there. Rebroff kept telling us all how wonderful we were. There was enough Corton-Charlemagne to float a battleship, and he seemed to find it highly amusing when we all got drunk and started pairing off. I practically had little Gloria on the couch, and Pogson was going great guns with that Chinese boy in the chorus. Jason, you know, Jason Tang. Tenor. Nice voice. He's going to join the Young Singers' programme next season."

"Of course I know Jason Tang, you tithead. I'm the casting director, remember? He's doing Alfred in this autumn's *Fledermaus*."

"Yes, quite," said Angus. "Sorry. Anyway, if our favourite oligarch doesn't end up diverting his dosh in our direction, I'm a Dutchman. Oh yes, Angus, nice bit of alliteration."

"What about Lindsey? Did she behave?"

"Well of course I was busy with Gloria's superb tits, but as far as I could tell you've nothing to worry about. Lindsey barely had a drink all night, and she kept going on about you and that delightful daughter of yours. Rather overdid it, in my opinion. She seemed a bit wary of doing anything wrong, if you know what I mean. So did Sergei. Didn't she say anything when she got in?"

"I'm afraid I was fast asleep, Gussie. But this morning she was terribly upset when Carly begged her not to go back to Salzburg."

"What, at four o'clock in the morning?"

"'Fraid so."

"Well, she sang like God last night, Jamie. She can't be suffering that much."

"She has an iron constitution. Famous for it. In public, that is. *Chez nous*, that's a different matter."

"You worry too much, James. Always have. Look, I'll tell you what, why don't you book that family holiday you keep talking about? It'll be something to look forward to, once she's finished Salzburg, and once Sergei's lovely money is on its way to the Company's bank account."

Not a bad idea, I thought. So I said goodbye to Angus – he was off for a siesta, lucky sod – and when Grace popped out for lunch, I logged onto Freshair's website and checked out flights to Montpellier in August. Then I rang Mme Dupuis, a charming little French divorcée who had a tiny but gorgeous pavilion in her back garden in Castelnau-le-Lez, just up the road from Montpellier. When she said it was free during that time I booked it on the spot, and then went back to Freshair and booked the flights.

Lindsey rang at the end of her day's rehearsals. I was still in the office. She sounded very excited.

"Jamie, I've got to be quick. I'm not wanted tomorrow morning, so I can come home tonight. I asked the Festival office to check about changing my flight, but it's Friday and the Freshair is full. I'd arranged to meet Sergei at 5.45 so I told him I wanted to go home but couldn't get a flight, and he immediately said I must use his private jet. He's coming with me. We're flying to City airport, leaving about seven. I should be home by nine your time."

I was trying to take this in. Sergei was in Salzburg yet again. My wife was about to spend the best part of two hours with him on a very expensive, very private means of transport. He probably wanted to do a great deal more for her delectation than be a trolley dolly.

"Lindsey you can't possibly accept such ridiculous generosity," I said. I sounded like a prep school headmaster.

There was a pause. Then, very crossly, she said: "Well, you can't stop me, Jamie".

And the phone went dead.

Calm down, Jamie. There would be the pilot, possibly two pilots. Maybe there would actually be an air hostess. There might even be an in-flight masseuse for all I knew. What the hell did happen on private jets? But anyway, there would be witnesses. Mutt and Jeff would be there, presumably. And Tatyana. Rebroff would never risk doing anything compromising. Would he?

I tried ringing about an hour later, but Lindsey's phone was switched off. I imagined them swilling champagne, and imagined him sticking his tongue down her throat again. I imagined all sorts of vile things.

With an effort of will I tidied the papers on my desk, let myself out of a now-deserted office (there was no show that night), and got myself to

Mum's to pick up Carly. Then I went straight home, where I shoved a Sainsbury's lasagne in the oven and tried to watch telly while Carly did her maths homework.

When supper was ready I called her, and while I dished up the meal she asked me some frightful question about fractions. I could no more have concentrated on anything mathematical than flown to the moon.

"Emma Anstruther-Fawcett's Daddy always helps her with her maths," she volunteered, helpfully. "When she's round at his I mean. He lives in Luton."

She made it sound like it was the most desirable place in the country.

"Doesn't her Daddy live with her Mummy?"

"Don't be stupid, Daddy, no-one's parents are still together."

"Well, Mummy and I are."

"You don't count. Everyone at school says so. Because Mummy's always away, I mean. Anyway, Emma says Mummy'll have an affair soon, then you'll split up. If you split up, will I live with you or Mummy?"

"Mummy and I aren't going to split up, Carly. We love each other. You know that."

"That's what Emma's Mummy used to say. Then one day a big black man appeared in their house, and her Daddy moved out. To Luton."

"Carly darling, tell me about your maths problem again," I said, between gritted teeth.

"And Emma says it's very odd you calling me darling all the time. She says people can be arrested for calling ten-year-old girls darling."

I bloody nearly hit her.

"Finish your tea, Carly. I'm not hungry. I'm going to do the washing-up."

"I'm not hungry either. Can we watch Bridget Jones?"

"No we can't, because Mummy's coming home."

"What, tonight?"

"Yes, tonight."

She squealed, and jumped up with her arms held high in a gesture of triumph. Her plate, still three-quarters full of lasagne and peas, fell off the table and smashed on the floor.

When Lindsey got home she was lit up like a beacon, with a slightly manic brightness in her eyes. I looked for signs of worry, or stress, or, let's face it, of recent sexual intercourse, but she was giving nothing away.

41

Carly was in her pyjamas, waiting up. She flew into Lindsey's arms, as if she hadn't seen her for months.

"Whoa, Carly, that's some hug," said Lindsey.

"Mummy, darling, I love you," said Carly.

"I love you too, Carly. Since when have you called me darling?"

"How long are you here for?"

"Till Sunday lunchtime."

"Can we go shopping tomorrow? I want a new phone, like Emma's. It's pink, and it flips open, and it's called eraser."

"Heavens! I should think so. What do you think, Jamie?"

"Well, I don't see any reason why we shouldn't," I said. "It's Saturday, and we've all got a day off."

Carly looked outraged. "*You* can't come. We want a girly day. Don't we, Mummy?"

"We'll see," said Lindsey. "You must go to bed. It's way past your bedtime."

"Please come and read me a story, Mummy."

"All right, little one, but it will have to be quick."

They went upstairs together, Carly talking nineteen to the dozen. I busied myself with the washing up.

"She's completely hyper," said Lindsey, when she came back into the room. "Has she been drinking Coke?"

"She had a glass at tea-time," I said. "It's not the Coke, Linds, she's just excited to see you. She'll go to sleep soon. Now, tell me about the flight. What was it like?"

"Oh, Jamie, it was incredible. Probably the most amazing thing was going through Salzburg airport. I mean, there was the queue for the Freshair flight, all waiting to go through security, looking irritated. And we breezed past the lot of them. There were two women, both smartly dressed in uniform, waiting by the security machine. They were apologetic, but really quick and efficient, and they inspected the contents of our pockets then waved us through. But it was only us, Jamie. They were there just for us!

"They kept bowing and scraping to Sergei and me, calling me "*Gnädige Frau*". Then, as we left the terminal building, more bowers and scrapers checked our passports, ushered us into a Mercedes that was miraculously waiting on the apron, and spirited us across to his plane.

"But the jet, Jamie. It's wonderful inside – olive leather seats and tables in between each seat. Sergei and I sat in two of them opposite each other. There were little bottles of cold champagne in the pockets at the side, and Sergei produced two glasses from nowhere. Before I knew it we were taking off. The tannoy came on, just like it would in an ordinary flight, except they hadn't closed the door through to the cockpit. I could see one of the pilots making the announcement, and I could see the Alps rushing towards us through the front window. 'Welcome Mr Rebroff,' they said, and then they said 'and welcome Miss Templeton. It's a great pleasure to have such a distinguished artist on board.'

"As soon as we were properly airborne, one of the pilots unstrapped himself and walked down the aisle towards us. Sergei told me he was English, and used to work for British Airlines. This pilot - Johnny, that was his name - was absolutely charming. 'Can I get you anything Miss Templeton?' he said. 'More champagne? Some caviar? A cheese sandwich?' They all roared with laughter when he asked about the sandwich. Obviously it's some kind of private joke that all English people like cheese sandwiches. 'Like on your famous British Rail,' Sergei said. Then he said to Johnny that he would look after me himself, and Johnny went back to the cockpit. Sergei was charming. The amazing thing is, Jamie, he's got all that money and power and everything, but underneath it all he's just a really nice bloke."

"So he didn't do anything, er, inappropriate," I said.

"No, he behaved beautifully. Oh, Jamie, stop worrying. I can't think what he was doing kissing me that first night in Salzburg. He talked about opera, and my singing. He's so excited to be a part of it all, just like a small boy. He's seen the heads of every opera company in Europe and he's just about to make up his mind. I think it's between the Salzburg Festival, and Opera London. But Sergei can't stand Knipe. I don't think he's all that keen on Göstl-Saurau, either, to be honest."

"Sergei not liking Greg the Dreg is anything but a problem," I said. "Did you get a chance to offer an opinion on where the money ought to go?"

"I really wanted to, darling, but I just couldn't find the right moment. It's hard when someone is treating you like Royalty. I'd have felt like a spoilt child wanting another ice-cream."

"Well, we've made huge progress, anyway. Angus says Sergei loved you all in the show last night."

"Oh, he was even more enthusiastic the second time. And he seemed delighted when his dinner party degenerated into what was practically an orgy. You should have seen Angus and Gloria Forrest. And Julian and that Jason Tang – Julian didn't have to go back to Salzburg, lucky thing, he wasn't called. So when they all started practically screwing each other, that was when I made my excuses and left. I had that flight to catch. I mean I'm sure Sergei wouldn't have done anything, but I was quite glad to have an excuse to leave. I'm exhausted, Jamie. It's been a hectic week."

"Darling, if you're tired, much the best thing you can do is go to bed. I'll finish the washing-up. We had a bit of a disaster earlier. Carly broke a plate. One of the Royal Doulton ones, I'm afraid. I shouldn't have used it, but all the others were dirty in the dishwasher. Sorry."

"Never mind, Jamie." She looked at me with those brown eyes. Then, quite unexpectedly, she gave me a huge hug.

"Sweetheart," she said, "I'm sure it's going to be okay. Don't panic." Thank God she went upstairs straight afterwards, because I cried like a baby for the next hour and a half.

We did our best to behave like a normal family over the weekend. Lindsey took Carly shopping for her phone on the Saturday, and on the Sunday went to the theatre for the matinée, before heading back to Salzburg to resume rehearsals.

I managed to persuade Carly to sit down and watch *The Sound of Music*, and within five minutes she had decided Emma was wrong, and that she loved it. I promised her that when we were in Salzburg the following month she and I would do the Sound of Music Tour together, and visit all the locations used in the film.

Meanwhile I tried not to fret about Sergei Rebroff. What was the point? There was nothing whatsoever I could do, except wait and see what was going to happen.

8

When I arrived in the office on Monday morning there was a note waiting on my desk. *Come up and see me as soon as you get in. Danieli's just cancelled. Five months pregnant, apparently. Dunwich.*

Lisa Danieli was an American soprano with a fearsome reputation, who had been engaged three years previously to sing the central role of Rosalinde in *Die Fledermaus*. The first night of this new production was in October, with rehearsals scheduled to begin on September the fourth. The chances of finding a replacement with an international reputation were not great.

I nipped up the stairs to the top floor, and tapped on Dunwich's window. His cheeks were even redder than usual, and I got the feeling that this was one problem too many for him. He was due for retirement in three weeks' time. He was not in a good mood.

"Bloody nuisance," he said. "Why the hell couldn't she tell us sooner? And who in God's name are we going to get? Lindsey's not free, by any amazing chance?"

It would have been a perfect role for her. In fact I had lobbied for her to get it. But there was too much opposition form within the Company, especially from Yvonne Umfreville, the Head of Music. She always fought tooth and nail whenever I wanted to cast Lindsey in anything. We were not best buddies.

"I'm afraid she's not, Henry. She's doing *Eugene Onegin* in Amsterdam. The dates clash almost exactly."

"Shit. Got any ideas?"

"I'll ring Graham Butterfield." Butterfield was the one British agent I could bear to talk to. We'd been in the Glyndebourne Chorus together.

"You're a bit too chummy with that Graham Butterfield, if you ask me," said Dunwich.

"Look Henry, Graham is the one chap I can trust. He'll find someone good, even if she's not his property."

"Oh, bugger it, I don't give a toss what you do. In three weeks' time I'll be fishing on the Spey, and the whole opera world can go screw itself."

"Graham, it's Jamie."

"About time you called, you old tart. Got something for me?"

"Might have, might not. I need to pick your brains. Who can I get for Rosalinde this autumn?"

There was a short pause. Then Graham said: "Oh, so Danieli's finally spilled the beans about being knocked up."

"You bastard. How long have you known?"

"Well, let's see. She told Pogson in Venice, when they were doing *Peter Grimes* – that would have been February. March April May June. Four months."

"Julian bloody Pogson. He's doing Eisenstein in the same run. Why didn't he tell me? Why didn't you tell me? Anyway, who the hell can I get? Who can I get that's any good, I mean."

"Funny you should ask now, actually. I've just been talking to Smits."

"Antwerp? Casting man?"

"Absolutely. He's like the cat that got the cream. They've found a new Australian girl. She's doing *Don Giovanni*, and Leclerc – he's conducting – thinks she's the greatest Donna Anna since Rosa Ponselle. But no-one else has ever heard of her, and she's got no work. She's a bit on the large side, but has a voice like an angel."

"This is too good to be true, Graham. Leclerc is conducting *Fledermaus*. So one assumes that he'd be happy with her. I'd only have Zimmermann to convince." Ursula Zimmermann was directing *Fledermaus*.

"What's her name?" I said.

"Get this." He paused again, then there was an audible intake of breath. "Evangeline Balls."

We both roared with laughter.

"She'll have to do something about that, obviously," Graham said, once he'd recovered.

"Look, Graham, this is serious. Can she act? *Fledermaus* is an operetta, remember. Dialogue. Comedy. All that sort of thing."

"Not fussy or anything, are you Jamie? Look, the première's tomorrow night. I'm going to see it, with a view to taking her on. Why don't you come?"

"Graham, this isn't a joke, is it?" He'd done it to me once before. Sent me on a wild goose chase to Nantes to hear some French 'tenor' called Prépuce, only to find that the guy was a drag act and sounded like Jimmy Clitherow.

"As God is my judge, Jamie, this one's for real."

"Okay, I'll come. Do they still do that direct flight from City Airport?"

"'Fraid not old boy. Airline's a goner. Just as well, with those hairdryers they used to run on that route. I was always in fear of my life."

"So how are you getting there? Can I come with you?"

"I'm going tonight. I've got a meeting with Smits tomorrow. You'll probably have to meet me there. Will you be lonely?"

"Fuck off. What time does it start?"

"7.30."

"And you absolutely promise me that this isn't just a load of balls?"

We both went into another paroxysm. Grace and the rest of the office were starting to laugh too.

"Got to go, Graham, this is getting embarrassing. Meet you in the foyer bar at De Vlaamse Opera at seven. Mine's a Duvel."

"Right you are, Jamie boy. But you're buying me dinner after if she's any good."

"I'll tell you what, Opera London can pay."

"Are we expecting some money in soon then, Jamie? A hundred million, that sort of thing?"

"You're pushing it, Graham. See you tomorrow."

I got Grace to fix my travel, while I rang Ursula Zimmermann. She had to approve the new Rosalinde, and since she was in Sydney directing at the Opera House this meant I had to persuade her to take my word for it. I knew her from a show she'd directed at College, which Lindsey and I had both been in.

"Hey, Jamie. How're you doin'?" She was German, but had learned her astonishingly fluent English in a San Francisco squat in the seventies, and her American twang practically blasted my eardrum off. "Danieli's cancelled? Terrific. Never did like her much. Who you got instead?"

"Wait for it, Ursula. I'm hoping to cast a girl called Evangeline Balls."

The scream of laughter which emerged from the earpiece of the phone was loud enough to make most of the people on the second floor look up. When she'd regained control of herself, she said: "come on Jamie. You're pulling my leg."

"As God is my witness, Ursula."

"I assume she can sing. Can she act?"

"I'll find out tomorrow – I'm going to Antwerp to hear her do Donna Anna."

"You won't find out much about her acting in that role. The last one I saw looked as if she was moving about on casters."

"Well if she's any good, can I book her?"

"Oh, sure, go ahead. As long as she turns up on the first day, and she can sing, I'll sort out the rest. She has to be up for a few evenings out, though. I don't want to be bored witless for six weeks."

"I'll bear that in mind, Ursula."

"Great. I can't wait, Jamie. I love *Fledermaus*, I love London, and I'm sure I'm going to love Evangeline Balls."

And with another deafening peal of laughter she rang off.

I rang Lindsey when I got home. She'd told me everything was going to be okay, and I wanted to believe her, but I needed to know if Sergei had followed her back to Salzburg.

"Oh, Jamie, hello. I'm sorry, darling, I should have rung you. Have you been worried?"

"No. Well, not really. I'd have had a call from the Festival if there'd been a problem. But I needed to ring you, to tell you that I'm going to Antwerp tomorrow."

"Heavens, Jamie, what's Carly going to do? You can't send her off to your parents again."

"It's okay. I spoke to them earlier. Mum wasn't all that keen, but I placated her by offering to drive over there as soon as I get back, and take them to Carly's Sports Day – she's got a great chance of winning the high jump this year, apparently. Mum's going to bring a picnic. Afterwards I'll drop them off and take Carly home."

"Well, that doesn't sound too bad. But Jamie, we must get another nanny. I know we had a nightmare with the last one, but we really don't have any option. I'll look at some agencies on the internet tomorrow."

"Have you got time?"

"I'll make time."

"Okay then, that would be great. I'd do it, only I've got to get off fairly early. Grace has booked me to fly Stansted-Brussels. Well, they call it Brussels, but apparently it's some god-forsaken airfield half way between Brussels and Antwerp. There's supposed to be a bus to Antwerp, but no-one can find out what time it leaves. So she's booked me on a twelve o'clock flight, in case I get lost."

There was a brief silence. Suddenly, Lindsey said:

"Oh my God, it's seven o'clock. I've got to go out to supper."

"Who with?" I said, a little more forcefully than I'd intended.

"Er, Sergei's taking the whole cast out to Der Triangel."

"He's back in Salzburg, then?"

"Er, yes, yes he is."

"He's slumming it a bit going to Der Triangel, isn't he? What's he going to do with the entourage?"

"He wants to experience the authentic atmosphere of the Festival." She sounded defensive.

"Will you ring when you get back?"

"I will if I can. I might be late."

"I'll wait up," I said. "See if you can put in a good word about the money."

Short pause. "The money. Right then. I've got to go."

Ten o'clock came and went, eleven, twelve, one. No call. There was the hour's difference to contend with, but even so, I knew she wouldn't ring that late.

Eventually I tottered up to bed. I had finished a bottle of Talisker I had in the cupboard, and I was drunk. Carly had been in bed for hours – we'd had a row when I tried to give her a goodnight kiss and she told me I smelt of booze.

I dreamt about Lindsey, who was at Kings Cross station, running for a train to Salzburg. Carly and I were trying to keep up with her. Eventually she jumped onto the train, and the guard slammed the door. "So sorry, Jimmy," he said. Carly and I were left on the platform.

Lindsey pulled the window down and laughed at us. Sergei was beside her, and he started throwing tenners out of the window.

As I tried to gather up the money from the platform, the train started moving. Lindsey called: "'Bye Jamie, 'bye Carly. Love you lots." She laughed again, her eyes unnaturally bright, like they had been when she'd arrived home after flying on Sergei's jet. I shouted at them both, telling Sergei to leave my wife alone, but as the train disappeared he just threw more money onto the platform. Carly shouted "I hate you, Daddy. You made Mummy go away". Just as she started crying, I woke up in a muck sweat.

I was in such a state that I contemplated ringing Lindsey to check everything was okay, but of course she'd be fast asleep, and there didn't seem to be any real reason to wake her up.

Instead I contented myself with checking on Carly, who was flat out. My heart melted, as it always did when I saw her sleeping, so I fetched myself a glass of water and a couple of Nurofen, and got back into bed. After a few minutes I lapsed into a fitful, dream-free slumber, and when my alarm rang at seven o'clock I turned it off and went back to sleep.

9

All hell broke loose when I woke up again. It was eight forty, and Carly had ten minutes to get to school. She was still asleep as well, and I ran into her room while pulling on my trousers. My head felt like a bomb had gone off inside it.

"Carly, get up now. It's twenty to nine. I slept through my alarm."

"Oh, no! I've got Mrs Bodley first lesson. She'll kill me."

"I'm sorry darling. Get dressed as quick as you can. You can have a piece of toast in the car."

I threw on the rest of my clothes, tore downstairs, shoved a couple of bits of bread in the toaster, and made myself a very instant coffee. Carly appeared looking dishevelled. I buttered the toast, aimed a dollop of marmalade at each slice, and gave one to Carly. Then we picked up her homework and roared out of the house. I just stopped her in time from banging the door to, ran back in and got my keys, then we jumped in the car. By five to nine when I arrived to drop her off, the usual crush of Shoguns and Discoveries around the school gates had dispersed, leaving only a couple of stragglers – both mothers who looked as harassed as I felt. I beat a hasty retreat, and flew home to shave, and pack a bag. Fortunately the Queens Park Police were not at Vigilance Level One that morning – I have no doubt I was still way over the limit.

I ran down the road to the station, having by some miracle remembered to put my passport in my pocket, but it wasn't until I was trundling through a tunnel underneath South Hampstead that I realised I had forgotten the confirmation slip from Freshair with the reservation number on it. I'd just have to wing it.

The rest of the journey – Victoria Line to Tottenham Hale, then the Stansted Express – went fairly smoothly, and I got into the check-in queue at 11:05. Fifteen minutes to go before they shut the desk.

At eleven fifteen it was my turn. I handed my passport to the young lady at the desk. She looked fed up. "Hi, my name is Consuela", said her left breast.

"Ressevvation nomber, pliss", she said.

"I'm awfully sorry, I'm afraid I've left it at…"

"We nee' ressevvation nomber. No nomber no fly."

"But I've left it at home. I'm terribly sorry, but I did book this flight yesterday. The name should be on the list. There, I can see it."

She handed the passport back to me. "Nest pliss."

"But there's my name, on the list."

"No nomber no fly. Nest pliss."

A man with facial hair from ear to ear, but no moustache ('A Belgian Beard' Angus called this) barged in front of me. His face was clammy and grey, and he was breathing heavily. He looked as if he was about to have a nervous breakdown, as indeed was I. But at least he was guaranteed a seat on the plane. It was eleven seventeen. I pulled my phone out of my pocket, plus all the receipts I'd accumulated since paying Lindsey's taxi driver last week (these fell in a jumble on the floor), and dialled Grace's direct line. Thank God she answered straight away.

"Don't tell me Jamie, you've forgotten your reservation number. It's EC2XLRP."

"Grace, you're a genius. What would I do without you? What did you say the number was?"

"EC2XLRP. Write it down, Jamie."

"Can't. No pen. I'll remember it. Thanks a million."

When the Belgian gentleman had finished, I took his place. Eleven nineteen.

"Ressevvation nomber, pliss."

"EC2LXRP. No, the other way round, sorry. EC2XLRP."

"Passport."

Could I find the bugger? I'd had it two minutes previously. I checked my left breast pocket (it was not called Consuela) for the third time, and found my passport hiding behind the scrunched up front page of last month's Opera Magazine, which had a picture of Lindsey on it. I handed the passport in triumph to Consuela.

"Check-in iss cloz. Iss elebeng twengty."

"Please, I beg of you. I have to get on this flight." I think I was about to cry.

Perhaps Consuela thought so too. "Hokay. I mek excepssiong. Dong do it ageng."

"Thank you so much, Consuela," I said. She smiled. It was not all that pleasant.

As I waited in the endless security queue, my phone bleeped with a text. It was from Lindsey.

Something to tell you Jamie. No time now, I'm in rehearsal. When can I ring?

The contents of my bowels did a familiar dive towards the floor.

I texted back *due to land 2.10. Ring then if convenient.*

What in hell did she have to tell me? That she was madly in love with Sergei, that they'd danced the Light Fantastic in his hotel suite until dawn, and then made passionate love between the silk sheets that he had had flown in from Kamchatka, or wherever they make silk sheets?

Having arrived last at check-in, I had a high security number. When they first started issuing these a few years previously I thought this meant you were being singled out as Very Likely To Be A Suicide Bomber. Now I was a seasoned low fares traveller, however, I knew it meant I would not be able to sit where I wanted, and would probably have to sit next to someone ghastly.

Sure enough, I had just got myself reasonably comfy in the last window seat in the aircraft, when the Belgian Beard came and sat in the seat next to mine. He spent the next ten minutes settling himself – getting up to take something out of the overhead locker, sitting down and fiddling with it, and then getting up to put it back. All this activity wafted in my direction the delicious scent of armpits, thinly masked by the free sample of **DKNY** *Red Delicious* he'd tried in the Duty Free. Lindsey retreated to the back of my mind while I contemplated the start of World War Three.

The situation was not improved when a German-speaking gentleman sat down immediately behind me. The entire aircraft shook, and the scent of *knoblauch* from the *Wurst* he'd brought with him for the journey compounded the stench from my left. This same gentleman had kept half the passengers waiting an extra minute on the aircraft steps, while he stowed his bags in the luggage bin, then changed his mind about his seat, and moved all his baggage across the aisle. Now he was finally settled he began to talk loudly in cod English – "velcome to ze airplane, ladies und gentlemen. Your lifejecket iss unter your seat" – and then roared with laughter, as did about ten other people all around me, who I realised to my horror were all in the same party. They had clearly been drinking beer since breakfast time. I knew this not only because of the loudness of the conversation, but also because of the smell, now an explosive mixture of garlic sausage, sweat, recycled Beck's and DKNY *Red Delicious*.

I tried to take my mind off this by concentrating on the trickle of inane drivel which was dripping out of the public address system. We had one fey Irish voice whose owner thought he was funny, and kept making private jokes for the benefit, presumably, of the rest of the aircrew, despite the fact that they all seemed to be Spanish. The Irish gentleman informed us all that "The doors are cross-dressed". None of the crew (or passengers, naturally) could even raise a titter at this exceptional bit of comic repartee. Maybe I hadn't heard correctly.

Three new members of the cabin crew appeared at strategic points down the aisle, and we prepared for the safety demonstration. A cross female voice said something which may have been in English, which appeared to be aimed at the German speakers in the seats around me. Its burden seemed to be "stop arsing around and listen to the public address system". How these Germans, if indeed they were Germans, were supposed to make head or tail of this incomprehensible Spanglish is a mystery, but many weary glances of the "we've got a right one here" variety from the three poor saps in the aisle, left us in no doubt that we'd all been naughty, and must from now on pay attention to the information that my own oxygen mask should be fitted before that of my daughter, were she with me, just in case there should be any attempt at altruism on my part.

During the flight I tried to sleep, but each time I started to drop off I was woken either by the smell, or by another announcement. At one point we were offered "hegg and bacong sangwishes, cheese ploughmeng ang cheeken ang stuff-em". Later I was woken again by a voice saying: "ledeez ang yentlemens, we are abou' to cong through the haircraf' wib scrash cardss, costing ongly wong poung orr two Euross. Some ob de money goss to charitee. You cang wing a carr, ang you haff a wong ing four chance ob weenging." How many of the passengers bought a card because they thought they had a one in four chance of winning a car is anyone's guess, but the cabin crew were doing a roaring trade.

Finally the captain said "cabin crew ten minutes to landing", which was the first recognisable thing I'd heard. I strapped myself in, made sure my tray table was stowed and my seat was in the upright position, and waited for the moment of impact.

We landed at two o'clock precisely. Ten minutes until The Call. We trailed through passport control (*Welcome to Erps-Kwerps international airport,* it said. *Gateway to Europe and the Low Countries*). As soon as I'd gone through customs, my phone bleeped at me. I was all fingers and thumbs as I tried to get it out of my pocket.

"*From Telenorth*," said the message. "*Switch to Telenorth for the best rates. You can also dial 343 for your messages, just like at home.*" I deleted it angrily. Two more of these texts came in before the phone rang properly. It was Lindsey.

"Hi, Jamie, how was the flight?"

"Smelly. What's this news?"

" Jamie it's terribly exciting. Sergei has agreed to give his money to Opera London."

"Christ. Well done Linds. Brilliant. I must phone Angus. Bloody hell. Did he say anything about who he wants in charge?"

"Yes, of course, that's the whole point. He thinks it's a great idea for you to do it."

"Me? Fantastic! Why?"

"As soon as I told him that you and Angus had this ambition to run the Company, he jumped at it. He said he particularly wanted you. Not Angus, although he's thrilled about that too, but you. He admires you enormously."

"Blimey." I remembered something I'd once read about never slagging off a married woman's husband if you wanted to have an affair with her. Not a happy thought. So I said:

"How much, by the way?"

"Up to a hundred million, he says. Pounds."

"Jesus. So last night was a success, then? You obviously got a chance to speak to him alone?"

"Yes, yes I did. After dinner. I mean, obviously I had to wait until the rest of the cast had disappeared. So I talked to him after dinner. After they'd all gone."

"Bloody marvellous, Linds! You've transformed the lives of you, me, Carly, Angus, well, everyone we know. And everyone who works for

Opera London. You deserve a Damehood. Fantastic! Well done, darling. I'm proud of you. Are you pleased?"

"Of course I am. It's a pretty wonderful thing for Sergei to have done, isn't it? Don't forget him in all this. It's his money, after all."

"Yes, yes of course. When are you next seeing him, by the way?"

"Oh, tonight. He's taking me out to dinner."

Fuck.

"Great! Is he coming to London at all? I suppose Angus and I should set up a meeting."

"Oh yes, he asked me to tell you to ring Tatyana to make an appointment. Have you got her number?"

"Grace has got it. Look, I ought to go. I've got to ring Angus. Thanks a million, Linds. You are a star."

"Oh, that's okay Jamie, anytime. How's Carly?"

"Fine, absolutely fine. Looking forward to going to stay with your Dad next week."

"I'll ring her tonight. She's at your Mum's, right?"

"Yes, that's right."

There was a silence. I supposed neither of us could say goodbye. Eventually I said:

"Linds, are you all right?"

"Of course I am, Jamie. I'll talk to you later. Bye."

"Bye Linds. And thanks for everything you've done."

But that was the point, wasn't it? I was pleased, of course I was. I was thrilled. But I was also, once again, in a state of complete panic. What exactly *had* my beautiful wife done?

Angus nearly ruptured my eardrum, he screamed so loud.

"Oh my GOD! He screamed. FAN-bloody-TASTIC! And he wants us to do the top jobs? This is insane, Jamie. Unbe-fucking-lievable! What do we do to make it all happen?"

"We've got to ring Tatyana – that's the secretary – and make an appointment to see him. I'll get Grace to ring her and set it up."

"How much does Gracie know about our plans?"

"Nothing yet."

"Then don't tell her. Do it yourself. We need to keep this under wraps, Jamie. It's the biggest bit of news there's practically ever been in British Opera. Can you come over now and talk about it?"

"No, I'm on my way to Antwerp. I've got to listen to a girl doing Donna Anna tonight. I'll tell you all about it."

"Not interested. When are you back?"

"Tomorrow, late morning."

"Ring me when you land, then come straight round."

"You're on. See you then."

"And Jamie…"

"Yes?"

"Not a word to anyone. Do you understand?"

"Absolutely. Bloody hell Angus, we're made."

"Not quite, old thing. We still have to work out how to get rid of Knipe. Don't forget The Establishment's very keen on him. And he's busy forming his syndicate of donors. Even if we get Sergei's money, he's a formidable enemy."

"Okay, we'll talk about it tomorrow. See you then."

"Can't wait, old boy."

I had been dimly aware during all this telephoning that lots of people were trailing past me. Now I'd finished, I put my phone back in my pocket, picked up my briefcase, and went to the information desk, where a uniformed girl with dazzling blonde hair and full red lips was busy filing her nails.

"Please could you tell me where the Antwerp bus goes from?" I said.

"Over there." She pointed over her shoulder. Her English was a deliciously inflected mid-Atlantic drawl. She was Flemish, presumably. I'd always had a thing for the Flemish.

"Thank you," I said.

"You will have to hurry," she said. "It is due to leave."

I looked up. A bus trundled past the plate glass window behind her.

"It has gone," she said.

"What time is the next bus?"

"Seven thirty. After the next Freshair flight."

"But I have to be there by seven," I said. "What can I do?"

"You will have to hire a car, sir."

You know, don't you, Miss Erps-Kwerps of the gorgeously pouting lips? That I left the house in a frantic rush this morning, only just remembering my passport, and that there is absolutely no way I would have thought to transfer my driving licence to the pocket of this jacket?

57

But you're going to make me empty everything onto the floor for the second time today, just in case it's hiding somewhere.

She stopped filing her nails for a moment, and stared quizzically at me while I searched. Eventually I gave up, and said to her:

"I'm afraid I haven't brought my driving licence with me. Is there any other way of getting to Antwerp by seven o'clock?"

"Yes, you can take a taxi to Erps-Kwerps station, which is about ten minutes away. There are regular trains to Brussels. You will need to change at Brussel-Noord, and take the fast train to Antwerp. There is one each hour."

"Thank you," I said. "It was a bit stupid to miss the bus, wasn't it?" I smiled at her.

"If you say so, sir." The face didn't crack.

"Where do the taxis go from?" I asked.

"You can ring this number," she replied. "Taxis only wait here when a flight lands. They will all have gone by now."

I looked at my watch. It was quarter to three.

"Thank you so much for your help," I said. I rather desperately wanted her not to be cross with me.

I tried the taxi number ten times. Each time there was a sound reminiscent of the Barlow breakfast-time frying pan, followed by silence. Eventually, at the eleventh attempt, the crackles turned into a voice.

"Ja?"

"Do you speak English?"

"Little."

"Please could I have a taxi from Erps-Kwerps airport to the station?"

"Ja."

"When could you come?"

"Ja. Which station?"

"Erps-Kwerps."

"Ja. Which station?"

"Erps-Kw... Oh bugger it. Please could you take me to Antwerp? Antwerpen."

"Ja. When?"

"Now, please."

"But I am in Kent."

This was a bit odd. "Whereabouts in Kent, exactly?"

"Ghghghghent." Jesus, what a sound. He must have covered half his dashboard with mucus.

"Oh, Ghent. Sorry. When can you come to Erps-Kwerps?"

"One hour, maybe one and half. Erps-Kwerps International Airport, yes?

"Yes, fine, thank you. Where shall I meet you?"

"I come to the information desk."

I went to the little coffee bar in the corner, and asked for a cappuccino. The woman behind the counter looked at me oddly.

"With whipped cream?" she said.

"No, frothy milk." I thought they knew about coffee in Belgium.

"Ah, you want café crème."

"Oh. Yes of course. Thank you." On a whim I bought twenty Marlboro. The sign on the bar said "no smoking here", so I put the cigs in my pocket, picked up my coffee and briefcase, and aimed for the "Smoking Area" notice which I could see in the distance. I sat down in a pale green plastic chair, lit up, and contemplated life as the boss of the best-funded opera company in the world.

The taxi driver arrived two hours later. I went to meet him at the information desk, where he said "one moment," and proceeded to lean over the desk and lock his mouth firmly onto the lips of Miss Erps-Kwerps. When he came up for air, he said something to her in Flemish, and they giggled, and looked at me. Then he said to me: "One hundred twenty euros. Okay?"

Opera London can pay, I thought, it's rich enough. "Fine," I said. We went outside, and climbed into a spanking new Mercedes. As soon as we got onto the motorway, I fell fast asleep.

When I woke up we were on the outskirts of a City, and the driver's clock said 18:45. "God," I said. "Are we nearly there?"

"Block," he said. "Accident. Where you want to go?"

"The theatre," I said. "De Vlaamse Opera".

"We arrive five minutes."

"That's okay."

I rang Graham Butterfield. "Get me that Duvel," I said.

"So tell me then, James. What's happening with Sergei Rebroff?" said Graham, when I arrived.

"Nothing much," I said. Angus had told me to keep my mouth shut. "We're hoping to get the money, but then so are ENO, and Salzburg, and probably most of the other companies in Europe. Watch this space."

I took a glug of my Duvel. Heaven.

"Where is he now?" said Graham.

"Salzburg, I think. He saw Göstl-Saurau yesterday. No idea what happened."

"When will you know?"

"No idea, Graham." Dangerous ground. "Tell me about Evangeline Balls."

"Disappointingly she turns out to be called Bolls. B-O-double-L-S. Bloody funny name, but not as funny, you have to admit, as it could have been. Smits talked about her all through lunch. As far as I can remember, that is. We drank two bottles of wine, then started on the grappa. I'm feeling shocking. But at least I managed to get a sleep this afternoon. Look at Smits."

Geert Smits was standing at the far end of the bar, looking grey. He had a large cup of something in front of him.

"He's going to have a job being the life and soul tonight, isn't he?" I said.

"Absolutely. Shall we give the post-show party a miss?"

"Christ yes. I don't want to see anyone. Anyway, Graham, aren't we going out to dinner? On Opera London, if I remember rightly."

"Yes of course, very generous of them. My second subsidised meal in a day. Great stuff."

Evangeline Bolls was sensational. She was a bit on the large side, but had real steel in her voice, and the top was magnificent. The recitative before Donna Anna's monumental act one aria "*Or sai chi l'onore*" was spine-chilling, and so was the aria itself. She was a bit less happy in the quieter, more rapt beginning to the act two aria "*Non mi dir*", but the fast-running *coloratura* at the end was immaculate. Her acting was feisty and accomplished, and she'd undoubtedly be a great Rosalinde. I was delighted that she wasn't as finished an artist as Lindsey, but she would be a damn sight more interesting than Lisa Danieli would have been. Before the applause had finished, Graham and I went through the pass door, and headed at top speed for her dressing room. We arrived there just before she did. She was running her finger underneath the lace at the front of her wig, and pulling it off, causing hairpins to cascade to the floor. We followed her into the room, and Graham shut the door and leant against it so no-one else could get in.

"Miss Bolls," I said. I caught Graham's eye, and he smirked slightly. "I am James Barlow, casting director of Opera London. You were absolutely marvellous – I can't believe I haven't heard you before."

"Thank you Mr Barlow."

"Miss Bolls, may I ask who is your agent? I must speak to him. Or her."

"I'm afraid I have no agent yet, Mr Barlow."

Graham's eyes lit up.

"Well, then I must ask you direct," I said. "Are you free this autumn? To do Rosalinde in our new *Fledermaus*."

"Y-yes, oh yes I am, how wonderful," she stammered. "When exactly?"

"Rehearsals start on September the fourth, and the performances go on until mid-November."

"I'd love to do it," she said. Her face was alight with excitement.

Graham extended a hand towards her. She shook it, in some confusion.

"Jamie is right, Miss Bolls. You were fantastic. My name is Graham Butterfield, and I have a very successful agency, based in London. Would you like me to represent you?"

"Oh well, yes, of course. What do you think, Mr Barlow?"

"He's the perfect man for the job," I said. "You need look no further. Graham, you seem to have just taken on one of the most talented young singers I've heard for years."

"Oh dear, this is all a bit sudden," said Evangeline. "I think I'm going to cry."

"Yes, of course, you must be exhausted," I said. "We'll leave you in peace. But may I just take a telephone number before we go?"

Graham and I both entered her number into our phones, and then made our excuses and opened the door. The corridor outside was filling up rapidly. At the head of the queue was Stephen Gibson, Lindsey's former agent, and sometime lover of Janet Hopkirk.

"You got here first, then, Graham," he said. "Did she say yes?"

"Yes, Stephen, I'm delighted to say I now represent Miss Bolls. Hard luck."

Gibson said "Fuck," very loudly, and slunk off in a huff.

"Graham," I said. "I cannot possibly leave without saying bravo to Olivier Leclerc. I don't care if he is a poisonous little queen, I must at least make contact. He's conducting our *Fledermaus*. Evangeline Bolls, as of five minutes ago, is in it."

" I should come too," he said. "Wouldn't be doing my job if I didn't."

So off we went down to the bowels of the theatre, just by the entrance to the orchestra pit, and knocked on the door of the conductor's room.

I'd been worried Olivier would already have left, but he answered the door, looking sweaty and dishevelled. Fair enough, I thought – it was a strenuous business, conducting an opera – but Olivier Leclerc looked exceptionally unattractive. He was in any case an unprepossessing individual. Pale as death, he had almost transparent skin, with barber's rash on his neck. There was a large wart on his chin, with three long, wiry hairs emerging from it. He had purple semicircles under eyes which managed somehow to be both sunken and bulging, with intense green irises and enormous pupils. His whole grotesquely thin face was framed by vast, bat-like ears and a shock of chaotic ginger hair. As unhealthy-looking a specimen as you could meet. But possessed of an almost uncanny ability to shape music of the eighteenth century.

He was now branching out into new repertoire – hence his forthcoming *Fledermaus* for us. He was also, as Angus had acidly pointed out when we'd had lunch in Bacchus, the other main contender for Music Director of Opera London. Whatever I thought of that notion, he would have been a frightening enemy, so I needed to keep him sweet.

"*Maestro*," I said. They liked being called maestro. "Bravo, you were terrific. Such brave *tempi*. I heard so many things in it I have never heard before."

"Good sings, Hi 'ope."

"Yes, of course, magnificent things. The whole evening was a real revelation. Many congratulations."

"Hand what you are doing 'ere, Jemms?" he asked.

"I'm glad you asked that. I came over to hear Evangeline Bolls."

"She eez fantastic," he said. "Ze best Donna Anna since Ponselle."

"I quite agree. Graham Butterfield is going to represent her, aren't you Graham?"

"Yes, absolutely."

"Anyway," I said, "I've got something to ask you, Olivier. How would you feel about Evangeline Bolls singing Rosalinde with you in our autumn *Fledermaus*?"

"Hi sought Danieli was doing eet."

"Not any more. She cancelled today. She's five months pregnant."

"Merde. Zese women, zey are a pain in my asshole."

"Well, Olivier, if you say so. But what about Bolls as her replacement? Can I go ahead and book her."

"Do what you fucking like," he said.

10

I felt absolutely bloody the next morning. I managed to down two cups of coffee and a couple of nasty croissants before I paid my bill, and left in a screaming rush to try and find the Hilton Hotel in Groenplats. From there, with surprising ease, I caught the Freshair bus, which left at eight-thirty.

The newsstand at Erps-Kwerps airport, to my astonishment, had a copy of that morning's *Statesman*. There was a picture of Gregory Knipe staring at me from the front page. I thrust my hand in my pocket, found a two-Euro coin, bought the paper, and read the following:.

STATESMAN 2 page 5: JANET HOPKIRK INTERVIEWS GREGORY KNIPE, CHAIRMAN OF BELEAGUERED OPERA LONDON.

They'd been fixing up this interview at the *Figaro* party, I thought. Something to do with Rebroff. It had to be.

For a ghastly moment I thought that the foreign edition didn't have the supplement with it, but then I realised that it had been shoved inside the main body of the paper. I sat down and turned to page five.

They had photographed him at his most saturnine, and therefore his most repellent. In a box half-way through the article, the following text was printed in large letters:

REBROFF'S FORTUNE WILL NO DOUBT SECURE THE FUTURE OF SOME OPERA COMPANY. BUT AT WHAT COST?

I read it eagerly, pausing to take in every detail and nuance of Knipe's argument. He had taken the opportunity to distance himself from the whole Sergei Rebroff phenomenon. His own syndicate of donors was nearly complete, he said. Opera London would be able to forge ahead with an artistic policy untainted by *the demands of a Russian oligarch whose money has been made in less than savoury circumstances.* The Arts Council would otherwise, he said, have had to look seriously at its long-term commitment to the Company.

God knows what he had done to nobble Hopkirk, but she was in gushing form, finishing the article with *to the relief of all true opera lovers, Opera London is in safe hands. Gregory Knipe is the man to save us all from Slavic Slavery.*

A voice on the public address system announced, in heavily inflected English:

"Would passenger Barlow, wishing to travel on Freshair flight 312 to London Stansted, please go <u>immediately</u> to gate two, where your flight is fully boarded and awaiting departure."

I tucked Knipe's grinning face under my arm, picked up my briefcase, and ran all the way to the plane.

As soon as we landed at Stansted, I phoned Angus.

"Have you seen Hopkirk's article?" he said.

"Yes, I picked it up in Brussels. What are we going to do?"

"You'll have to find Tatyana's number, then come straight over to my place. We'll ring her when you're here. You'd better go into the office yourself and get it. I don't want anyone knowing we're talking to her."

"Right then. I'll be as quick as I can."

The whole of the first floor was in a rictus of excitement when I arrived at the office. The words "Knipe" and "Rebroff" were being thrown about the open-plan room like footballs. I tried to be unobtrusive as I went over to my computer to retrieve Tatyana's number, but I failed miserably.

"Jamie, I thought you weren't in," said Grace. "Have you seen Hopkirk's piece?"

"Absolutely, Gracie. What do you all think?"

"What a disaster! We all thought there was a really good chance of getting Rebroff's money. Now it looks like we get no money, AND we're stuck with Greg the Dreg."

"Yes, it's not good, is it? Anyway, I'm not here really. I've just got to pick up a phone number."

"Whose? And why couldn't you just ring and ask me to get it?"

"I didn't want to bother you." I lowered my voice. "Look Grace, it's nothing very important. But I can't tell you about it right now, okay? "

I found Tatyana's number on my computer and keyed it into my phone.

"Sorry, Gracie. All will be revealed soon, I promise."

I tried to sneak out. The calls of "Jamie, wait" which followed me down the stairs told me I had been as unsuccessful as when I went in. As I walked out into the street I looked at my watch. It was twenty to one. I had a vague feeling I had forgotten something, but couldn't for the life of me remember what it was.

I got to Angus's flat in West Hampstead half an hour later. He was still in his pyjamas, and extremely dishevelled.

"Gloria left at ten o'clock," he said. "It's just that I haven't bothered to get dressed. I've been plotting."

"Plotting what?"

"How to get rid of Knipe, you cretin. Are you up for a bit of serious skulduggery? With Sergei's help, of course. He's reputed to be something of an expert at it."

"Well, I can't see why not, Gussie. As long as it's not actually illegal."

"Bit of a moot point. Depends how clever we are."

"Jesus Christ. All right, let's hear it."

"Okay. We've already discussed our friend Gregory's unwise predilection for members of his own sex, and in particular for Olivier Leclerc."

"Please don't tell me you're going to persuade Olivier into a bit of kiss-and-tell."

"Of course not. I am going to tell you a story. This story concerns Julian Pogson, our very own Opera London Company Baritone. He, believe it or not, found time over the weekend to sashay off to some monstrous gay party on the Belgian-Dutch border. Pogson, of course, is supposed to be rehearsing Antonio in Salzburg as well as singing The Count with us, but rehearsals in Salzburg are going extremely slowly, and they haven't scheduled Act Two until the end of this week, so Julian's got a few days off. After the *Figaro* matinee on Sunday he got in the car and whizzed through the Tunnel, getting to Breda, which is where the party was, at about midnight. Quite a journey, you'll agree, but my experience is that these chaps have never minded a bit of international travel when willy needs attention.

"So anyway, Pogson walks into this haven of peace and tranquillity, and waits while his eyes adjust to the darkness. A certain sombre gloom is, I gather, *de rigueur* for this sort of do. Eventually he sees something quite unmentionable going on in the corner of the room. Julian thinks he might like to join in – I know, I know, it's not a pleasant thought – but he changes his mind as soon as he realises that one of the tangled mass of bodies belongs to none other than up-and-coming maestro Olivier Leclerc, who's jumped in the car and driven up from Antwerp for the occasion. Pogson is, to my relief, and I'm sure to yours as well, somewhat put off by this astonishing bit of synchronicity, so he simply makes a mental note, and then swans off to sow his own wild oats elsewhere.

"As soon as he gets back to London he phones me to let me know what he saw. He does this sort of thing for me on a regular basis, does Julian. I think he thinks it'll enhance his career."

"Dear God, Angus. This is getting worse and worse."

"Shut up and stop being such a bloody prude. As far as I'm concerned, the moral of this story is that dear little Olivier is clearly not averse to a bit of group sex, even when he appears to be involved in what is laughingly called a long-term relationship with our beloved Chairman. Now, I have been pondering in my heart how to use this nugget of information in the fight against Knipe, and this morning I have come up with a rather good plan. First, however, another teeny little bit of background. There was an interesting moment at Sergei's little do in his suite at the Savoy after the *Figaro* performance on Thursday night."

I must have flinched slightly. A look of concern briefly crossed Angus's unshaven features.

"Don't worry old boy, nearly finished. You may or may not remember that two of the participants in that night's near-orgy were Julian Pogson (remember him?) and little Jason Tang, shortly to be the newest Opera London Young Singer. This liaison almost passed me by at the time, since as you may remember I was engaged in my own bit of slap-and-tickle with Gloria. But this morning I put two and two together, and formulated my nefarious scheme."

He gave me a smug little smile.

"I suggest we arrange a *ménage-a-trois* in which the participants are Gregory Knipe, Olivier Leclerc and Jason Tang. I am pretty sure this is achievable because I know Leclerc fancies Tang. Jason told me he auditioned to him the other week, and Leclerc's eyes nearly popped out of their sockets. When Jason had finished singing, Leclerc called him down into the auditorium to talk to him. He said he loved his voice, and invited him to come over to Antwerp to sing in some Baroque opera he's conducting in a couple of years' time. At the end of the conversation Leclerc reached out to shake hands, and pressed into Jason's hand a piece of paper. It said *you have a very cute ass*, and had his mobile number on it.

"What I suggest is that we persuade Jason to go and see Leclerc, and convince him that what would really float his boat is a threesome with him and Greg. Olivier, whose tongue will be hanging out, will need no second bidding. He will swallow it whole. If you'll pardon the expression."

"But how the hell do we get Jason to agree?"

"Asked him on the phone this morning. Told him what a boost it would give to his career when I take over."

"But we're not supposed to be telling anyone."

"Needs must, old chap. Anyway, Jason ummed and ahhed a bit, but eventually, bless his little cotton socks, he laughed and said it might be quite fun, as long as we protect his reputation, anonymity, all that."

"So how do you intend to exploit this extraordinary liaison? How do we actually make sure Knipe leaves?"

"That's the simple part. Jason goes and tells Knipey he's going to the tabloids. He feels duty bound to tell the British public about the three-in-a-bed party at Olivier's. Unless, that is, Gregory offers to resign from the chairmanship of Opera London. Job done. Oh by the way, I offered Jason ten grand to do it. Hope you don't mind."

All I could think of was poor innocent little Jason Tang becoming the nastiest kind of *agent provocateur*. Sod it. I was already in it up to my eyeballs.

"Looks like it's a done deal, then, Gussie."

My phone bleeped at me. It was a text from Carly.

L o Daddy I won th high jmp. Were r u?

"Jesus Christ" I said. "What time is it?"

"One-fifty-five, old bean. Why?"

"Fuck and fuck and fuck. I've missed Carly's sports day. Mum was doing a picnic. Sorry Gussie, I've got to go."

"Wait, for God's sake. We've got to arrange the appointment with Sergei."

"Oh, Jesus, so we have."

I rang Tatyana, and tried to sound like an international arts administrator. Apparently Sergei would be in London tomorrow, the twenty-ninth of June. Of course he bloody would – he'd be coming to *Figaro*, wouldn't he? We fixed an appointment for eleven o'clock, at the Savoy, then I hurtled out of Angus's house and jumped in a taxi.

I told the driver to go straight to the school. On the way I sent Carly a text to say I was on my way, and that she should wait for me.

When I got to the sports field the first sight that greeted me was Mum and Dad and Carly, all sitting on a groundsheet, munching their way through delicious-looking bits of quiche.

"James. How good of you to join us," said my mother. "Would you like some quiche? Or is my little picnic beneath the dignity of a grand personage like you?"

"No, of course not. Look, I'm really sorry Mum. How did you manage to get here?"

Dad looked at me sadly, as if I'd really let him down. "We waited for about half an hour, then Pauline said we really ought to get the car out and drive over, because we might just arrive in time to see Carly's event. We didn't quite make it in time."

"Sorry Dad. Not one of my better efforts."

Mum wasn't letting this opportunity pass by. "Don't say sorry to us, dear. It's Charlotte you should be apologising to. She won, by the way."

"Yes, I know, Mum. She sent me a text."

Carly was sitting cross-legged on the groundsheet, with her eyes fixed firmly on the floor.

"Where were you, Daddy? I jumped really well, and I beat Pandora Aitken, who's the best in the school."

"Well done darling. I'm really sorry I wasn't here."

"Don't call me darling."

"I had to go and see Uncle Angus."

"You forgot, didn't you, Daddy?" She looked dangerously as if she was about to cry. But then her phone made a funny sound, like a bird in labour. She squealed.

"It's Mummy ringing me. It says so." She picked it up. "Hallo?" She listened for a while, then said: "I won Mummy. I beat Pandora Aitken. But no-one was here to see me… yes, I was really upset. I've been crying. Do you want to talk to Daddy now?" She pressed a button and looked curiously at the phone, then handed it to me. "Daddy, I think I might have switched Mummy off."

She hadn't switched Mummy off. Mummy was marshalling her forces for the attack.

"Jamie, how COULD you?" she said. She was talking awfully loud. "You knew how important this was for her. Or I thought you did."

"Well you weren't bloody well here either, were you Miss Perfect?" It was the guilt which made me say it. The effect was immediate.

"How dare you? Everyone thinks you're so marvellous, Jamie, did you know that? The husband who does everything for his family while his Diva wife is swanning around the capitals of Europe. And what's really happening? I'm here working my tits off, and you can't even remember our daughter's Sports Day. Well, I'll tell you what you can do. You can stop ringing me, stop texting me, and stop asking me to get money for your shit of an opera company."

And that was that. The line went dead, and I handed the phone back to Carly, who was looking at me a bit oddly. So was Mum.

"James, I don't think you should let Lindsey shout at you like that. Everyone on the sports field heard your whole conversation."

Several tardy picnickers were staring at me. Jesus Christ, that was why Lindsey was making such a racket. Carly had switched it to loudspeaker by mistake.

"Look, I'll tell you what," I said. I'll go and get a bottle of Coke for Carly, and a bottle of Gewürztraminer for us, and we can at least have a bit of fun. What about that?"

There was a long pause. Eventually it was my Dad who answered.

"James, we can't always wave a magic wand and make everything better, as your mother has been telling me these last forty-three years. We were all looking forward to our picnic, and Carly really wanted you to see her jump. Now we've all listened to you having an embarrassing row with your wife. You're not a bad lad, really, but today you've made a complete mess of things. Now, have a piece of your mother's excellent quiche, and shut up."

"Thank you, Derek," said Mum, quietly. "Very occasionally, you remind me why I married you."

11

Lindsey was due back at midnight in readiness for the next day's performance. At about seven-thirty, while Carly was upstairs doing this term's last bit of homework, she rang from the airport.

"Oh, Jamie, hi. Look, I'm sorry about going off the deep end this afternoon. You were quite right – it was as much my job to be at Carly's Sports Day as yours. I was feeling guilty enough about her as it was."

"It's me who should say sorry, Linds. I completely forgot, which is unforgivable. But I can't pretend it's not difficult, managing here without you. Did you get anywhere with nannies, by any chance?"

"Actually, I did go online yesterday and have a look at some agencies. But this morning I got a call from Miep in the Company Office in Amsterdam. You remember Miep?"

Certainly I remembered Miep. Legs up to her armpits, and the smile of a Botticelli Angel.

"Yes, of course I do," I said.

"Well, this is probably nothing, but Miep has an eighteen-year old daughter called Saskia, who wants to do a gap year in England, living with a family. Miep asked me whether we might be interested. I said yes, definitely."

Jesus. If Saskia looked anything like her mother, I was going to be in serious trouble.

"Linds," I said, "don't you think we ought to look at some more agencies first? We've no idea what this girl is like with kids. Carly will probably run rings round her."

I looked behind me nervously, in case Carly had sneaked in to the room, but there was no-one there. I quietly pushed the door shut.

"Nonsense, Jamie, this is a really good idea."

I didn't much fancy another row, so I said "okay, okay. I'll ring Miep and talk to her."

"Hang on Jamie, it looks as if we're boarding. I'll have to go. Listen, when I get to Stansted can I get another taxi home? I know it's expensive, but I'm so tired."

"Yes, of course you must get a taxi, Linds. You've got to stay at the top of your game, for all our sakes. But please would you pay him yourself tonight? I really need to go to bed. Angus and I have got to see Mr Sergei Ivanevitch Rebroff tomorrow morning."

A slight catching of the breath? I wasn't sure.

"You're working fast. Okay, I'll pay the taxi, and I'll sleep in the spare room so as not to wake you."

"And I'll try not to wake you tomorrow morning, Linds. Have a good flight."

The next morning, I was up in plenty of time for once, and the bacon and egg was top-class. Carly was talking excitedly about the end of term, and her forthcoming holiday in Rutland with Albert, Lindsey's Dad. I rushed about trying to get everything done, with much shush-ing, and you'll wake your mother-ing.

I dropped Carly at school clutching end-of-term presents for her piano teacher and Mrs Bodley – Mum had remembered to take her shopping for them, thank God. Then I rushed home, and dialled Miep's direct line in the Company Office in Amsterdam. She answered straight away in her sexy Dutch accent.

"Oh, Jamie, hi, really good to hear you. Are you ringing about Saskia?"

"Yes, I certainly am. Lindsey says she might be interested in coming to be our *au pair*."

"She is more than interested. I spoke to her last night. She was so excited she could hardly speak."

"Well, we'd definitely like to have her," I heard myself saying.

"Fantastic, Jamie. When should she start?"

"Beginning of September would be ideal."

"Fine. Shall we make it Sunday the third? The day before Lindsey flies over to us to start *Onegin* rehearsals."

"Perfect."

"That's settled then. I'll ring to let you know when and where she's arriving. I'm sorry to rush you, Jamie, but I have to go down to the rehearsal room before the morning session. We'll speak again before September."

I scribbled a note telling Lindsey that it was all fixed up, and left it propped up on the kitchen table. Then I quietly let myself out of the house.

I arrived at the Savoy, dressed in my best bib and tucker, at ten to eleven. Angus was waiting in the foyer with Tatyana. The first thing she said to me was "ah, good morning Misterr Barlow. Very punctual. Sergei likes punctuality. Before we go up, would you be so kind as to arrange four tickets for us for performance tonight? He insists on paying."

He couldn't keep away, could he? But then if he was planning to give us all that money maybe that wasn't so unreasonable.

"Of course," I said. "Mr Knipe is away, so once again I will arrange for you to have his box. I imagine Sergei wants to be as discreet as possible? After yesterday's interview in *The Statesman* everyone is talking about him. Do you know if he has seen the article?"

"Of course. Now, tickets, if you would be so kind."

I tried to look cool as I dialled Grace's number.

"Gracie, would you mind fixing Knipe's box for tonight? I need four tickets in all, and I don't want anyone else in there."

"Sounds exciting, Jamie. Who's this for, then?"

"Secret."

"Ooh, sorry I spoke. Comps presumably?"

"No, to pay for. Okay?"

"Consider it done, oh mighty one." I flipped my phone shut.

"All done, Tatyana. The tickets will be at the box office in my name. Will you be able to pick them up?"

"Of course."

The three of us walked straight across the small Art deco foyer, and down a single step to a discreet little lift. From nowhere appeared one of Sergei's heavies – the one with the ear-ring. He terrified me, so to make myself feel better I decided that if the two of them were called Mutt and Jeff, then he was Mutt.

There were two businessmen waiting there. When the first lift arrived, Angus and I let them get in first. Mutt put out a swift hand to prevent us following them.

When the next lift came, Tatyana put a plastic card through the reader and pressed the button for the top floor. When we arrived the doors slid open, and we were greeted by Jeff, the other bodyguard. He looked at Angus and me closely, then said something in Russian to Tatyana.

"I am sorry gentlemen, but my colleague must check you both for weapons," she said. Gawd. Jeff proceeded to frisk us thoroughly, then nodded at Tatyana. She said "follow me, please," and unlocked a large door with the same plastic keycard which she had used in the lift.

Sergei was sitting behind a huge desk, talking on the phone. He was speaking Russian.

"Even though he is currently most interested in opera, he has of course other business to attend to," said Tatyana.

I looked at Angus. He was nodding earnestly, as if he were quite used to this sort of thing. Presumably he'd been through it all once already, at the post-*Figaro* party.

Eventually Sergei put the phone down, and smiled at us. The film-star smile. Yuck.

"Angus, we meet again, what a pleasure. And Jimmy, thank you for coming. Lindsey has told me much about you. Judging by cast you put together for *Figaro*, your work is of highest quality.

"Thank you, Mr Rebroff."

"Call me Sergei, please."

"Yes, of course. Thank you Sergei. But I wonder if I might ask you to call me Jamie, rather than Jimmy? I have hated that name ever since I was a child."

He laughed. "Of course Jamie, please forgive me. So, let us get down to business. As you know, I would like to endow Opera London with a gift of many millions of pounds. And I would like you, Angus, to be Musical Director, and Jamie to be General Director. 'The Dream Team,' Lindsey tells me. She was quite clear that I must give my money to Opera London, and she left me in no doubt who should be doing top jobs."

"This is astonishingly generous of you, Sergei," said Angus. "All of Opera London is profoundly grateful to you."

"It is I who am grateful to you, Angus, for agreeing to accept my gift. Those of us who are lucky enough to have money must spend it wisely. My mother was herself singer with most beautiful voice. Since she died while I was still child, I look for opportunity to fulfil promise I make to her, that I will devote my life to opera. Sadly I myself cannot sing. So for me now is, instead, great privilege to give money. I believe I can free your company for ever from its financial difficulties."

Angus was ready with his most unctuous smile.

"The privilege is ours, Sergei. We will do our best to justify the faith you have shown in us."

"Good, gentlemen," said Sergei. "I have no doubt that we will make most successful partnership." He picked up from his desk a copy of the previous day's *Statesman*. "But we have problem, as you know. Mr Knipe says publicly that he does not want my money. How easy do you think it will be to proceed without him? Angus?"

"Our problem," said Angus, "is that in any fight over the future of Opera London, the Arts Council may well favour Mr Knipe, because he has been assiduous in his wooing of its members, and very careful to keep the public on his side. His interview with Miss Hopkirk is just the latest part of his public and private campaign to retain control of the Company."

"But does he have money to secure Company's future?" asked Sergei.

"Clearly he doesn't have access to the kind of funds you are so kindly offering." said Angus. "But, as he mentioned in the interview, he has put together a syndicate of wealthy donors, and must be confident that sufficient money is available to clear Opera London's considerable debts. The Arts Council will almost certainly not be prepared, as it has been in the past, to come up with this money itself. Our best chance of success, it seems to me, is to persuade the Arts Council that, under Jamie and myself, the Company is in safe hands artistically, and that with your money it is secure financially."

"For me it is advantage that Mr Knipe is not interested in working with me because I wish myself to become Chairman of the Company."

Angus looked at me, a bit startled. It seemed an obvious solution. But neither of us, as far as I know, had thought of it.

"Is this in keeping with your wishes, please? Jamie?" Sergei sounded a bit desperate. It occurred to me to wonder what privileges he would expect as the new Chairman. Twice-weekly sex with the General Director's wife?

"It seems a very reasonable suggestion, Sergei. I'm sure we would work together admirably."

Sergei nodded. "Angus?"

"Yes, I agree with Jamie. But we are left with the central problem. How do we get rid of Knipe?"

Sergei smiled a rather chilling smile. "I think to get rid of him will not be difficult. But we must do it with care, as we are operating within your revered British democracy. We must do nothing to arouse suspicion. For this reason, I have had my people do little research into Mr Knipe, and have come up with incriminating information. This information we call *kompromat* in my country. It is great help when solving problems of this kind."

What *kompromat* did he have on us, I wondered? But Angus didn't seem to be worried about a thing. Like an eager schoolboy, he said, "you may be interested to know, Sergei, that we have some excellent *kompromat* of our own on Mr Knipe. And a very good plan for making him resign as Chairman."

Sergei raised his eyebrows. "Please tell me your plan, Angus."

Angus went into the whole Knipe/Leclerc/Tang idea with enormous relish, furnishing Sergei with every unpleasant detail.

"Am I right," asked Sergei, "that this Jason Tang was at party I gave here after *Marriage of Figaro?*"

"Yes, absolutely, Sergei," said Angus, who was clearly beginning to enjoy himself. "He was getting up to all sorts with Julian Pogson."

"This is excellent. Angus, you have a surprising talent for this sort of thing. As well as being world-class conductor." He laughed. "And great ladies' man, as I also noticed at my soirée. I think we should set plan in motion immediately. Angus, please speak to Jason Tang as soon as possible."

Angus looked a bit worried. "Of course, Sergei, I will be more than happy to talk to Jason. But I would not turn down any help you, or your people, can give me. I am beginning to realise the enormity of the task. And, er, I'm afraid I kind of offered Jason ten thousand pounds to do it. I might be a bit pushed to find that sort of money myself."

Sergei roared with laughter. "Angus my friend, ten thousand pounds is not big problem to me, as I'm sure you know. But you must of course offer him much, much more. If he were to go ahead with this plan, and then sell his story to any of the newspapers, they would pay him at least six-figure sum. I suggest you start by offering him one hundred thousand, and see what he says. There are, I think, very few young singers who could afford to turn down this kind of encouragement."

Angus looked flabbergasted. "Yes, yes I understand, Sergei, I'm sure you are right, now I come to think about it. That's what I will do, then. Thank you."

"In any case, Angus, all of my resources are at your disposal. You need only ring Tatyana, and she will pass all requests onto me personally. At this stage, I would, however, like to say that opera business, especially in this country, is very small. You must be discreet. I am happy, nonetheless, to leave this in your capable hands, Angus. Please keep Tatyana informed as to your progress. She has my absolute trust. And please remember that at this stage I want you only to talk to Jason, and to go no further."

"Of course, Sergei," said Angus.

Sergei paused and looked at each of us in turn. "But there is one more problem which we must at all costs solve."

"The Arts Council," I said.

"Yes, indeed, the Arts Council. What can we do to convince them that our team is as strong as any other? Financially *and* artistically, I mean."

Angus cut in: "financially you have obviously provided us with a far stronger bid than the rival faction. But artistically, I am afraid they may be perceived as the safer team. This is absurd, when Jamie and I are planning to take the reins. However, I can see one further contribution which the two of us can make here."

"Please tell me," said Sergei.

"Jamie and I have a friend from University. His name is Archie Foster. He is about to become Opera Manager for the Arts Council of England. We have always got on very well, and he admires my work – in fact it was at last Sunday's matinee performance of Figaro when I re-encountered him for the first time for some years. He told me with glee that his new job would involve him in deciding which of the Arts Council's clients should receive money, and which should be cut off to make way for new enterprises. I think we should approach him soon, and tell him of our plans. With any luck he will regard me, and of course Jamie too, as safe pairs of hands artistically."

"Maybe he can be persuaded to endorse my Chairmanship without our having to impugn Mr Knipe," said Sergei.

Where in God's name did he learn a word like *impugn*?

"Sergei, I don't think any of us should underestimate Mr Knipe," said Angus.

"No, no, I quite agree. Then maybe you are right, Angus. You should speak to Jason as soon as possible, and Jamie should see Archie Foster, also as soon as he can."

"Where will you be for the next few weeks?" said Angus. "In case we need your help?"

"It is not yet clear, Angus. I may have to go back to Russia. But rest assured that my funds are available whenever they should prove necessary. Now, I have only one further request."

"Anything you like, of course Sergei." I sounded like a fawning sycophant.

"Every business deal must be secured with glass of vodka," he said. "I rarely drink alcohol, but I always make exception for such occasions. I hope you will both join me here after performance tonight, to seal our collaboration?"

Carly would have to spend yet another night at Mum and Dad's. Mum wouldn't be pleased.

"Yes, of course," I said, "it will be a pleasure, Sergei. Angus?"

"Great idea, Sergei. Can I bring Gloria?"

"Of course, Angus. Nothing is complete without women." He turned and favoured me with his smarmiest smile. "And you will bring Lindsey?"

"Of course," I said, looking him straight in the eye. For a second he looked distinctly uncomfortable, then began to tidy the papers on his desk.

Angus and I emerged from the foyer into the hotel's little time-warp of an access road, and he climbed straight into one of the waiting taxis, pausing only to give me Archie Foster's number.

I decided to walk back to the office, and on the way I called Lindsey. She sounded tired, and when I told her that Sergei had asked us to celebrate in his suite after the show, she flatly refused.

"You go, Jamie. I'll have to go straight back home to bed".

I was hugely relieved, and didn't argue. I didn't fancy it much myself, but it would be easier on my own. I immediately called Tatyana, told her that Lindsey wouldn't be coming to the Savoy after the show, and arranged that Angus and I would meet them there. I sent Angus a text telling him I'd meet him at the stage door and that we'd get a taxi together.

Next I dialled Archie Foster's number, but he wasn't answering, so I left him a message.

"Archie, it's Jamie. Huge congrats on your new appointment – I've only just heard. Look old chap, I'd really like to see you. It's business.

Maybe we can have lunch? Give me a ring. Oh, and it's a bit hush-hush, so keep it under your hat."

As soon as I arrived back at the office, I had to sell the idea of Evangeline Bolls singing Rosalinde to Yvonne Umfreville, who as Head of Music took her casting responsibilities extremely seriously. I dialled her number.

"Yes, James, what do you want?"

"Yvonne, you know Lisa Danieli's cancelled *Fledermaus*?"

"Yes I bloody do. Stupid bitch. Hasn't she got enough children?"

Poor Yvonne was considered somewhat unlikely to have children of her own. She didn't have much time for other people's.

"Can I pop down and see you about it?"

"Fine." She put the phone down.

I ran down the stairs to her office and knocked on her door – she had a room with a Steinway piano in it in the old part of the theatre. Nobody, especially singers, ever walked through that door without experiencing a frisson of terror. She was Head of Music, which meant she was in charge of the coaches who helped prepare the singers for their roles, and who played the piano at the early rehearsals when the orchestra wasn't there. She herself was a pianist of astonishing technical prowess, and an administrator of fearsome efficiency, but her bedside manner left much to be desired, especially when engaged in one-to-one coaching sessions. With one dismissive comment – "that's simply not good enough – flat, late and it sounds like a banshee on cocaine" – she could render international stars incapable of setting foot on stage. I did my best to keep her away from all but the most resilient singers.

"Come," said an impatient voice.

She was sitting behind an immaculately tidy desk, studying a score. She was the most extraordinary-looking creature: short and plump, shaped a bit like a football, really. She had a pudgy face topped by close-cropped blond hair. Her mouth was twisted into a permanent sneer, and one ear had at least ten silver rings hanging from holes evenly spaced from the bottom of the lobe to somewhere around the ear's unattractive middle. Today, as usual, she was dressed in black canvas fatigues, which gave her a disturbingly masculine appearance.

"Well?" she said.

"Yvonne, I've found a cracking replacement for Danieli."

"Who? Please say it's not Lindsey."

"No, it's not Lindsey. She's busy, as a matter of fact."

"I've heard Lindsey's been *very* busy, just lately."

I decided to ignore this. "Lindsey will be doing *Onegin* in Amsterdam, so isn't free. I want to cast a girl called Evangeline Bolls."

"Oh, I know. Olivier Leclerc's doing *Giovanni* with her in Antwerp. Says she's marvellous."

"Then it's okay with you if I go ahead and book her?"

"Well Olivier's conducting the bloody thing, isn't he? If he likes her, it's fine by me."

Normally I would have expected far more of a struggle. But what I had forgotten was that Yvonne and Olivier were bosom pals. Apparently she and her girlfriend Olga frequented the same late-night bars as Olivier when he was in Town. There were rumours of the most lurid kind, involving everything from whips to cocaine.

"Terrific. Thanks, Yvonne."

"Keep me posted on any developments on Sergei Rebroff and Lindsey." She smirked unpleasantly. "Individually or severally."

"I doubt if I know any more about Sergei Rebroff than you do. Anyway I've got to run. I'll get Grace to confirm about Bolls in writing." And without waiting for an answer, I let myself out of the room.

Rumours about Lindsey and Sergei were obviously circulating. Bugger the whole bloody lot of them, I thought.

12

With much tutting and sighing Mum agreed once again to have Carly for supper and for the night. I went home after work to shower and shave, and spent about two hours trying to decide what clothes would be appropriate for an intimate post-show party in a private suite at one of the world's most exclusive hotels. I had nothing at all suitable, and no Lindsey to advise me – she had long since left for the theatre. I ended up looking a complete dork in a ten-year-old Ciro Citterio suit that had definitely seen better days.

There were problems on the Tube, and by the time I made it to the stage door Angus had been waiting for a good five minutes. Gloria was there too, wearing the lowest-cut dress I'd ever seen. My eyes, I'm embarrassed to report, were out on stalks.

"It's a lovely dress, isn't it Jamie?" said Angus, somewhat acidly. "We bought it on Tuesday afternoon, after you'd called to say we were getting the money. It's Armani and it cost a bloody fortune, didn't it little Gloria?"

"Ooh, yes, a fortune."

"Worth every penny," I told them both. "Now let's get a move on."

There was a queue of fans outside. I guessed they were really waiting for Lindsey, but a couple of them proffered photos for Gloria and Angus to sign. We managed to get away fairly quickly, then we legged it to the Victoria Station taxi rank.

On the way to the Savoy Angus quickly filled Gloria in on the deal we had made with Sergei. He had kept it quiet until now, he said, because it was very important that no-one else in Opera London should know what was going on. He left out the controversial bits – about the Knipe entrapment, and about Archie Foster. Gloria smiled brightly throughout the whole speech. I suspected Angus valued her more for her sexual prowess than for her intellect.

It wasn't long before we turned right off The Strand into the hotel's grand entrance. Tatyana was waiting for us on the pavement. She allowed one of the grey-suited commissionaires to open the taxi door, then gave him something which looked suspiciously like a fifty-pound note for his trouble.

We went through the same meet and greet rigmarole with Mutt and Jeff, and Tatyana let us in to the suite with her pass card. We walked through the office into Sergei's inner sanctum. Tatyana quietly shut the door behind us.

The room was sumptuously decorated in cream and gilt, with prints on the walls of the original productions of all the Savoy Operas. The incongruity of the situation was not lost on me. Draped over a slightly sinister-looking black velvet sofa was Mother Russia's newest oligarch, ready to celebrate his decision to bestow millions of his ill-gotten petrodollars on our little opera company. And behind him, leering at me from within a gilt frame on the wall, was George Grossmith dressed as Bunthorne in *Patience*.

Sergei's sofa was one of four arranged in a square around a low, painted, cream-and-gilt table which was laden with huge numbers of the most delicious-looking canapés. Beside them stood a bottle of vodka and four bottles of Staropramen beer. All five bottles had condensation dripping down them.

Sergei got up and pumped Angus's hand.

"Angus, I am so proud. To be part of such extraordinary artistic achievement is something I have dreamed of since childhood. Now, finally, I am within reach." Then he seized Gloria by the shoulders, and pulled her towards him so he could kiss her on both cheeks. Her breasts wobbled precariously.

"Gloria, I have seen three times your Susanna, and you are quite captivating. Thank you for being so wonderful."

"Thank *you* Sergei," she simpered. "What wonderful news about you taking over the Company, and giving us your money, and everything. Angus says it's all terribly hush-hush."

"Yes indeed. There are many hoops we must jump through before we can say Company is mine. We must not tell anyone just yet."

Then he turned his attention to me. "Jamie, finally I have chance to entertain you here in my private rooms. My sadness is only that Lindsey cannot come, but I understand she has to rest."

He gestured for us to sit down, perched himself on one of the sofas, poured vodka for us all, and opened the beers. "Don't worry," he said. "There are many more Staropramens in fridge. And of course more vodka in freezer." He picked up his glass of vodka, said "*nazdarovye*", and downed it in one. We all followed suit.

Gloria looked momentarily as if she was going to explode, and then said: "wow, Sergei, that's quite something. Mind if I pour myself some more?"

"You must have beer first. Then you repeat the process. As many times as you wish."

We all got roaring drunk very quickly. I suspected that Angus felt he should be concentrating on Sergei, but he was quite unable to resist when Gloria stuck her tongue down his throat. Within a short time she and Angus were behaving extremely inappropriately on the sofa.

Sergei was soon absolutely wasted. He watched the other two for a while, a sad smile on his face. It reminded me of me of my teens, when I went to those parties where everyone except me ended up snogging behind the drapes, while I sat there staring at them. Then he poured himself another vodka and said:

"I watch Angus and Gloria, and I feel sad. They are so happy, and enjoy each other with a kind of innocence which is very touching." I would have described Gloria as many things, but innocent was not one of them.

"This innocence," he went on, "is something which I have lost when still child. Because, you see Jamie, since my mother died I am unable to form easy relationships with women. No woman can ever be as perfect as my mother was. For me, therefore, my great love is opera. Opera is my way of paying homage to this wonderful woman." His words were very slurred, and he looked as if he was about to cry. "I have promised to her on her deathbed that I will devote my life to it. I loved her so much. And I have in Russia my wife Nadezhda, who is not perfect like my mother, but whom I have learned to love. And she is herself mother to my boys Aleksandr and Mikhail, whom I love madly. These people are my life, but I see them so very rarely. So instead I have opera, which is for my mother but also for me, for my soul. When I hear Lindsey singing *Dove Sono*, with its great sadness, I am transported to place which I cannot reach by any other means."

Gloria and Angus were becoming increasingly difficult to ignore. But Sergei took not a blind bit of notice.

"Jamie, I congratulate you. You have best wife in world. For first time, I love woman like I loved my mother. I am sorry, but is true. You must listen to me carefully. You maybe are worried that I will take her away from you. But is not possible. I cannot hurt her. And she loves you so much, and she loves too your Carly. Maybe one day Carly will marry Aleksandr, or my little Mikhail."

He began to cry, huge wracking sobs making his whole body shake. I didn't know what to do. Was I supposed to comfort him, or hit him? Gloria came up for air, and looked quizzically at this sad drunken wreck of a man, but he didn't retain her interest for long. She pulled Angus's face towards her, and glued her lips back onto his.

Eventually Sergei recovered himself slightly. "Jamie, I love you too. But I must see Lindsey, I must spend some time with her, I am sure you understand. I will not take her away from you, because I love you too much. I love her too much, also. She has fiery temper, this I find very sexy."

I considered decking him, but I was so pissed I doubted if I was in a fit state to do so, so I simply said:

"Sergei, I can't listen to any more of this. Lindsey is my whole life. I like you and all that, and I'm terribly grateful for all that fucking money, but you can't have my wife, so would you be kind and leave her alone? Now I think I should go before I say something naughty, so goodbye and thanks for absolutely everything."

At the third attempt, I managed to get off the deep-cushioned sofa and remain more or less upright. I attempted to focus again on Sergei, and said: "Probably by tomorrow we'll both have forgotten this conservation, so I think's better if I totter off home. 'Bye Angus, Gloria. Perhaps you'd better let Sergei join in. He's lonely."

I negotiated my way out of the door and out into the office, where Tatyana was doing some writing at a small desk on the other side of the room. She looked up and smiled the same pitying smile.

"He is no doubt very drunk – this always happens when he has even small amount of alcohol. In morning he will remember nothing of what anyone said. Tomorrow we must all return to Russia, Sergei has important business to attend to. Please if you wish to speak to him ring my cell phone. I hope you have enjoyed yourself. I will call car for you – this will be outside front door of hotel very shortly. Goodbye, Misterr Barlow."

She picked up the phone, and told it that she wanted a car immediately, to be added to Mr Rebroff's account, please. I let myself out of the door into the corridor, where Mutt sat on an upright chair, somewhat surprisingly playing Sudoku. He looked up at me, said "*Dussvidanya* ", and carried on with his puzzle. I took the lift to the ground floor, and turned left, sadly failing to spot the step which the management had thoughtlessly put in my way. I fell flat on my face and swore loudly. This brought a uniformed flunky running in my direction. He picked me up, none too gently, and frog-marched me across the foyer to the revolving door, where for logistic reasons he had to leave me on my own to negotiate the rest of the journey to my waiting Mercedes.

I tapped on the driver's window, which was parked facing the pavement. I remembered something Dad had told me when I was a boy – that the access road to the Savoy is the only street in London where the cars drive on the right. The memory made me unaccountably sad, and I started to cry. The driver looked at me, and somewhat reluctantly pressed his little button to open the window.

"Queens Park, please." I opened the back door, plonked myself down on the black leather seat, and wept piteously all the way home.

When we got there I spent about ten minutes trying to force money onto him, telling him I didn't want anything else from Sergei fucking Rebroff, thank you very much. Eventually he managed to extricate himself and drive off.

Lindsey was fast asleep in the spare room. Carly's bed was empty, which caused me a moment of panic, but then I remembered she was at Mum's. Pretty much convinced that I was going to lose both wife and daughter before very long, I went to the loo, crashed onto our bed fully clothed and put the light out. My last thought before falling into a deep, drunken stupor, was that we were all due to spend the weekend at Albert's, where the three of us had spent some of our happiest times. Please please please God let Stockencote work its magic, and make everything all right again.

13

If you wanted to experience the English Rural Idyll, you needed to look no further than Albert Templeton's farm at Stockencote. It overlooked Rutland Water, Europe's biggest man-made lake in England's smallest county. While to me Rutland Water was a thing of wonder, to the old denizens of the village of Hambleton it was nothing more than The Puddle, which had been foisted on them in the seventies by a succession of Governments more interested in the water supply than the picturesque English countryside. Rutland used to be the loveliest county in England, they complain. Pretty villages like Lower Hambleton, nestling in a deep green valley full of sheep and wonderful pubs, where they served local ale from the cask. Now it was fifty foot deep in water to supply the newly emergent economic area of East Midlands. Centuries of tradition brutally cut short by The Peterborough Effect.

But Stockencote had not only survived the depredations of Harold Wilson, or Ted Heath, or whoever perpetrated this act of vandalism, it had positively benefited from them. The Puddle was to Stockencote a private lake at the bottom of the garden – the magnificent old farmhouse had been just far enough up the hill to be on the peninsula instead of under the water.

The drive really did sweep round past the front of the house – a Georgian façade with real pillars on either side of the door. There was a pale blue carpet in the hall which was sheer folly – it meant everyone had to take their boots off – but then no-one ever went in the front door, only special visitors on their first visit, or guests coming for one of Albert's famous parties. Carly would sail up and down that carpet pretending that it was the sea.

The kitchen was the nerve-centre of the house. Flagstones which must have been there since it was built – polished by generations of wellies to a deep, reassuring shine. Eating cornflakes with a jug of milk fresh from last night's milking, with a thick layer of cream still on it. They had to be crisp – a newly-opened packet was ideal – and then that enormous metal milk jug, cold from the fridge. And tea – 'Builders' Tea' the Queens-Parkers called it, but at Stockencote it was just 'A Good Cup', the colour of tomato soup. Two spoonfuls of sugar, and not a Baby Gaggia in sight.

But the real joy of Stockencote was the people. Not just Albert, Lindsey's wonderful father. Not just Gordon Brewster, the pink-cheeked old farm manager from the cottage just up the hill. But Lindsey herself. She only had to arrive through the kitchen door and the cares of the world dropped off her shoulders. She need never walk on a stage again. They didn't recognise her in the village – not as Opera's Next Big Thing anyway. She could walk into the Finches Arms in Hambleton and she was just Albert's girl, back from The Smoke. All the lads in the village had fancied their chances with her, but she suddenly went off to make her fortune as an opera singer, if you please, and she came back with some wimpy chap she'd met at College. Mind you he wasn't a bad lad either, just a bit arty. At least he looked after Lindsey and that little tomboy who'd called herself Carly at the age of two.

But Lindsey on a horse, that was the thing. Looked like someone at Hickstead, or the Olympics, bolt upright and gut-wrenchingly gorgeous, in total harmony with the bay thoroughbred she'd been grooming and polishing all morning. All they were doing was hacking across the fields, but you had never seen anything so magnificent. And when she came in for lunch, the front end would be grinning from ear to ear, and the back end would be winking at me through her jodhpurs. You lucky bastard, it seemed to say, this arse is yours and yours alone – treat it with respect or some fucking Russian billionaire will shaft her away from you, before you can say Novosibirsk.

We arrived after a surprisingly good run up the A1. There had been the usual jam at Welwyn, but otherwise we had sailed through. And as we travelled north, both Lindsey and Carly gradually transformed from urban harpies into relaxed country girls, full of anticipation for their forthcoming stay at Stockencote. Lindsey and I were only coming for the weekend, and she had to get the train down to London and back the following day, to sing a performance of *Figaro*. But this didn't seem to worry her.

The journey had begun with: "Jamie, are you still drunk? Then: "why did you jump that red light? Do you want to get us all killed?" But it ended up with "Thank you for doing all that horrid driving, darling. Isn't it wonderful to be here?" Carly leapt out of the car, which we'd parked in the yard at the back of the house, and tore through the kitchen door. I heard Albert say "whoa there, Missy, what a big girl you are now. You'll have me over next time. My goodness, that's some hug, Carly. Or do we call you Charlotte, now you're so grown up?"

Ethel, Albert's elderly and odiferous pug, charged up to Lindsey as she walked in, and released a volley of piercing yaps as she snuffled ecstatically around her legs. Lindsey gave the dog a friendly pat, then enfolded Albert in a hug which lasted for at least thirty seconds. Albert looked over her shoulder and winked at me.

"Been treating her rough then, Jamie? She seems very keen on her old Dad today."

Life had dealt Albert Templeton a hideous blow. How do you cope with your wife dying when your only daughter is two? Car crash. She's on the motorway, it's pouring with rain, and suddenly she's faced with a lorry-load of tyres bouncing down the carriageway towards her. Bang. The end. Well, they all hope it was the end, and that she died quick. By the time it had all finished there were four lorries and thirteen cars all in a pile, and Lottie Templeton lying at the bottom, surrounded by bits of her ancient Land Rover. I've never asked, but I don't think those old buggers even had seat belts. She was practically unrecognisable – Albert had to go and look at six different corpses before he found what was left of the woman who was his soulmate, best friend, lover, well everything really. Poor bastard had never re-married. How could anyone ever match up? So instead he became a beaming, life-and-soul-of-the-party widower, every gold-digging divorcee within fifty miles making eyes at him at the Hunt Ball. But the one person he doted on was Lindsey.

You might have expected him to be furious when a failing baritone from Middlesex spirited her off to a two-up two-down in super-expensive Queens Park, a hundred miles away from the Family Pile. But even that didn't seem to faze him – often turning up in London for Sunday lunch having left the farm to Gordon for the day. Champagne in hand, and always a smacker for Lindsey. "Is this good-for-nothing office boy looking after my famous daughter?" he would say. "And here's Carly. By heck you're a pretty little thing Carly – where's a kiss for Grandad?" And from nowhere he would produce a mint humbug – a mint humbug for God's sake, surely they stopped making those things twenty years ago? He'd pop it into Carly's perfect little 'o' of a mouth, and she'd shove it in her cheek as she kissed Grandad right on the lips, and she'd say: "thank you Grandad. I love you," which was just what she was supposed to say.

It wasn't long before Albert said "now then, the sun's well and truly over the yardarm." He paused for a moment, then his face broke into a grin. "What about a G and T?"

He sent Carly off to the fridge to find the old-fashioned ginger beer which she loved, and which only Albert seemed to be able to get. Then he busied himself with our drinks – "Gilt, it is, you must always remember, G. I. L. T. Gin, Ice, Lemon, Tonic. And the tonic has to be fizzy, or you might as well be drinking meths." He made the same speech every time. It was your Welcome To Stockencote ritual.

Carly was due to stay at Albert's for the best part of a month. His elder sister – a spinster called Evie with a sharp tongue but a heart of gold – was due to come in every day from Monday onwards to look after her. A couple of years previously she had retired from being matron of a local nursing home, and liked nothing better than making herself useful to Albert, especially when Carly was in residence.

Carly, who adored Evie quite as much as Evie adored her, would spend every day helping Albert or Gordon round the farm. And they would all come in for their lunch, and instead of the doorstep sandwiches which Albert and Gordon would have when they were on their own, Evie would have cooked shepherd's pie, or beef stew and dumplings.

But over the weekend we were managing the cooking ourselves. Albert could cook a bit, but loved to have a break when we were visiting, so I cooked on the Saturday while Lindsey read the paper and rested in preparation for the show. We had a huge lunch so she wouldn't need to eat again that day – I cooked a lasagne, which was about as close as Albert would get to Funny Foreign Food. After lunch I took Lindsey to Peterborough station to catch the train to London, and then drove back to Stockencote to do a bit of relaxing myself. Evangeline Bolls and Ursula Zimmermann seemed a world away. So, thank God, did Sergei Rebroff, although I did remember while I was washing up the lunch things, that Tatyana had told me while I was drunk on Thursday night that Sergei had gone back to Russia for a while, which could only take the pressure off Lindsey and me.

Even the fact, which we had forgotten, that on Saturday nights the Inter-City trains stopped at eight-thirty, and Lindsey had to take the milk train back after the show, didn't dampen her spirits. When I picked her up from the station at twenty to one, she was full of how fantastically the show had gone. She didn't mention Sergei, and it was pretty clear by now that she also knew he'd gone back to Russia. And although she wouldn't have sex when we got into bed – too tired she said – we slept soundly, and together.

Sunday was the day for riding, and for Sunday lunch, which Lindsey was cooking. She had not gone to sleep until one-thirty, and she and I had to leave that afternoon at four to get her to Stansted for the seven-o-clock Freshair back to Salzburg. But she was determined to pack as much as possible into her short stay, so she got up at seven-thirty, and went out at eight-fifteen with Carly to fetch Cedric, the Welsh cob, in from the field. Albert always dispensed with his groom during the summer months ("bloody hell, Jamie, I'm not a bottomless pit. Got to save a few quid somewhere"), so the horse needed grooming and tacking up before Carly's riding lesson, at nine, with a local woman called Fliss. Fliss was a former Olympic horsewoman with a reputation for striking the fear of God into her young pupils, but Carly always had lessons when she came to Stockencote, because she had inherited Lindsey's passion for horses and seemed to thrive on Fliss's military style of teaching.

I went out at nine to watch them. The lesson had already started. As I walked up to the manège I heard Fliss's stentorian voice screaming: "Tits and teeth, Carly, tits and teeth." God knows what she was on about. But Carly was doing really well. She jumped a three-foot fence which Lindsey and I had to put up in the middle of the manège where the lesson was taking place. Fliss was pleased with Carly – "all that time in London doesn't seem to have affected her talent", she said – and Cedric behaved immaculately.

Lindsey, to my surprise, decided not to ride herself. But she was in a radiant mood all day, and for lunch she cooked the most succulent roast chicken. Although Albert wasn't about to tell Carly why the bird had such a fine flavour, I knew it was one of the hens which wandered about all day, picking bits of God-knows-what up from the yard. We had all the trimmings: chipolatas from the next-door farmer's pigs, stuffing and bread sauce. It was my favourite meal, bar none, and the couple of glasses of Albert's excellent Chablis which I allowed myself only added to my sense of wellbeing.

But after lunch it was time for a quick getaway. Before Lindsey got in the car, she and Albert had an emotional farewell. "I know it's only been a couple of days, Dad," she said, "but Stockencote's cast its spell on me as usual. I've been so tired, and so utterly fed up with being away and working, that I was afraid I wouldn't enjoy it this time. But it's been wonderful to see you, and to spend some proper time with Carly. I don't want to leave."

He pulled her into a warm embrace.

Lindsey, lass, you've always got a bed here, you know that. You're my little girl and I love you more than anything in the world. Don't you worry, we'll see each other very soon."

"What about you Dad. Will you be all right?"

"I'm lucky, I've got Carly staying here, so I'll be fine. Don't you worry about me. Now be off with you, before I make an exhibition of myself. Jamie, look after her."

"I will, Albert, of course. Thanks for a wonderful time."

He lifted Carly into his arms to wave goodbye. As he did so, he winced slightly.

"Dad, you keep doing that," said Lindsey. "Are you all right?"

"Little touch of sciatica, sweetheart. Comes of being an ancient old sod. Take no notice."

"As long as you're sure."

And off we went, down the A1, and the A14, and the M11 to Stansted bloody airport, leaving Carly and Albert waving at the kitchen door. As we drove, Lindsey's lips got tighter, and conversation became strained.

Shortly before we arrived at the airport she suddenly seized my hand.

"Jamie, this life's no good for me. You know that, don't you?"

"Um, yes. I mean no. I don't really know what to say."

"I'm sorry, Jamie. I don't make life easy for you, I know that. It's just that I've had the most wonderful weekend, and I don't want to go back to my horrible little flat in Salzburg. Can I come home with you?"

"Don't be daft, sweetheart. I mean it would be fantastic, but you're in the middle of the most exciting job of your career. And you've got to earn the dosh. Just see this one through, then we can all go off to Montpellier and have a fantastic holiday."

We drew up in the short term car park, where I had to drop her off. She opened her door, then before getting out she turned to me and gave me a whacking great hug.

"Jamie, I'm sorry about all this. I don't deserve someone as wonderful as you," she said.

Without waiting for a reply, she got out of the car, picked up her bag, and walked off into the terminal.

14

Lindsey away in Salzburg, until Tuesday night anyway. Sergei, thank the Lord, in Kamchatka or somewhere. And Carly in Rutland. I was left to my own devices, to play politics with Angus, and Gregory Knipe, and Archie Foster.

My phone rang at about eleven o'clock on Monday morning.

"Jamie? It's Archie. Long time no see. What's this you want to talk to me about? It sounds exciting."

"It's a bit difficult over the phone, Archie. When do you start your new job?"

"I'm starting next Monday, as a matter of fact, so my predecessor can show me the ropes, although I shan't get into harness properly until September."

"Can we meet for lunch this week?"

"Yes fine, Jamie. Tomorrow okay?"

"Yup. Where and when? Somewhere up near you, maybe. You still in Belsize Park?"

"Yes. Are you by any chance looking to put a certain distance between you and the premises of your opera company?"

"Got it in one, Archie. So where are we going?"

"There's a Chinese in England's Lane, just round the corner from me. Called Mr Ling's. Not much to look at, so people don't go there, but the nosh is excellent."

"Perfect. One o'clock?"

"See you there."

Angus had rung me earlier, saying he wanted to talk, and we'd arranged to meet for a take-away at my place at seven. I picked up a Chinese (two Chinese meals in a row, but I hated Indian, and couldn't face cooking, so what the hell?) and found a couple of bottles of Pinot Grigio in the fridge. It was like being back at Cambridge.

"Right, who's starting, you or me?" said Angus.

"The food, or the talking?"

"The talking, you idiot. We can both eat at the same time. Got any chilli sauce? I need to dip this prawn toast into something."

I fetched some worrying-looking red goo out of the kitchen cupboard. It was two years past its sell-by date. I told Angus, but he didn't seem to care.

"It would have mould on it, or smell, or something, if it was no good, and it hasn't, and doesn't, so I'm going to risk it."

"Fine. You talk first."

He dipped the prawn toast into the red sauce, then into some crispy seaweed, and stuffed it in his mouth. "It tastes fine. Right then, Jason Tang. Do you want the good news or the bad news?"

"Bad news first, please."

"He's got cold feet." He picked up a spring roll, and went through the same procedure with the chilli sauce and seaweed. "Jason," he said, with his mouth full, "has a bit of a problem with the Knipe halitosis."

"God, who can blame him? And the good news?"

"When I offered him a hundred grand he nearly fell off his seat. Said he'd take them both home and have the threesome on the carpet in front of his Mum for a hundred grand."

"Why couldn't you say so straight away? That's brilliant news."

"Do you think so? I think the mother might not agree to it."

"Angus, stop being a pillock. When's the deed going to be done?"

"I rang Tatyana this morning to ask her that very question. She said she'd ring Russia, and later on I got a text back. I'll read it to you." He pulled his phone out of his pocket.

"Here it is. It says *Angus, boss says go ahead when you like. Please report back when it has been done. Our young friend must not say anything at present. He must just perform task, no more.*"

"Have you spoken to Jason again since the text?"

"Yes, this afternoon. He rang Leclerc straight away, then rang me back."

"How did their conversation go?"

"Well I'll spare you the gory details, old thing. But the gist was, hallo Olivier darling, sorry it's taken me so long to reply to your little note but I have fancied you since the day I was born. Please can we make the beast with two backs as soon as convenient?"

"Without Knipe? What's the point of that?"

"The point is, oh naïve little Jamie, that until Olivier's got a bit of a taste for young Jason, he's going to smell a big rat if he's asked for an immediate ménage-à-trois with one of the most foul-smelling men in England. They need to do it in a more normal kind of way first – if this kind of thing can ever be described as normal. Then, in the post-coital glow, Jason can ask him about doing it with Greg the Dreg."

"Yuck. Doesn't he want two hundred thousand for having to do it twice?" I said.

"There's no need. Young Jason, you may find it somewhat alarming to know, is champing at the bit to get into Leclerc's knickers. Don't ask me why. Odd birds, these chutney ferrets. Sorry. Mixed metaphor."

I went out to the kitchen to get the crispy duck. When I got back into the room Angus was helping himself to the last spare rib.

"You don't want it, do you old boy? Good. Tell me about Archie."

"Archie and I are having lunch tomorrow. I think it wouldn't be a bad idea if you came too. You, after all, are the talented one, and it's my guess that Archie and his future cronies at the Arts Council will only go with us if we can persuade them that you're the prime mover."

He stuffed an untidy pancake into his mouth. "Too much duck. You're a flatterer, Jamie."

"Will you come, then?" I said.

"Where are you going?"

"Some Chinese in Belsize Park. Excellent food, apparently."

"And discreet? We don't want to meet any singers. Or anyone else, really."

"Apparently so."

"Then I'll come. As long as you're paying."

"Angus, you're an arsehole. Make sure you're nicer to him than you are to me."

"Oh, I will be, old boy, trust me. Any more of that Pinot Grigio?"

When we arrived at Mr Ling's Archie was already sitting there. He was a bit gormless-looking, with gap teeth and freckles, but he had the most fearsome intellect.

"Angus, you here too," he said as soon as he saw us. "The plot thickens."

"Hallo Archie, old thing. Twice in ten days. I'm not sure I can cope with such excitement. Jamie's paying, by the way."

We sat down, and a cross-looking woman hurled menus at each of us. We ordered Set Meal C, which included everything but the kitchen sink, and a bottle of house white.

"Right," said Archie, once Madam Mao had gone. "Spill the beans."

Angus took over immediately. "Archie, old son, we have an exciting prospect in store. How do you think the Venerable Old Tossers of the Arts Council would like it if we could rid them for ever of the financial burden of Opera London?"

"I guessed this was what it was about. Does Rebroff want to favour your company, then?"

"Strictly off the record," said Angus, "he would be willing to cough up one hundred million quid."

"Bloody hell, quite a decent sum. Enough to pay off the debt, and then provide a substantial income, provided the Arts Council is prepared to carry on with the grant at its current level."

"Exactly," said Angus. "That's a hefty incentive, surely?"

"You have a point. And I should stress at this stage that I haven't spoken to any of the Venerable Old Tossers, as you so diplomatically put it, about the overall funding situation for the Arts in England. But my reading of it is that there may be trouble even sustaining the current level of funding. There are those who are so fed up with the financial difficulties of Opera London that they would willingly pull the plug completely."

The cross Chinese woman brought us our wine, which was surprisingly pleasant. But Archie scarcely paused for breath.

"So the important point here, chaps, is that Opera London must continue, with or without the Rebroff money, to pursue an acceptable artistic policy. And the Old Tossers are unlikely to regard a Rebroff bid as being artistically suitable. However, I do know that for some extraordinary reason you, Angus, are regarded very highly by the Powers That Be. Indeed I know that they have on at least one occasion tried to persuade Knipe to appoint you as the new MD without any further ado. But I gather Gregory is rather keen on this young chap Leclerc. He won't be swayed, apparently."

"So what we need to know," I said hurriedly, trying not to catch Angus's eye, "is how wedded are The Old Tossers to The Rt Hon Gregory Knipe?"

"They approve of him strongly. Artistically he is regarded as a safe pair of hands, and financially they feel he has the right credentials. I gather his syndicate is nearly complete, by the way."

"What does that mean, exactly?" said Angus. "How much have they got?"

"Ten million, give or take."

"Not bad. But it's not in Sergei's league."

"The fact that you use the gentleman's given name with such ease suggests that you are quite intimate with him. Is this the case?"

"Archie, I don't think we have to apologise. I think it's necessary for you to know that Jamie and I have had substantive negotiations with Mr Rebroff, and that he is willing to give his millions to the Company only on the understanding that the two of us form the nexus of the management team."

"For God's sake Gussie," I said, "This is Archie and me you've got here, not some Government Think Tank. Speak English – you're one of the few people who are still good at it."

"I agree with Jamie, actually Angus. We haven't a chance of sorting this lot out unless we all remember that we're artists, not members of some Downing Street focus group."

Our starters arrived. Yet more spring rolls, prawn toasts, spare ribs, seaweed and crispy wontons.

"Right then," said Angus, when she'd gone. "You have a point. I'll try and summarise, without the jargon. Rebroff's willing to give Opera London the cash as long as Jamie and I are in charge. But he wants rid of Gregory Knipe. Otherwise the deal's off."

Archie looked slightly mollified. "That's better. Now we know where we are."

"So the question we haven't asked," I said, "is what happens to the Arts Council's attitude if Knipe, for whatever reason, has to resign."

Angus shot me a sharp look from behind a prawn toast. But Archie looked at me with some interest, even amusement. "And how are you going to make our lovely Gregory do that, pray?"

"Let's just say he decides to go. Political ambition, needs to spend more time with his family, whatever. What happens then?"

"As far as I'm concerned," said Archie, tearing a grotesquely large chunk of meat off a spare rib, "we all shout Hallelujah and start looking for an alternative. But I'm warning you, the Tossers will not take kindly to it. My guess is they'll need to see cast-iron evidence of two things. Firstly, and most importantly, will there be enough guaranteed long-term income to keep things going, without them playing Fairy Godmother yet again? And coming a very close second: can we guarantee that the ancient institution of Opera London is not going to turn into some kind of Slavic circus, putting on wall-to-wall Moussorgsky? Or, even worse, foisting on the unsuspecting public an unending stream of bad Russian musicals, starring Yevgenia Rebroff, Sergei's long-lost Aunt, in the Old Bag roles?"

He was getting a bit pissed. So was Angus.

It was left up to me to pull them both together. "The question is simple, Archie. If Angus and I were the management team, would The Tossers be able to stomach a Knipe-less Opera London?"

"Cards on the table," said Archie, letting out a huge burp. "Bloody good grub, isn't it? I'm fairly convinced that you two are the best hope the archaic and insane art-form known as Opera has in this country. In addition to this, I personally don't want that little jerk Leclerc getting his unpleasant hands on one of my favourite companies. So I will push the two of you, in tandem with the Rebroff millions, as hard as I can. But Knipe has to resign, or you haven't a prayer."

"Consider it done," said Angus. "Hey, Jamie old bean, this bottle's empty. Can we get another one? I think we should celebrate all being together round a table again for the first time since Cambridge."

"Absolutely, Gussie," said Archie. "Quite like old times."

By the time we'd got through the rest of the meal, and two more bottles of wine, we were all well away. Archie had tried to find out what the plan was for Knipe, but we'd managed to fob him off. I paid the bill, and we all got up to leave.

"One last thing," I said. "Not a word to a soul about any of this. Agreed?"

They both said "agreed," and then burst out laughing.

"I think we're going to do this," said Angus.

"Too bloody right, Gussie," laughed Archie. "Just get rid of that shite Knip. Shorry, that shit Knipe. Okay?"

I went to *Figaro* the following evening – Lindsey had arrived home late the previous night while I was asleep, and I hadn't had time to speak to her. As always her singing made me fall in love with her all over again. On the way home she told me about the production of *Cosi* in Salzburg. Apparently it was set in a funfair. Don Alfonso and Despina were the proprietors and kept making the four lovers, of whom Lindsey was one, get on different rides. It sounded odd, not to mention expensive, but was very much in Göstl-Saurau's style. They were performing it in the new *Haus für Mozart*, which was just finished – they'd knocked down the old *Kleines Festspielhaus* to make room for it. During the whole taxi ride Lindsey didn't mention Sergei Rebroff once. We slept together, and at four o'clock in the morning I got up to cook her some bacon and egg to send her on her way back, once again, to Salzburg.

She rang the odd time during the next couple of days, and we were very civil to each other. Whether or not she was also talking to Sergei on the phone was not clear, and I wasn't sure that I wanted to know. When she got home late on the Friday night, all she said was, "Hi, Jamie, here I am. Last time thank God. You're not getting up early are you? Only our bed is so much more comfortable than that bloody spare. Good. Lock up, then, will you? I'll almost certainly be asleep when you come upstairs."

Saturday July the eighth was the last performance of Figaro, and the last night of Opera London's season. Knipe's PA rang at about eleven, when Lindsey and I were having brunch.

"Mr Knipe would like to invite all of the *Figaro* cast to dinner tonight after the performance. Will Miss Templeton be able to make it?"

"Yes of course. Are partners invited?" I wasn't missing this opportunity to see how Knipe's plans for the Company were shaping up.

"Oh yes. It's at the Athenaeum, Mr Knipe's club. Taxis will be laid on. Please wear a tie, Mr Templeton."

Stupid cow. "Mr Barlow, actually. Yes of course I'll wear a tie. Thank you very much."

When we arrived, Knipe was in expansive mood. He was wearing a bright yellow linen suit – Pakeman, Catto and Carter, he said. Bought at The Badminton Horse Trials. Angela, his wife, was wearing a twinset, which looked as if it had come from M&S many years earlier. She looked, as she always did, faintly embarrassed to be there.

The Athenaeum had hauled itself into the twenty-first century, and provided us with foie gras and turbot, not the mixed grill or fish-and-chips I'd been expecting. Gloria and Angus's hands were anywhere except on their knives and forks, which made it a tad difficult for them to eat, and Julian Pogson was on superb form, entertaining the party with scurrilous stories about the Great and the Good of the opera business. Everyone was very well-oiled by the time Knipe got up to make his speech. Everyone except Lindsey, that is. She'd offered to drive home. Who was I to say no?

"Firstly may I say," Knipe began, "how thrilled I am that so many of you could come tonight at such short notice? This production of *Figaro* has been, for me, the highlight of my time so far at Opera London. You have all given extraordinary performances, and the critical reaction has been everything we could have wished for. It is invidious to single anyone out, but I would just like to thank Julian Pogson, and in particular Lindsey Templeton, for being such troupers, and carrying on without any sign of tiredness while both have been rehearsing in Salzburg."

There was applause, and Angus yelled "Bloody good effort, chaps."

Knipe went on: "It has also, I am quite sure, been difficult for you all to sustain this level of excellence while the whole Company has been in a ferment about Mr Sergei Rebroff, and his bid to buy an opera company." I avoided looking at Lindsey. "I feel that now is as good a time as any to announce that, under my chairmanship, Opera London has no intention of accepting a single penny of Mr Rebroff's money."

There was an audible groan around the room. But Knipe still had his trump card to play.

"I can however also announce that, as of yesterday evening, I have definitely secured the co-operation of over thirty friends and colleagues, who are each willing to give a substantial sum to the Company, in order to pay off its well-publicised debts, and put it back on an even keel. This syndicate of donors be known as the Gregory Knipe Circle, and will look to stand behind the Company now and into the future. Its first contribution will be ten million pounds, to be in the bank by Christmas. For me the pleasure of this evening is multiplied many times over by the knowledge that, owing to the extraordinary generosity of my Circle, I am at last able to confirm my long-term tenure of the chairmanship of this wonderful company."

Angus caught my eye when Greg talked about his generous Circle. We both giggled like schoolboys.

"You are all, quite rightly, in celebratory mood. I am delighted to note that this is not quite the end for this production, and this cast. I look forward; as I'm sure you all do, to the semi-staged performance of *Figaro* at the Proms at the beginning of next month. In the meantime, let us all, without further ado, drink a toast to Opera London."

Everyone got up, said with varying degrees of enthusiasm: "Opera London", and drank the toast. Then to my surprise, Lindsey got to her feet.

"I'm sure someone should reply on behalf of the cast," she said. "So may I just say, Mr Knipe, how much we appreciate your generosity in treating us to such a lovely meal this evening. This is a great company, and always will be. Thank you."

Good one, Linds. We all partied long into the night, and at about two-thirty taxis were called to take us all home.

I ran to the loo. Angus caught me up, and we pointed Percy together.

"Jason's all set," he whispered. "He's already done the deed for the first time with Leclerc, and it went swimmingly. Olivier's invited him to dinner, and is going to ask Greg to come too. Jason's going to take along a nice bottle of Grand Marnier – they like stickies, apparently, these shirtlifters – and once they're well lubricated they're both hoping that one thing will lead to another. Keep your fingers crossed."

He zipped himself up, and went back to where Gloria was waiting, pissed out of her head. I rejoined Lindsey, then we walked back to the car and she drove home.

Apart from the Prom performance, that was the end of *Figaro*. I wondered what the bloody hell *Cosi* and the Salzburg Festival held in store.

ACT 2: COSI FAN TUTTE

15

I dropped Lindsey at Stansted at six the following evening. We'd had a perfectly pleasant day, and I waited while she queued for security. She turned and waved, smiling, as she disappeared. It was the last time I heard from her for over a week. Apart from the text she sent me the following morning, that is.

Hi Jamie, arrived safely. Forgive me, but I need space for a while. I will be fine here, & can talk to Carly at Dad's, but need time to think. Please don't ring unless it's an emergency. Love Lindsey.

There had been no sign of Sergei. For all I knew he might still be in Russia. Of course he could have made his way back to Salzburg, but if so he was keeping a low profile. I did succeed in getting hold of Pogson towards the end of the week, on the pretext of checking his availability for an extra *Fledermaus* rehearsal in September, and managed to work Sergei into the conversation. Pogson claimed he hadn't seen him for over a fortnight.

I knew Angus had been in touch with Tatyana – Knipe had buggered off for a quick holiday in Umbria with the entrancing Angela, so the dinner party at Olivier's hadn't happened yet. Of Sergei's whereabouts Tatyana had revealed not a word.

I tried to occupy myself at work, catching up with the likes of Evangeline Bolls and Ursula Zimmermann, and I rang Stockencote a couple of times to speak to Carly, who was having far too much fun to bother much with me.

So when my phone said *Lindsey calling* at about eight o'clock the following Monday evening, I nearly jumped out of my skin.

"Linds, at last, how are you, for God's sake? What's happening?"

"Jamie, are you sitting down?"

"Yes, what on earth's the matter?"

"I'm pregnant."

"Jesus Christ. How do you know?"

"I've done a test, Jamie. Actually I've done both the tests that came in the packet." She sounded as if she was in a total panic.

"When were you supposed to come on?"

"Sometime around the weekend we were at Dad's. But I don't know when. My periods haven't ever been all that regular because of the endometriosis. And I don't know for certain when I last had one."

"Fifth of June," I said. I always knew exactly what her dates were.

"Yes, I thought it was around then, but I wasn't sure. I didn't really start to worry until the end of last week. Then on Friday morning I felt a bit sick, but it went off, and I thought nothing of it. I'd arranged to meet Julian for lunch – we both had a free afternoon, and I told him I'd woken up feeling a bit rough. He asked me if I had a hangover, and I said no, I hadn't been feeling much like alcohol for some reason. Then he said, 'bloody hell, Lindsey, you're not pregnant by any chance?' I must have gone white as a sheet. He said, 'oh my God, you are, aren't you?' Then he said, 'you look as if you've seen a ghost. What's the matter?' Jamie, I didn't know what to say. I mean Julian knows we've been trying for a baby for years. I should have been thrilled. So I just said 'sorry Julian, but it's a bit of a shock. If I'm pregnant I'm going to have to cancel an awful lot of really good work.' I think he swallowed it. But I couldn't think straight for the rest of the meal."

"But I don't understand, either," I said. "You don't sound pleased at all."

"Well, I am, Jamie, of course I am. But like I told Julian, it's a shock."

"You're sure the baby's mine?"

"Yes, Jamie, I'm sure it's yours." She'd obviously been expecting me to ask.

"Lindsey, is there anything you should be telling me?"

"About what, precisely?"

"About Sergei, for instance. Has anything been going on?"

"No. Well. Not really. Look, Jamie, I admit I like him. And he likes me. And you know he kissed me, that first night I was here. But that's as far as it went."

"Last Monday you told me not to ring. We haven't spoken for over a week. Is that because you've been with Sergei?"

"Jamie, I've spent the last week worrying that I'm pregnant. I'm not exactly likely to have been doing anything with Sergei, am I?"

"But if nothing's been happening between you why have you been worrying about being pregnant? You've wanted this for years, you just said so."

"Look, Jamie, will you stop giving me the third degree? I'm pregnant, the baby's yours, and nothing important has happened with Sergei. All right?"

"No, Lindsey, it's not all right. What exactly did happen with Sergei, and when?"

"I've told you we like each other, and I've told you nothing's happened. That's it."

"You didn't say nothing had happened, you said nothing important had happened. Has Sergei been there this week?"

"Yes, but we haven't done anything, I keep telling you. For Christ's sake, Jamie, will you stop it? I can't handle this kind of conversation on the phone."

"Me neither. I'm coming over tomorrow."

"What do you mean you're coming over? Where?"

"To Salzburg. To see you, and talk about this properly. I'll get the 6.40 Freshair."

"Jamie, don't be ridiculous, you can't possibly come. You've got work to go to. Anyway, this place is crawling with singers. You'll be recognised."

Now I was really angry. "Jesus, Lindsey, if anyone's got an excuse to come to bloody Salzburg it's me. I'm the casting director of an opera company, remember? And the world of international opera might just find it rather touching that hubby makes a special trip to see his missus while she's in the middle of rehearsals. Unless everyone knows something I don't."

"Jamie, you have no right to speak to me like that."

"No, no-one ever speaks to you like that, do they? You're too fucking important, aren't you?"

"This conversation is about to finish, Jamie. Don't you dare come tomorrow."

"I'm coming, and there's nothing you can do about it. You're on stage tomorrow night aren't you?"

"We've got a stage and piano rehearsal at six."

"Then you won't be rehearsing during the day. I'll come to your apartment."

"You are not coming to my apartment."

"Oh yes I am, Lindsey. I'll beat the door down if I have to."

"But…what if there are no seats left on the plane?"

"You can always get a seat on Freshair. I'll be there by ten-fifteen tomorrow morning, if the flight's on time."

There was a long pause. She didn't hang up, as I'd thought she would, but just waited. I heard sniffling. It always softened me up when she cried.

"Look, Linds, I'm sure we can sort this out. But I've got to know what's been going on. I'll see you at ten-fifteen. You can make me a cup of coffee while we talk, then I'll be a good boy and come straight home. Promise."

"All right, Jamie, if you must. 'Bye."

"'Bye Linds."

And that was that. I got straight onto the Internet. There were still seats on the flight. I had to pay £249, plus taxes and charges. Wouldn't it have been nice if I could have got on my Lear jet instead?

The Freshair flight was vile, but at least it was on time, and I hadn't checked a bag in, so I was in a taxi heading for Lindsey's apartment in Reichenhallerstraße just after ten their time. I dialled Grace's number at work.

"Hi, Jamie. Where are you?"

I'd worked this out on the plane. "Grace, I've had to take a last-minute trip to Salzburg. I've got to listen to the bloke singing Bartolo in their *Figaro*. We're trying to cast Fiesco in next season's *Simone Boccanegra*. This guy is willing to sing to me during their lunch break, so I've just popped over for a few hours.

"Very international we are these days, aren't we Jamie?"

"Yes, thank you Grace. Just field my calls for me would you? I'll be back first thing tomorrow morning."

This was a tissue of lies, except that we were doing *Boccanegra*, and hadn't found a bass yet. So I rang the Festival Office, and spoke to Göstl-Saurau's secretary, whom I happened to know quite well. She gave me the number of the guy doing Bartolo, and confirmed that he would be rehearsing morning and afternoon in the *Großes Festspielhaus*.

107

I phoned him immediately. He was American, and jumped at the chance to audition to me at lunchtime.

"Hey, man, I'd be delighted. Fiesco you say. Yeah, sure, that's in my repertoire. I'll get a score from the library, and fix the pianist from the *Figaro* rehearsal. And I'll fix a room, too. There are some decent-size practice-rooms on the fourth floor of the *Großes Festspielhaus*. Come to the auditorium at one-thirty. We'll walk up from there."

Thank God he was American. The most organised singers in the world. He'd be brash, with a great voice like all Yanks. Maybe he even might be the guy for our *Boccanegra*, although if he was singing at Salzburg, he'd be expensive. So what? Sergei wouldn't mind coughing up.

The taxi drew up outside Lindsey's apartment. I paid the driver and got a receipt, then rang Lindsey's doorbell.

"Jamie, is that you?"

"Yup."

"Come up. Second floor, first door on the right as you get out of the lift."

When I got there she was still in her night things. She looked terrible. I tried to kiss her. Bad move. She turned on her heel and went into the kitchen.

"Coffee?" she said.

"Yes, please, darling."

"I wish that word 'darling' didn't trip so easily off your tongue, Jamie. It doesn't mean anything. You just sound like some luvvie opera singer."

"Sorry. Where do we start?"

"Oh for God's sake, Jamie, you decide. You're the one who chose to make this mad journey. This coffee's not bad, by the way. Although I've been feeling sick the past few mornings, which puts me right off it. Do you want a biscuit?"

"Yes, please. I'm starving. I haven't eaten anything except a bowl of Cornflakes at four-fifteen this morning."

"It's no fun doing that journey at that time of day, is it?"

"No, darling. Sorry. No, Lindsey."

When the coffee was brewed, she put everything on a tray and took it into the living area. I could see her double bed through the open bedroom door. She saw me looking.

"No, Sergei has not been to this apartment, in case you were wondering, which you obviously were. He won't risk going somewhere like this without his minders, and we both agreed it was nicer when they weren't around."

"So you're telling me you haven't had an affair with him, is that right?"

She poured my coffee. Her hands were shaking ever so slightly, and the jug clinked a few times against the mug.

"We haven't had sex," she said eventually. "We've done a few other things."

"What, like Bill Clinton? 'I have not had sexual relations with that woman,' that sort of thing?"

"Jamie, I'm doing my best. If you're going to be rude or sarcastic you'll just have to leave now."

"Okay, I'll try to keep my temper. What exactly *have* you done with Sergei?"

"I am not prepared to go into details. But I am prepared to say that the baby can't possibly be his. We've been extremely careful."

"And that's all I get, is it?"

"Yes, Jamie, that's all you get. But, well, I decided, when I knew you were coming here, to tell you that I still love you. Oh no, that came out all wrong. I'll tell you again. I want you to know that I still love you."

"You might have thought of that before you started anything with Sergei."

"For God's sake, Jamie. Sometimes we're not all perfect like you. I get lonely when I'm away, and I need companionship. And he is so charming, and I really like him, and he really likes me. And yes, I like the fact that he flies me to London in his private jet. It's a bit grander than your clapped-out Passat. But I know you haven't done anything to deserve all this. I wish it had never started."

She paused to take a gulp of her coffee, then grimaced and put her cup down.

"But anyway, Jamie, the baby's yours. So we need to do everything we can to stitch our marriage back together. I can't exactly expect Sergei to look after your baby, can I? Even though he's now your number one buddy."

"Linds, I wish it was anyone else who was giving all that dosh to the Company. But it's the best opportunity I'm ever going to get in this business and I'm not going to blow it."

"Okay, then, Jamie. Here's the deal. You go on with this unbelievable scheme to rescue your beloved company. I'll go on seeing

Sergei when he asks me to, but we won't do anything physical. And you and I will both do our level best to play happy families whenever we're together, and we'll hope we get through all this intact."

"I'm not happy about you going on seeing Sergei."

"And I'm not happy about you taking his money."

There was a long pause. Eventually I said, "right then, I suppose you've got yourself a deal." I finished my coffee. "I'd probably better go, had I?"

"Yes, please, Jamie. I'm feeling awful."

"You look shocking. I should be here looking after you."

She looked at me, and the flicker of a smile crossed her face.

"I'll be fine," she said. "You're coming with Carly at the end of next week, for the first night. Let's all try to be nice to each other, for her sake."

"How's the show going, by the way?"

"Oh, fine. Giotti, the conductor, wants to book me for practically everything he's doing for the next five years. But I've got to be at home, Jamie. This can't ever be allowed to happen again."

"No, Linds, it can't. I'll go then. Hope you're feeling better."

She opened the door. I aimed another kiss at her lips, but she turned her face sideways and it ended up being a peck on the cheek. As I waited for the lift she called out to me.

"Jamie, I'm really, really sorry to be putting you through this."

I looked at her for a moment, then the lift arrived. I watched the door open, unable to decide what to say. By the time I'd turned to say a last goodbye she had disappeared back into her room.

As I walked out of the apartment building I looked up at her open window. She was looking down at me, tears streaming down her face. I waved half-heartedly, then turned and walked down Reichenhallerstraße towards the *Großes Festspielhaus*, and my new life as a cuckolded husband.

Anthony Giovanelli, the American bass turned out to be fantastic. He sounded like Boris Christoff – a huge rolling voice that seemed to emanate from somewhere around his bowels. I asked him instantly whether he would be interested in coming to London to sing Fiesco the following year.

"Wow, yeah, sure thing. That would be just fine. Can you get me a work permit?"

"It might be a bit tricky," I said, "but we usually persuade the powers that be to let us have who we want. Can I ask you what your fee is?"

"Jeez, ah jes' leave that to my agent."

So I took his agent's number, and waved him a cheery goodbye.

The Freshair flight didn't leave until eight-fifty, so after shopping for a little while, I decided to walk to the airport. It wasn't far, and even dawdling along trying to enjoy the sunshine it only took me forty minutes. I arrived at four-thirty. I had nothing to do but wait, so I inserted myself into the bar, ordered a glass of Grüner Veltliner – the wonderful lemony, grassy Austrian wine – and half a dozen Mozart Balls. I began to eat and drink myself into a stupor. By the time I went through security, I must have had at least a bottle and a half.

There had been a huge alert at Heathrow or somewhere just a week or so previously. As a result the new rule was that you weren't allowed to take much through security, but that once you'd gone through you could take anything on you wanted. It all made me a bit nervous.

However, procedures did not appear to have changed one iota since the last time I made this journey. I was perfunctorily frisked by a very grumpy Austrian gent, and walked through to the shopping nirvana that was Salzburg Airport's departure lounge, where I had a printed sheet shoved into my hand. Ah, I thought, this will shed light on the new regulations, and maybe give me some reassurance. The notice read as follows:

Salzburg Airport W.A. Mozart would like to inform you:
YOUR SAFETY IS OF THE UTMOST IMPORTANCE TO US!
All products in the TravelValue/DutyFree shop have had a thorough <u>security check</u>.
So please feel safe to carry on shopping as normal!
All products purchased can be taken on board <u>the airplane</u>!
We wish you a good and safe trip!
Salzburg Airport W.A. Mozart.

So that was all right, then. I could shop away to my heart's content. Anyway, how bloody stupid could you get, calling an airport after a composer? It was like calling Heathrow after Edward Elgar. Or Stansted after Andrew Lloyd Webber. "*Lloyd Webber balls can be purchased in the Duty Free Shop!"* Maybe one day they would call an airport after Sergei Ivanevitch Rebroff. Then we might be able to purchase a couple of his balls, and crush them very hard under our feet. Wondering whether the Grüner Veltliner had been through a thorough <u>security check</u>, I went to the airside bar to have a couple more glasses before we left.

The flight was even more ghastly than the one that morning. I was so full of booze that I had to go three times to the loo, which was a source of enormous irritation to the felt-hatted Austrian lady in the aisle seat to my left.

I took a taxi home (if Lindsey could do it, why the hell shouldn't I?), and got back about half past eleven. I opened the fridge. A bottle of Pouilly Fumé sat winking at me. I opened it, and sat down with the express intention of getting roaring drunk all over again.

Three-fifteen. Asleep in front of the telly. Shit. Pissed, needless to say. Never mind. Any more of that Pouilly Fumé? Little drop. Yum. What could be nicer than a scrummy glass of white wine with little pearls of condensation sitting on the outside of the glass? Except this stuff's warm, why is that? Oh yes, went to sleep in front of the telly, and it's three-fifteen.

Something's wrong, isn't it? What? Can't remember. Oh yes I can, Lindsey's pregnanski, isn't she? Lovely news, exciting, 'cept that I might not be the Daddy. Oh, she, *says* I'm the Daddy, but there's a look in her eyes while she says it, like she thinks someone else might just have done wiggle-wiggle-and-out at the wrong time of the month. Who might that be now? Oh yes, of course, Sergei Ivanevitch Rebroff, saviour of Opera London and of Jamie Barlow's poxy little career. Well I know what I know. That baby might easily be Sergei's. She *says* they didn't have sex, but I bet they did. Probably doing it now. All that crap about not knobbing last week 'cos she was worrying about being pregnant – it never stopped her last time, did it? We bonked like rabbits until she was eight months gone. But she says the baby's mine. When did we last fuck, actually? Oh I remember, when she came home before the second *Figaro*. Bloody good sex. The last time, probably ever. But you might as well go out with a bang. A bang! Bloody funny, Jamie. Any more of that wine? No. Bugger it. Let's see what there is in the fridge.

Only box. And it's almost finished. Squeeze the bag, that's right. Almost a full glass there, look. How lovely. Mind you this stuff's foul, isn't it? Jolly Shopper's own brand Soave. Never mind, at least it's cold. Pro'bly won't notice the difference. Wedding at Cana and all that, and anyway, when I'm this far gone I don't care if it tastes like Cillit Bang.

So here we have it – finally I've got it all sorted. Lindsey, my wife of the splendid tits, is having sex with Sergei Rebroff even as we speak. He is using the withdrawal method, but worries that sometimes he might pull out his little willy a bit too late, and thinks he might have got her knocked up. But it doesn't matter, because the husband – what's his name, oh yes, Jimmy, that's right – won't dare say anything 'coz he needs his money to make a living, and he thinks the sun shines out of his arse.

Masterly summing-up, if I may say so. Do you find the suspect guilty or not guilty? Oh, guilty, m'lud, definitely.

There we are. Finished. Four o'clock. Time for bed, said Zebedee. Don't bother to set the alarm. No-one'll notice if I'm a bit late for work. They're all on hols, anyway.

16

In the end, though I had swallowed a vast quantity of white wine that day, it had been spread over a long period, and I must have metabolised most of it by the time I woke up at nine. I had a thumping headache, but otherwise felt more-or-less human. Except of course that I was supposed to be at work at ten, so I had to run around the house like a blue-arsed fly, and didn't manage to shave.

"How was the trip?" asked Grace, when I finally made it in.

"Bloody quick, but very successful," I said. "That guy is fantastic. Anthony Giovanelli his name is. I want to fix him straightaway for Fiesco. Better talk to Dunwich. Is he in?"

"Yes he is, Jamie, but you can't possibly talk to him looking like that. He'll think you're trying to sell him a copy of The Big Issue. For God's sake go and shave."

"Christ, Grace, you're a hard bloody task mistress. I've only got that ancient Philishave with the blunt blades. It'll give me barber's rash so bad everyone will think I've got scarlet fever."

"Better that than looking like a tramp. Go on Jamie, go and do it now. You need taking in hand."

The idea of Grace taking me in hand was rather appealing, and caused a brief stir in the Calvin Kleins, but I went and did as I was told. Grace promised to ring Dunwich while I was gone, to see if I could go up straightaway.

When I got back, slightly cleaner shaven than before, she said to me: "Jamie, I'm worried about you. You and I are going out for a sandwich at lunchtime. I need to know what's going on."

Dunwich was beaming at me through his window when I arrived at the top floor.

"Jamie, splendid to see you. Looking a bit rough, if I may say so. You need a new blade in your razor."

"Yes, Henry, how right you are. I just popped up to okay a bit of casting with you."

"I know all about it, Grace filled me in. Cracking girl that. Hope you're taking her with you when you get my job."

"Henry, do you know something I don't?"

"No, not really dear boy, wishful thinking I'm afraid, but you're my favoured successor. You're a decent cove, I've always thought. And with that magnificent wife, too. Only trouble is, the board will back Knipe, and I think Knipey's got his own candidate."

"Who?" I said.

"Oh God, some drip from Paris. Likes that frightful little Olivier Leclerc, who is also favoured by Mr Knipe."

He was talking about Damien de la Chapelle, an absurdly young but brilliant Frenchman who was currently Artistic Administrator of the Théâtre du Châtelet in Paris. He was known to be part of an infamous Parisian group of bohemians which included Leclerc. They indulged, according to operatic folklore, in every conceivable modern vice.

"They're all poofs, you know," said Dunwich. "I have a sneaking suspicion that our own dear Gregory Knipe might also be a bit suspect on that score, don't you think?"

His Lordship was in expansive mood. He was also much more astute than he made out.

"Surely not, Henry? What about Angela?"

"Bloody Norah, the last time those two had rumpy-pumpy must have been before the Ark. Angela likes Coronation Street much better than sex, anyway. Probably suits her to be married to a pooftah."

"Henry, you're a rogue," I said. "I shall miss you. When do you actually quit these four walls?"

"Friday of next week. I'm the first General Administrator in five to walk out, rather than being pushed. Knipe's invited God knows how many people to lunch at Spencer's. You're not coming, by any chance?"

"Can't, Henry, I'm so sorry. I've got to go to Lindsey's first night in Salzburg."

"Bugger. It'll be ghastly. I suppose there might be a decent piece of beef, but the rest will be simply hideous – seaside landlady's vegetables, that sort of thing. What the bloody hell did the old fart have to book Spencer's for? Never mind, there'll probably be a decent drop of claret. By the way, cast who the fuck you like as Fiesco. Basil Brush if you want. Actually, that's not a bad idea. *Boccanegra* could do with a few laughs."

Grace and I bought our crayfish and watercress sandwiches, and sat down.

"Right then, Jamie," she said. "Time to tell me what's going on."

"Okay, Gracie, I'll come clean. But for God's sake keep it under your hat."

"You got it, boss."

"I've got several big problems. Problem number one is that I'm worried Lindsey's having an affair. I don't imagine that comes as much of a surprise."

"No, Jamie, I'm afraid not. Sergei Rebroff, presumably?"

"Got it in one. They clearly have a big thing for each other. But it's worse than that."

"What could possibly be worse than that?"

"Lindsey's pregnant."

Grace let out a low whistle. Several people looked round.

"Gracie," I whispered, "for God's sake be quiet. This is for your ears only."

"Sorry. It's a promise, boss."

"Good. Well, it's very early days. She's only about four weeks gone. She says the baby's definitely mine, because she hasn't had sex with anyone else. But I don't believe her. I think she and Rebroff have been doing the deed in Salzburg."

"That's what Julian Pogson thinks, too."

"He told me he hadn't seen him. Bastard. In any case, what the fuck's it got to do with Julian bloody Pogson?"

"I'm afraid he's been ringing me from Salzburg with regular progress reports."

"So I suppose it's all round the office, then?"

"Of course it's not, Jamie." She was annoyed. "I can keep things to myself, you know."

"Okay, okay, sorry Gracie. So what's Pogson been saying?"

"That last week they were together practically every evening. And, as far as he knows, quite a lot of nights, too."

I picked up a crayfish tail which had dropped out of the sandwich onto my plate, and shoved it in my mouth. It tasted vaguely gynaecological, and I spat it out. "But he has no inside information on whether they've actually screwed."

"No."

"So we're no nearer finding out whose the baby is."

"But you're telling me that Lindsey says it's definitely yours?"

"Well that's what she says. But I don't think she knows."

"Why not?"

"Because of the look on her face when she told me."

She took a bite of her sandwich, and thought for a moment.

"If you're right, and she genuinely doesn't know which of you is the father, she won't have a clue what to do. But the one thing she won't want is an abortion. She's been wanting another baby for years. It'll be far too precious to get rid of."

"How can you be so sure?"

"A woman's instinct."

"Does your woman's instinct tell you who she wants to end up with?"

"I doubt if she knows, Jamie. My guess is she's feeling terribly guilty about the whole Sergei thing."

"Then why did she do it, Gracie?"

"Swept off her feet. If I got whisked off in a private jet, I might find it a bit difficult to turn a guy down."

"How did you know about the private jet?"

"Everyone knows, Jamie. Lindsey couldn't keep it to herself."

I'd given up with my crayfish. They lay higgledy-piggledy on my plate looking accusingly at me.

"What you think she'll do, Gracie?"

"Okay then, let's see. Lindsey doesn't know who the father is, but is too frightened to find out, because she's determined to keep the baby. She also wants to come back to you and Carly so you can be a proper family. Therefore she's told you it's yours, and is determined somehow to ditch Sergei and make it work with you."

"But what if the baby turns out to be his?"

She took another bite of her sandwich. She didn't seem to be having the same trouble as me.

"I don't think she can face thinking about that," she said. "On the other hand, if Sergei thinks the baby's his, he may decide he wants her,

117

and will jettison his Russian wife and family to get her. Then you have a real problem on your hands. It'll be up to you to warn him off."

"There's just one more small issue. Lindsey has persuaded Sergei to give his money to Opera London."

Grace whistled again. More people looked at us.

"Stop it, Gracie, this is really serious."

She smiled at me. "Okay, boss, I'll be discreet I promise."

"In some ways," I said, "the most amazing bit is yet to come. He's going to give his money to us on one condition. Well. Two conditions, actually."

"I'm all ears."

"That Angus Lennox becomes Music Director, and that I become General Administrator."

"My God, Jamie. You'll be the big boss."

"So it makes it a bit difficult for me to get heavy with Sergei."

"Yes, I can see that. You'd like to knock his brains out, but you're a teeny bit worried that it might mess up your career prospects."

"Something like that."

"It's not going to make Lindsey feel a whole lot better, is it?"

"What do you mean?"

"Jamie, listen. What Lindsey thinks she wants is this. She thinks she wants you to be all chummy with Sergei, so she can feel less guilty about having sex with him, if she has. That'll be why she's told Sergei to give his money to Opera London, and it's probably why he's insisting on you being General Administrator. But my guess is what Lindsey really wants, deep down, is for you to make the problem go away by thumping the living daylights out of him. He crawls away with his tail between his legs, and you're the Alpha Male."

"That might be a bit tricky. He has armed minders with him 24/7. Apparently most of his enemies are six feet under."

"I see your problem. I'm not surprised you've been looking a bit stressed."

"Grace, I can trust you, can't I? Not to tell anyone any of this?"

"Of course you can, Jamie. In any case, I'm off on holiday next week, so I won't have much chance, will I?"

Lindsey didn't ring, and despite an almost overwhelming urge to do so I didn't feel I could ring her. Apart from anything else, she was doing a monumentally difficult role in the most important Mozart Festival in the world. So, aware that anyone who knew what was going on must think me a terrible wimp, I left her to the tender mercies of Sergei. I assumed he was still in attendance, sympathising when the conductor shouted at her and mopping her up when she had morning sickness.

I rang Stockencote on the following Sunday evening. Albert answered.

"Jamie, my dear chap, long time no hear. Everything okay?"

"Fine, Albert, thank you. How's Carly? Is she driving you mad?"

"Not at all. She's lovely – a breath of fresh air. She's been riding every day – Fliss is delighted with her – and she's had that little Hattie from the pub round a few times, and she's no trouble either. They've both been helping me no end on the farm. Nice to have able-bodied people around – an old crock like me needs all the help he can get. And Carly's been watching that DVD of *The Sound of Music* whenever no-one's been there to look after her."

"Blimey, Albert, has she really? It's not long ago she couldn't stand that film."

"Well, she's pretty keen on it now, Jamie. I think she knows the whole thing from memory. And she keeps singing bits – she's got a lovely little voice, you know. Just like her mother at that age."

"I'm so grateful to you for having her, Albert. She adores it there."

"We adore having her, Jamie. We're having a great evening playing Monopoly – Carly, Evie and me. Carly's winning, which is just as well. I have to confess she's not at her most charming when losing at Monopoly."

"I won't disturb her then. But we have to arrange my picking her up this week. Is Thursday all right?"

"Good heavens, is it time for her to leave already? I thought she had another week. I'm going senile, of course. Yes, Thursday's fine. Come for lunch."

The phone went five minutes later. It was Carly.

"Daddy, why do I have to come home? I much prefer it here."

"Because we're going to Salzburg on Friday to see Mummy, darling. Thursday's the last possible day I can pick you up."

"Oh, wow, I'd forgotten. Are we going to all the Sound of Music places?"

"Yes darling."

"Awesome, Daddy, awesome! Can I go back and play Monopoly now? It's probably my go. I'm going to put hotels on Park Lane and

Mayfair. I've already got four houses on each. Evie's very cross 'coz she's losing."

"See you on Thursday,then."

But she'd already gone.

Angus rang me at six the next evening.

"Just had Jason Tang on the phone. Tonight's the night. Olivier is putting on his apron as we speak. Something with monkfish, apparently. Jason's got the Grand Marnier in his hot little hand, and Greg the Dreg, newly *bronzato* from his week in Umbria, is preparing his corpulent body for a bit of prodding and pulling. Apparently Angela thinks he's going to some meeting in his constituency, and might have to stay the night. Although how she can be stupid enough to believe he can't get home from Penge is beyond me."

"Perhaps Angela's got a beau of her own, and is glad to see the back of him," I ventured.

"Yes, absolutely, that'll be it. A young black boy with a huge cock. They'll watch Coronation Street together, then fuck all night."

"Stop it, Angus."

"Yes. Sorry. Anyway Jason said he was going to ring me as soon as he got home after the party. But Tatyana phoned me this morning, and said the Boss had left specific instructions that nothing was to be said on an open phone line. Jason's rehearsing all day tomorrow, so he's coming round here at seven-thirty to tell me all about it."

"It's all getting very cloak and dagger, Gussie."

"Ridiculous, I quite agree. But I s'pose this is what Sergei's used to, all this John Le Carré stuff. And he's the guy with the dosh, so we'd better do what we're told. I know, why don't you come round tomorrow as well? I'll cook carbonara. Bring a couple of nice bottles of Italian red – Brunello di Montalcino or something."

"You'll be lucky. I might run to Valpolicella. But anyway, of course I'll come, thanks. One last thing."

"What's that, old chap?"

"If we're not supposed to be talking on an open phone line, what are we doing having this conversation right now?"

There was a short pause.

"Yup, absolutely, take your point. See you at the pre-arranged time in the pre-arranged place then, Number One."

In order to show willing at work the next day, I stayed on until after seven, checking my notes from the latest casting meeting, and making a list of small roles which still needed sorting out. I arrived at Angus's at seven thirty-five. Jason was already there. He normally looked immaculate – his small, olive-skinned face moisturised to a state of shiny perfection, and each item of clothing in perfect harmony with the others. But today he looked an absolute wreck.

"Hi, Mr Barlow," he said. "You're going to be the new boss, I hear." Originally from Hong Kong, he'd learned his almost perfect English at Public School. Small wonder he liked boys better than girls.

"Partly depends on you, I think Jason." I was mortally embarrassed. The last time Jason and I had spoken, he'd just finished auditioning to me, and it had all been very formal. Now I was about to hear about how he'd got on at a sex party to which he'd only gone because Angus and I had put him up to it.

"Oh, no worries on that score, Mr Barlow. I'll tell you all about it."

"I'm sure just the basic outline will do, aren't you Angus?"

"Absolute bloody nonsense, Jamie, I want every gory detail. And will you stop behaving like a schoolma'am?" He went off into the kitchen to cook the supper.

I opened one of the Valpolicellas. "Some wine for you, Jason?"

"I suppose I might as well, Mr Barlow. What's the expression? – the hair of the dog that bit you? Actually I'd need some Grand Marnier for that, but I don't suppose Angus has got any. Probably just as well, actually."

Angus called from the kitchen: "I've got tequila."

Jason went an extraordinary shade of green. "No, I think that might be a bit of a disaster, Angus. Wine will be okay, thank you. Maybe Mr Barlow would just get me some Badoit as well?"

"For God's sake call me Jamie," I said. "And I should think the chances of Angus having Badoit are about one in a million. Am I right, Angus?"

"I've got a bottle of Perrier, will that do?"

"Yes, thank you," said Jason. "I'd like that."

I went into the kitchen. Angus was draining the pasta. "Quick-cook pasta, and sauce in a packet from Marks and Sparks. All ready."

We went back into the living room, where Jason had re-arranged himself decoratively on Angus's white leather sofa. I handed him his Perrier. Then I poured three glasses of wine, and put them on the low glass table in the middle of the room. Angus handed us all plates of food, and we sat down.

"Get that down you Jason, that'll make you feel better," said Angus. "A bit of bulk, I always say. Best cure for a hangover."

"It's very nice," said Jason. "Do you want me to start telling you about last night?"

"Fire away old thing," said Angus.

So Jason began his saga. "I arrived at Olivier's flat at eight-thirty, as we'd arranged. Mr Knipe was already there. They'd had some wine, and Mr Knipe knew someone else was coming to dinner, but Olivier hadn't told him who it was. It was a surprise."

"A nice surprise, I'm sure," said Angus.

"Oh, yes, I think so," said Jason, and suddenly went into peals of girlish laughter. "His eyes nearly popped out of his head when I walked in. But Olivier just said, 'Gregory, I don't think you've met Jason Tang? Jason, this is Gregory Knipe.' So I said, 'very nice to meet you Mr Knipe,' and winked at him. I think he nearly came in his pants."

I put my fork down. My M&S carbonara had lost some of its appeal.

Angus appeared to have no such qualms. "Great stuff so far, Jason," he said, shovelling a huge quantity of food into his mouth. "What did Knipey do?"

"Olivier wouldn't let him do anything," said Jason. "He said: 'well now gentlemen, Hi sink it is time for our deenerr. Hi 'ave cooked lotte – 'ow you say? – monkfeesh. But first we must 'ave huîtres. Haffrodeeziaque.' "

Jason, like a lot of singers, was a terrific mimic. He sounded exactly like Olivier. He ate a forkful of pasta.

"This is good, Angus," he said. "Please can I have another glass of wine?"

"Of course, help yourself."

Jason poured himself some more Valpolicella, and carried on telling his unpleasant tale. "So we sat down to eat our oysters, which were excellent – the first time I have ever eaten them – then Olivier brought in the main course. 'Lotte au poivre', he said. And he served it up – slices of delicious fish with a pepper sauce on it. 'Heet weel 'eat you erp', he said. 'Hi want everyone to be nice an 'ot by ze time deenerr is ovverr.' Then Mr Knipe spoke for the first time since I'd arrived. 'Olivier, what exactly did you have in mind for us after dinner?' he said. Olivier just looked at me, and I smiled again at Mr Knipe. 'Jason 'as brought a bottle of Grand Marnier,' he said. 'Hi sought we might 'ave a leetle dreenk of zat. Hand maybe a leetle will get spilt. Zen we will 'ave to lick it up, no?' "

"Had you planned all this in advance, then?" said Angus. "You and Olivier, I mean?"

More girlish laughter. "Of course not. But Olivier was doing it so brilliantly. It was fun. Mr Knipe was getting redder and redder. He had to remove his tie – I think he was finding it difficult to breathe. So we finished our fish and concentrated on our wine for a while. Meursault, Olivier said it was. And before long we'd got through two bottles. That was when Olivier said: 'time forr some Grand Marnier, Jason. Greg, you like Grand Marnier, yes?' Mr Knipe found it difficult to reply at first. He tried to say 'yes', but his vocal cords didn't come together properly. It was more of a croak. Eventually he managed to say 'yes, darling, I love it'.

"So come on, Jason, what happened then?" said Angus. "You're just getting to the good bit."

Jason had finished his carbonara. "Well actually," he said, "that's where the good bit finishes, I'm afraid. Olivier went out to fetch the Grand Marnier, and I moved over to the other side of the table, and knelt down next to Mr Knipe. Then I undid his trousers, and was just about to start properly pleasuring him when…" and here he paused… "it was all over. I think this happens with older men when they get very excited. It was suddenly very messy, and Mr Knipe said 'oh my God, I'm awfully sorry, Jason. It's too much for an old queen, I'm afraid.' Olivier came back into the room, and saw what had happened, and was furious. 'Jesus Christ, Gregoree,' he said, 'eez zat ze best you can do? Hi was looking forward to eet.' 'I'm so sorry, Olivier,' said Mr Knipe. 'As you know only too well, this does happen to me sometimes. Look, maybe I'd better go home, and leave you two young things to your Grand Marnier. Actually I'm not feeling all that well. I think I might have had a bad oyster. It's happened to me before.' He did look a bit green. So we helped him into his jacket, and he put his tie on and left. I think he was going to call a taxi."

"Christ, Angus," I said. "Are premature ejaculation and food poisoning enough for a kiss-and-tell story in the tabloids?"

"If you were hoping to become a Cabinet Minister in the next Tory Government, old boy, don't you think you'd want to hush up Jason's story?"

"Well, yes, of course I would, Gussie." I opened the second bottle of wine, and filled everyone's glass. We'd all by now either finished or abandoned our supper, and there was only red wine, and maybe a bit of cheddar from the fridge, between me and another solitary night in Queens Park.

"What do you think, Jason?" I said. "Do you think Knipe will be worried enough to resign?"

"Actually I feel sorry for poor Mr Knipe."

"Bugger poor Mr Knipe," said Angus. "There's a hundred grand waiting for you when this is all over."

"Oh, yes, of course." He gave a sheepish grin, which made him look about fifteen years old.

"Look, Angus," I said. "Surely Sergei God-Almighty Rebroff can help with this? I think Jason's performed his task admirably. Now we need to take what we know to Sergei, and let him tighten the screw on Greg the Dreg. If you remember he offered to help."

"Yes, I s'pose you've got a point, Jamie," said Angus. "Right then, I'll ring Tatyana in the morning, and set up a meeting with Sergei. How many of us should go, do you think?"

Jason looked truly horrified. I said quickly: "Just you, Gussie, if you don't mind. Jason's done enough, and I don't particularly want to see Sergei at the moment. I'm sure you can tell him what happened."

Angus looked mildly irritated. "Okay, if I must. Oh, bugger it, I'm sick of you two sitting there with long faces. I think we should celebrate clever young Jason's scoring with our beloved Chairman. Even if it was a bit quick, I'm sure it still counts. I've got one bottle of claret left over from Christmas. I've been waiting for an occasion to drink it. Jamie, you go into the kitchen and find us a bit of something to eat with it."

I went out to the kitchen, and rummaged around in Angus's fridge. To my amazement I found some reasonable-looking cheese and a new packet of water biscuits in one of the cupboards. I took them in triumph back to the living room.

Angus opened the wine. Château Ducru-Beaucaillou 1982. Things were looking up. The cheese was okay, the wine was sensational, and we managed to enjoy ourselves for the rest of the evening.

Eventually Jason said: "It's time for little Chinese queens to go to bed. Thanks for the wine, Angus, and the food."

Angus yawned. "Absolutely. Time to go, both. Just one more thing, Jase."

"What's that, Angus?"

"What happened to the Grand Marnier?"

"Oh, Olivier and I got through the whole bottle after Mr Knipe had gone home. We had a lovely time."

I felt very queasy indeed as I hailed a taxi and went home to my boring little two-up, two-down. No-one there to greet me when I got back. Christ, how I missed Lindsey, and Carly too. But at least I didn't have to spend the night licking Grand Marnier off Olivier Leclerc's willy.

17

The phone went the next morning at work. It was Angus.

"I've been in touch with Tats."

"Who?"

"Tats. You know, we're supposed to be talking in code these days."

"Oh, right, fair enough. Tats. What did she say?"

"I've made an appointment to see the Big White Chief on Friday. He's flying me out to Salzburg on his private jet. Thursday evening, I'm going."

"Well, at least that confirms his whereabouts, then," I said. "No great surprise, it has to be said."

"Yes, sorry old chap. Bit of a raw nerve I know. But anyway, I thought I'd stay over for Saturday night's première of *Cosi* with your good lady wife. Are you going, by any chance?"

"Yes I am. I was asked to this lunch that our premature friend Mr Knipe is giving for Dunwich, but I'd booked months ago for Carly and me to fly out on Friday morning."

"Is Carly going to the show?"

"No, I daren't take her to a Salzburg Festival first night. Black tie and all that."

"Are you taking anyone else?"

"No."

"Can I have Lindsey's other comp then?"

"Yes, probably, I'll check tomorrow. In any case I refuse to sit next to my Russian nemesis, and I can't think who else she'd want to give it to, so assume it's okay unless I ring."

"Top hole. Meanwhile I suppose we just sit tight and let Knipey stew, overcome by guilt for what he's doing to his poor wife. Do you think he'll get over his bad oyster by Friday, in time for his little lunch?"

"I have a feeling we're not supposed to be discussing this over the phone. I'll see you on Friday."

"Right, Jamie, that's good then. Where shall we meet?"

"*Der Triangel* at six-thirty. Do you know it?"

"I've been there once. Remind me how to get there."

"I haven't been since the new *Haus für Mozart*'s been finished. But you basically stand facing the *Großes Festspielhaus*, turn left past the front of the new theatre, and then turn left down *Wienerphilharmonikergaße*. It's just there, on the right."

"They named a street after an orchestra?"

"Every bloody street in Salzburg is named after something musical," I said. "If you play your cards right, in thirty years there'll be an *Anguslennoxstraße*."

"Nice idea. I could live with that."

The next day, Thursday, dawned clear and sunny, but for the first time ever I wasn't much looking forward to going to Stockencote. Albert had an uncanny way of knowing when something was wrong, and I was concerned he would ask awkward questions.

But I needn't have worried. When I arrived just before lunch he was out on the combine, according to Evie. He sent his apologies for being so rude, she said, but they weren't sure about the weather forecast, so he felt he couldn't stop even for lunch.

Ethel the pug made up for his absence, though. She made a huge fuss of me, and leapt onto my knee at every available opportunity. And Carly was really pleased to see me, which cheered me up no end. Albert had let her have a ride on the combine the day before. She'd loved it.

"It was great. You're miles off the ground, and there's this huge wheel thing at the front cutting all the wheat. Then behind you, you can hear this really loud noise, where another great big machine is getting the wheat out. Grandad said I'm not to tell anyone I went on it, because of someone called Helen Safety."

"Health and safety," I laughed. "I won't tell anyone, I promise."

We had cold ham and salad for lunch. Carly actually ate a bit of her lettuce, which amazed me. She shared my natural aversion to all things green and if we'd been at home she wouldn't have touched it.

When it was time to go, Evie came to the door with us, and gave Carly a terrific hug.

"I've so enjoyed you being here, Carly dear. Come back soon."

"I will, Auntie Evie, I promise. If Daddy lets me."

"Give my love to your Mummy for me, won't you?"

"Yes, I'm going to see her tomorrow."

"I know darling. What a lucky girl you are, to have such a lovely Mummy and Daddy."

"Bye, Evie," I said. "Thanks for everything. You're wonderful with her. And please thank Albert. Sorry not to have seen him, but I quite understand."

We drove away from the back yard. Ethel was barking like mad, and Evie was waving, and rummaging in her sleeve to find a hanky. I said:

"Auntie Evie's awfully sad to see you go."

"It's not just that. She's worried about Grandad. But I don't know why, he seems fine to me. He's just got a bit of a pain in his back. I get those all the time."

Carly and I were up at four the next morning for the journey to Stansted. The Freshair experience was made all the more joyful by having a ten-year-old in tow. She complained from the moment we left home to the moment we arrived at Salzburg Airport. It was entirely beyond me to contemplate any means of transport to Lindsey's apartment but yet another taxi.

I rang the doorbell, and Lindsey's voice answered straight away.

"Second floor," she shouted, and the buzzer rang.

Carly pushed the door and roared up the stairs, while I hauled our bags up. When I arrived, the two of them were in a giant embrace. Lindsey made a brave attempt at a smile, over Carly's shoulder. She looked dreadful.

"Oh, I've missed you," she said. And: "hallo Jamie. Nice to see you." Six months before she'd have had just as big a hug for me as she did for Carly.

We all sat down at the table. Carly said: "Mummy, can I have something to eat?"

"Yes, darling, of course I'll get you some breakfast," said Lindsey.

"No, no, Linds," I said, "you look exhausted. I'll find some food for Carly. What about something for you?"

I went into the kitchen and opened the fridge. Half a pint of milk, two eggs, some low-fat spread, and a bit of soapy-looking cheese wrapped in cling film. Then I opened the cupboards, one by one. Some spaghetti, a small tin of tomato purée, and the end of a bottle of extra virgin olive oil. There was a bit of runny honey, and two individual helpings of Marmite in little round plastic pots.

More promisingly there was most of a loaf of sliced brown bread. But when I looked inside the packet it was covered in little green spots of mould, like some kind of hideous disease.

I went back into the other room. Carly was telling Lindsey something about Auntie Evie, and Lindsey was smiling.

"Linds, with the best will in the world I can't really rustle up anything worthy of the name breakfast. Maybe I'd better nip out and get something."

"Can't you make some toast?"

"Not with bread that's got the pox."

"Oh God, I'm sorry, I haven't felt much like shopping."

"Have you been eating?"

"Oh yes, after the rehearsals. I've been going out with, well, with the cast."

"Does that mean you haven't eaten since Wednesday night?"

"No, it doesn't mean that. I went out for supper yesterday, too."

"Who with?"

She paused.

"Was it with Uncle Sergei?" said Carly.

Lindsey banged her hands down on the table. Not hard, but loud enough to make Carly jump.

"Look, I'd really like something to eat, actually Jamie. There's a bread shop just across the road – they do nice croissants. Would you mind?"

The day continued in much the same vein, but somehow we all managed to be civil to one another, and that evening we got another wildly expensive taxi to take us half way up the Gaisberg, to the east of the city. There was a hotel there called the Gersberg-Alm, with wonderful views back down the valley. Carly ran and laughed in the play area, and we all ate well. Lindsey wasn't drinking, but I got through a whole bottle of Grüner Veltliner, which for once made me mellow rather than agitated or sleepy.

After another taxi ride we arrived back at Lindsey's apartment, and before long Carly flopped into bed, exhausted after her long day. Lindsey and I sat down together.

"So," I said, "do we risk a discussion about The Situation, or not?"

"I think we have to, Jamie. The thing is… I've decided to tell Sergei I won't see him again."

"But that's brilliant, Linds. Why didn't you tell me earlier?"

"Couldn't with Carly about. But anyway, it's not all roses, so you'd better let me finish."

"Okay, go ahead."

"I am actually in love with Sergei, I'm afraid. I wish I weren't, but I am. And he's in love with me, too. But the stupid thing is, I'm still in love with you."

"Did you have sex with him?"

"Yes."

"Properly?"

"Yes."

"Shit. But you're certain the baby's mine?"

"One hundred per cent. The dates only work with you."

She didn't look convinced. And anyway, I knew Lindsey's monthly cycle better than she did. What she said could only be true if she and Sergei had waited at least two weeks before starting their affair.

"I'm having a devil of a job believing you, if I'm honest," I said. "You say you're giving him the boot. You're assuming, I take it, that I'll have you back?"

I thought she'd hit the roof. But actually all she said was: "no, Jamie, I'm not assuming anything. Would you have me back?"

"Yes, I think so, as long as I knew it was really over between you."

"All I can say, Jamie, is I'm going to try."

"Have you told him yet?"

"No. I haven't known what to do. I've been feeling dreadfully sick, although that went off a bit today, with you and Carly. I'm also terribly nervous about tomorrow night. I don't know why, but it's worse than it's ever been. And I've been feeling guilty and weak and…"

She started sobbing. Really huge, dreadful sobs that seemed to be tearing the very soul out of her. I tried to put my arm round her, but she gently pulled away from my embrace. Her face was streaming with tears, and she looked sort of blank, as if the pain was too much to bear. I had no idea what to do, so I just sat there.

Eventually she said: "I'll have to go to bed. Are you coming?"

"Do you want me in your bed?"

"No, not really."

"Okay, then, I'll sleep on the sofa bed. My case is here anyway – I haven't unpacked yet."

"All right, Jamie. Good night."

She stood up, then hesitated.

"Jamie, I want you to know that I'm really sorry to be putting you through this. God knows you don't deserve it. But I have to work this thing through."

She sighed heavily, then without another word she went into her bedroom and shut the door.

18

Carly roared into my room at eight o'clock the next morning. After Lindsey had gone to bed, I'd had to rummage around the flat for ages before I'd found anything remotely resembling bedclothes. In the end I'd stretched out underneath a hideous shiny orange throw, which I'd found gathering dust on top of a cupboard. Shaking the dust out of it had occasioned a monumental sneezing fit which I'd been frightened would wake everyone in the apartment block, but thank God both Carly and Lindsey were, in their different ways, too far out of it to notice.

Lindsey had her first night, of course, so was Not To Be Disturbed. I did my best to concentrate on something nice. Today was the day for the much-anticipated *Sound of Music* Tour.

Albert was right. Carly had become obsessed with the film. She'd learned all the songs and all the children's names. She even knew about something about the historical background, and was full of admiration for Captain von Trapp's heroic opposition to the evils of Hitler and the Gestapo. She had already decided that when she grew up she was going to enter the Nonnberg Convent to be a Benedictine Nun.

The Sound of Music turns out to be almost unknown in Austria. Whether this is because of the Hollywoodisation of its subject matter, or because of its unquestioning opposition to the evils of Hitler and his cronies, it is hard to say. Certainly, if you head south-west out of Salzburg towards the magnificent Alpine scenery of the Berchtesgaden National Park, you can if you wish visit the village of Obersalzberg where Hitler held court at the Berghof. You may also go by bus up the mountain road and then take the lift, through the rock, to the tip of the

132

Kehlstein, the site of genial, friendly Adolf's infamous Eagle's Nest. It's all a bit like a Theme Park.

However, notwithstanding the film's uncompromising stance on the *Anshcluß*, the Salzburgers realise that *The Sound of Music* can be exploited to release a large number of euros from the pockets of the tourists and opera professionals who descend on the City each summer. The various tour coaches wait in a long line in front of the Mirabell Gardens, where Fräulein Maria and her gaggle of curiously-dressed children cavorted around the Statue of Pegasus singing *Do-Re-Mi*.

Our tour guide was a raven-haired creature called Adriana, who turned out to be Italian. In her delectable Mediterranean-infused English ("in this region they are farming porks, for example") she told us about the palaces, mountains and lakes so familiar from the film. Why is it that all non-British eighteen-year-olds appear to be educated to the eyeballs in the high culture of European history? She knew the intricacies of the *Risorgimento*, the operas of Mozart as well as his personal habits, and the lurid peccadilloes of Archbishop Markus Sittikus, founder of the Palace of Heilbrunn, whose gardens we visited because they now housed the little glass pavilion used for the filming of *You are Sixteen*.

Carly, with Adriana's encouragement, ran inside the pavilion, and began to dance around, jumping on and off the bench which ran around the perimeter, and singing *You are Sixteen* word-and note-perfect to the gaggle of waiting tourists. They all applauded and took photographs.

We sped past *Schloss Frohnburg* – used in the film as the front of the Von Trapp Mansion. "It is now a University," said Adriana. "They do not support visitors." Then we stopped at the private lake belonging to the Palace of Leopoldskron, But we were close enough for Carly to recognise it, and she took a couple of undecipherable snaps on her phone.

Several kilometres later we drew up in a car park on the edge of the private lake of Leopoldskron. Across the other side of the water was, unmistakably, Captain von Trapp's Palace. There, Adriana informed us, we could just pick out the place where the von Trapp children fell out of their boats into the water. The little girl playing the role of Gretel, apparently, had been terrified because she was unable to swim. This led as a direct consequence to the extreme brevity of the scene in the finished film, as the cameraman had suddenly had to abandon his filming to dive into the artificial lake and rescue poor little Gretel, who had just fallen in.

Carly absorbed it all with rapt attention, and was the first to the front of the bus when Adriana invited vocal contributions from the tour party.

She was half way through *The Lonely Goatherd* ("Lay-ee-oddle-ay-ee-oddle-ay-ee-hoo") when my phone rang. A British woman with a steel-grey bun and a Crag Hoppers rucksack on her knee looked round crossly.

I fished the phone out of my pocket. *Lindsey calling*, it said.

"Hi Linds," I whispered. Several more people in the bus began tutting their disapproval. "How are you getting on?"

"Terrible, Jamie. My throat's on fire, I'm feeling sicker than ever, and I'm sure I'm coming down with something."

It was not unknown for Lindsey to do this before exceptionally frightening premières. Nerves did funny things to singers. I knew almost no-one in the profession who didn't believe with absolute certainty that on first nights they were coming down with bird flu, or mad cow disease, or whatever civilisation-threatening epidemic happened to be in vogue. The crucial thing was to take their symptoms absolutely seriously.

"Your speaking voice sounds fine," I said, as encouragingly as I could. "Can you sing?"

"I'm okay at the moment. I've just sung an E flat."

A top E flat. Verified by the green and black plastic Melodica she carried round with her and blew into regularly in a most unhygienic fashion.

"Do you think you need the doctor?"

"Yes. No. Perhaps."

"How about the sickness? Is it much worse than usual?"

"Oh God, I don't know. I had the scampi salad at the Gersberg-Alm last night, but then so did you."

There was a doctor retained by the Salzburg Festival, who carried a laptop round with him to record his notes and diagnoses. If you sneaked a look over his shoulder you'd see the names of at least fifty of the grandest singers in the world, all having the vapours about the state of their precious instruments. But it looked as if we might get away without having to call him in.

"Linds, I should make yourself a cup of pineapple tea and get yourself to bed. If it gets any worse ring me again."

"If you're sure, Jamie."

"I'm sure, Linds. See how it goes."

"Ok, then." She still sounded very dubious, but eventually said we said goodbye and she rang off.

Carly was by now into the second verse of *I have Confidence*. We crested a hill, and there in front of us was the bright blue shape of the Mondsee dotted with white sails. The little boats looked impossibly jolly and carefree, filled no doubt with Austrians whose daughters were not about to have their innocent childhoods interrupted by marital infidelity and, God forbid, divorce.

To my relief no further call came, and the Tour began to peter out. Carly had finally exhausted her repertoire, and the other members of the party were unwilling to expose themselves to ridicule, so the musical entertainment reverted to selections from the Soundtrack of the Original Motion Picture. We stopped for lunch at the picturesque town of Mondsee, which is home to the Church whose magnificent Baroque interior was used as the location for the wedding of Fräulein Maria to Captain von Trapp, but my heart was no longer in it. Carly managed to extract some pleasure from the monstrous-looking banana split which ended her meal, but once we were back on the bus she fell sound asleep, and had to be woken when we arrived back in Mirabellplatz.

We said goodbye to Adriana, who thanked Carly for her lovely singing, and managed to feign surprise when I gave her a ten euro tip for giving us such an informative tour. Then we walked through the Mirabell Gardens, crossed the River Salzach, and wound our way through the maze of alleyways towards the three theatres, side by side: the *Felsenreitschule*, where the von Trapp Family Singers had sung their way to freedom from the tyranny of the Nazis; the brand new *Haus für Mozart*, where Lindsey was about to perform, and the *Großes Festspielhaus*. Then on into *HerbertvonKarajanplatz* and left through the Siegmundstor tunnel.

Finally we turned right down Reichenhallerstraße towards Lindsey's flat, and the imminent task of forcing my nervous spouse through the first night of *Cosi fan Tutte* at the most important opera festival in the world.

Lindsey was already preparing to leave for her pre-performance meal. Not that she fancied anything much to eat, so she said. She looked pale and gaunt. Her throat was still sore, but she assured me, thank God, that she didn't need the doctor. She was going to buy a bag of oranges on the way to the theatre and was sure they would do her as much good as any doctor.

She was probably right. Doctors regularly consulted by opera singers mostly seemed to have the idea that cortisone was the universal panacea. True, a dose of cortisone will temporarily stop the symptoms of almost any of the performance-threatening throat complaints which afflict singers. Indeed, singers will often report that their voices are functioning better than usual. The after-effects, however, are not so desirable, often rendering the singer unable to perform for weeks afterwards.

"You don't want company at lunch, I suppose?" I said.

"Not really, Jamie. I'm too petrified to be good company, I'm afraid. I'm best left to myself, I think."

"I'll come, Mummy," said Carly. "I need to tell you all about the *Sound of Music* Tour. You can buy me an ice-cream."

Dear God it was only a couple of hours since the banana split in Mondsee.

"No, I don't think so, Carly," said Lindsey. "Mummy needs to concentrate on the show".

Within ten minutes she was gone.

19

Lindsey had organised a babysitter recommended by the company manager, but I needed to make Carly's tea before going out to the performance. Carly and I made an expedition to Spar, which was just round the corner, to buy some more spaghetti, some Coke and some Barilla Bolognese sauce. Anything more elaborate was beyond the meagre capacity of Lindsey's kitchen. But Carly pronounced it "much nicer than the spag bol you make at home, Daddy", which was convenient if not particularly flattering, and she ate every last morsel.

The babysitter, whose name was Reinhilde, arrived on the dot of six o'clock. She was an extraordinary-looking creature: bull-necked, and with cropped hair and a beer belly, and Carly looked terrified of her. But with fearsome efficiency and prescience Reinhilde had brought with her the entire *Lord of the Rings* trilogy on DVD, so Carly was soon mollified. They both settled down to watch Part One, in English with German subtitles, while I changed into my dinner jacket and left for my meeting with Angus.

Der Triangel was heaving when I arrived, and for a moment I thought Angus hadn't made it. Then I spotted him, squeezed into a corner between a huge soprano, whom I recognised from Glyndebourne the previous year, and the very effete and heavily made-up director of her show. I managed to catch Angus's eye without being seen by any of the others, and he excused himself and slid out from behind his table, causing a great commotion as they all had to stand up to let him out. I meanwhile had snuck back outside, and by some miracle a couple got up to leave just in time for me to grab their table.

Angus came and sat opposite me, plonking a glass of Grüner Veltliner down in front of me as he did so.

"Bloody hell old boy," he said, "couldn't we have gone somewhere more private?"

"Sorry, Gussie. There's nowhere in Salzburg which isn't stuffed with opera people. Anyway, thanks for the drink. Now, tell me what our lord and master had to say about Greg the Dreg."

"He made it all sound very easy. He has some friend, or employee, or acquaintance, who will communicate to Knipe that his recent indiscretions with Jason are about to become public knowledge if he doesn't resign."

"What's this acquaintance going to do? Cut letters out of the newspaper and stick them together to form a message?"

"I haven't the slightest idea. For all I know Uncle Sergei will call his chum Mr Putin and get the KGB to do it."

"I don't think the KGB exists any more," I said. "What happens to Jason?"

"Sergei promises that he won't come to any harm. And he is about to become a hundred grand richer, so I don't think we should feel too sorry for him."

"It's too much for me, Angus, that's all I know."

"Oh for God's sake, Jamie, you're like a wet weekend. I've just told you that nothing now stands in the way of you becoming General Administrator of Opera London. We'll have champagne in the interval to celebrate."

What with one thing and another, I wasn't in much of a state to appreciate the beginning of Act One. The three men, Ferrando, Guglielmo and Don Alfonso came on at the end of the overture. In this new production Don Alfonso was the proprietor of a fairground, and appeared to be trying to persuade the two younger men to climb onto a magnificent, working roundabout, which had lifelike models of naked women on all fours instead of the usual fairground horses. One of these women bore a striking resemblance to Lindsey, and when Ferrando, a young American tenor called Randy Youngman, finally climbed on top of her I was uncomfortably reminded of Lindsey and Sergei.

There was a seamless scene change, during which the roundabout was replaced by a similar model, the difference being that the women-horses were now replaced by naked kneeling men, two of whom were clearly intended to represent Ferrando and Guglielmo. Sure enough, when Lindsey and the German mezzo singing Dorabella began their first duet *Ah Guarda Sorella*, they caressed the models, and a little later on they started humping them.

The show continued in much the same vein – when the two men were called off to their pretend war by Alfonso their models were carefully draped with uniforms by the girls, and when they came back as 'Albanians' the uniforms were changed for Arab *dishdashas* and *keffiyehs*. The girls kept hitching up their skirts and hopping on and off the models.

It all looked pretty silly to me, but the singing was fantastic. Lindsey in particular had a commitment and purity of tone which surpassed anything I had previously heard from her. *Come Scoglio*, in which her character Fiordiligi sings a defiant aria declaring her fidelity to Guglielmo, was sensational – the insanely difficult *coloratura* runs delivered with pinpoint precision. At the end of the aria the auditorium erupted. Lindsey tried to stay in character throughout the prolonged cheering, but she was visibly astonished by her reception.

When the interval came the audience went mad, and as we all trooped out of the auditorium there was an excited buzz of conversation. Angus and I joined the queue for the champagne bar.

"She's singing up a storm, your wife," said Angus. "Bloody fantastic. Better even than in *Figaro*. Best Mozart soprano in the world, if you ask me."

"Yes, I have to say I agree. I'm just finding it a bit more difficult to take than usual."

"Oh, come on, Jamie. I've told you, this thing with Sergei's just a blip. Nothing really wrong with your marriage, I'm absolutely bloody certain there isn't. I mean even if she has done the deed with our friend from Novosibirsk you'll still have her back, won't you?"

"Christ, yes of course I will."

"Well take her off on holiday, buy her lots of nice meals and presents, then fuck her brains out. You'll sort her out in no time."

"We're going to Montpellier, actually Gussie. As soon as this *Cosi* is over. But there's a major complication which you don't know about."

"What's that, old boy?"

"She's pregnant. And I don't know whose it is."

"Oh fuck," said Angus.

The super-smooth barman sashayed over to us. "Ja?" he said.

Angus seemed incapable of any response.

"Zwei champagne, bitte," I said.

"Gerne," said the waiter, and picked two minuscule glasses of the fizzy stuff off a shelf behind him. "Funfundzwanzig Euro, bitte."

"Angus, he wants twenty-five euros for those two little glasses. I've only got twenty."

Angus quickly fished a five euro note out of his pocket. I handed the twenty-five to the barman, who gave me a withering look.

We made our way through the people behind us to the far side of the bar, where we managed to find a low white wall to put our tiny glasses on. Angus was still looking poleaxed.

"It's a bit of a tough one, isn't it Gussie?" I said.

"Christ old boy, I should say so. I mean it does put a bit of a different complexion on things. Do you think Lindsey knows who the father is?"

"She says she's certain it's mine, but I don't believe her. I mean it easily could be mine – we knobbed at the right time and all that – but she's admitted to having sex with that Russian wanker, and although she says that the dates don't fit, I can see a look in her eyes which makes me think she's worried."

For almost the first time in the twenty-odd years I'd known him, Angus was lost for words. He took a sip of his champagne. Finally he said: "doesn't seem a very appropriate drink now, does it? Sorry, old thing."

"Be that as it may, Gussie, I'm going to need your help. Where do I go from here?"

He sighed. "I have got an idea, actually. Something a friend did a few years ago. But it's nasty, I warn you."

"Can't be any nastier than what I'm already going through.

"Ok then, brace yourself. We haven't got much time before the second half, so it'll have to be brutal. First a couple of questions. To establish the ground rules, so to speak. Will Lindsey have an abortion?"

"Not a chance. She's longed for another child for the last ten years. There is absolutely no way she'll agree to a termination. Next question?"

"Would you bring it up if it was Sergei's?"

"I've asked myself that a thousand times. I keep trying to tell myself that it would be okay, that I'd get used to it. But the real answer is I'm not sure."

"But she wants to come back to you whatever happens, right?"

"So she says. She's going to end it with Sergei, apparently. Then she'll come home and have the baby. That's the theory, anyway."

"So the only real solution is to find out for certain that the baby's yours?"

"Well, great, Angus, yes, that's the solution. But what happens if it's not?"

"If it's not yours then I simply have no idea what you'll do. But surely not knowing is just as bad, if not worse?"

"You have a point, I suppose. But how in God's name do you propose that we find out?"

"You'll have to do a paternity test, Jamie."

"Oh, fuck, don't be ridiculous. I mean there are limits. She's my sodding wife, for fuck's sake."

Several people looked round. "Try and keep your voice down, there's a good chap," said Angus. "Look, Jamie, I warned you it'd be nasty. But this is the rest of both your lives we're talking about. Not to mention Carly's. Don't you think you owe it to them?"

"Okay, maybe I do. But I doubt if Lindsey will agree, because she'll be too worried I'll insist on getting rid of the baby if it's his."

Angus drained his glass, and then paused for a moment. "You could do it without Lindsey's permission."

"Oh yes, sure, Angus, that'd be easy."

The bell rang for the end of the interval. There was an announcement in German, which was then repeated in a different voice in perfect English.

Ladies and gentlemen, please return to your seats. The performance will resume in five minutes.

"Bugger," said Angus, "got to rush to the loo. Follow me to the gents."

We walked quickly towards the little man picked out in green neon on the wall. There were two unoccupied urinals at the far end.

Angus unzipped himself. "What's the name of that gynaecologist you're friendly with?" he whispered.

"John Standish. What the hell's he got to do with this?"

"Shut up and listen. Do you think Lindsey'll have an amniocentesis?"

"What, the test for Down's Syndrome? She didn't have one with Carly. I think she's more likely to have one now because she's classed as a geriatric mother, but I'm not sure."

"If she does you can use the results to test against your DNA. A friend of mine did it recently. He paid some unscrupulous wallah in Harley

Street a fortune to do it without telling his partner. I bet you could get Standish to do it for a couple of top-price stalls seats at Opera London."

The bell went again.

Please take your seats, the performance is about to resume.

"Shit, Gussie. We'll have to talk about this some more."

"Bollocks. You know what to do. But don't say it came from me. Let's go."

By the time we made it into the auditorium, Maestro Giotti was already tottering to the front of the orchestra pit and receiving the rapturous applause of the audience. We had to vault over the backs of our seats from behind, and there was a deafening chorus of tuts and sighs from the glittering opera-goers around us. I distinctly heard one very loud whisper saying "*Englisch*".

When the curtain rose the men- and women-horses had been replaced by couples in various states of congress. Some were copulating; some were indulging in oral sex. There was even a couple who had finished, and were smoking post-coital cigarettes.

The audience gasped, then immediately burst into more applause. The Despina, a scorchingly beautiful Slovakian girl called Anna Jenkerova, had to make four separate attempts to start the first recitative.

She and Don Alfonso were seated on a podium above the stage, and were both now dressed in black leather. Whips and chains were lying around them. During the course of the act they would periodically fondle each other as they encouraged the four lovers into ever more unseemly acts of physical contact. During the Dorabella-Guglielmo duet, *Il core vi dono*, the two new lovers had rather satisfying sex up against the pole in the middle of the roundabout.

I dreaded what the rest of the proceedings had in store for Lindsey. However, to my relief, Fiordiligi was clearly regarded by the director as The Pure One, and she and Ferrando subjected us to nothing more than a bit of token humping.

All the singing was of an astonishingly high standard, and when Lindsey sang her second great aria: *Per pietà*, the whole audience held its breath. The repeat of the first section hung on the merest thread of tone – a sound of the most exquisite beauty. And again her *coloratura* at the end of the aria was brilliant. The horns of the Vienna Philharmonic were flawless, even in the hideously difficult final *obbligato*, and Lindsey's final B flat was triumphant, declaring her determination to remain faithful at all costs to her first lover.

142

The audience did not wait for the postlude to finish before starting to shout their approval. The performance stopped for a good five minutes, during the course of which Lindsey stood, visibly moved, in the middle of the stage. Normally she would have made her exit before the end of the aria – Fiordiligi off to gather herself before setting off to join Guglielmo on the battlefield – but the production dictated that by this stage all six singers were on stage watching each other's scenes. I couldn't for the life of me work out how this fitted with Mozart and Da Ponte's plot, but this didn't seem to worry the Salzburg audience, who were spellbound throughout.

At the end of the show, they went berserk. As each new singer walked onto the stage to take his or her call, the volume increased, and when Lindsey came on, the last of the six to take her bow, the noise was deafening. She had never been much good at the heart-clutching and head-shaking which was *de rigueur* for most international sopranos on receiving the rapturous approval of the audience, and she tried to get away with a simple curtsey and a smile. The Salzburgers were having none of it. Time and again they renewed their screams of '*brava, diva!*' and time and again Lindsey tried unsuccessfully to join the line-up with the other five. Eventually she walked off the stage to get Giotti from the wings, and as he tottered on, arm in arm with my wife, the cheering began all over again.

When the production team of director, designer, and lighting designer walked on, there was more deafening noise. At this point one or two rather feeble boos attempted for a short time to compete with the cheering, but the ayes had it.

On and on went the applause. By now the audience was standing – half in ovation, half in readiness to depart. I nudged Angus, and we took the opportunity to work our way to the end of the row, and down towards the backstage area. Lindsey had given me her pass, and I swiped it through the reader. It opened to let us into the prompt side wing. We made our way quickly to Lindsey's dressing room, the applause and cheers still ringing through the theatre. I opened the door and Angus and I walked in, to be confronted by Mutt and Jeff, who looked more agitated than ever. Behind them were standing Tatyana, and the great oligarch himself, Sergei Ivanevitch Rebroff.

"Ah, Jamie, Angus, what pleasure." He waved Mutt and Jeff aside. "Lindsey was sensational, was she not?"

I hadn't in any way prepared for this moment. I stood there speechless, looking at the extraordinary group in front of me. Angus had to reply for me. Not that he made a very good job of it.

"Absolutely sensational, Sergei. The best I've ever heard her shag – er – sing."

Angus went puce. But as usual Sergei smarmed on as if he'd heard nothing untoward.

"I want her for my new company. I hope all will be fixed for money, and for me to be Chairman, by autumn. She must sing in opening production."

This made me really angry. Who the bloody hell did he think he was?

"I'm so sorry, Sergei, but that will not be possible. The opening production of the season is already cast. Rehearsals begin a week on Monday. The artists will already have been working on their roles for some time. And in any case, Lindsey is not free – she is contracted to sing Tatyana in *Yevgeny Onegin* in Amsterdam."

For the first time, I saw a flash of anger in Sergei's eyes.

"Your Russian pronunciation does you credit, Jamie. We will speak again about this, perhaps with Lindsey."

At that moment the door swung open and in she walked. She was prising her wig off her forehead, and was followed into the room by a clucking wig technician, who was trying to catch up with her before she tore the lace.

When Lindsey saw the reception committee waiting for her, she looked horrified.

"For God's sake. I can't cope with all of you at once. Sergei, please ask the boys to wait outside. I don't think anyone in here is likely to shoot you."

They slunk out, looking a bit disgruntled. Tatyana followed them, saying to Lindsey as she left: "forgive us please. Your performance was magnificent."

That left Lindsey with Sergei, Angus and me. There was an awkward silence as we looked at each other, then the three of us all began to speak at once, telling her how wonderful she was. To my astonishment, she burst out laughing.

"My God, you three should see yourselves. Why don't you go to the bar and get a drink? I've got to have a shower – all that humping's left me pouring with sweat. We'll meet back here in fifteen minutes. By then I might have worked out how to cope with you all."

I looked at Angus. He gave me a rueful grin, and said: "never been known to turn down an opportunity for a lotion. What's yours, Sergei old bean?"

For a moment Sergei was at a loss for words. Then he said: "Lindsey, you were superb. We will come back in fifteen minutes. Angus, it would be pleasure to have drink with you."

We trooped out to join the others in the corridor. I looked back at Lindsey as we left, but she was busily rubbing her face with make-up remover, and didn't notice.

Sergei had recovered his *sang-froid* by the time I closed the door.

"There are too many people here. We go to bar."

Mutt and Jeff made as if to complain, but Sergei said something to them in Russian, and it appeared to mollify them. We walked back through the wings to the pass door, which from this side could be opened by pressing a button. Then we joined the slow procession of people making their way out of the auditorium towards the bars and the street beyond. Mutt and Jeff were standing one either side of Sergei, constantly looking round in case one of the *lederhosen*-clad gentry in the audience should make an unexpected move against him, but they were all far too excited about the performance to bother.

There followed an agonising period of ten minutes at the bar, during which Tatyana, Sergei, Angus and I discussed the performance in general, and Lindsey in particular. My contribution to the conversation was pretty perfunctory, because all I wanted to do was shove Sergei's perfect white teeth down his throat, but Angus held the fort manfully, explaining to Sergei why he had so enjoyed the show. The production had been okay, he said, but it was the performance of Giotti, with his masterly control over the orchestra and his pacing of the opera, which had made the evening so satisfying. Sergei mostly nodded and tried to look wise. Prat.

Angus and I had both managed to get tickets for the jamboree afterwards, and obviously Sergei had magicked some up as well, so when we had finished our drinks we all went back through the wings to Lindsey's dressing-room. As we arrived, she walked out of the room, dressed in some new, outrageously expensive designer gown which she had presumably bought specially for the occasion. She looked fabulous. With my stomach churning, I followed them out of the theatre, and along the road to the neighbouring *Großes Festspielhaus*.

20

Salzburg First Night Parties were legendary. Not for them a shepherd's pie buffet in the Telenorth Bar, which was all Opera London could usually manage. We all trooped onto the stage of the *Großes Festspielhaus*, whence the set on which the *Figaro* cast had been rehearsing that afternoon had been spirited away to some far-flung corner of the enormous theatre. The whole performing area was groaning with tables, chairs for 150, and bone china platters filled with exquisite little canapés. There were tiny squares of smoked salmon sitting on bits of blini, with dollops of sour cream in between, topped with a sprinkling of chives; mozzarella and tomato crostini, carpaccio on toast, and crayfish tails in pastry barquettes with some unidentifiable but delicious orange goo in between. Bottles of *Grüner Veltliner* and *Blaufränkisch* wine were lined up next to the *Mineralwasser*, sensibly provided for those with voices or reputations to preserve.

The whole stage erupted into applause as soon as people spotted Lindsey. Göstl-Saurau made an instant beeline for us. His face was wreathed in smiles. "Lindsey, my dear, you vere simply sensational," he said. "Not since Jurinac heff I heard such exqvisite control, such dazzling *coloratura*."

"Thank you, Graf von Göstl-Saurau. I think you know my husband, Jamie."

"Yes, of course. You are ferry velcome to ze *Salzburger Festspiele*."

Göstl-Saurau shook my hand, but he wasn't looking at me. His eyes were focussed on something behind me.

"Herr Rebroff." Göstl-Saurau managed to maintain his smile, but obviously at some personal cost.

Sergei inserted himself between Lindsey and me, leaving the rest of his party, including Angus, hovering behind him. "Graf von Göstl-Saurau, how splendid to see you. Please allow me to congratulate you on astonishing performance."

Göstl-Saurau was looking rattled.

"Ve are lucky to heff such a fine cast. I'm sure you agree zet Miss Templeton gave us a vunderful Fiordiligi."

"I could not possibly disagree. She is my favourite artist."

It would have been such a pleasure to thump him in the face. Göstl-Saurau transferred his rictus of a smile to me.

"You must be ferry proud off her."

"Of course I am. I have always considered myself extremely fortunate that Lindsey is my wife. She is a great singer."

Eventually Göstl-Saurau excused himself, and sashayed off to the front of the stage, where a podium had been set up for him. He climbed onto it, and a raucous voice called in German and English for silence.

Göstl-Saurau spoke first in German, so I only got about half of what he said. He began by thanking every cast member individually, and then went into diatribes about Giotti and the director. Then, to my total amazement, he turned his attention to Sergei Rebroff. At this point he switched into English, which was just as well because I wouldn't have wanted to miss one word.

"Ve heff viz uss tonight vun off ze most talked-about figures in world opera. Es I am sure you all know, Sergei Ivanevitch Rebroff hess promised to give vun opera company a ferry large sum off money. Many people vere excited about ziss, end hoped zet ziss money might come to Salzburg. How-effer, Mr Rebroff hes decided to giff instead hiss money to Opera London. He iss off course entitled ziss decision to make, but I kvestion vezzer it is vise. My friend Gregory Knipe, Chairman off Opera London, iss here tonight, end I know he iss not heppy to receive ziss money, because he regards it as ill-gotten, end sinks zet if ziss kind off money is used to prop up a publicly-subsidised opera company, ze Arts Council off England may altogezzer vissdraw its support."

I had that sense of time standing still which always seems to accompany an event of profound significance. First nights were never used for this kind of inflammatory speech. I looked at the shocked faces around the room, and there in their midst was our very own Greg the Dreg. He was staring resolutely at Göstl-Saurau, hanging on his every word.

"I em afraid zet sumsink ferry bed may be about to happen to opera in Britain. Ve all know vot terrible sinks are happening in Italy since ze budget cuts of Signor Berlusconi. Many opera companies vill be forced to close unless sumsink iss done to restore the missing money. I fear zet if zere iss now in Britain a bettle between Mr Rebroff end Mr Knipe, it vill be a disaster for everyone who luffs opera. Perheps Mr Blair vill giff all of British opera's money to hiss beloffed Olympic Games. I vould like on ziss occasion tonight to urge Mr Rebroff to sink again. Perheps, like hiss friend Roman Abramovich, he vould like instead to use hiss shtinkink millions to buy a football team."

He said this with a nasty smile on his face, and there were a few nervous titters around the room. It was at this point that Sergei said, rather loudly, "Lindsey, Jamie, Angus, I regret that we must leave party immediately."

Everyone turned to look at us. Sergei started to make his way out between the tables. He did not look round. It was Angus who made the decision to go with him.

"Come on Jamie, for Christ's sake, we have to stick with him, or the whole bloody game's up."

"Angus is absolutely right." I said. "Are you coming, Linds?"

Lindsey had gone white as a sheet, and looked as if she was about to faint. "Of course," she said in a whisper.

We all trooped out, following Sergei like a flock of sheep. I tried to avoid everyone's gaze, but unfortunately our exit took us right past where Knipe was standing. As Angus and I tried to edge past him, he planted himself squarely in front of us. When he opened his mouth to speak, I got a noisome blast of halitosis.

"I don't know what the bloody hell you think you're doing leaving with that odious man. I would like you to know that whatever the game is, you're backing the wrong horse."

Angus said: "mixed metaphor, Mr Knipe. I'm surprised at you." There was a brief stand-off, then Knipe smirked unpleasantly and stood aside to let us all out. Lindsey looked at the floor as she passed him. She had taken my arm. I didn't flatter myself that she did it for any other reason than to stop herself falling over.

As we walked through the front doors of the theatre, a policeman to our left was waving through a black Mercedes limousine. It drew softly up in front of us, and the driver jumped out to open the rear door for Sergei.

How the hell he'd arranged for it to appear to get through the police cordon so quickly was a mystery. He turned around to look at the rest of us.

"I am sincerely grateful that you have all chosen to stay with me after disgraceful display from Graf von Göstl-Saurau. Please come with me, all of you, to Hotel Sacher. It would be my privilege to entertain you to supper, now I have deprived you of your meal on stage of *Großes Festspielhaus*. We can all go in my car – my bodyguards will follow with Tatyana."

I looked to my left, where a second car had drawn up behind ours. Mutt and Jeff said something in Russian, which I took to be an effort to persuade Sergei to allow at least one of them to ride with him, but he waved them away, and they wandered reluctantly back to the other car. Lindsey and I climbed into the back with Sergei, and Angus was shown into the front seat by the driver.

As we drove across the bridge to the hotel the River Salzach was at its most captivating. Everywhere lights were winking at us, and the moon cast a luminous reflection on the water. It was all impossibly romantic. Except that my left thigh was rubbing up against the Savile Row-clad right thigh of Sergei Ivanevitch Rebroff, with whom my life was now more firmly linked than ever.

Sergei's suite, again on the top floor of the hotel, was sumptuously furnished. Gleaming wooden floors throughout were carelessly scattered with Persian rugs. The walls played host to the kind of furniture you see on *The Antiques Roadshow,* and which used to make Arthur Negus nearly wet his pants with excitement.

Sergei gestured for us all to sit down. Lindsey was looking distinctly uncomfortable, but made a point of sitting on a two-seater sofa next to me. Angus, who didn't seem happy either, sat on his own opposite us. And Sergei busied himself on the telephone, ordering in irritatingly fluent German some late-night repast for us all.

He put down the phone, and went out to the room beyond. Within thirty seconds he had returned with a tray bearing a bottle of ice-cold vodka and four glasses. Without asking us what we wanted, he poured us each a vodka, and placed the glasses in front of us. Lindsey said demurely: "I don't think I'll have any vodka, thank you Sergei. Have you got any mineral water?"

"I have ordered mineral water with gas."

There was a knock on the outer door.

"Kto?"

A female voice said something in reply, and Sergei said "Da". In walked Tatyana.

"Sergei I am sorry to disturb you, but I am here to check all here is okay."

"Yes, thank you Tatyana. I am happy that there are no Ingushetyan terrorists hiding in the kitchen. I have ordered food, wine, and mineral water. The boys will no doubt want to check the poor unfortunate from room service who brings it up. Then I ask you please to bring it in for us. Please ring down for separate order of food for yourselves. And then leave us to destroy Graf von Göstl-Saurau in his absence."

"Of course, Sergei. Thank you."

She left the room. Sergei, with no further preamble, drained his glass of vodka, then poured himself another. He drained that, too. He then repeated the process a further three times. Then he slammed his glass down on the table, and said, simply, "shit".

We sat there like lemons for several seconds longer. It was Angus who broke the ice. "Well, Göstl-Saurau was on form, wasn't he? What a load of bollocks. He and Knipe deserve each other, if you ask me."

"Quite," said Sergei. "I am amazed that they consider themselves to be in position to look Sergei Ivanevitch Rebroff's gift horse in mouth. But I am not accustomed to losing this kind of fight. Battle is joined, Mr Knipe. And no-one need be in doubt who will win.

"But what makes me so angry is the way they treat artists. The way they treat you, Lindsey. They fawn on you for your great performance. But they cannot even show you respect of allowing triumph of such evening to be yours. You should all be in no doubt that when your wonderful Company is mine, those who produce this magnificent thing that we call opera will be accorded the respect they deserve. Singers, players, dressmakers and wig technicians. Stage crew and electricians. Conductors, directors and stage managers. These will all be important people in my opera company. Not politicians who celebrate great achievement in Arts one minute, and withdraw funding the next.

"Jamie, I understand what you said to me in Lindsey's dressing room. Job of casting is yours and yours alone, and will remain so when I am in charge. But this one issue is to me most important. You must look for production very soon in which Lindsey can sing. If it cannot be first of season, then it must be as soon as possible."

150

He paused, but he clearly hadn't finished.

"We all, I suspect, know that Lindsey is pregnant – this subject cannot be pushed under carpet any longer, because it will affect plans of Company."

Lindsey said quietly: "Sergei, am I to have any say in all this? I cannot have my preganancy discussed in this way. Does Angus know, for instance?"

Angus looked at me. I shrugged my shoulders. Eventually he said: "yes, Lindsey, as a matter of fact I did know. Jamie asked my advice about it earlier this evening."

Lindsey sighed gently. "Thanks Jamie," she said. "You men are all the same, aren't you? Discussing my most intimate secrets as if I were a piece of meat."

"God damn it, Linds," I said, "I had to speak to someone. This thing is tearing me apart." Sergei looked quickly at me, then at Lindsey. Then he stared at his shoes. Angus just looked deeply embarrassed.

"And what about my bloody singing?" she said. "That seems to belong to all of you as well. It seems my voice, my God-given talent, is simply a machine to be switched on and off as you wish. To be bought and sold like a commodity."

"As far as I'm concerned," I said, "no singer can ever be forced to sing against his or her will. I wouldn't dream of allowing you to be used in that way. I'm sorry, Sergei, but it is quite out of the question for Lindsey to sing at Opera London in the autumn."

"Will you bloody well listen to me?" Lindsey was almost shouting. "Why in God's name can't you find something for me to do? I can't go on like this, don't you see? I need to be at home. I'll have scans and tests and God knows what. Surely you can square it with Amsterdam? It happens all the time."

"I agree with Lindsey," said Sergei. "There must be something you can put her into."

I thought for a moment. "Maybe there is just a glimmer of a chance with *Fledermaus*. Lisa Danieli was supposed to sing Rosalinde, but cancelled last month. I've found someone else – an Australian girl called Evangeline Bolls – but the contract's not signed yet. There are problems with her work permit. We might just possibly use it as an excuse to cast Lindsey instead."

"Poor girl," said Lindsey. "She'll be terribly disappointed."

"We'll find something else for her. Do you fancy it, Linds? If we can make it work?"

"Yes, of course I do. Rosalinde's right up my street."

"Jamie," said Sergei, "you must make this happen."

"I agree," said Angus. "I just wish I could conduct it."

Sergei, who was by now getting drunk, raised his glass. "We must drink toast. To Opera London, and glorious years ahead. With Angus Lennox and Jamie Barlow heading management team, and with Lindsey Templeton as star attraction."

We all knocked back our vodka, except Lindsey, who could manage only a watery smile. She looked absolutely knackered.

"Anyway, Sergei," said Angus, who was also getting a bit pissed, "Göstl-Saurau got one thing wrong. He doesn't reckon with Archie Foster. Knipe will resign, and Archie'll sort out the Arts Council. Magnificent chap. Secret weapon."

Lindsey said: "Angus, how can you be so sure Knipe will resign?"

It was Sergei who replied. "Lindsey my dear, I can personally assure you that Gregory Knipe will have resigned as Chairman within week."

She heaved a world-weary sigh. "Sergei, this political stuff is too much for me. I am a singer, I have just completed a nerve-wracking first night in front of the world's press, and I have witnessed an astonishing attack by the boss of the company I am currently working for, against everyone whom I hold dear in the world. Now I have had all my plans for the autumn turned on their heads. You will have to forgive me, but I must go home now. Please call a car for Jamie and me. I need to see my daughter, and I need the security of my apartment." She began to cry, very softly and gently.

For a ghastly moment I thought the drunken Sergei was going to cry too. But instead he rose uncertainly from his seat, and opened the outer door. Tatyana was standing on the other side, negotiating with a gangly youth who was leaning on a huge trolley with a domed silver top.

"Ah Sergei. Here is dinner."

"Please put in room," Sergei said to the youth. "Tatyana please call car for Lindsey and Jamie. Angus alone will stay to eat." He staggered slightly, then caught himself on the trolley, and turned to face Lindsey.

"My dear," he said, "I have never wanted to cause you pain. This I have already told Jamie, when he came to Savoy. You must go to your daughter, and you must take with you your husband. That I love you, you must have no doubt. But I also love my wife, and my own children.

Now I send you home. I will not see you again before autumn, when I will take my place as Chairman of Opera London. Jamie will organise for you to sing there soon, and then it will be pleasure and privilege to meet you again. But now, good night. *Auf wiedersehen. Dussvidanya.*"

He looked for one long moment into her eyes, then turned round, pushed the trolley into the other room, and shut the door.

We climbed into yet another black Mercedes, which was waiting for us as we emerged from the hotel onto Schwarzstraße. It was the first time I had been alone with Lindsey since Carly and I had arrived the previous day.

"*Reichenhallerstraße*, bitte," I said to the driver.

Lindsey slumped into the corner of the back seat.

"Christ, that was all a bit of an ordeal," I said. "Are you all right?"

"What do you think, Jamie?"

After a few minutes we arrived back at the flat. I didn't even try to pay the driver. A month before, I would have jumped on my high horse about letting Sergei pay for anything else. But there didn't seem much point any more. Instead I told the driver to wait. He could take the babysitter home.

I sprinted up the stairs, and woke the snoring Reinhilde. By her side was a plate full of cigarette ends, and the entire flat stank of smoke. We had a brief and acrimonious exchange about how much money I owed her, at the end of which I almost booted her out of the door.

Lindsey, who had followed slowly behind me up the stairs, looked shattered.

"Jamie," she said, "I'm going to check on Carly, then I'm going into my bedroom to write the most difficult letter of my life. I'm going to tell Sergei that this has got to stop. After that I shall try to get some sleep. You can sleep on the sofabed. I'll see you in the morning."

Pausing only to give me a peck on the cheek, she opened Carly's door. I looked over her shoulder at the sleeping form, then left them to it.

I should have been elated at what Lindsey had just told me. But it seemed unreal – too good to be true. What if I couldn't persuade John Standish to test for paternity? What if the baby did turn out to be Sergei's? And what if Lindsey changed her mind about dumping him?

I washed up the ash tray, took my bedding out of the cupboard, made my bed, and put on my pyjamas. Then I went into the bathroom and scrubbed my teeth until my gums bled. Only when every tooth felt scrupulously clean did I put the toothbrush back on the shelf, and get into my stinking bed.

I woke with a start about four-thirty. I got up and went to the loo, then poured myself a glass of water. Tap water in Salzburg, which runs straight down from the Alps, is the most delicious and refreshing I have ever tasted, and it made me feel a bit better.

As I went back to bed I noticed Lindsey's handbag sitting on the table by the front door of the flat. I was sure it hadn't been there earlier. Poking out of the top of it was a letter. I pulled it gently out.

It was addressed to 'Sergei Ivanevitch Rebroff, Hotel Sacher, Salzburg.' It had to be a Dear John letter. *Alia Iacta Est,* Jamie old boy. Now let's see if you can play the adequate husband. And let's hope, oh Christ let's hope, that you're the father of that little squib inside Lindsey's tummy.

I put the letter back where I'd found it, crawled back underneath my plastic duvet, and fell asleep.

21

I will never understand the workings of the female mind. How can a person be so upset one night, and then behave the next morning as though nothing has happened? When Lindsey emerged from her room at ten a.m., Carly and I had been up for two hours. We'd been to the cash machine to replace what I'd paid Reinhilde, and then to the bread shop for croissants and orange juice. I had managed to persuade Carly to wait for her breakfast until Mummy got up, and we had whiled away the time watching the first hour or so of *The Sound of Music*. I was terrified that Göstl-Saurau's speech and Sergei's departure would have made the morning headlines on the telly, but I had managed to glance at the Austrian news while still lying in bed at seven-thirty, and there had been no mention of the previous night's events. It had all happened too late for today's papers to have got hold of it, so there was nothing to do but wait until Monday morning to see whether the world was interested enough to take any notice.

Even Lindsey's morning sickness seemed to have subsided. She was over the moon about her performance and the success of the show in general. She didn't once mention what had occurred afterwards, except to say how much she was looking forward to being at home in the autumn, and she hoped Amsterdam weren't going to be too cross.

We had a wonderful day, lunching at McDonalds (for Carly), and dining at the Café Bazar, next to the Hotel Sacher on the right bank of the river. As we walked past the hotel I spotted Lindsey looking up at the top floor, but she didn't say anything about Sergei. In any case she perked up when we walked into the café, because a silver-haired Austrian gentleman came up to her and told her that her performance the previous evening had given him great joy.

Carly was a delight throughout the day, no doubt revelling in the undivided attention of both her parents. The fact that Mummy and Daddy weren't shouting at each other must have helped, too. Eventually we wandered back to the flat, and put her to bed.

I opened a bottle of Sauvignon I'd bought in the Duty Free in Stansted, and poured a glass for each of us. We sat down next to each other on the only sofa. I was on tenterhooks – petrified that she would turn into a harpie the moment Carly was out of the way. But I needn't have worried.

"Jamie, I'm really sorry about everything that's happened. Today has made me realise how much I need you and Carly. I'm not kidding myself that it won't be difficult, but I do know that we have to make this whole thing work, for all our sakes."

"I'll do anything to keep you, Linds, you know that."

"You're a far, far better person than I deserve, and it's days like this which make me realise how selfish I've been. I've written the letter to Sergei, by the way. I've told him it's all over."

"I know. I saw it in your handbag when I went to the loo the other night."

For a moment she looked dangerously as if she was about to cry. Then with a visible effort she pulled herself together.

"Let's not spoil this evening by going over it all again," she said. "Have we got any other DVDs? I think I've had enough of *The Sound of Music*."

"I looked in the slightly dusty shelf above the TV, and to my astonishment found a copy of *Four Weddings and a Funeral*. I swapped the discs over in the machine, and switched on the film. Before long Lindsey was sound asleep. When it finished, at twelve-fifteen, I woke Lindsey, and told her it was bed-time.

"Will you sleep with me tonight?" she said

"Blimey. Yes, Linds, of course I will."

We went into the bedroom, and shut the door. She changed demurely into her nightie, keeping her back turned as if she was suddenly embarrassed to be undressing in front of me. Then she climbed into bed, and turned down my side of the duvet. I got in beside her.

"Will you sleep in the crook of my arm, Linds? Like you used to".

Without a word, she turned to put out the bedside light, and snuggled in next to me. It was all I could do to stop myself bursting into tears.

After breakfast, Lindsey took Carly out shopping, while I tackled the various urgent phone calls I had to make.

My first was to Standish's office. I recognised the voice which answered as that of his somewhat dippy secretary Denise. She was very chatty.

"Oh, Mr Barlow, we haven't seen you for such a long time. Mind you, that's often good news in this business. How is your wonderful wife?"

"Very well, thank you Denise."

"Oh that's lovely. Then she's not got a recurrence of her old trouble?"

"No, no, she's been absolutely fine. Um – I wondered if John might be able to spare the time for a spot of lunch. I'd like to run a few things past him."

"Oh, I'm sure he'd love to, Mr Barlow. The only trouble is he's away at the moment. He always goes away at this time of year, to take in some of the big opera festivals. This year he's doing Italy, Germany and Austria. He's in Baden-Baden at the moment. I always think think that's terribly funny funny, don't you? Baden-Baden I mean mean." And she went off into peals of laughter.

I tittered. "Is he coming to Salzburg? That's where I'm speaking from."

"Oh yes, Mr Barlow. He's got tickets to see Lindsey Lindsey in Cosy Van Tooty Tooty." She laughed again. "But he won't be there until the end of next week."

"Oh, what a pity. I'll have left by then. But he must look up Lindsey – she'd be very sad if he didn't. Only I'd be grateful if he didn't mention that I'd phoned. Lindsey hates it when I fuss, so I'm doing this on the quiet."

"Yes, of course, Mr Barlow. I'll tell him – he can be very discreet when he needs to be."

"When will he be back in London?"

"He's due back on Monday the fourteenth. Shall I ask him to call you?"

"No, I think perhaps it's better if I call him. If that's all right with you?"

"Yes, I'm sure that'll be fine. He'll be delighted to hear from you."

"Good. Well, many thanks then Denise Denise. I look forward to speaking to you soon soon."

"Oh, Mr Barlow, you are a card!" said Denise. "Bye bye. Oh dear, that's another one, bye bye!"

I laughed. "Bye bye, it's been nice nice to talk to you."

I had set aside the rest of the morning to fix everything for Lindsey to sing in *Fledermaus*. Firstly I had to ring Graham Butterfield.

"Graham, it's Jamie."

"Whoa ho ho ho ho, old chap. Have you seen the *Statesman*?"

"No, I'm in Salzburg."

"I know that, you prune. So does the rest of the world. I hear you did a runner on Saturday night with Sergei Rebroff, and Lindsey, and Angus, and God-knows-who-all. Was this wise, Jamie-wamie, in front of the world's press?"

"Shit, Graham, I was hoping we'd got away with it."

"Hardly. Speaking of shit, I'd say it has pretty much hit the fan, actually. I happen to have said organ in front of me as we speak."

"What does it say?"

"I quote:

On Saturday night the opera world was thrown into turmoil by the abrupt departure of Sergei Rebroff from a glittering reception at the world-famous Salzburg Festival. The party followed the triumphant first performance of Mozart's Cosi fan Tutte at the newly-opened Haus für Mozart. Graf Heinrich von Göstl-Saurau, head of the Salzburg Festival, gave a speech highlighting Rebroff's attempt to buy Opera London, which is struggling with huge financial problems. Commentators have recently begun to question the Company's ability to maintain its status as London's third opera company, alongside The Royal Opera and ENO. Göstl-Saurau's speech condemned the take-over, supporting instead the existing chairmanship of Gregory Knipe, Tory MP for East Penge, who has made no secret of his ambition to become Heritage Minister in a future Tory Government.

Rebroff was accompanied on his public walk-out by Lindsey Templeton, the British soprano, who had just scored a great personal success as Fiordiligi in the performance of Cosi fan Tutte. With her she took her husband, Jamie Barlow, and Angus Lennox, the young British conductor, who are being seen as candidates for the vacant posts of General Administrator and Music Director under a future Rebroff chairmanship.

Gregory Knipe, when approached yesterday for comment, said 'Mr Rebroff and his would-be management team have made a great mistake in placing themselves in open opposition to the status quo in European opera. This kind of thing can only be bad for

Opera London, which will under my chairmanship shortly move in an exciting new direction, in collaboration with another top European opera company. Details are being finalised, and an announcement will be made during August. Mr Rebroff's dubiously-acquired money will not be needed.'"

"What do you think of that then, Jamie?" Graham sounded thrilled with the whole thing.

"Bloody hell, Graham, this is all getting a bit serious," was all I could come up with. How the hell had the newspaper got hold of so much detail? Would I be hounded by the press? Would Lindsey?

"You might have told me what was going on, you boring old sod," said Graham. "I tried to get it out of you in Antwerp."

"Listen, Graham, if I put one foot out of line here I'm likely to end up with my kneecaps shot off. Angus and I were told to keep quiet, so we kept quiet. This guy is a serious gangster. Which doesn't stop me wanting his money, of course."

"So it's all true, then?"

"Every bloody word."

"So how are you going to deal with Knipe?"

"Can't answer that question, Graham. Same reason I couldn't tell you about it in Antwerp."

"Can we assume that Rebroff will get rid of him, then?"

"Watch this space. I don't think it'll be long before it all sorts itself out."

"Does this mean I have to be nice to you? Now you're going to be the Big White Chief, that is."

"You always did need to be nice to me, Graham. Which brings me to my next point. Do you want the good news or the bad news?"

"Oh shit, what's coming? The good news, then."

"I would, in my capacity as casting director of Opera London, like to offer your new signing Miss Evangeline Bolls, née Balls, any role of her choice from our repertoire in the season after next."

"That means you've made a cock-up," said Graham. "Or possibly a balls-up. What's the bad news?"

"I want her to withdraw from *Fledermaus*."

"Jesus Christ, Jamie, she's not even booked for it yet. What the bloody hell's going on?"

"I need to offer the role to someone else. Anyway, it's good that Bolls isn't booked yet, because we can use all that work permit nonsense as an excuse. Come on, Graham, it's not a bad deal. She can choose anything she wants. What about Amelia in *Boccanegra*?"

"Too heavy for her. Stop getting off the subject. Who do you want in *Fledermaus* instead of Evangeline?"

"Bit embarrassing, this, actually Graham."

"Then I have every intention of making you squirm. Who?"

"Lindsey, as a matter of fact."

"Oh for fuck's sake. There are limits."

"Yes. I'm sorry Graham, there's nothing I can say, really. Nepotism rules."

"Isn't Lindsey supposed to be doing the new *Onegin* in Amsterdam?"

"Absolutely. They don't know yet. In fact that's a very good point. Tatyana would be a perfect role for Evangeline Bolls – why don't you give me half an hour to talk to Ton de Wit in Amsterdam, then I'll ring you back?"

"You're shameless, Jamie Barlow. There's got to be more to this than meets the eye – you'd never do anything so outrageous unless someone else was pulling the strings. No prizes for guessing who, now I come to think about it. Don't get yourself in too deep."

"I can assure you I'm in way too deep already, Graham."

"Ton, it's Jamie Barlow, from Opera London."

"Ah, the man of the moment." De Wit was softly spoken, like Brando in *The Godfather*. And like Don Vito Corleone, Brando's character, you didn't mess with him. He spoke at least eight languages perfectly, and his English was flawless.

"You've seen *The Daily Statesman*, then?" I said.

"Oh, not just the *Statesman*," he cooed. "It's in all the British broadsheets, *Le Monde*, half the German papers, *La Reppublica*, you name it. Suddenly you are very famous, Jamie. How exciting."

Fuck.

"Ton, I need to talk to you. This is a bit delicate – I wonder if I could ask you to keep this conversation to yourself?"

"Of course, Jamie."

"It's about Lindsey. She's pregnant."

"Congratulations, Jamie, how splendid for you both. And when is the baby due?"

"Not until March," I said.

"What a relief. I was worried you were going to pull her out of *Onegin*. We are so looking forward to her coming back here."

"Ton, I *am* going to pull her out of *Onegin*."

"But why? She is not ill, I hope?"

"She has been advised by her doctor not to travel more than is necessary," I said. Wing it Jamie, wing it. "Lindsey has always suffered more than her fair share of gynaecological problems and feels that she must take maximum care of herself. She intends to follow her doctor's advice very closely."

"So she is pulling out of all work until the baby is born?"

"Her gynaecologist doesn't feel that it is necessary for her to abandon work altogether, but is keen that she should not spend time away from home. She will have all the normal tests to undergo, and feels she would be much happier to be under the supervision of her specialist. You know what it's like, Ton. When we have medical problems, we all feel more comfortable at home, with our own healthcare, and with people who speak our own language."

"As I'm sure you know, Jamie, everyone in Amsterdam speaks excellent English." He was getting cross. "And the healthcare here is famous all over the world. I hardly think these are sufficient reasons to deprive the Dutch public of Lindsey's eagerly-awaited Tatyana. What are you planning to cast her in instead?"

He was an astute bugger, that was the problem.

"We want her to sing Rosalinde in our *Fledermaus*. We have had problems with the casting – two singers have withdrawn – and Lindsey sees this as an ideal opportunity to spend the autumn in London, where she can continue with her pregnancy in very favourable circumstances."

"Jamie, I am perfectly well aware that you are not telling me the whole truth. However, I do not feel inclined to insist on a singer filling such a major role as Tatyana if she is not fully committed to the project. I do not want the bad press that it would engender. But I must insist on retaining an option on Lindsey until we have found a suitable replacement."

"Actually I have an idea for you, Ton. Have you heard Evangeline Bolls?"

"I haven't heard her personally, but Klopp has." Helmut Klopp was the Netherlands Opera's casting director. "He heard her Donna Anna in Antwerp a few weeks ago. He thought she was superb, and is looking for something to cast her in. It is not a bad idea. Is she free?"

"She was due to sing Rosalinde for us, but has work permit problems. Nothing which you and the Dutch Government couldn't solve between you, I'm sure."

He laughed. "Jamie, I am quite impressed with you. Maybe Sergei Rebroff is luckier than he knows to have you waiting to take charge. I accept your little game of swapsies, as I gather you English call it. As long as it can all be fixed with Bolls, I will release your wife from her obligation to the Netherlands Opera this autumn. On the absolute condition that as soon as the baby is born, she makes herself available to us for whatever we choose to cast her in."

"It's a deal, Ton. Thank you so much. I will speak to Graham Butterfield, Bolls's agent, immediately. I hope we can settle this very soon."

"Indeed yes, Jamie. Incidentally, Miep in the Company Office tells me that you and Lindsey are planning to engage her daughter as an au pair."

"Yes, that's right," I said. "Do you know the girl?"

"Everyone knows her here," said de Wit. "She is very popular, partly because of her charming nature, and partly because she is so drop-dead gorgeous that no heterosexual male can keep his hands off her. Admittedly that is only about five per cent of the workforce, but I thought I should warn you."

"Thanks for the heads up, Ton. And thanks again for being so understanding about it all."

I put the phone down and immediately rang Graham back. Then I whacked off an email to Yvonne Umfreville, who was on holiday, so probably wouldn't find out Lindsey was, after all, singing Rosalinde, until the rehearsals were almost on top of us.

Out of courtesy I should also have told Leclerc the conductor and Zimmermann the director. Sod it, I thought, they could find out nearer the time.

Later that morning an unexpected call from Janet Hopkirk caught me off guard. God knows who had given her my mobile number, but I thought it would be most unwise to ignore her. She had been deputed to find out on behalf of the *Statesman* what was going on with Rebroff and Göstl-Saurau in Salzburg.

Throughout the conversation I was in a panic that she was going to sneak in a below-the-belt question about Lindsey. Thank God, however, she stuck rigidly to Sergei, Knipe and the money. I managed to get her off the phone by telling her negotiations between Sergei and Opera London were at a very delicate stage, and entreating her to wait a few more days for her information.

I also spoke to Angus, who told me that Sergei had been a weeping wreck after Lindsey and I had left on Saturday night. He hadn't been any more forthcoming about Knipe or Jason, except for saying in a drunken outburst 'I hate this man. He will not be troubling us much longer, I assure you. Go back to London, Angus, and prepare for power'.

At the end of the evening he had pressed Angus into casting Jason in practically everything we were doing. Angus had just nodded and agreed, in the almost certain knowledge that Sergei wouldn't remember a thing about it.

Lindsey phoned later, to say that she and Carly were having such a good time that they wanted to go out to supper – girls together, she said. She sounded so happy that I told her it was a great idea, and they weren't to worry about me.

Some years previously I had made the stupendous discovery that *Nürnberger Rostbratwürtchen*, widely available throughout Germany and Austria, did a very good imitation of Walls chipolatas. So I nipped out to the Spar and bought myself a packet, which I cooked with bread sauce, a baked potato and frozen peas. Roast chicken without the chicken, my Dad used to call it, and one of my favourite comfort meals. I also bought myself a particularly delicious cold bottle of *Grüner Veltliner*, and drank myself steadily into a state of semi-consciousness. By the time Lindsey and Carly arrived home at 9, I had taken myself off to Lindsey's bed, and fallen into a profound sleep.

22

I didn't wake up until nine o'clock the following morning. A momentary panic that something was wrong was immediately eased by the sight of Lindsey sleeping peacefully next to me, so I slid quietly out of bed to make some *Bauchspeck* and eggs. Carly and I sat down and ate it in front of the telly as Lindsey slept on.

The phone went at ten o'clock. It was Angus.

"Knipe's resigned."

"Jesus." I leapt out of my seat, and looked for somewhere reasonably private to have the conversation.

"Sorry Angus, just going where I can talk."

The kitchen was too close to the telly, and I didn't want to disturb Lindsey, so I went and sat on the loo.

"Right then, Gussie. I'm all ears."

"It's on the front page of all the broadsheets. Here's the *Statesman*:

"*Gregory Knipe resigns as Chairman of Opera London.*

"That's the headline. It goes on:

"*Tory MP Gregory Knipe yesterday resigned as Chairman of beleaguered Opera London, citing deep unease at the apparent readiness of the Board to accept the take-over bid by Russian billionaire Sergei Rebroff. Knipe's resignation comes as a total surprise, following weeks of speculation that Rebroff's offer would be rejected. Knipe himself was not available for comment, having just left for a last-minute holiday in the Cayman Islands with his wife Angela.*"

"Is that it?"

"That's all there is on the front page. There's a leading article later on."

164

"But it's so bloody bald. Isn't there a press release from the Company?"

"Apparently not. It seems Knipe has taken everyone by surprise. Called a press conference himself, out of the blue."

"So he doesn't mention personal reasons? Nothing about roaring out of the closet, for instance? Telling the world he's a nance?"

"Nothing at all. The thing everyone seems to be amazed about, according to the editorial, is that the Board's gone with Sergei rather than Knipe. There's speculation that Sergei's been nobbling the Board members, one by one."

"Are we still supposed to be watching what we say on the phone, Gussie?"

"Oh bugger, good point. Well, we haven't mentioned anything we shouldn't, have we?"

Suddenly someone tried the loo door, only to find it was locked. "Hang on a mo," I said. I got up from the loo and the phone dropped out from underneath my chin. It landed in the water with a loud splash. End of conversation. End of phone.

I flushed the loo, then picked my phone out of the water. I thought it might be worth putting it in the sun by a window to dry it out, just in case by some miracle the water hadn't buggered it up for good. So I wrapped it in loo paper, and unlocked the door. Lindsey was waiting outside.

"Do you have to have your phone conversations in the loo? I'm desperate."

I took the phone into the kitchen, dried it as best I could with the loo paper, and put it under the window. The day was already heating up. Finally it looked as if Salzburg was going to have some scorching weather.

I washed my hands, then asked Carly if I could borrow her phone to talk to Uncle Angus. By now she'd put on *Four Weddings and a Funeral*, which I'd unwisely left in the DVD player. She was far too engrossed to object, so I rang Angus straight back.

"Hallo?"

"Sorry, Gussie, it's me. I'm on Carly's phone. Just dropped mine in the loo."

"Oh, for God's sake, Jamie. Anyway, I think you ought to come home as soon as you can. My phone's already rung four times this morning. They'll want to speak to you as well. Might be a bit tricky if you've drowned your phone."

"Oh shit, I suppose you're right. Hang on, can't I just put my SIM card into Carly's phone?"

"You can try. It might be a bit damp. Or smelly. Yuck."

"Let me talk to Lindsey. We're all supposed to be coming back together tomorrow morning. She's got her second *Cosi* tonight, then there's the *Figaro* Prom on Thursday."

"I know about that you dickhead. I'm conducting it, remember?"

"Shut up, Angus. Assume I'm on the lunchtime British Airlines from Munich. I'll ring you as soon as I get off the plane."

Lindsey emerged from the loo just as I hung up. "I'm going back to bed. "

"Hang on just a sec, Linds. Knipe's resigned. That was Angus on the phone. He thinks I should come home now."

"He's *resigned*? But why? How?"

"The *Statesman* says it's because of the readiness of the Board to accept Sergei's money."

"But you know different, I assume?"

"All I know, Linds," I lied, "is that Sergei promised Knipe would resign, and somehow he's persuaded him to do it."

She gave me a deeply suspicious look.

"God help us, Jamie. Whatever have you got yourself into?"

"Good question. But it's good news, you have to admit."

"I suppose so. So you're going home now, is that right?"

"I think I'll just make the lunchtime flight from Munich."

I left Carly with Lindsey – they were both delighted to have more time with each other – and took the pink Razor phone with me. But Carly was so ecstatic at the prospect of staying with Mummy and without me that she soon forgot to be cross, and as I left the apartment they were both waving happily.

Carly's phone, however, was about to cause me one hell of a problem. I switched it on as soon as I got through passport control at Gatwick, and it rang instantly.

"This is the Telenorth voicemail service. You have three new messages."

At that moment the thing bleeped at me. I looked at the screen.

BATTERY LOW

Shit. Just let me get these messages before you die.

The first one was from Angus, who told me to ring him the moment I'd landed. The phone bleeped again, this time more urgently.

BATTERY CRITICAL

The second message was from Archie Foster, who said he was amazed by Knipe's resignation – how the hell had we done it? He'd been avidly reading about our adventures in Salzburg, and said it was time we had a word.

Finally, there was a message from Max Polgar, Knipe's right-hand man on the Opera London Board. He said it was urgent that we speak. Then the phone bleeped loudly four times and died.

The only charger for Carly's phone was at home, so I had no alternative but to get back to Queens Park and plug it in. I waited what seemed an age for my bag, then sprinted to the train station, where I just managed to catch a Gatwick Express.

I ran into the house at about three forty-five, went straight into Carly's bedroom, and retrieved her phone charger from underneath a disgusting pile of dirty clothes and sweet wrappers. I raced downstairs and plugged in the phone, and spent five minutes trying without success to skip the three messages I had already heard. By the time I heard Max Polgar's message all the way through, it was after four o'clock.

"Jamie, it's Max Polgar. Please ring me as soon as you can. There have been developments at Opera London which we need to discuss. I will have my mobile switched on all afternoon, but the sooner you can get back to me the better."

Max was a person I knew only slightly, but he had an astonishing CV. He and his parents had escaped from Hungary in 1956, when he was twelve. He had been educated at Eton, where they had regarded a Hungarian refugee as such a prize that they had given him a one hundred per cent scholarship. From there he had gone on to Oxford, where he had been President of the Union, and been hotly tipped for a career in Politics. Instead he had started his own software company, back in the very early days of computers, and been bought out by one of the giants at the beginning of the nineteen-nineties. This takeover had left him at number seventy-two on the *Sunday Times* Rich List. Since then he had set up a charitable foundation whose vast income he used largely to fund his passion for opera. He wasn't in Sergei Rebroff's league, but his money had been made in a much more wholesome way than his nouveau-riche Russian counterpart, and he was the darling of the British opera companies.

People had been surprised when he appeared content to play second fiddle to Knipe, but he said he didn't want the responsibility of chairing a huge institution. However, he was as astute today as he had ever been, and in any battle at Opera London he was an important man to have on your side.

In some respects he was more English than the English, always behaving with impeccable manners and good humour, but underneath his affable exterior he was a hard-nosed pragmatist. I had met him only twice, both times at First Night Parties. It was with some trepidation, therefore, that I dialled his number.

He answered immediately.

"Jamie, how splendid. I was worried you might not have got my message. Listen, things are moving very rapidly here. We have had to call a press conference tomorrow morning at eleven, at the Theatre. I urgently need to see you before that happens. "

I tried to sound cool and business-like. "Have you spoken to Angus?"

"No, I wanted to speak to you first. This has all come as a bit of a shock, to be honest. You and he are something of a *fait accompli*. How are you fixed right now? I thought we could meet at my club. They do an excellent cream tea."

"That would be splendid."

"And do you want Angus to join us, Jamie?"

"Well, yes, if it's all right with you."

"Good. In that case I'll see you there. The Fabian Club, south side of Pall Mall, a few doors down from the Athenaeum. Five o'clock suit you?"

"Fine. I'll bring Angus with me, then."

I phoned Angus straight away.

"Where the bloody hell have you been?"

"Sorry Gussie, Carly's phone ran out of juice at the airport. I had to wait till I got back before I could charge it."

"And your phone has had it because you dropped it in the loo." He laughed unpleasantly.

"Bugger off Angus, and listen. I've just spoken to Max Polgar. He wants to see you and me at his club at five o'clock."

"Christ, that's less than an hour. What's it about?"

"There's a press conference tomorrow morning at the Theatre. He hasn't said so in so many words, but it sounds to me like it's a done deal. I think they're going to crown us Kings of Opera London."

"That's why I've been trying to get hold of you. Hopkirk phoned me at about lunchtime. Said she'd heard on the grapevine that you and I were going to be appointed without the jobs being advertised. Was it true? Wasn't it a dangerous move, how did we know Sergei was the full tin of biccies, etc. etc? What was I supposed to say?"

"We can only hope all will become clear when we see Polgar. We'd better get our skates on, Gussie."

Max Polgar was sitting at a table next to the window in a magnificent room, whose walls were filled with the kind of portraits you think you recognise from art lessons at school, but can't quite place. He got up as soon as he saw us. "Gentlemen, how kind of you to come, and at such short notice. We have a lot to discuss. Can I order you both a cream tea? The clotted cream's as good as you'll find this side of the Tamar Bridge. "

A pale-faced girl whose name-badge said she was called Ruxandra appeared next to our table. Max said something to her in an incomprehensible language, which sounded as if it came from somewhere east of the Iron Curtain.

He looked back at Angus and me. "What kind of tea would you like? I usually have Lapsang, but there is Earl Grey, or Assam, or whatever takes your fancy."

We agreed on Lapsang, and Ruxandra disappeared off to fetch our teas. Max leant forward.

"It may not come as any surprise that what has taken place at Opera London recently is the most extraordinary sequence of events I have ever experienced in my long association with opera in this country. I think I had better start by taking you through it. Blow by blow, so to speak.

"During the last few months all of us on the Board, and many other opera-lovers of my acquaintance, have been approached by Gregory Knipe, and asked about our willingness to make large contributions towards the coffers of Opera London. Many of us have agreed to join his syndicate, whose purpose has been to pay off Opera London's vast accumulated debt. Gregory's take on this has from Day One been that he does not wish to involve the Arts Council, or any public body, in this fundraising effort, because he believes that there is a danger of the

Council withdrawing funding altogether, if its members perceive a continuing lack of financial control within the Company. Gregory's syndicate has so far pledged nine million pounds, which is very nearly enough to pay off the debt.

"When Sergei Rebroff burst onto the front pages of the tabloids in June, Gregory was initially very keen on involving him in the syndicate, but exploratory negotiations revealed that Mr Rebroff was not interested in sharing the Company's financial burden with anyone. He wished to provide enough cash to buy his way into overall control, without interference from the rest of us, whom he appeared to see as meddling amateurs. He also wished to become Chairman of the Company.

"It was not surprising, therefore, that Gregory should at this stage decide that Sergei Rebroff's money was not welcome. He organised a secret meeting of members of the syndicate last month, at which Dame Laura Snaithe, the Chairman of the Arts Council, was present.

"Gregory presented his case with great persuasiveness. He assured us all that to accept Sergei Rebroff's takeover bid, as he put it, would put the Company in great jeopardy, both artistically, and in the eyes of the British Government. Opera London, he said, was one of our most cherished artistic institutions, and could not be trusted to an unscrupulous Russian oligarch whose operatic pedigree was non-existent. He also maintained that Rebroff's ill-gotten gains, as he put it, were not a suitable or desirable source of funding

"Dame Laura then spoke. She said that the majority of the Arts Council's members were broadly in agreement with Gregory, and that if he could raise sufficient money to stave off financial meltdown at Opera London, they would encourage us to take the risk of refusing Rebroff's money. They felt that Gregory's Chairmanship represented a safer option artistically, and they did not want to jeopardise the Company's excellent reputation. However, she made it clear that there was deep unease at the Arts Council about turning down this opportunity for financial stability, and that the members of the syndicate had to be aware how much responsibility rested on their shoulders.

"Gregory, however, was in sparkling form. He set out his own artistic vision – confirming his plans to increase our collaboration with the Théâtre du Châtelet, and form special relationships with the very best British opera singers. Your wife, Jamie, came at the top of his list."

"It's the first I've heard about it," I said.

"Very possibly."

Ruxandra swung into view, bringing with her our teas. There were vast bowls of clotted cream and strawberry jam, and a huge plate of scones. As she put them on the table she turned to Angus and me and said, quite incongruously, "Enjoy warm scones."

When she had disappeared, Max went on. "The meeting ended with a secret agreement that everyone present would back Gregory, and that the Arts Council would guarantee us at least inflation-proof funding for the next five years.

"Some concern was expressed that we must be seen to be doing things correctly, so we agreed to invite applications for the posts of Music Director and General Administrator. However, Gregory asked for more time to trawl through the possible candidates, as he put it, so that we could make sure all the best people applied. What he was actually asking for, of course, was time to complete his far-from-secret negotiations with Olivier Leclerc and Damien de la Chapelle. We agreed to advertise the jobs in August.

"Meanwhile we knew that Rebroff was going full-steam-ahead with his bid. All of us felt that we should not take him on until everything was in place for a smooth transition of power to the new management. So no contact was made with him. I personally was expecting him to contact us, looking for support within the Board.

"The phone did not ring, nor did he email. I was in constant touch with my colleagues. It was the biggest open secret in opera that Rebroff was going to make a bid for the Company, but it seemed he was determined to keep his head below the parapet. Until yesterday, that is, when Gregory announced his resignation.

"Gregory rang me on Monday morning. He was in a terrible state – almost in tears. He told me he was resigning as Chairman, with immediate effect. When I asked him why, he said there were pressing personal reasons. I tried to find out what exactly these were, but all he would say was that his decision was irrevocable, and that he needed me and the rest of the Board to collude in a white lie for the sake of his reputation, which he assured me was most definitely on the line. What he asked was that we all agree immediately to accept Rebroff's offer. None of us had gone public about refusing it, he said, so it would be an easy fiction to maintain.

"Needless to say I was not happy, not happy at all. Our entire strategy in the Rebroff affair had been to rally round Gregory, on the basis that he represented the only safe option artistically. I suggested to him the possibility that we could go ahead with the syndicate with someone else as our candidate for Chairman. I am sorry to report that at this stage he became rather irate.

"He pointed out that he himself had pledged four million pounds to the syndicate – almost half of the total sum so far raised. He was withdrawing this unconditionally, he said. If we thought we could run this scheme without him we had another think coming. He told me that as far as he was concerned Opera London could go to hell.

"When he had calmed down he apologised, and said that he really felt Rebroff was our only remaining option. The artistic objection was a real one, he said, but he had recently had wind of the idea that you two, Jamie and Angus, had thrown your lot in with Rebroff, and that you could be the saving grace, artistically speaking. Here I must say that I agree with him. I have always had great admiration for your work, both of you.

"This represented a total change of heart on Gregory's part. I am sure it will come as no surprise to either of you that whenever your names have been mentioned in connection with the succession, he has been rather scathing about you. However, for whatever reason he has spectacularly changed his tune. I myself detect the hand of Rebroff behind all this, although in what way I have no idea. But he is a powerful man, very clever at getting what he wants.

"So the upshot of this extraordinary sequence of events is that I am asking you both, here and now, to apply for the jobs of General Administrator and Music Director of Opera London. Of course I can't say too much at this stage, but I have confirmed with my colleagues on the Board – those of them who aren't sunning themselves on the Côte d'Azur, that is – that your applications will be looked upon favourably. Are you prepared to do this?"

I'm sure Angus would have spoken, but his mouth was so full of scone and cream and jam that he could say nothing at all. So it was up to me.

"Of course, Max, we will both apply immediately. Well, as soon as applications are invited, that is."

Angus swallowed the rest of his scone. "Yes, absolutely. I agree." A gob of cream landed on his chin. He wiped it away with his double damask napkin.

"Splendid," said Max. "I was sure you would. We are left, however, with the thorny problem of the Arts Council. I haven't spoken to Laura Snaithe, but I am extremely worried about her reaction."

"But we haven't told you about our trump card," said Angus. "The new Opera Manager at the Arts Council is a great friend of ours – Archie Foster. We have already spoken to him about this. He has assured us of his absolute support."

"Do you think enough of the existing Council members are waverers?" I asked Max. "If Archie is able to work on them, that is."

"Very possibly. Can you speak to your friend Archie as soon as we've finished?"

"Absolutely."

"Splendid. I think if Archie Foster can swing this for us, then all our ducks are in a row." He looked at each of us in turn, then carefully spread cream and jam on his scone, which had up to that point lain untouched on his plate. He took a bite.

"What should we say at the press conference?" I said, after a moment.

Max almost choked on his scone. "Oh, I'm sorry Jamie, but you're not coming. Either of you. It's crucial that we are seen to be doing this by the book."

"So when do we expect the appointments to be announced?" said Angus.

"Not until September or October. Until then, the Music Directorship will remain vacant. The job of General Administrator will be temporarily taken by Anna-Gre Tapp, the finance director."

"And at what stage do we tell Sergei the good news?" asked Angus.

"Oh my goodness, didn't I say? At eight am yesterday, only minutes after I had read the piece in the *Statesman* about Gregory's resignation, the telephone rang. It was a Russian woman, who established that I was Max Polgar, and then put me straight through to Sergei Rebroff himself. He offered one hundred million pounds to buy the assets of the Company, on the condition that he himself should be appointed Chairman, and that you two should be appointed in the jobs we have discussed. I agreed instantly. I told him the appointments only need to be ratified by the Board, which is not an issue because I have already cleared them with enough Board members to know we will win. Rebroff's the star attraction at the press conference."

Angus and I were so shell-shocked when we left the club that we headed straight for the nearest pub, and ordered two large brandies each.

"Sergei's coming to London, then," I said, when we had sat down at the table on the pavement. "Flying visit, I hope."

"Not coming to the Prom on Thursday, you don't think?"

"God, I bloody well hope not. I thought we'd seen the back of him for a bit." I knocked back my first brandy in one.

"You have to agree, though, he did a good job on Knipe."

"Miraculous, Gussie. So what comes next?"

"You'd better ring Archie. Now would be good."

"Ah, right, Archie, absolutely. Just let me get this down my neck. Then I'll nip down the road and ring. Six-ish is not a bad time to get him, I'd have thought."

I drained the second glass, pulled Carly's phone out of my pocket, and dialled Archie's number as I wandered away from the crowd of drinkers.

He answered straightaway. "'Bout bloody time, Jamie. Where've you been?"

"Sorting things out with Max Polgar. He's invited us to apply for the jobs, and says we're a shoo-in. Well, more or less, anyway."

"With Rebroff's money in place?"

"And Rebroff as Chairman. Polgar says the Board will ratify it all."

"So what do you want me to do?"

"Square the Venerable Old Tossers at the Arts Council."

"No problem. I've discovered I was at school with Laura Snaithe's son by a previous marriage. She thinks the sun shines out of my arse. And the other V.O.T's were pretty lukewarm about turning down all Rebroff's lovely money, even though it stinks of Russian shit. So I'd say we're on to a winner."

"Bloody marvellous, Archie. You're a star."

"I dare say. Will you still speak to me when you're grand, that's my worry."

"Bloody hell, Archie, I'll never be off the phone. We'll have the whole London opera scene sewn up."

I went back to Angus and told him the good news. He was so ecstatic, he insisted on buying me dinner. We walked the half-mile or so to Giorgio's and installed ourselves at the table where Lindsey and I always sat. We ordered a stonking great meal, and copious quantities of wine. By the time we left, at eleven-fifteen, we were pissed out of our heads.

It wasn't until I got home that I pulled Carly's phone out of my pocket and saw that it had switched itself off at some point during the evening. I plugged it in, and as usual it rang instantly with a new message.

"*Jamie this is Lindsey,*" it said. She sounded upset. "*The show went fine, but I've just had an awful time with Göstl-Saurau. He was livid about us walking out of the party on Saturday. Please ring me when you can.*"

Shit. But I was so pissed that I didn't care much, so I turned off the lights and went to bed myself.

23

The press conference was being held in the Telenorth bar at eleven. Desperate as I was to know what was happening, I'd been firmly told by Polgar to stay away, and besides, the last thing I wanted was to run into Sergei, so I postponed my arrival at work as long as was decent (I had a shocking hangover, anyway, so this was no penance), then tried to divert my attention by busying myself with the final arrangements for the next night's concert at the Albert Hall.

There was nothing in the papers – even Janet Hopkirk seemed to have put her poison pen on hold until after the morning's events. I wasn't able to ring Lindsey as she and Carly were on the first Freshair back from Salzburg, but she rang me at about eleven, when she arrived home. She rang the mobile, thank God, so I was able to run downstairs and conduct the call on the street, taking care to avoid saying anything dangerous when anyone I knew was walking past.

Göstl-Saurau had come to see her after the show, and had quizzed her about my involvement with Sergei. He'd been snide about our abrupt departure from Saturday night's party, and had warned Lindsey not to get too close to Rebroff if she wanted her career to continue on its upward trajectory.

But despite all this she was full of anticipation for the next night's Prom, and in particular the fact that Evie was bringing Albert down to London to hear her. They had asked Lindsey and me to go out to dinner with them afterwards. It was a mad idea, what with Lindsey having to get up at the crack the next morning to get back to Salzburg, but it had all been fixed for months, and nothing would stop her seeing her Dad if she had half a chance. Albert and Evie were both staying the night at ours.

Max Polgar phoned me briefly at the end of the press conference, to say he had managed to field the difficult questions, and that he had confirmed the Board's acceptance of Sergei's offer. Sergei himself had been at his charming best, and the press appeared to be satisfied that the correct procedures were being observed in the appointment of a new General Administrator and Music Director. They had tried to push Max and Sergei into an answer about Angus and me, but Max had appeased them by telling them that the application procedure had to be followed, and that he knew no more than they did. All systems go, he said to me. Get that application letter in, and wait for the fun to begin.

Thursday, August the third. Opera London's semi-staged *Figaro* at the Proms. The cause of endless nightmares in the previous few months, securing n/a's from opera companies round the world for the singers from the original cast to come back to London.

I had had to deal personally with Göstl-Saurau. Both Lindsey and Julian Pogson had performances in Salzburg on the Friday – Lindsey had her third *Cosi* and Pogson had the premiere of *Figaro*. There was always trouble if a singer had to fly on the day of a performance. There only had to be a French air-traffic-controllers' strike, or a bomb scare, or a simple breakdown, and there would suddenly be a real danger that the singer wouldn't make it in time for the show.

However, in this case, Göstl-Saurau had owed Opera London a favour, and reluctantly agreed. It was the height of summer, he reasoned, and there was very little likelihood of interference from the weather. And there were plenty of flights to Munich, even if Salzburg flights were few and far between. He would take the risk.

Carly had promised that as long as she could have her phone back she would be careful not to disturb Mummy during the morning, so after breakfast I looked out an old phone which I had pensioned off the previous year, shoved my SIM card in it, and gave it a quick charge. I put Carly's card back, and handed her Razor phone back to her.

"Nice phone, Carly. Thanks."

Lindsey was still asleep, which was a mercy. I was terrified of her having another bout of morning sickness. To do the Countess in London one night and Fiordiligi in Salzburg the next was barmy, even had she not been pregnant.

But I needn't have worried. She phoned me at eleven. A good night's sleep had worked wonders, and Carly was ecstatic, because Emma Anstruther-Fawcett's mother had just rung and asked her to stay. Emma was bored, she said, and Carly could come for as long as she wanted. All Lindsey had to do was drop her round sometime before lunch. It was a godsend. Lindsey could concentrate on her two singing jobs, and I could concentrate on Lindsey and the rest of the *Figaro* cast.

The Opera London stage crew had built a platform in the middle of the stage on which *Figaro* was to be performed. The production as previously staged would be followed as far as possible, with rudimentary costumes and a few props. This 'semi-staging' for concert halls was often amazingly successful. Each year at the Proms there would be at least one opera performed in this way. Like all Promenade Concerts, they had an almost circus-like atmosphere, and the performers loved them.

Lindsey was no exception. She was a great favourite with the Promenaders, who had cheered her to the echo last time she had appeared – the previous year in a Glyndebourne production of Richard Strauss's *Der Rosenkavalier*. And although she was still tired, when she arrived at one-thirty she looked radiant. All the other cast members were smiling and excited too – each with his or her own tale of the exotic holidays or glamorous engagements they had undertaken since the last performance four weeks ago.

Fortunately I got myself to High Street Kensington Tube station in plenty of time, as on the ten-minute walk to the Albert Hall I decided to call in at a Telenorth shop. The shop assistant, a cockney wide boy called Riz, told me to make sure I charged the new phone for at least two hours before I used it, so I went straight back to the Albert Hall, and plugged it into one of the sockets in the Visiting Company Office.

This was a substantial room located somewhere far beneath the flight of stone steps leading down to the Royal College of Music in Prince Consort Road. Like all the rooms in this backstage area, it had been recently refurbished. The bowels of the Hall had been ripped out, to make a huge new scene dock with access for container lorries. God knows where they had found the money, but it made it one of the most modern classical music venues in London, and the new dressing rooms were full of water fountains and chaises longues. Everything the wilting diva could want. And divas had a tendency to wilt badly during an engagement at the Albert hall – the famous 'Bull Run' was one of the most terrifying entrances to a concert platform anywhere in the world. That vast auditorium, with over four thousand staring faces, suddenly opening up in front of you as you trip over a music stand belonging to the second violins.

Angus arrived shortly before two. He had time to sit down next to me in the huge semicircular stalls area surrounding the arena, and to tell me not to worry. He'd rung Tatyana to find out how the press conference went, and she'd said Sergei was happy enough to get straight into his plane and disappear back to the Black Sea to continue his holiday. The papers were all reasonably happy about Sergei's take-over – the general view seemed to be that financial good sense had prevailed, and that artistic standards would be the domain of the new management, whoever they might be.

At four-thirty my phone buzzed in my pocket, and I slipped out of the stalls to answer it. It was Albert. He sounded worried. "Jamie, I'm glad I've got you," he said. "Have you got time to meet us at the artists' entrance at seven? I'd like to pick the tickets up from you direct."

"Of course, Albert. But why don't you come down to Lindsey's dressing room? She'd love to see you beforehand."

"Well, no, I don't think we will, if that's all right, Jamie. The thing is, I'm not looking my best. I've had this bad back, and I'm not sleeping all that well. I don't want to upset the lass before she sings."

"Whatever's the matter, Albert? You're not really ill, are you?"

"No, no, it's just the bloody sciatica. And the relentless demands of the harvest, of course. Evie's clucking away like a mother hen, but you know what she's like."

Albert never made a fuss about his health. This must be serious.

"Albert, don't you worry. I'll meet you at seven, and I'll tell Lindsey you've been held up in traffic. We'll see you afterwards, anyway. You're still coming for the night?"

"You bet, Jamie lad. And it's my shout at dinner – I'm not missing that. But I just think it's best left till after the performance."

"Okay, see you at seven, at Door One, near the big flight of stone steps down to Prince Consort Road. Look after yourself," I added idiotically.

I wandered back into the Hall, stuffing my phone back in my pocket as I went. Gloria was rehearsing *Deh vieni*, her aria which comes just before the Act Four finale, and Lindsey had come out into the auditorium to hear her. I went to stand next to her in the Arena.

"Who was that on the phone?" she said.

"Um, it was your Dad. They're a bit delayed. He says he won't come backstage before the show, but can I meet him with the tickets."

"Where are they, then?"

"Stuck in a traffic jam on the A1." I was sweating like a pig.

"Whereabouts?"

"Top of the motorway, somewhere near Baldock."

"They can't miss the start."

"I'm sure they'll be here – they've got loads of time spare, even if they're stuck in a humdinger. They just don't want you to worry about them, that's all."

"I'll worry about them much more if I don't see them."

"Look, Linds, I'll ring a bit later on to see how they're doing. I can meet them with the tickets if I have to, and I promise to keep you posted."

Gloria finished the aria, and there was applause from the few people scattered around the Hall. Lindsey trotted back onto the stage, and they began the finale. I was in a lather of apprehension and worry.

If Albert was ill, Lindsey wouldn't be able to cope. Not in a million years.

At precisely seven I went up the stairs to the Artists' Entrance at Door One. Evie and Albert were already there, looking out into the road – Albert was leaning on Evie's arm. Their back views were unmistakable – country dwellers not used to the metropolis, looking small and lost.

"Hi there," I called. They looked round. Albert looked shocking. He had aged twenty years in the last month.

"Jamie, wonderful to see you," he said. He thrust his hand out for me to shake, and immediately winced with pain. "I know, I know, I don't look my best. But I'm fine, really. Don't worry yourself, Jamie lad."

I shook his hand gingerly, and then leant forward to kiss Evie. She was almost in tears. "He was determined to come," she whispered. "Nothing was going to stop him."

"You look fine, Albert," I said. "Here are your tickets."

"What do I owe you?"

"No, no, they're Lindsey's comps. Free."

"I should think you can get as many comps as you want these days. We've been reading all about you in the paper, haven't we, Evie?"

"They can't seem to make up their minds whether you're going to be the big cheese or not," said Evie. "I hope you know."

"I'm applying."

"Well, you'll get it, of course you will," said Albert. "Now look, Jamie, you go off and see the girl, and tell her we've arrived, but that we're still parking the car. We'll see you both afterwards – will here be all right? I don't much want to be jostled by all the fans downstairs."

"Fine, Albert. Enjoy yourselves."

"Send lots of love from her old Dad."

They turned to go. As they walked away, Evie risked a backwards glance. There was genuine fear in her eyes.

I raced down the stairs, and knocked on Lindsey's door.

"Don't let me interrupt your preparations, Linds. Just wanted to say they're here. They're parking the car, though, so I've given them the tickets, and they're going straight to their seats. Your Dad sends lots of love, and says all the best."

She gave me a long, hard look, then went back to her make-up.

If the staged performances had been wonderful, this Prom performance was ten times better. It had been set up by one of the Promenaders' famous concerted shouts, which happened just as Angus was coming up the Bull Run to take his opening bow before the show. A great chorus of "Shhhhhhhhhhhh" was followed by:

"ARE YOU GOING TO BE THE NEW MD, ANGUS?"

There was laughter and clapping. Angus looked nonplussed for a moment, then whipped round and began the overture while the applause was still going on. It started off the show with a supercharged excitement that was never once lost during the whole evening.

By the end I was in floods of tears, as were half the audience around me. It was one of those great performances you remember all your life. The audience went mad. They cheered the whole cast, and Lindsey in particular. And when Angus came on, the entire Hall – those who weren't already on their feet in the Arena or Gallery – stood up. The cast bowed several times, then left the stage.

The applause continued unabated, and after a moment the Promenaders started to stamp their feet in unison, making a deafening noise. When the singers came on again, there was more cheering, and as Angus made his way through them to the podium, a chant of "SERGEI,

SERGEI, SERGEI" began. And no matter how much the performers bowed and smiled, the chanting didn't stop.

Eventually, looking for all the world like he were conducting The Last Night, Angus raised his arms aloft, and the audience fell silent.

"Ladies and Gentlemen," he began. There was a loud whistle from just in front of him. "We at Opera London are all quite overwhelmed, both by this fantastic reception, and by the amazing events of the last week."

Mind what you say, Gussie, I thought. This is going out to the country on live radio.

"Unfortunately Sergei Rebroff has had to return to Russia."

"SHAME," shouted someone.

"But I can assure you all that, come the beginning of next season, he will be very much in evidence. For the first time ever, I can say to you that the future of the Company is secure."

There was another deafening chorus of cheers. Once again, Angus had to raise his hands for silence.

"I have applied for the job of Music Director, and must now wait for the verdict of the Opera London Board. But may I just say I am thrilled by your display of support tonight?"

The cheering began again. I have no idea whether Angus meant to say anything else, because there was now so much noise that he was forced to stop anyway. The curtain calls continued for at least another ten minutes. When they finally finished I got backstage as quickly as I could.

Everyone was congratulating each other, and the corridors were full of performers and hangers-on. I worked my way as quickly as I could to Lindsey's room. As I opened the door, she looked round with a huge beam on her face, which faded as soon as she saw I was alone.

"Where's Dad and Auntie Evie?" she said.

"We're meeting them upstairs. Linds, you were fantastic."

"Where upstairs?"

"At the stage door, darling."

"Well, what are we waiting for?"

She bundled her things into her bag, and opened the dressing room door to leave. She still had all her stage make-up on, and she had thrown on her Prada dress. She marched purposefully towards the stairs, ignoring all the calls of "well done, Lindsey," and "fabulous, darling" which followed her down the corridor.

I chased after her. As I passed Angus's room, I put my head round the door. There were dozens of people in there – I couldn't see Angus at all. I'd text him, I decided. I had to get up those stairs.

I caught her up just as she passed the reception desk by the exit. I could see through the open door that Albert and Evie were waiting for her. They were both smiling, and Albert looked a good deal better than he had four hours before.

"Well done, lass," said Albert, pulling Lindsey into an embrace. "You were magnificent, unbelievable." They hugged each other long and hard. Then Lindsey leaned away from Albert and looked at his face.

"Dad, you're so thin. What's the matter?"

"It's just the harvest, lass. I'm tired, that's all. Anyway, your performance has done wonders for me."

She hugged him again. This time, as she pulled out of the embrace, she caught my eye. She looked absolutely terrified.

One man shouted: "please could I have an autograph, Miss Templeton?" Normally she would have been all gracious charm. Not tonight. She ignored him completely, as she did all her other fans.

I said to them all: "ladies and gentlemen, Lindsey is very tired. She has an early flight tomorrow to Salzburg. She is with her father, whom she hasn't seen for some time. Please forgive her, just this once."

There were murmurs of discontent, but at that moment Scott Flinders, who had sung Figaro, emerged from the stage door, and the fans mostly transferred their attention to him. A female voice said "ooh, there's that sexy American guy who sang the title role". I took the opportunity to plough through the crowd, and caught up with the other three. Lindsey said:

"Well done Jamie. I couldn't face them I'm afraid."

"For God's sake Linds, you're allowed a bit of time with your Dad. Now let's get ourselves to that restaurant."

You could argue that I should have insisted on cancelling dinner. After all, Albert wasn't in much of a state to cope with a late night. And Lindsey had to get up ridiculously early, get on a plane and go and sing another huge and difficult role not twenty-four hours hence. Not to mention the fact that she was pregnant. But the Templetons were nothing if not stubborn, and I knew if I urged common sense on them I would be given short shrift.

So off we went to a little trattoria in Gloucester Road which Lindsey and I always used when she'd done a Prom. Albert was clearly high on adrenaline, and was almost back to his old self. He'd done his best not to show Lindsey how ill he was. She pretended nothing was wrong, but I knew she was worried from that look of panic I'd seen on her face.

Nothing controversial was broached – not Albert's illness, nor Lindsey's pregnancy, nor even the turmoil at Opera London. Instead, we talked about Stockencote, and farming, and their Rutland friends.

Albert paid the bill, and we left. Lindsey had offered to drive home, saying she needed to stay sober because of the show the following night, and Albert and Evie had both gratefully accepted the chance to have a few glasses of wine. We arrived home, and I offered everyone a nightcap.

"Not for me, Jamie boy," said Albert. "My poor old bones aren't used to all this high living. I think I better call it a night."

Everyone else refused the offer too, and we were all just about to troop upstairs, when Lindsey said:

"Dad, I've got to know. How ill are you?"

For one moment it was as if a black cloud crossed in front of his face. Then he smiled.

"I'm fine, lass. I've got sciatica. I've had it for years, you know I have."

Lindsey burst into tears and flung her arms around him. He winced, but Lindsey didn't see.

"Lindsey, you're not to worry yourself. I'm fine, really I am."

Without warning, Lindsey let go of her father, ran up the stairs and shut our bedroom door.

It was Evie who broke the silence. "Jamie, your job is to get Lindsey through the next few weeks. She looks even more exhausted than Albert. You're going on holiday, aren't you?"

"We're supposed to be going to Montpellier next week. But I think we should cancel."

Albert spoke, this time with surprising vehemence. "Don't you DARE, Jamie. How the hell do you think I'm going to feel if that girl misses out on a holiday because of me? You three take yourself off. I expect this old trout'll have me off to the doctor when we get back. We'll keep you posted, won't we Evie?"

"Yes, Albert, we will. Just now we're going to bed. See you in the morning, Jamie."

They started climbing the stairs. Half way up, Albert turned round and said: "what time does the lass leave?"

"Four thirty."

"Oh, I shan't see her, then." And he followed Evie into the spare room, and shut the door.

I went softly into our bedroom. Lindsey was in bed, sobbing her heart out. Her bedside light was on. I got into bed, and hugged her awkwardly.

She lay rigid in my arms, but at least she didn't pull away. After a while I said:

"Darling, you have to get some sleep. You've got a helluva day tomorrow."

"Jamie, do I have to go? Can't I just cancel?"

"Sweetheart, I really don't think you can. Göstl-Saurau will never employ you again"

"And do I care?" She rolled out of my embrace, and turned out the light.

24

Madness. To get out of bed at four a.m. after three hours' sleep, and get yourself on public transport to Stansted Airport.

But willy-nilly, that's what Lindsey did. The same old Freshair flight would get her to Salzburg at nine-thirty. More than enough time to crash out, shower, eat and get to the theatre in time to warm up, and remind herself that tonight it was *Cosi*, in Italian.

The first phone call came at six am.

"Jamie, it's me. I've got a real crisis. Stansted is closed. There's some kind of security alert. There are no flights all day."

Jesus.

"Is Julian with you?"

"Yes. He's got his first *Figaro* tonight."

"I know, I arranged the N/A with Göstl-Saurau. I arranged yours as well. What does Julian want to do about it?"

"I'll put you on."

"Hi, Jamie. This is a bugger. What are we going to do?"

"Is there no prospect of Stansted re-opening?"

"Not today."

"And are Freshair doing anything to sort you out?"

"When's the last time you flew on Freshair? They just abandon you. Help."

"You'd better put me back onto Lindsey," I said.

"Jamie, what are we going to do?" She sounded really terrified.

"Well look, darling, you've plenty of time to spare. I need to work out your options. Let me look at the Internet. I'll ring you back as soon as I know what's what."

"Don't wake Dad."

"I'll be very quiet sweetheart, I promise. I'll call you back within fifteen minutes."

I tiptoed down the stairs, and into the office, brought up Google and typed in 'Salzburg flights'. It arsed about with me for a bit, offering me a hot air balloon trip in the Alps, then it put me onto the Gatwick Airport web site. Promising, I thought. Maybe one of the cheap airlines had started a Gatwick-Salzburg flight.

And then I found it. Unbelievable. On Fridays, it said, an Austrian airline called Air Franz ran an eleven-thirty service from Gatwick to Salzburg. I booked it straightaway for both of them. *This is a business airline*, it said. *First-class service for first-class people.* The two single fares cost me just under a thousand pounds. I'd sort it out later with Freshair, or perhaps with Sergei.

I rang Lindsey straight back.

"How soon can you get yourselves to Gatwick?"

"Jamie, you don't understand. We can't move here. The train station is closed, because all the platforms are full. The taxi queue is right round the front and side of the terminal building. And the car hire places all have about a hundred people at them, and I've just heard someone say there aren't any cars left anyway."

"What about a bus?"

"Bloody hell no. We've been down there. The only buses with any spaces on them are the ones going to the hotels. There's an ambulance crew in the car park dealing with a woman who got crushed in the stampede when they announced a bus was leaving for London."

"Hasn't Julian got any ideas?"

"Jamie, you know the answer to that question."

"And he's standing right next to you, yes?"

"Absolutely. It's all down to you."

"Right then. I'll come to Stansted and pick you up, then take you to Gatwick. There's an eleven-thirty flight on something called Air Franz. That's Franz with a zed."

"Where to?"

"Salzburg."

"Can't we go on a proper airline?"

"None of the proper airlines flies to Salzburg. You'd have to go to Munich."

"We don't have much alternative, then, do we? This was mad, Jamie. What if I don't make it?"

"You'll be fine, Linds. You'd have had to cancel the Prom if you hadn't been prepared to make this journey. I need to get a move on. Why don't you two get on the next bus to the Hilton, which is near the M11? Get yourselves some breakfast. I'll pick you up there, in something like an hour and a half, depending on the traffic."

"What are you going to do about Dad and Evie?"

"I'll go in and wake them just before I leave. They can get something to eat, then pull the door to when they go."

"Okay then. Don't tell Dad what's going on. He'll insist on coming himself."

"Okay, sweetheart. I'll ring when I'm close."

I threw on some clothes and went across the corridor to knock on Albert and Evie's door.

Albert answered instantly. "I'm not asleep, Jamie. Come in."

Evie was fast asleep, with the bedclothes all curled around her. Albert on the other hand was wide awake, his duvet on the floor, and his hair all messed up. He'd probably had a vile night.

"Albert, I'm so sorry," I whispered, "but something's come up. I'm going to have to go. Can you get your own breakfast?"

"Yes of course. What's wrong? Is it Lindsey?"

"It's one of the other singers from *Figaro*. He's stuck. He needs a lift to Gatwick."

Well, it wasn't a lie, was it?

"Can't I go? We don't have to get home until later."

"No, really Albert, thanks anyway. Just as long as you're going to be all right. To get your breakfast, I mean."

"We'll be fine, Jamie, don't you worry. Shall I lock up?"

"Just pull the door to. I must go, and I don't want to wake Evie. Thanks so much for dinner."

"Pleasure." He winced suddenly, and caught his breath. "Bugger this bloody back. Jamie, you need to get off. Ring us later, when you've had time to catch your breath."

I ran down the stairs, picked up my keys, and let myself out of the front door. It was six thirty-five.

As I approached junction eight of the M11 the traffic ground to a halt. I'd heard on the radio that the congestion was severe, and that everyone should avoid the area if at all possible – the airport was closed, they said. The last half-mile was stop-start, and I didn't make it to the Hilton until eight forty. I stopped at the car park barrier, and pulled a ticket out of the machine. It opened, and a digitised voice said "Welcome to the Hilton Stansted Airport." I drove right up to the front door, and jumped out of the car.

"You can't leave that there," shouted a burly commissionaire.

"Got to, sorry. Frantic hurry. Shan't be a moment."

I'd phoned Lindsey from the car, and she and Julian were standing in the lobby waiting for me. I grabbed her bag, and ran straight back to the car.

The commissionaire was standing over it, looking cross.

"Do you realise you could have caused a security alert, sir?"

"There's already one of those. I don't suppose another one would have made much difference."

We all climbed into the car, and I drove to the exit barrier. I put my ticket in the machine.

TICKET NOT VALID, it said.

I pressed the red button for assistance, and after half a minute of ringing another disembodied voice said: "Yes".

"My ticket won't let me out."

"Have you paid, sir?"

"No. I've only been here two minutes."

"Ten pounds for a day, or part of a day, sir. It's clearly marked at the entrance to the car park."

"Oh for God's sake. Don't you have twenty minutes' free parking?"

"No sir. Ten pounds for a day, or part of a day. You can pay at the reception desk."

I slammed my fists down onto the steering wheel. The horn sounded.

"For heaven's sake, Jamie," said Lindsey. "Just go and pay it."

I looked in my mirror and saw a silver Audi drawing up behind me. I gesticulated wildly at the driver to back off, and after a few inconclusive shoulder-shrugs he reversed, giving me space to make my way to the front door.

"Not you again, "said the commissionaire.

"Yes, sorry, I've got to pay for the car park. I'll be back in a tick."

He looked at me with something between pity and contempt, as I ran inside again, and slammed ten pounds on the desk.

"Don't you want me to validate your ticket, sir?" said the receptionist.

"Oh yes, thank you." I had no idea which pocket I'd put it in. It took me at least a minute and a half to find it.

The commissionaire was laughing when I got back to the car. But Lindsey and Julian weren't. He was sitting on the back seat, pale as death, with a fine beading of sweat covering his top lip.

I looked in my mirror. "Julian, are you all right?"

He didn't reply. For a ghastly moment I thought he was going to burst into tears.

We got straight onto the motorway, which in this direction had hardly any traffic on it, and sped off towards the Dartford Bridge. It was nine o-four.

All was fine until we got to within two miles of Gatwick. Then the traffic slowed to a crawl, just as it had at Stansted. I parked the car in the South Terminal car park at ten-eighteen, an hour and twelve minutes before the plane was due to leave.

I went up to Departures with them. There was no queue at the Air Franz check-in desk, and Lindsey and Julian handed over their passports at ten-thirty precisely.

The check-in girl was called Nancy. She was blonde, and very young, and her face wore an expression of concern.

"You do know there is a delay of at least two and a half hours on this flight?"

The three of us spoke in perfect unison. "Oh my God."

"What's the problem?" I said.

"The aircraft which was due to form this service is unserviceable. There is another aircraft coming from Austria."

"When did it leave?"

"It has to go from Vienna to Salzburg to pick up passengers. It will fly on here as soon as possible."

Julian spoke next. "In that case it will be a great deal more than two and a half hours late, won't it?"

"Yes, I'm afraid it could well be. Air Franz is very sorry for this delay. Refreshment vouchers will be issued shortly."

"Refreshment vouchers aren't really the issue," said Julian. "We both have to be in Salzburg by six at the latest."

190

"Air Franz does not guarantee prompt arrival times, sir."

"You don't understand," I said. "These two passengers are both opera singers, and simply have to be in Salzburg this evening for performances of two different operas in the Salzburg Festival."

She looked gratifyingly impressed. "Are you famous, then?" she asked Lindsey.

"Not really. Well, a bit perhaps. Do you like opera?"

"Ooh, yes. Do you know Charles Danvers?"

Charles Danvers was the latest *Wunderkind* "opera singer" to hit the classical charts. Like all his predecessors he'd never sung a complete performance of an opera in his life.

"No, I'm afraid not," said Lindsey.

Nancy appeared to lose interest. "Oh. Well anyway, you'd better tell me what you want to do. Shall I check you in?"

"Hang on," I said. "Let me just see if I can find any other flights which will be any good. We'll pop over to the British Airlines desk."

The three of us trailed across to the other side of the Departure Lounge, to a very small British Airlines kiosk in the opposite wall.

All British Airlines flights go from the North Terminal, said a notice. *Tickets and Information only at this desk.*

I asked a smiling girl called Indira whether here were any Munich flights leaving soon. She was most helpful.

"Yes, indeed, sir, we have one at one-thirty. Would you like to make reservations? I'm afraid we only have business class seats left."

"When is it due to arrive?"

"Four fifteen, local time."

"And how much do the tickets cost?"

"Six hundred and eighty five pounds including taxes and charges, sir."

"I think we'll go back to the Air Franz desk and see if there's any more news."

Back we trooped once again. Nancy took one look at us, and the colour drained from her face.

"Oh gosh, I'd forgotten about you. We've just sold the last two seats on the plane. We've had a bit of a rush this morning – some problem at Stansted, I gather. I'm afraid you can't go on this flight."

"But what do you mean, you've sold the tickets? My wife and her friend were here first."

"I'm afraid they've been bumped off, sir."

"Does this mean Air Franz will pay for us to go on a different airline?" said Julian.

"Yes, it does. Oh dear, I'm going to be for it."

"In that case," said Julian, "we'd better change to British Airlines quick. At least it means we can get a taxi at Munich – presumably Air Franz will have to pay for that, too?"

"Yes, I'm afraid we will."

So back we went. Indira was delighted to see us.

"Yes, indeed, we have two seats available on the Munich flight. Oh, you have a voucher from Air Franz, that makes things a lot easier. Passports, please."

Lindsey had hers in her hand. Julian on the other hand, a man after my own heart, had to spend five minutes searching. Eventually he found it in the back pocket of his unreasonably-tight jeans. As he pulled it out, his phone pinged out of the same pocket, and landed on the floor.

"Shit," he said, as he picked it up. "It's switched itself off."

He handed his passport to Indira, and then proceeded to poke and prod at his phone as she worked at her computer. After a minute or so, he said:

"The bugger's broken. I don't believe it."

Indira handed him his tickets. "You have a nice flight now, sir." She seemed to find us all, and Pogson in particular, rather amusing.

Julian looked cross. He turned camply on his heel and minced off towards the North terminal shuttle train, with Lindsey half-running to keep up with him.

"Julian, hang on. I'm going to have a miscarriage unless you slow down. This is all too much for me."

Before long we were at the North Terminal security queue.

"I suppose I'll have to love you and leave you here," I said. "Are you all right?"

Julian gave a brittle laugh. "Oh, yes, Jamie, little short of superb. On cracking form."

Lindsey wasn't in the mood for levity. "I'd be fine if I wasn't in mortal fear of having to cough up a six-figure sum to the Salzburg Festival, not to mention worrying about my career coming to an end. And if I weren't pregnant, and frightened about losing the baby with all the stress."

She was right about the money. It had happened before – singers who had left too little time to get to a venue had been fined enormous sums by opera companies forced to compensate entire audiences for the cancellation of the show.

"I'll be on the end of a telephone if you want anything," I said. "You'd better go through."

The two of them set off to where boarding passes were being checked, then Lindsey disappeared through a barrier. Julian turned round and gave a camp little wave, and then he was gone too. It was eleven thirty-eight.

They really should be okay, I thought. The British Airlines flight was due to land at four fifteen, local time. Neither of them had checked in a bag. If they jumped straight in a taxi at Munich Airport they would be on the motorway by four thirty. Given a decent run, the journey would take an hour and a half, so they should be there at six. Lindsey didn't have to be on stage until seven forty-five, a quarter of an hour into the *Così* performance. And Julian wasn't on until the end of the second act of *Figaro*, meaning he didn't really need to be there until nine. No need to ring Göstl-Saurau at this stage.

Unless there was terrible traffic between Munich and Salzburg, that is. The thought began to gnaw away at me as I drove back up the M23 towards London. The first Friday in August – did it make any difference in Germany? It bloody well did in France. What did they call them? '*Journées rouges*', I think. When every self-respecting Frenchman north of the Loire, plus the entire Belgian nation, launched him- or her-self at the *autoroutes* in a frantic attempt to get to the sun. I had once been stuck trying to get round Lyon for six hours.

I was just driving across Battersea Bridge when my phone went. It was Lindsey, who was little short of hysterical.

"This flight's delayed by an hour. Late arrival of the incoming aircraft. What in Christ's name are we going to do?"

"Oh my God. I'll have to ring Göstl-Saurau."

"But Jamie, I'll be in the most terrible trouble."

"Not you, darling, me. I fixed this up, remember? And Göstl-Saurau agreed. He can put someone on standby. There must be hundreds of sopranos in Salzburg who know Fiordiligi."

"I suppose you have a point. I mean, a big part of me would like not to have to sing tonight. Can we do without the money?"

"Not really, but hey. I'll ring him now. What does Julian want me to do about him?"

193

"Here, talk to him. I'll pass you over."

"Hi Jamie," said a male voice, after a moment. "This is super, isn't it?"

"Julian, I'm about to ring Göstl-Saurau. If he offers to put someone else on to do Antonio, how do you feel about it?"

"I don't think he will offer, Jamie. This is the first night, remember? We've been rehearsing for weeks and weeks. The director said to us all the other night that if anyone cancelled they'd be shot."

"I'll ring him anyway. Is your phone still buggered?"

"Dead as a dodo."

I rang off, then dialled Göstl-Saurau's number from memory. His secretary answered.

"Oh, mein Gott, zat iss a problem. Miss Templeton END Mr Pogson. Graf von Göstl-Saurau iss not here in ziss moment. I vill call him immediately."

I rang Lindsey back straightaway. "Any news," I said.

"They still think the flight's going to depart at two thirty." She sounded marginally calmer than she had a few minutes earlier . "We're in the business class lounge. I'm feeling a bit sick."

"Göstl-Saurau's not in the office at the moment. His secretary's going to ring him. I'll ring you to let you know what he says."

"That could be a problem, Jamie. I forgot to bring my phone charger home from Salzburg the other day. I thought it would last, but I've just noticed the battery's really low."

"Jesus Christ. And Julian's is broken, yes?"

"Apparently so."

"How the hell am I supposed to manage all this if I can't even talk to you?"

"Don't you shout at me, Jamie. I'm exhausted, I'm feeling sick, I'm pregnant, I sang the Countess at the Proms last night, and I've probably got to sing bloody Fiordiligi in one of the most important festivals in the world tonight. This is all your fault anyway. DON'T get on at me about forgetting my phone charger, which, by the way, is something you do about three times a week."

"Okay, okay, I'm sorry. You'd better get off the phone, so as not to waste any more battery. Leave Göstl-Saurau to me – you don't really need to know what he says anyway. "

"Right. Fine. Goodbye."

I looked at the clock on the dashboard. Twelve forty-six.

Göstl-Saurau didn't ring back till two fifteen. By then I'd been back at home for a quarter of an hour, and had had time to check the Internet. Their flight was still expected to leave at two thirty.

"Mr Barlow. Ziss iss a disaster in ze makink. Because of your UNprofessionelity not vun, but TWO off our productionss are in jeopardy. Ze premiere off our new *Figaro*. End our megnificent *Cosi*, in vich your vife, notvisstendink her disGRACEful display et ze opening night party, iss ze star attraction."

"I'm so sorry Graf von Göstl-Saurau…"

"SORRY? IT ISS NOT SORRY! ZISS ISS DUE TO YOUR GROSS UNPROFESSIONELITY."

"But the airline delays are quite beyond my control," I said.

"ZET ISS VY VE DO NOT PERMIT SINGERS TO TREFFEL ON ZE DAY OFF A PERFORMANCE!"

"I understand completely. But they have had very bad luck."

"BED LUCK! It iss NOT bed luck. Because of your UNprofessionelity zese two whole shows may heff to be cancelled. Maestro GIOTTI iss conducting *Cosi*. Sir Simon RETtle iss comink. How cen you justify ziss extraordinary ceffelier attitude to our great Festival?"

"Could you not have other singers standing by?"

There was a short, angry pause. The he began again, speaking in a low, menacing growl.

"Let uss look et ze two cases. First, ze less important vun – Herr Pogson. In *Figaro* he sinks only ze schmal role off Antonio ze gardener. Nonezeless, he hess been rehearsink viss ze rest off ze cast for many veeks. Ze director, your ferry own Sir Leslie Saunders, hess told me personally only yesterday zet iff any off ze cast should sink off cancelling ze openink night, he vill remoof hiss name from ze production, and vill not appear on stage before ze public, vich vill cause somesink off a scendel. I voss off course concerned zet somevun vould be ill, but ve heff good luck, end all singers are, es I believe you English heff it, in ze pink. But your Mr Pogson, who sinks zis schmal role, iss late, becoss a leetle English opera company viss a lot off filsy Russian money hess decided to send him beck from London on ze day off a show. Howeffer, in ziss role ve cen at least put on a younk men from ze chorus, who heppens to know ziss role, end who hess made a point on hiss own PERsonal responsibility to learn Sir Leslie's production. I heff already informed him zet he may heff ze chance to go on. He iss ferry excited. He iss also Austrian. I say ziss becoss it may be instructiff for you to note zet he hess more responsibility in hiss little finger zen you British people heff altogezzer.

"But ze case off your vife iss entirely different. Despite her unfortunate allegiances to you end to Herr Rebroff, she iss a ferry great singer. Ze refiews heff been extraordinary. All of Europe now vants to see ziss *Cosi*, largely because of her performance. I simply cennot allow her to cancel."

"What if she had been ill, Graf von Göstl-Saurau?"

He screamed his reply. "But she iss NOT ill. If she vere ill ve vould send her to a SROAT specialist. End if ve hed to replace her ve vould do so. But I vill NOT replace her if she is simply late, because off your UNprofessionelity."

There was a lot of heavy breathing after this tirade. I thought it better to keep quiet.

"Vell, I attempt to calm down. Ve must, after all, face ze situation in vich ve find ourselves. Please tell me exactly vere Miss Templeton end Mr Pogson are now?"

"They are about to leave London Gatwick airport on a British Airlines flight bound for Munich, which is an hour late. Its new expected time of arrival is five-fifteen your time. They have no bags to collect. They are therefore expecting to be in a taxi by five twenty, or at the latest five twenty-five. All being well, they should arrive in Salzburg by seven. This will give Lindsey enough time to put on her costume, wig and make-up, and be on stage for her first entry at seven forty-five approximately."

"Vot if zere iss bed treffic?"

"We have to take that risk, I'm afraid."

"Ho ho ho, you are ferry, vot iss ze vord, zenkvin."

It took me a moment. Sanguine, I realised.

"We have no alternative," I said. "I will telephone you again as soon as they are in a taxi. I trust there will be no further delays."

"If zere are more delays ve may heff to cencel ze performance. Ziss iss preferable to putting on some ozzer, inferior singer in ze role off Fiordiligi. You must face ze fect zet eizer Miss Templeton herself, or else Opera London in her place, may heff to pay. Ziss vill be ferry bed for you. But of course Herr Rebroff cen pay ziss kind of money, ess I sink you put it, fallink off a log. Vezzer he vill be ferry please viss ze man who vishes to be his new General Administrator…" he gave a nasty little laugh, "iss a different metter. I do not vish to speak viss you again. Please give me ze hendy phone number off your vife."

"Her mobile phone is almost out of battery."

"Mein Gott, her hendy iss almost out off bettery. Zen ze phone off Mr Pogson."

"I'm afraid it is broken."

For a second I thought he was sobbing down the phone. Then I realised he was laughing.

"It gets better und better! You English heff a unique telent for ziss sort off sink. Zen sedly I must speak again to you, Mr Barlow. Please rink, as you say, ven zey are in a texi. How vill you know?"

"Lindsey is going to text me. She should have just enough power left for that."

"Zen I vait by ze phone."

The line went dead. It was two twenty-four.

I kept checking the Teletext to see how they were doing. This was not too onerous a task – the fourth Ashes Test had begun the previous day, and I watched it through the whole of that dreadful afternoon. Kevin Pietersen was busy notching up the fastest century in Ashes history, which was a pleasant counterpoint to the panic which had taken possession of my entire being. I had rung work when the extent of the problem had become apparent. I reckoned this was Opera London business, so I told them I was working from home all day.

The expected time of arrival didn't change, and at four sixteen our time I checked again to discover that the flight had landed five minutes before. Sure enough, at four twenty-one my new phone made a noise I'd never heard before. It was a text coming in from Lindsey.

"In a taxi. Very quick through customs, so should be okay. Feeling like shit. How the hell am I going to sing? And what did G-S say?"

I texted back: "G-S is cross. He won't put anyone else on. Julian might get away with it. Keep me posted by text." I mean I'd like to have dressed it up, made it sound a bit less aggressive. But what can you do in a text message?

I rang Göstl-Saurau's number immediately. The secretary answered. Thank God.

"It's Jamie Barlow," I said.

"Ah, Herr Barlow. Vot iss happenink?"

"They are in a taxi. All should be well now."

"Graf von Göstl-Saurau vill be ferry please. I vill tell him."

And she rang off. I went back to the cricket, allowing myself to feel relieved. They were in their taxi, in enough time to make it. They even had a bit of time to accommodate bad traffic. And they'd had enough bad luck for one day, hadn't they?

It was the home phone which rang next. Pietersen had just been dropped on 94 by Gilchrist off Warne, which made me very happy indeed. I was convinced he was going to whack the next one for six. So I was irritated by having to walk into the hall to answer the fixed phone – needless to say all the portable ones had gone walkabout.

I looked at the display. It said '4.46', and, beside that, 'INTERNATIONAL'.

"Hallo."

"Jamie it's me. You're not going to believe this. The taxi's broken down."

"Oh Christ. Where?"

"Thank God it was right by a service station – Vaterstetten it's called. The car started to buck like a bloody-minded pony. The driver didn't seem to know what to do. So I shouted at him to pull in to the services, and thank God he did, otherwise we'd have gone sailing straight past and we'd have been totally sunk."

"So what's happening now?"

"The driver has spoken to the guy behind the counter and they've ordered another cab. They say it could be ages."

"And where are you ringing from?"

"A phone box in the garage. My mobile hasn't actually switched itself off yet, but it keeps bleeping at me."

"Do you want to ring Göstl-Saurau from there? It might be better if you talked to him yourself."

"For Christ's sake, Jamie, do you want me to go off pop? If anyone shouts at me now I haven't a hope of singing anything. I'm not likely to be much good anyway, am I?"

"Well can't Julian ring him? He's only got to do Antonio."

"Julian is sitting at a table in the far corner of the room in floods of tears, Jamie. He's worse than useless."

"Oh God, I suppose I'll have to do it."

"Don't play the martyr with me, Jamie. Do you have any idea what it's like being stuck here on the motorway, not knowing whether you have the slightest chance of getting there in time? I should have thought that ringing Göstl-Saurau was the least you could do.”

I had to concede she had a point.

“Okay, then. Give me the number you’re ringing from. I’ll ring you back as soon as I’ve spoken to him.”

So she gave me the number, which was written with typical German efficiency just above the handset cradle. Then I rang off, and dialled Göstl-Saurau’s number yet again.

“It’s Jamie Barlow again. We have a problem.”

The secretary said: “I vill put you srough to Graf von Göstl-Saurau immediately.”

Oh shit.

“Yes?” said a very cross male voice.

“The taxi has broken down.”

There was a sharp intake of breath, and then a long pause. Eventually he said: “vere are zey?”

“Vaterstetten.”

“Mein GOTT zey are only in Vaterstetten? Zen zey heff no chance.”

“How far away is it?”

“Et least vun end half hours. Heff zey ordered anozzer texi?”

“Yes.”

“Und how long vill it be?”

“They don’t know.”

“Ziss iss ferry bed.”

He no longer sounded angry. He sounded defeated.

“What shall we do?”

“Ve cen do only vun sing. Ve cen hope. You vill please to phone me again ven ze texi hess arrived.”

“I may not hear when the taxi has arrived, Graf von Göstl-Saurau. Linsdey’s phone may not even have enough power to text me. And we can’t wait for her to ring me from the fixed phone in the garage.”

“No, you are correct. Zen you give zem a message. You cen ring zem beck now?”

“Yes, as long as the taxi hasn’t already left.”

“Zen pleass tell zem zet if zey are not goink to be in my office in ze *Großes Festspielhaus* by seffen twenty, zey must shtop, vereffer zey are, und phone me. Und you tell my secretary ven you heff deliffered zis message. You understand?”

“Yes. I must ring them straightaway.”

He didn't even bother with finishing the conversation. He simply put the phone down. I rang Lindsey back, and she answered immediately.

"Any sign of the taxi?" I said.

"Not yet. What did Göstl-Saurau say?"

"That you are to stop the car if you don't expect to be in his office by seven twenty, and telephone him. Have you got the number?"

"Yes, we've both got lists of contact numbers from the Festival."

"Fine. Any sign of the car?"

"Shut up Jamie, you are a prick."

"Okay then, text me when you're in it. If you have any juice left, that is."

"And if I haven't?"

"Then we'll just have to leave it to chance."

"Jamie, don't you EVER do this to me again." The line went dead.

I rang Göstl-Saurau's secretary to tell her I'd delivered the message, and then went back to the telly. I didn't feel like watching any more cricket, so I switched it off and stared at the wall. It was four fifty-two in England, and five fifty-two in Germany and Austria.

There was no text. Nor was there any further phone call. I just had to sit and wait. I didn't get any more news until six twenty-nine, when my mobile made the same odd noise as before. It was a text from Lindsey's phone.

"Made it. Feel terrible. Borrowed charger 4 phone. No time 4 more. L."

And that was it. I texted back: "well done, darling. You must be so relieved. Toi-toi, I know you will be great."

Toi-toi. Was that the best I could manage? The opera world's time-honoured code for "have a good show", supposedly based on people spitting over each others' shoulders? I felt in my pocket, pulled out a squashed packet with four Rothmans left in it, went into the kitchen to get a plate to use as an ashtray, and found some matches. Then, totally ignoring our rule about never smoking in the house, I lit up.

I went to the drinks cupboard, and looked for the strongest thing I could find. I'd finished that bottle of Talisker, I realised, a few weeks before. There was some nasty cooking brandy, and a bottle of Grappa which Albert had brought back from some holiday in Italy.

I chose the Grappa, then plonked myself down on the sofa. Five huge glasses and three cigarettes later, I felt just about strong enough to pick up the remote, and flick through the channels on the telly. I found some crappy soap opera, and set myself to concentrate on it, desperate to take my mind off what was going on in Salzburg. But I needn't have worried. Within five minutes I was fast asleep.

My mobile woke me up. I fished around to try and find it. Eventually I realised it had slipped down the back of the sofa. I pressed the button with the little green telephone on it, and put it to my ear.

"Jamie it's me."

"What? Who?"

"Lindsey. Your wife."

"Oh sorry. Fell asleep on the sofa. What time is it?"

"Just after nine. Eight your time. We're in the interval. Are you drunk?"

"Well, a bit maybe. Sorry. How's it going?"

"Terrible. I can't sing at all."

"Oh, bollocks, Lindsey. You can always sing."

"Well, tonight I can't. It's hardly surprising. I didn't have time to warm up, or eat, or anything."

"Have you seen Göstl-Saurau?"

"We got here at seven-eighteen. The taxi driver was going a hundred and eighty all the way. So we went up to Göstl-Saurau's office and clocked in. I thought he'd shout at us, but instead he smiled, and I burst into tears. I only just managed to recover myself in time to throw on a bit of make-up and my costume and wig, and run onto the stage to sing."

"Well never mind, darling. At least you got there."

"Jamie, do you have any idea what I'm going through? I CAN'T SING, for fuck's sake."

I desperately tried to force my mashed-up brain cells to concentrate – Lindsey had never before rung during a show to say she wasn't singing well. I'd better say something good.

"Darling, I'm sure you're fine." Terrific, Jamie. A triumph.

"I am NOT fine, Jamie. I completely missed the B flat at the end of *Come Scoglio* – I just did a sort of squawk. The *coloratura* was hopeless – no definition at all. I ran out of breath on that high quiet phrase in *Soave sia il vento*, and all the ensembles have been really frightening. I don't know how I'm going to get through Act Two. I've got *Per pietà* coming up. Jesus Christ."

I heard the tannoy say "*Damen und Herren vom Orchester, Ihr erstes Zeichen. Ladies und Gentlemen, your first call.*"

"Oh my God, I've got to go, Jamie. Help me!"

What the bloody hell was I supposed to say?

"Just go out there and sing wonderfully, like you always do, sweetheart. Ring me as soon as you've finished."

"I'll do my best. Bye."

She sounded as if she was going to cry. How on earth were you supposed to sing if you were crying? In any case the line went dead, and yet again I had to wait.

When she phoned back at ten thirty our time, I'd sorted myself out a bit. I'd opened all the windows, thrown away the contents of my makeshift ashtray, and had some beans on toast. It was the first time I'd eaten all day. Several cups of black coffee later, I felt slightly more as if I could face whatever Lindsey had to say.

"How did you do, Linds?"

"They booed. After the aria, and again at the curtain call."

"Shit. Where are you now?"

"Back at the flat."

"Did anyone say anything?"

"The cast were all nice to me – they said it wasn't too bad, and my technique must be fantastic to have got through it at all. Giotti ignored me completely. I never saw anyone from the management – they're all at the *Figaro* premiere, thank God. But as I walked out of the stage door someone shouted 'maybe you should not have sung in London last night'. Quite bloody right. Of course I shouldn't."

"Look, darling, it's been a nightmare, but at least you got through it. People understand, you know - we're all human."

"Jamie, there's nothing you can say. I messed up big time. How's Dad?"

Christ, I'd completely forgotten to ring. I didn't dare tell her.

"They got back fine, darling. I didn't have time to talk much, but he said they both loved last night. I'll speak to him properly tomorrow."

There was silence at the end of the phone. I had to fill the gap.

"Maybe you'd prefer to speak to him yourself, sweetheart?"

Another long pause. Then she said: "the last thing Dad wants is to have to cope with a hysterical singer who's just given the worst performance of her life. You ring him in the morning."

And with that the line went dead. I thought about ringing her back, but I was just sober enough to realise that it wouldn't do any good. I picked up the remote and found some crap to watch, then poured myself another large grappa and lit my last cigarette.

25

Saturday August the fifth began for me, at eleven forty-three am, with a lurching realisation that our world was in danger of falling apart completely. Not only that, but yet again I had a throat like something the parrot had sicked up, and a screaming headache. I was stark naked, and I had no recollection of going to bed. It occurred to me that I was quite lucky to have survived the night. It also occurred to me for an ignoble moment that I wished I hadn't.

I seriously considered turning over and going back to sleep, but some vestigial sense of responsibility forced me to get up and face the day. The mess downstairs was indescribable, but I set to and cleaned up. At two o'clock, after a restorative bacon-and-egg lunch, I decided I could postpone the awful moment no longer, and rang Stockencote.

Evie answered the phone. This in itself was unusual – when there was no Carly to look after, she was seldom there, in normal circumstances anyway. She sounded very anxious.

"Oh, Jamie, thank you *so* much for having us the other night, and for the tickets. Albert absolutely loved it. So did I, of course." She paused.

"How is Albert?" I asked.

"He was terribly tired when we got back, but he's a bit better today. The trouble is, as soon as he feels better, he will insist on getting back on that combine."

"How ill is he, Evie?"

"Oh dear, Jamie, I really do need to talk about this to someone, but I don't know if I should."

"Evie, please."

"All right then, on the strict condition that you say nothing to Lindsey. Albert's far more worried about her than he is about himself."

"Understood."

"He insists he's just got sciatica. And he may even be right. But I've seen it before - the patients at the home often used to suffer like this. I'm about eighty per cent convinced he's got cancer."

"I had an awful feeling you were going to say that. Has he been to the doctor?"

"He refuses to go. I've tried times out of number."

"But Evie, for God's sake, if he has got, you know, the big C, then he needs treatment as soon as possible. Doesn't he?"

"Yes of course he does, Jamie. I just haven't been able to persuade him to go. But I think I'm nearly there – he really frightened himself with the trip to London. I had to drive back yesterday, because he felt so terrible. As soon as we got home, he went to bed. And he didn't get up till this morning."

"You should never have come."

"There was no stopping him. And if it's persuaded him to get his head out of the sand then maybe it's done some good."

"How long have you suspected this, Evie?"

"Well, he's had a bad back for years, so I didn't think much of it at first. It was a few weeks ago I started to worry. The pain seemed to be there all the time, whereas before it would come and go. I wanted to say something to Lindsey but Albert absolutely forbade it."

"Have you told Albert what you think?"

"I haven't mentioned the C-word. But he knows I'm worried. He keeps telling me not to fuss."

"Maybe Lindsey should ring him and tell him to go the doctor."

"Jamie, I've told you, Albert insists that Lindsey know absolutely nothing of this. Not until we know for certain what's wrong. And not before she's finished this job in Salzburg."

"I suppose he has a point. The singing voice is a very fragile thing. I've known singers lose their voices overnight because of stress."

"Jamie, if that happened to Lindsey Albert would never forgive himself. And he insists that you go ahead with your holiday, by the way."

"We can't possibly go away on a jolly while all this is going on. Can't I speak to Albert now? I'll be very careful what I say."

"Heavens, do you think I would have spoken to you so frankly if he'd been in the house? He's on that blooming combine again. He probably won't be in until it gets dark."

"God, poor you, Evie. Are you staying at Stockencote?"

"Yes, I've moved in for the moment. At least I can cook and clean for him. He's my brother, the stubborn old bugger, and I want to do everything I can."

"Then for pity's sake get him to the doctor."

"Yes, yes, Jamie, I promise I will. I'll drag him there if I have to."

"You're a saint. Thank you for being so honest with me. I'll ring Lindsey now, and tell her that he's got sciatica, and that she's not to worry. I expect she'll ring him later."

"Well, tell her not to bother until at least ten-thirty. I'm going to make him eat a decent tea when he gets in. After that I should think nothing could be better for him than to talk to his daughter. He loves her so much, you know. Carly too. Make sure you look after them both."

"I will, Evie. Bye."

"Bye bye Jamie. And thanks."

And so I turned my attention to Lindsey. Of all the hideous phone calls I'd had to make to her over the past few weeks, this was by far the worst. I'd never been any good at lying.

She answered straightaway. "Oh, hi Jamie."

"Hi darling. How do you feel today?"

"I keep telling myself I'm fine."

"Have you done any singing?"

"A bit. My voice seems more or less okay, but I haven't put it under any pressure. It was odd last night. I don't know what was wrong. I mean of course I had an excuse to sing badly, but normally pressure doesn't get to me like that. And basically, it felt fine, until I came to the difficult bits. I kept thinking 'I bet this is going to go wrong', and every time I thought that, I messed it up."

"Are you in a state about your Dad?"

"Of course I am, Jamie."

"Well I've spoken to Evie properly now. They seem to think it's just a bad dose of sciatica. And that he's very tired because of the harvest."

"Nothing worse than that?"

"Apparently not."

"Oh God, I'm so relieved. I've been worried sick."

"Evie could see you were worried. She says why don't you ring? He'd love to talk to you. Only it'll have to be when he gets in from combining."

"Yes of course I'll ring. What sort of time?"

"About ten thirty, she says – nine thirty your time."

"Great Jamie, thanks. You've made me feel so much better."

After she had put the phone down I tormented myself for a good hour about whether I had done the right thing by lying. Of course I knew deep down that I was laying the foundations for terrible trouble when she found out how ill Albert was. But it was on his express instructions, wasn't it?

I had another shocking nightmare. This time Sergei was having a riding lesson from Fliss. The horse he was riding had Albert's face. Fliss was shouting at Sergei:

"For God's sake, man, you can ride him harder than that. Kick like mad, then he'll jump."

Sergei kept presenting the Albert-horse to a huge fence, which turned out to be the front of the Opera London Theatre in Victoria. Albert kept refusing, and running out down the side of the fence.

Eventually Fliss shouted "you get on," and Lindsey, heavily pregnant and wearing full riding gear, got up on Albert's back. He uttered a blood-curdling cry, half a human scream of pain, half an equine whinny. The Albert-horse reared over backwards, crushing Lindsey beneath him.

"Bugger," said Fliss. "The horse has got bloody cancer. It'll soon be dead. Sergei, and you, Jamie, you two push him off Lindsey. I've seen this kind of accident before, and I don't like it."

Sergei and I ran to the scene of fall, and manhandled the unconscious Albert-horse off Lindsey. She was crying.

"There," she said. "I'm fine. But Dad's dead, and just look at the baby."

On the ground next to where Lindsey was sitting was a pool of blood, with a small dead pig lying in the middle of it. Sergei said:

"It must have been yours, Jimmy, because Rebroffs are not farming porks."

At this point the horse miraculously came back to life. It now had the face of Gregory Knipe. It kicked out with its hind leg at Sergei's balls. He fell, shouting "Curse you, Red Baron", and where when his head hit the ground the wound opened up, releasing a stream of what looked suspiciously like Grand Marnier. Lindsey was crying, and screaming "Jamie you bastard, you've killed him. You've killed them all."

I woke up, pouring sweat. I found some old Marlboro in the bedside table, and had to have three to calm down, before I lay back down on the bed and tried to dismiss the hideous visions that were still crawling round my head.

The following morning I couldn't shake off the anxiety. I was in urgent need of something normal and reassuring to do. For once I was regretting not having Carly to see to – the routine would have taken my mind off it.

I decided to ask myself round to Mum and Dad's for Sunday lunch. I needed a decent feed – roast meat and two veg might just help correct the imbalance caused by two days of booze, cigarettes and anxiety. I picked up the phone, and dialled the number.

Mum sounded really pleased I was coming, which was great. I felt a bit like I had when I was away at school – home might be a bit irritating but it was still home, and sometimes nothing else would do.

Also I was going away the next day, to Bregenz. I had to see two shows – one on the floating stage, and one in the *Festspielhaus* the following night. Bregenz was a nice place, and normally I would have been quite happy to jump on a plane on my own, and stay the night in some hotel. But loneliness was crowding in on me, so before I left for Mum and Dad's I rang Angus, on the off chance that he would be free and able to make the trip with me. In any case as the new Music Director he needed to get to know as many singers as possible.

He jumped at the idea. Could he bring Gloria, he said? She had a few weeks off before starting our *Fledermaus* – she was singing Adèle – and they'd been looking for a chance to get away together. We arranged to meet at Stansted at one o'clock the next day.

I got to Mum and Dad's at about one, just as she was serving up roast chicken with all the trimmings. Proper English food, with Mum's famous bread sauce, for which I would happily die. Dad opened not one but two bottles of Claret, and we spent the afternoon watching Steve Harmison skittling out the Aussies, with an incredibly hostile display of fast bowling. When Strauss scored the winning runs for England, at ten past six, a splendid afternoon was made perfect. While there was home and bread sauce and cricket, life couldn't be that bad after all.

26

The floating stage at Bregenz is one of the most spectacular opera venues in the world. Every two years they build a new set, which then plays host to between twenty and thirty performances of the chosen opera in each of the two following summers. The set is a semi-permanent structure, which dominates the skyline as you look at the town from the other side of Lake Constance.

In England you'd never get planning permission. But in Austria this magnificent eccentricity is celebrated as a cultural jewel, and big business sponsors the event to the tune of millions of Euros. Just like in Salzburg, everywhere you look there are huge silver limousines with Festival logos on the sides, transporting the Great and the Good around town. The only difference is in Salzburg these cars are Audis, while in Bregenz they are Mercedes.

This year there was a new production of Verdi's *Il Trovatore*. It was a tremendous undertaking. The members of the orchestra played in the orchestra pit of the indoor *Festspielhaus*, and were broadcast from huge speakers around the set – the sound system had won awards for its magnificence. This meant that the conductor, who stood with the orchestra, was only visible to the singers on a giant television screen. The problems of balance and ensemble that this arrangement occasioned could occupy hours of precious stage rehearsal time.

The performance was not due to start until 9.15, by which time it would be dark enough to use the stage lighting effectively. So, after a suitable amount of ooh-ing and aah-ing at the floating stage, with Lake Constance as its astonishingly beautiful backdrop, Gloria, Angus and I walked down to the Kornmarkt, where there was a little Greek restaurant called the Avgolemono. We ate meze and souvlakia, and drank an indecent quantity of retsina.

I was afraid I might fall asleep during the show but I needn't have worried. The production was full of real fire effects, and there was even a speedboat which drove into the middle of the set, setting down its passengers at the stage's very own drop-off point. I'd made the trip specifically to hear the tenor, an Australian whose name was whose name was Shane Campbell, and he was fantastic. Angus actually let go of Gloria's thigh for a moment when Campbell got to *Di Quella Pira*, with its whacking great top C at the end.

When it finally came to an end after eleven, the huge audience shuffled out, and I imagined that the three of us would wander back to our hotel for a nightcap, before chastely (well, in my case, anyway) turning in for the night. But to my astonishment and delight, just as we emerged onto the Platz der Wiener Symphoniker, I saw John Standish, wearing his traditional spotty bow-tie.

As soon as he caught sight of me, he screamed 'Jamie' at the top of his voice. About three thousand people looked round, startled, and there was Teutonic tutting of the Salzburg Festival kind. Once again, the word *'Englisch'* was on everyone's disapproving lips. We went over to where John was standing. He was wreathed in smiles.

"I've been on this trip for weeks now, and you're the first friend I've run into in all that time. I was beginning to think opera wasn't the private club it used to be. How the devil are you, you young whippersnapper?"

"I'm fine, John, just fine. I'd heard from Denise that you were on your annual opera jaunt. Angus, Gloria, this is my great friend and opera lover, John Standish. John, you remember Angus Lennox, my Best Man?"

"Of course I do. Gussie Lennox, the Great White Hope of British opera. And if I'm not very much mistaken, Madam, you're Gloria Forrest, and you have recently given London its finest, and if I may say so, sexiest Susanna for many a long year."

Gloria flashed a full set of dazzling white teeth at Standish. "Mr Standish, you're too kind."

Standish looked deep into her cleavage. "No, no, Madam, I assure you I only issue this kind of extravagant compliment when it's entirely deserved."

Angus took Gloria's arm in a proprietary way. Standish looked a bit disappointed.

"John," I said. "Have you read about last week's goings-on at Opera London?"

He peeled his eyes away from Gloria's breasts. "Not a thing, I'm afraid, dear boy. I very seldom either switch on the box or look at a newspaper. And never when I am away from home."

"Very wise," I said. "Then you won't know that it's all confirmed about Sergei Rebroff giving the Company his millions, and becoming Chairman?"

He whistled. "What's happened to our dear Gregory Knipe, then?"

"Skedaddled," said Angus. "Buggered off."

"Hooray! And what's going to happen to you boys? I heard one rumour you were taking over the top jobs."

"It's a possibility," Angus said quickly. "We're applying. We'll have to wait and see about the outcome."

"Don't give me that load of cobblers, Angus," said Standish. "I can read young Jamie here like a book. When do you both start?"

I couldn't get the grin off my face, and after a moment of feigned irritation, nor could Angus.

"Well done the two of you. This calls for a celebration. Night club, I think."

"We're a bit male-heavy," I said. "Don't you have some sensationally beautiful female travelling companion?"

"Always travel solo on these jaunts. Leaves one open to all possibilities. I'm sure Bregenz can turn up a bit of talent to entertain a rapidly ageing old gynaecologist. I also suspect you need a bit of female company, Jamie, what with the missus off in Salzburg. I'm going, by the way, on Thursday. I hear she's sensational. You two," he looked with some amusement at Angus and Gloria, still arm in arm, "don't look as if you need any help at all. Come on, where are we going?"

Angus was one of those people who by some miracle always know The Place To Go. We walked beside the lake to the level crossing, then crossed back into the Kornmarkt. We walked past the front of the Avgolemono, and then turned up to the right. Before long we came to an open doorway with loud rock music pumping out of it.

A shaven-headed bouncer said something aggressive. Standish replied, in impressively fluent German. Whatever he said the bouncer smiled broadly and stepped back to let us in. We handed over thirty Euros each to someone on a desk and went inside.

The place was heaving, and the air was thick with cigarette smoke. Standish worked his way through the crowd to the bar. Meanwhile Angus said something in what was meant to be a voice loud enough to carry over the music.

"Can't hear," I shouted into his ear. "You'll have to speak up."

"Don't forget to ask him about the DNA test." I'd have worried about Gloria overhearing, but the music was so loud anyone who didn't have their ear pressed directly against the mouth of the speaker was unlikely to hear anything at all except the Red Hot Chili Peppers, or whoever the hell they were.

Standish reappeared, bringing with him not only a tray with a bottle of Moet and six glasses on it, but also two sensationally beautiful leggy blondes, who had grins on their faces the size of Lake Constance.

"Ulrike and Agathe," he yelled. "They'd like to meet you, Jamie."

I have never known how people do this. Pull a couple of birds, that is. I found out that mine was called Ulrike, but that's about as far as we got before she grabbed the back of my neck and thrust her tongue down my throat, only stopping when she got to my tonsils. Percy enjoyed this more than was in any way decent, which I'm afraid Ulrike noticed almost immediately, pulling my crotch towards hers. She lifted her mouth off mine for just long enough to say "ooh!" in an approbatory sort of way, then slid her hand round behind me and pulled me in even tighter. Her tongue resumed its original position down my throat.

I was dimly aware that I shouldn't be behaving like this. Not only was my wife languishing in a nasty little flat a few hundred kilometres to the east, trying to get some beauty sleep before a frightfully important show the following evening. She was also a close friend of the gentleman opposite me, who had his tongue down Agathe's throat, and who had procured Ulrike for me not five minutes previously.

But if Standish didn't care – and he clearly didn't give a damn – then who was I to complain? I ran my hand up under Ulrike's T-shirt to discover a deliciously unfettered pair of tits.

The champagne was sitting untouched in the glasses, which seemed a shame, so I reached over with my spare hand and grabbed one. At the same time I pulled away from Ulrike's slightly manic embrace, and took stock. She was quite pretty, but up close she wasn't as unmissable as I had originally thought, so I handed the champagne to her with what I hoped was a boyish giggle, and took another glass for myself. I was aware that Angus and Gloria were staring at the two of us with looks of incredulous amusement on their faces.

At this point Standish and Agathe also came up for air. He raised his glass and motioned for us all to do the same. He said something in Angus's direction, and something else in mine. Then he finished his in one gulp.

Presuming it was a toast, I did the same, then reached into my pocket for my cigarettes. Before I had a chance to get one out, Ulrike presented me with one of hers, and lit it.

I was only slightly drunk, which made me more rational than might otherwise have been expected. Here I was, puffing away at a cigarette in some hideous dive in the back streets of Bregenz, about to commit adultery for the first time in my life. And there was my gorgeous wife, pregnant with what I devoutly hoped was our child, thinking that however irritating I might be, I was at least faithful.

"Ulrike, I'm sorry," I yelled, "but I've got to get back to my hotel. I'm not feeling too good." She looked absolutely livid. "Angus, I'll call you tomorrow morning. Have a great evening all of you. John, I really need a word with you before we go."

They were all stunned. I don't think it had crossed any of their minds that I might be about to cut and run. Ulrike had a face like tripe.

Standish gestured for me to follow him. We made our way through the crowd, and into a disgusting little loo beyond. There were just the two urinals side by side, and both were occupied. We had to wait for a couple of blokes to finish, which seemed to take much longer than was necessary. But they were far more concerned with each other than with Standish and me, so I just kept my mouth shut and waited. An unwelcome image of Olivier Leclerc and Jason Tang crept into my brain.

Eventually they left , and we were able to relieve ourselves in relative peace.

"You said you wanted to talk to me?" said Standish.

"Yes, it's rather urgent, actually John. I need to have lunch with you – something hush-hush."

"Problem?"

"Yes, a big one."

"Operatic, or gynaecological?"

"Both, in a way. When are you back in London?"

"Next Monday."

"Any chance of meeting up that day?"

"Of course, dear boy. Where are you taking me?"

"Somewhere near you. I don't want to be spotted."

"Right you are. I'm working at UCH. Let's say one o'clock, at Warren Street Underground. We'll go to a little French place I know in University Street. Bring your cheque book. It's pricey. But very discreet."

"Terrific, John, I'm awfully grateful."

"Now if you don't mind, you surprisingly boring old fart, I'm going back to Agathe. She and I will be romping until dawn. For Christ's sake slip Ulrike enough for the taxi home, or we'll have her in tow as well. Actually there's something to be said for that idea. She and Agathe make a lovely couple."

He zipped himself up, and left. I followed him, pressed fifty Euros into Ulrike's hand on the way out, and made my chaste way back to the hotel.

Absurdly, given my heroic forbearance the night before, I woke racked with guilt. I felt I had let Lindsey down. And I couldn't bear to think of her so lonely in the flat in Salzburg, with the terrifying mountain of that night's performance of *Cosi* to climb. I also, following my close shave with Ulrike, really wanted to see her.

While I was in the shower, I came up with the idea of getting a train to Salzburg, and going to Lindsey's show. I could reassure myself her singing was fully recovered, and spend the night with her.

There was a problem about Bregenz, though. Someone from Opera London had to see the Scarlatti opera in the *Festspielhaus*. We were thinking of hiring in the production the season after next.

I was in the middle of shaving when I had my brainwave. Since Angus was here, why shouldn't he see it instead of me? We could tell Geraldine Faulkner, the English *Intendant* of the Bregenz Festival, that Angus and I had high hopes of heading the new Opera London management team. I'd tell her that I had to go to Salzburg, but that Angus would report back.

As soon as I was dressed, I rang his room. I had to wait some time for an answer.

"Hallo." He sounded like some superannuated Russian bass.

"Angus it's Jamie."

"Jesus Christ you self-righteous bastard, leave us alone. Just because you behaved immaculately last night – for which huge congratulations, you ridiculous killjoy – the rest of us didn't. Gloria and I only got into bed at six. Ulrike wanted to come with us. What's the time now?"

"Eight fifteen, I'm afraid. Listen, I need to talk to you."

"I supposed you must have rung for a reason, you tosser. What about?"

"I want you to represent the Company at this Scarlatti show tonight. I need to go to Salzburg."

"Don't be ridiculous, the world doesn't know I've got anything to do with Opera London. You're the one who's casting director, remember?"

"We'll say you're coming as Sergei Rebroff's personal representative. And we can tell Faulkner that you and I are a shoo-in as the new top management team."

"What if she's planning to apply for your job herself?"

"That's hardly likely. Bregenz is a high-profile position for her, and she only has to be here about three months of the year. It gives her scope to go off and direct her own shows elsewhere during the other nine months. And it probably pays her as much as she'd get in London for being there all year round. I think she'll be an ally."

"Oh all right then. Anything to get you off the phone. But set it up with her before you go. Why in hell do you want to go back to Salzburg, anyway? Haven't you had enough of the place?"

"I just need to see Lindsey. I miss her."

"Oh bloody hell, listen to you."

"Angus, all you have to do is turn up at the box office at seven, and pick up your tickets. Then afterwards, find Faulkner and say her production of this Scarlatti piece is revelatory, life-enhancing, the usual crap. Then buy her a couple of drinks, or maybe dinner. The Company can pay – I'll put it through on my expenses. I'll liaise with her afterwards by email, then when you get into harness you can fix up bringing it to London. It'll be a feather in your cap."

"What if it's a load of rubbish?"

"Doesn't matter a bugger, Gussie. If it's the emperor's new clothes, half the world won't notice anyway. And it's Sergei's money, when all's said and done, so who cares?"

"You are considerably too much of a cynic to be doing this job at all, James Barlow. I need to go back to bed."

He hung up. I went down to breakfast feeling rather pleased with myself.

After breakfast I rang Lindsey to tell her the good news.

"Darling it's me."

"Oh God, what time is it?"

"Nine forty-five."

"I was still asleep. Is there something wrong? Is it Dad?"

"No, Linds, this isn't about your Dad. It's just that I want to come and see your show tonight."

"Why? Are you spying?"

"Linds, don't be ridiculous. I just want to see you – I miss you, that's all."

"Sounds mighty suspicious to me, Jamie. Where are you now?"

"Bregenz. That's why I thought it would be a good idea . There's a train which leaves at twelve forty-five, and arrives at five thirty."

"Well, I suppose you can come if you want to. It'd be nice to have a friendly pair of ears."

I hung up, then immediately rang Geraldine Faulkner's secretary, and told her Angus and Gloria would be coming to the Scarlatti in my place. I told her that he was representing Sergei Rebroff, which made her go all girly and excited. Then I rang Göstl-Saurau's secretary in Salzburg, and fixed myself a ticket for *Cosi*. She made a fuss, and I had to pay full price for my seat. But I had no real alternative, so I gave her my credit card number, and arranged to pick the ticket up from the box office.

I hadn't heard from Evie, so I thought a quick call to Stockencote was necessary, to see whether she'd been able to persuade Albert to go to the doctor. She answered straightaway.

"Evie, it's Jamie. Did he go to the quack?"

"I managed to drag him along yesterday evening. Dr Storey took one look at him, and booked him straight into Peterborough hospital for an MRI scan. The appointment's next Tuesday, the fifteenth, at eleven o'clock. A week's an awfully long time when you've got what Albert's got."

"You're sure it's the big C, then?"

"The look on Storey's face was enough. He's an old friend, you know."

"Can't you get them to move the appointment forward?"

"Apparently not."

"Evie, in the circumstances I think I really have to tell Lindsey."

"Albert won't hear of it. You don't realize how stubborn he is, Jamie. How's Lindsey now? Has she said anything?"

"She says she's not worried, but I'm sure she is deep down."

"As I say, Albert's determined not to upset her. So I suppose we have to respect his wishes. Will you be able to keep it to yourself?"

"Yes, Evie, of course I will. I'll phone you on Tuesday evening next week to see how the scan went. In the meantime if Lindsey asks, we all still think it's sciatica. Agreed?"

"Yes."

"Keep your chin up. It must be terribly hard for you. But he needs you, and you're doing a fantastic job."

"I don't know so much, Jamie. Anyway, I'll keep going, for his sake."

I packed my bag, paid the bill, and left for the short walk to Bregenz station. The train journey through the Alps was spectacular – wonderful weather and sensational views of the mountains. I arrived at Salzburg *Hauptbahnhof* at five-thirty, and had to go straight to Göstl-Saurau's office in the *Großes Festspielhaus*.

Thank God neither Göstl-Saurau nor his secretary was there when I arrived, so I picked up the tickets from a stunning girl in her early twenties, who couldn't have been more charming, or more apologetic when she took the three hundred Euros off my credit card. She was excited that she was talking to Lindsey Templeton's husband, and told me that everyone at the Festival thought Lindsey was this year's star turn. No mention of her vocal problems the other night.

There was an excited buzz around the theatre, just as there had been on the first night. I heard the words 'Lindsey Templeton' on a lot of lips, and most of the speakers wore bright smiles of anticipation. Just once I heard an effete young man say in a waspish voice: "*Lestes Freitag war die Templeton nicht gut*". I tried to tune into his conversation, but he saw me earwigging, and crossly moved his companion away from me.

At about seven I texted Lindsey the following message: *Sweetheart, I arrived safely, and have picked up my ticket. I know you will be as wonderful as you were on the first night. All my love J xxx.*

A moment or two later this arrived: *glad you're here. Have no idea what will come out of my mouth. X.*

In Lindsey's first scene everything seemed fine. Maybe she wasn't taking quite as many risks as she had, but her voice sounded rested and in splendid form. The first hint of any problem came towards the end of the hauntingly beautiful trio *Soave sia il vento*, sung by Fiordiligi, Dorabella and Don Alfonso when they think the boys have gone off to war. During her phone call on Friday night, Lindsey had mentioned that she had had trouble with it. Sure enough, when she got to the long high G sharp which Fiordiligi holds while Alfonso sings passing notes underneath, the old wobble which she had so completely eliminated at College started to creep in, and just before the end of the note she had to sneak a breath. She recovered almost instantly, though, and there was a conspicuous absence of that collective intake of breath which indicates an audience is worried.

When she got to *Come Scoglio*, my heart was in my mouth, but she got through it more or less okay. Perhaps the *coloratura* was a little less precise and jewel-like than it had been, and perhaps the B flat wasn't quite so magnificent, but there were a couple of *bravos* at the end of the aria.

So she reached the interval more-or-less unscathed. I texted her: *darling you're fantastic. Sounds like you're fully recovered.*

She texted back one word only: *bollocks*.

The second half went very much as the first had. Only twice did I clutch the arm of my seat in panic – as she began the final section of *Per Pieta*, when the *coloratura* went awry for a bar or two, and in the middle of *Fra gli Amplessi* – the duet during which she falls in love with Ferrando. In response to his entreaty to her to turn her eyes towards his, she repeats the words *giusto ciel*. Without warning the wobble came back with a vengeance. It was only for a couple of phrases but it threw me completely.

The audience reception at the end was, perhaps, not quite as rapturous as on the first night, but they were enthusiastic nonetheless. I fetched my bag from the luggage check, then went backstage and knocked on Lindsey's door. There was no gaggle of fans waiting for her. No sign of Sergei either, so that was at least something.

"Ja."

"Linds, well done darling. It was wonderful."

"Shut the door, Jamie."

I did so.

"Tell me honestly, what did you think?"

"You were terrific, sweetheart. Just like you always are."

"I want an honest answer."

"Okay then. Ninety-eight per cent of it was of the highest international class. The other two per cent was slightly less good. But it was still okay. The sort of thing other singers get away with all the time."

"You're talking about the Act One trio, the B flat in *Come Scoglio*, and *giusto ciel*?"

"Yes. And those bits weren't too bad. They just weren't quite your best."

"Jamie, I'm going to have to withdraw from the last two shows."

"Nonsense, Linds. You have to realise that almost all of your singing tonight was brilliant. You heard the reception."

"But why should I suddenly get my wobble back after all this time? That's new tonight by the way. In the trio I got worried because I ran out of breath the other night. I think it was the worry which made me wobble. But God knows why I wobbled again in the duet."

"Linds, you're knackered. Anyone would be, after the schedule you've had. And you're pregnant. Don't be too hard on yourself."

Her dresser had walked into the room while I was in the middle of the last speech. I offered up a silent prayer that she hadn't heard me say the word 'pregnant'.

"Cen I heng up zese close?"

"Yes, of course. I shan't be a moment."

Lindsey rapidly undressed, and put on some comfortable clothes. She left her stage make-up intact.

"Thank you, Hildegard," she said. "I am going home now. See you on Thursday."

So she wasn't actually planning to cancel.

"*Auf wiederschauen*, Frau Templeton."

Lindsey gave me her bag to carry. I picked up mine, slung it over the other shoulder, and we went off to the stage door, Lindsey somehow managing to look radiant, and me looking like an overloaded hotel porter.

There was polite applause as we walked into the street. Two or three hands were stretched out towards her, holding autograph books for her to sign. But it was noticeable that there were fewer people than there had been on the first night.

We walked back through the tunnel. Lindsey, who had been quiet ever since we'd left her dressing room, now said to me: "Jamie, do you fancy a Chinese? There's quite a good one just down there, on the corner of Neutorstraße and Rainbergstraße. We used to go there for lunch while we were in the rehearsal room in the mountain."

"Great idea, Linds. Lead on."

They were about to close, but when I mentioned that this was Lindsey Templeton, who had just sung Fiordiligi in the *Haus für Mozart*, they got excited and agreed to stay open. We had the place completely to ourselves.

While we looked at the menus and ordered, we exchanged pleasantries, and avoided controversy. But when the waitress had gone into the kitchen, Lindsey said to me:

"It's serious, you know Jamie. Something's happening to my voice. I don't know what to do about it."

"Sweetheart, you're tired, you're pregnant, and you're stressed. You just wait till we've had a couple of weeks' holiday, then you'll be as good as new."

"That's what I'm counting on, Jamie. Because I don't know what's wrong."

"Just do whatever you need to do to get through the last two *Cosi's*, then we'll take stock in Montpellier. You'll be at home in the autumn, now we've fixed everything for *Fledermaus*. We can go to all your scans together, just like we did with Carly. And antenatal classes, if you want."

"What if Dad's really ill?"

"They're sure he's okay, Linds. Don't worry about him."

The waitress brought us a proper Peking duck. She'd offered it to us as soon as we'd arrived, and it was all that we had ordered. Its skin glistened invitingly. She pulled it apart with two forks, then receded into the far corner of the room.

Lindsey ate ravenously. The sight of it gladdened my heart. I was hungry, too, and between us we almost finished the whole bird. Lindsey had one glass of *Grüner Veltliner*, and I drank the rest of the bottle.

But we never finished the conversation. Nothing about Sergei, nothing about Albert, nothing more about Lindsey's singing. Instead we exchanged pleasantries – Lindsey no doubt as aware as I was that there was an enormous amount left unsaid. I felt as if Damocles' entire armoury was hanging over our heads.

She insisted on paying the bill. I got the sense that she was really pleased I had made the effort to come, although she didn't say so. We walked the short distance back to the flat, and went straight to bed. No sex, but a fair bit of cuddling. Lindsey began to take regular, deep breaths, and to twitch slightly, and I knew she was asleep.

But I lay awake until three o'clock, turning everything over in my mind. If this was the calm, what the hell was the storm going to be like?

27

Lindsey was very sweet when I left, giving me as big a hug as I had had for a very long time.

"Thanks for coming, Jamie. I really appreciate it. Do you really think my singing was okay?"

"Yes, sweetheart, absolutely. Just rest as much as you can for the next thirty-six hours, then I'm sure you'll be right back on form tomorrow night. And even if you sing like you sang last night, everyone will think it's fabulous. I'm counting the days till next Wednesday, when we can all three jet off to the sun for a fortnight."

When I got back I picked Carly up from Emma's house. Emma's Mum was full of how beautifully they had both behaved, although they had clearly spent the entire time in front of a succession of DVDs, some of which sounded highly unsuitable. Nevertheless I thanked her effusively, and brought Carly home.

As soon as we got into the car she started to complain – about the lack of suitable DVDs in our house, about the fact that I wouldn't take her straight back to Salzburg or Stockencote, about everything, really. I tried shouting at her, then I tried bribing her with the offer of a take-away pizza. It was hopeless. At about six o'clock I more or less threw her into the car, and took her to Blockbuster, where we hired six new DVDs. Then I brought her home, shoved a plate of bacon and egg into her hand, and told her to stay put in front of the television and not to disturb me.

We had another battle at bedtime, made worse by the fact that by then I was the wrong side of one of the bottles of *Grüner Veltliner* I had brought back from the Salzburg Airport Shop. It wasn't until ten o'clock that I finally settled down alone in front of the telly.

The phone rang almost immediately. It was Lindsey.

"Jamie, I'm going to have to cancel the second half."

"Why? Are you all right? What's the problem?"

"I can't sing at all, that's the bloody problem."

"Is it any worse than it was on Tuesday?"

"About a million times. The wobble keeps on happening. It's worst in the sustained bits. *Soave sia il vento* nearly didn't happen at all."

"How was *Come Scoglio*?"

"The beginning was terrible, but when it started to move about it got easier. Stupidly I sang a stonking B flat. It's completely unpredictable."

"Has anyone been round? Göstl-Saurau, or any of the management?"

"No. And I haven't asked for anyone yet. I wanted to wait until I'd spoken to you."

"Can you sing me a scale now?"

She sang a two-octave scale from right down in her boots to right up in the stratosphere.

"It sounds great to me, Linds. Are you sure you're not worrying unnecessarily?"

"No. I told you, it's completely unpredictable."

"How do you feel about having a glass of something to get you through?"

"Jamie, I can't possibly do that. It's the slippery slope. *And* I'm pregnant."

"Linds, I don't believe one glass will hurt the baby, and it's not suddenly going to turn you into an alcoholic either. There are special circumstances."

"What special circumstances?"

"You're stressed."

"Well I'm not prepared to risk the health of the baby just to get through the second half of this fucking opera."

Then I had a brainwave. "Linds, I've got a great idea. How long have you got before you've got to go back on stage?"

"About fifteen minutes I think."

"I'm going to give John Standish a ring. He's in tonight."

"What, here in Salzburg?"

"Yes, he's on his annual opera holiday. I ran into him in Bregenz. I bet he'll have his mobile switched on during the interval. I'll ask him if it's okay for you to have a glass of wine."

"Jamie, you're a nutcase."

"I dare say. I'll ring you back in two minutes."

I hung up, then immediately brought Standish's name up on my phone, and pressed the little green telephone. Sure enough, it rang with a European bleep, and he picked it up almost instantly.

"Jamie, is that you?"

"Yes. I've got to be quick. How's Lindsey singing?"

"I've heard her sing better, to be honest."

"How bad is it?"

"Intermittent. There have been a couple of awful bits, but most of it has been okay, and just once or twice she's produced her best sound – the B flat at the end of *Come Scoglio* was unbelievable."

"The problem's in her head, I'm sure of it. Listen, I'll explain more on Monday, but she's pregnant. About seven weeks. Will it harm the baby if she has a glass of champagne to calm her nerves?"

He sniggered. "Much better for her to have some of the little happy pills I've got in my pocket. Don't ask me what they are, but you can trust me, I'm a gynaecologist. They'll kick in almost instantly, get her through the performance, and do no lasting damage either to her or to the baby."

"How are you going to get them to her?"

"My dear boy, I'm already half way to the pass door. I'll blag my way past the security guard. I'll be in her dressing room in about one minute."

"John, you're brilliant. Thank you."

I heard him say something in German, and heard a male voice laugh uproariously. Then I heard John say 'Danke sehr, mein Freund." Shortly afterwards, he came back on the line.

"I take it she's in the number one dressing room?"

"Yup. By the way, don't mention our lunch."

"Mum's the word, dear boy. I'm just getting to the door now."

I heard a knocking, then I heard Lindsey's voice.

"Mr Standish, how wonderful. I can't believe you're here."

"Take these."

"Whatever are they?"

"Nothing that will do you any harm at all, my dear. Or the baby."

"My God, you know about the baby?"

"Your husband's just told me. I think he's still on the other end of this phone."

"Please may I talk to him?"

Lindsey came on the line. "Jamie, are you there?"

"Yes, darling."

"Did you hear any of that?"

"All of it."

"What should I do?"

"Take them, for goodness' sake. You've got your own personal gynaecologist telling you they're okay."

"Are you sure, Jamie?"

"A hundred per cent."

There were some rustling noises, and then Standish came back on.

"All done, Jamie. She's swallowed them down like a good girl."

"Thanks John, you're fantastic. What in those things?"

"Hang on a second, Jamie…"

There was more rustling, and I heard Standish say "you'll be fine now, my dear. You'll see." Then the phone went quiet. After fifteen seconds or so Standish came back on.

"That's it. I'm out of Lindsey's dressing room now. She's going to give the second half a go."

"John you're a genius. Thank you. What the hell's in those pills?"

"Nothing that's going to do her any harm, dear boy. But I bet she'll sing brilliantly in the second half."

When she rang me after the show, she was full of how wonderfully the second half had gone. *Per pieta* and *Fra gli Amplessi* were both faultless, by her own account. Apparently the audience had gone mad at the end, and one wag had shouted, in English, 'Miss Templeton, you are sensational. I love you.'

The weekend was, quite simply, a nightmare. Carly and I both spent the whole of Saturday slumped in front of a succession of DVDs. By the time we got to the Sunday morning I couldn't cope with being at home on my own with her any longer. I persuaded Mum to have us for lunch again, but there was no joy in it. Instead I had too much to drink, and took offence when Carly started telling Mum and Dad what a terrible father I was. The aged parents laughed it off, but I could see in Dad's eyes a slight shadow, which told me he was worried about how things were going in our house. He wasn't the only one.

By way of more DVDs and a take-away on the Sunday night, we made it through to Monday, the day on which I had my lunch appointment with the newly returned John Standish. I had arranged for Carly to go back to Mum and Dad's, which at least meant she would be safe and well fed. I took myself off to Warren Street tube in plenty of time, and set myself to wait for Standish's arrival.

He turned up five minutes late, which was entirely in character. He looked bronzed and relaxed, and was wearing his pinkest, spottiest bow tie.

"Jamie, dear boy, an unalloyed pleasure. Follow me. This place isn't five minutes away."

We walked briskly down Tottenham Court Road, then turned left down University Street. On the left, just where the shops ended, was an unpretentious-looking place called *Gaspard de la Nuit*. We went into a room with gingham tablecloths, and mustard-coloured walls. On a shelf just above where we were sitting was what appeared to be a complete set of champagne bottles, from a nasty little airline-sized quarter bottle right up to what I suspected was a Nebuchadnezzar. Standish saw me looking at them.

"Don't worry, I'm not going to make you buy me one of those. I've got to work this afternoon. Why don't you choose us one bottle of decent claret, and we'll order our food around that?"

I ordered a bottle of Château Palmer 1981, and then we ordered poussin, quite simply roasted. After the waiter had gone off with our order, Standish said:

"Now then, I sense you have something rather weighty on your mind."

"Okay, John, let's plunge in the deep end. Lindsey, as you know, is pregnant. The problem is, I don't think she knows who the father is. She says it's mine, but I can see in her eyes that she's worried. And I know for a certain fact that she has been sleeping with none other than Opera London's sainted benefactor, Sergei Ivanevitch Rebroff."

Gratifyingly, Standish did the nose trick with his claret. A dribble worked its way down his chin, threatening to find its way onto his linen suit. He flicked it away impatiently.

"Bugger me, James. How long's this been going on?"

"It started when she was rehearsing the Salzburg *Cosi* towards the end of June. Sergei has been away on holiday with his family since the end of July, which means that for the moment it's stopped."

"So give me all you know about the dates, dear boy."

The waiter brought us a basket of cut-up baguette. No butter, no plates. When he'd gone I said: "Lindsey and I last had sex on June the twenty-first. That was day fourteen of her cycle. I'm pretty sure she didn't have sex with Sergei until Monday June the twenty-fifth, or day nineteen."

"And how regular has she been recently?"

"Not at all, that's the problem."

"Also no great surprise, given her gynaecological history. When did she discover she was up the duff?"

"She bought a pregnancy test in Salzburg on July the fourteenth, and it was positive. Don't bother to do the maths, it was day thirty-seven. Since then morning sickness has come and gone, but otherwise she seems healthy. Very stressed, however."

"As was quite apparent in the *Haus für Mozart* last Thursday. So what does she want to do?"

"Well, John, as I say she's insistent that the baby's mine. When talking to me, anyway. I think she's desperate for me not to ask too many questions, because she doesn't want me to leave her, and she's determined to keep the baby. I think she sees me as the best person to bring up the child with her, because it will keep the family together. But I also think that, while she recognises the sense of sending Rebroff packing, she has found it exceptionally difficult to do, because she is in love with him."

"And what is the current state of your relationship with her? You behaved immaculately in Bregenz last week. Poor Ulrike was beside herself."

"Ulrike was no real competition, I'm afraid. I still love Lindsey very deeply, and I think she loves me. But we are both finding the stress of her lifestyle very difficult. Discussing anything important necessitates my making an appointment with her weeks in advance."

"Yes, quite. I do see. And I could tell, of course, from the shocking sounds she was making during Act One last week."

"Those happy pills you gave her obviously worked a treat, John. Did you leave any with her?"

"Just enough for the last show, which if I'm not mistaken is tonight."

The waiter arrived with our plates of poussin. The skin was crisp and golden and lightly flecked with herbs, and it sat in a pool of unctuous-looking sauce. The waiter then brought a huge basket of the most delicious-looking little chips. That was it. "Bon appetit," he said.

I took a bite of my poussin, as did Standish.

"Quite delicious," he said. "Now why did Lindsey's voice go wrong so suddenly, do you think? Have there been any fresh developments in the last week or so? I heard she was magnificent in the Prom, for instance."

"Yes, John, I'm afraid there has been a new development. Lindsey's father is ill. His sister, who is a nurse of many years' standing, thinks it's cancer. She managed to drag him to the surgery last week. Apparently the doctor took one look and immediately booked him an MRI scan, which is happening tomorrow morning. Albert's sister is worried that he should have seen someone about it weeks ago, and she says the look on the doctor's face when he did his preliminary examination did nothing to allay her fears."

"And Lindsey knows?"

"Well, no, she doesn't. Her father is determined that whatever is wrong with him he won't tell her until she's finished in Salzburg. But she saw him, after the Prom, as it happens. She was very worried by how he looked. I've been instructed to throw her off the scent, but I have wondered whether her singing breaking down like this isn't a symptom of an underlying worry."

"She's got plenty to worry about."

"Quite. Anyway, I haven't come to the crux of this conversation yet."

"Fire away, dear boy."

"Okay then. I want a DNA test to establish paternity."

"No problemo. Assuming Lindsey agrees, of course."

"John, the last thing she's going to agree to is a paternity test. She won't even admit there's any doubt."

He took a sip of his claret. "It's not possible without her permission."

"But it is, isn't it? Possible I mean. It's just not ethical."

"You're too clever for your own good, Jamie. Yes it is possible, assuming she has an amniocentesis, or a CVS. The tests for Down's syndrome. If I have a sample of your DNA, I can in theory test it against the results of one of these tests. But they are not without risk, and I couldn't recommend her to have one unless she showed an increased likelihood of having a Down's baby."

"When will we know whether she's having one of these tests?"

"We decide about an amnio, which is usually the better option, after her first scan, which takes place around twelve weeks. One of the things we check at the scan is whether there is an increased risk of Down's."

"And if there isn't?"

"Then no amnio, and nothing against which to check your DNA. And in any case, I cannot possibly consider doing this without Lindsey's permission. I'd be struck off."

"I think Lindsey needs to know as much as I do."

"Then discuss it with her, man."

"Can't."

He looked at me crossly, then sighed and took another bite of his poussin, followed by another slow, considered mouthful of wine.

"Look, Jamie, you'd better book her in for this first scan. I take it you would like me to look after her during her pregnancy?"

"Yes, definitely."

"Only babies are not strictly my field , you know. I'm a gynaecologist, not an obstetrician."

"John, we went through all this last time. Of course I'd like it to be you."

"Then in that case I'll be doing her scan. We can usually date conception pretty accurately, you know. It might solve your problem. When will Lindsey be twelve weeks?"

"In about a month's time."

"Then that's the next step, isn't it? At that point, if I feel Lindsey should have an amniocentesis, I will advise you accordingly. What you do after that is up to you. Now if you'll forgive me, I am going to drop this subject, and address something a little more agreeable. I still have half a poussin in front of me, and I propose to give it the attention it deserves. Likewise this extraordinarily complex Château Palmer. Eat, for God's sake, and don't get yourself into such a stew – you still have a wonderfully beautiful wife, and you have just landed one of the plum jobs in British opera. You are, if I may be so bold as to offer an opinion, one lucky fucker. Lunch is on me, by the way. You need cheering up."

I felt better for having unburdened myself, but I thought I had handled the conversation badly. Standish was supposed to emerge from lunch having agreed to help me out, either because he adored me so much, or else because I was going to get him some free tickets for the opera.

228

Willy-nilly, I had to broach the subject of Lindsey's dating scan when she rang later on that evening. After I'd asked her how she'd sung, naturally.

"How was it, sweetheart?"

"Oh, unbelievable, Jamie. I sailed through it. John Standish left me some more of those little pills. I sang brilliantly. The audience went mad at the end."

"So all the problems had disappeared? No wobble or anything?"

"No, it was amazing. I kept waiting for it to happen , but it just didn't."

"So that's it, then. *Così*'s all over."

"Thank God, Jamie. It's been a real bugger."

"Didn't you want to go out with the others for a last-night celebration?"

"No I really didn't, I'm afraid. Göstl-bloody-Saurau turned up and fawned all over everyone. I couldn't stand it. So I made my excuses and left."

"At least you'll get a good night's sleep, then. Listen, there's something else I wanted to ask you. Shouldn't you be having a scan soon?"

"What, for the baby?" She sounded wary, defensive.

"Yes. You should have one at about twelve weeks, shouldn't you?"

"You've suddenly become a bit of an expert, Jamie."

"Not really, sweetheart. I want to look after you, that's all."

"Bollocks, Jamie. I know you – there's something more to this."

"No darling, really there isn't. I could book it for you, if you like. I could ring Denise, Standish's secretary, tomorrow."

"Why are you so keen to do this suddenly?"

"It's just that I'll feel much happier about going to Montpellier if we've got something fixed. Time's marching on, you know."

"Yes, thank you for pointing that out, Jamie. All right, then, go ahead and fix it. But I'm not sure that we should even go to Montpellier. What with Dad, and the baby, and everything."

"Of course we must go. We all need a rest, you especially. And your Dad is insistent."

"Jamie, you're a control freak. But I'm too tired to argue. The only thing I must do is ring Dad tomorrow, before we go, to make sure everything's okay."

"Fine, darling, of course. Now I need to go to bed, and I think you should too. You've got to get that early flight. Get a cab to the airport. No carrying heavy bags."

"All right, then. I'll see you tomorrow. 'Bye."

"Bye, darling."

I went upstairs, and checked on Carly, who'd still been in a fractious mood when I'd brought her back from Mum and Dad's. She was in a deep sleep, looking calm, untroubled, and gut-wrenchingly vulnerable. Not for the first time I asked myself what in hell our behaviour was doing to her.

Never mind, we'd have a lovely time in Montpellier, and it would all sort itself out. Wouldn't it?

INTERLUDE

28

The next morning I rang Standish's office to fix Lindsey's dating scan. Denise answered the phone, and was terribly excited when I told her Lindsey was pregnant.

"Oh, Mr Barlow, what wonderful news. I thought when I spoke to you last week that you might be keeping something from me. The patter of tiny feet – it keeps the world ticking over, doesn't it?"

"Yes, indeed it does, Denise. Does Mr Standish have any time around the fifteenth of September? We reckon that's about twelve weeks.

Yes, your wife can come on the fifteenth itself, to UCH at ten-thirty if that suits."

"Ten-thirty will be fine, Denise, many thanks."

"You're more than welcome, Mr Barlow. Oh dear, I'm so excited I can't speak. I'm going to get Mr Standish to tell me the sex of the baby, so I can start knitting. No, don't worry Mr Barlow, I'm only joking. That would be malpractice, and we wouldn't want any nonsense like that, would we? I'll just have to knit everything yellow."

Oh dear, Denise. We might have no alternative to a bit of malpractice, might we? Given that I needed to know whether the baby was, like Fry's Turkish Delight, full of eastern promise.

The rest of the day was spent feverishly washing clothes and packing suitcases. Lindsey phoned Albert as soon as she got home, and he told her that he'd been to the doctor, who'd just said again that it was sciatica, and that he had nothing to worry about. He was working as hard as ever, although he hoped to take a bit of time off once the harvest was done and dusted.

232

During the same call Lindsey had spoken to Evie, in an effort to confirm Albert's story. Evie had simply said Albert was fine, and that we were to go away and enjoy our holiday.

Lindsey, clearly exhausted, appeared to be satisfied with this. Underneath, I was sure she was deeply worried – indeed I was pretty certain that was the reason for her continuing vocal problems – but she seemed enthusiastic about our trip.

She and Carly both went to bed soon after nine. My turn to ring Stockencote.

"Jamie, thank goodness it's you," said Evie. "Albert's just gone up to bed. Lindsey can't hear this conversation, can she?"

"No, no, Evie, she's gone to bed too. Is it bad news?"

"The worst. Albert had his MRI scan. He's got prostate cancer. But the really terrible thing – the thing I've been dreading – is that he's got secondaries. There's one in his spine, and another in his brain God only knows why he's had no symptoms. The consultant talked half-heartedly about chemotherapy, but he thinks there may be no point in putting him through it, just to buy an extra couple of months. Jamie, they think it'll be all over within weeks."

Christ.

"Evie, for God's sake, surely it's worth doing something to try and cure him. He's so young."

"That's what I said to the consultant. He just looked at his feet, and said he was terribly sorry, but in all honesty it was really too late. Then he asked Albert what he wanted to do."

"And?"

"Albert smiled, believe it or not, and said: 'I'm a stupid bugger not to have listened to you, Evie. Anyway, I'm not going through all that business of losing my hair. It's the one thing I've got left.' Then he said no thank you very much, he'd save the NHS's money, and go home to die, if that was all right with the doctor. The consultant looked at me, and said could I cope, and I had to say I was a trained nurse and had done it far too many times before. That was it, Jamie. We came home, and we had our tea, and he went to bed. I've no idea how much longer he'll even be able to get himself to bed. At least he took his pills like a good boy. I was afraid he'd turn his nose up at those, too."

"What else did he say?"

"That there's one thing that's more important to him than anything else, and that's Lindsey. He insists she's not told until she gets back from

233

holiday. He says he'll have plenty of time to make his peace with her then."

"Bloody hell, Evie, does that mean I'm supposed to keep the secret, and have a jolly time for two weeks?"

Her reply was surprisingly vehement.

"Just do it, Jamie, do you understand? This is your Waterloo."

"She'll be furious when we tell her."

"She'll come round. And Albert's right, it won't make any difference in the end. I'm not taking no for an answer. When are you leaving?"

"Tomorrow morning, first thing."

"Then get yourself to bed, Jamie. And go and have a bloody good time."

"Will you be all right, Evie?"

"As long as you look after that girl, I'll be fine. Now get off the phone before I lose control."

Carly was excited about her holiday. She was looking forward to seeing Mme Dupuis's eleven-year-old daughter Sylvie – they got on like a house on fire, making light of the language barrier as only children can. I had high hopes that Carly might be speaking a fair amount of French by the time we got home.

Lindsey had a brittle smile on her face from the moment she got out of bed. She was determined to enjoy herself. To my relief she didn't mention Albert once.

There is a song in a fifties British musical called *Salad Days*, which begins with the words 'Summer, and sunshine, and falling in love', and goes on to describe a girl's idyllic days at university. The song came into my mind as we disembarked from the plane at Montpellier airport. The heat seemed to bounce off the runway and the sea and the sky were the colour of sapphires.

As we waited to collect our bags, I reached out for Lindsey's hand, and to my astonishment she didn't pull it away. We walked through customs, and made our way to the Europcar desk.

We hired a beautiful black Audi A4, and drove the short distance to Castelnau-le-Lez. The atmosphere in the car reminded me of other holidays, when our lives were simpler and less stressful. Carly was chuntering away happily about all the wonderful things she was going to do with Sylvie, and for once it didn't seem to be necessary to tell her to shut up. We arrived at Mme Dupuis' villa in as sunny a mood as I could remember. Although the hideous prospect of what I knew we had to face when we got back kept butting in to spoil my mood.

Mme Dupuis was all smiling Gallic charm. The moment the three of us had unpacked our bags she insisted we join her in the big house for lunch. She had prepared it specially, she said, to welcome back her favourite guests.

She had cooked *beignets de fleurs de courgettes*. Carly asked what they were. To my amazement she said she liked the idea of eating flowers, and enjoyed them as much as the rest of us did. This certainly impressed Sylvie, who had presumably been told that British kids only liked fish and chips and McDonalds.

Then came a *Reblochon* cheese, in perfect condition, and finally a *tarte au citron* from the local *boulangerie*, which sent both Lindsey and Carly into raptures.

Lindsey had felt a bit nauseous first thing, but with our arrival in France her sickness seemed to disappear. It was an idyllic lunch, and was followed by a luxurious siesta, while Carly and Sylvie went off up the steps to play by the pool, and later in it.

At about five o'clock Lindsey, who hadn't indulged in the pink *Côteaux d'Aix-en-Provence* which Mme Dupuis had produced for lunch, drove us both to the huge *Carrefour* at Lattes, and we stocked up on cheese and *saucisson*, and *jambon de Bayonne*. We got home to find Carly had been whisked off into the big house by Sylvie, and that Mme Dupuis was going to give her some supper. Lindsey and I opened our bottles – pink *Bandol* for me and *Badoit* for her, and watched the sun go down. We dined off our haul from *Carrefour*, and for the first time in months all was right with the world.

While Carly was out, Lindsey took the opportunity to broach a subject which had been at the back of my mind for a while now.

"Jamie, when are we going to tell Carly I'm pregnant?"

"Funny you should mention that. I've been leaving it till we got here. Why don't I tell her tomorrow?"

"Good idea. I've been hoping you'd do it. You'll be better than me if she asks any awkward questions."

"We're still working on the assumption that it's mine, aren't we?"

"I've told you, Jamie, it can't be anyone else's. Don't get me started."

The atmosphere was a bit tense for a few minutes, but then we drifted back into our sense of wellbeing, and when Carly came back from the house we went to put her light out together. Lindsey and I went to our room shortly afterwards.

We both climbed into bed stark naked, and I tried an exploratory kiss. Lindsey pulled away from me gently, and said:

"Sorry Jamie. I've gone right off sex. They say a lot of women do when they're pregnant. How about spoons?"

So I cuddled up to her back, and we both fell into as blissful a sleep as I'd had for months.

The garden looked ravishing at eight o'clock when Carly and I walked through it to the little *boulangerie* where Mme Dupuis had bought the previous day's *tarte*. Carly had been practising her French, and was determined to order the bread herself.

"Bonjour, ma petite," said the rotund lady in the *boulangerie*.

"Trois pains au chocolat, deux croissants et une baguette, s'il vous plaît."

"Mais oui ma petite, bien sûr." The lady smiled indulgently, first at Carly and then at me. "Avec ça?"

Carly looked at me for help. "Non, merci," I said. I doubted if it was right, but the woman seemed to understand. She looked at Carly again, then reached into the glass-fronted cabinet and picked out a little round *brioche*, covered in big white dots of sugar.

"C'est offert."

I didn't know what that meant, but she appeared to be giving it to us, so I said "merci, madame," and said to Carly: "say thank you to *madame*, sweetheart."

"Merci madame," said Carly, with a beatific smile on her face.

We paid and left the shop. As we walked back through the garden to our pavilion, two of Mme Dupuis's army of tortoises were humping right in the middle of the little path.

"What are Sarko and Ségolène doing, Daddy?" They had different coloured dots of paint on their shells, to tell them apart, and she knew all their names. It was Mme Dupuis's little joke to call them after French politicians.

"They're making babies, darling."

"Eeeuu. That's gross."

"No, it's not gross, darling. It's just like what people do when they want to make babies. Although it must be quite difficult for tortoises, what with their shells and everything."

Carly was dumbstruck. She watched the two reptiles making what appeared to be very uncomfortable love. Sarko was making the most extraordinary noise – half squeak half grunt – in time with his rhythmic thrusting.

"Do you and Mummy do that sometimes?"

"Yes, sweetheart, sometimes. That's how we made you."

"Did you squeak like Sarko?"

"Not exactly, darling. But a bit."

"Eeeuu. More gross."

"Carly, did you know we've just made another one? Baby I mean, not tortoise."

"Can I see it?"

"It's in Mummy's tummy, darling. You're going to have a brother or a sister."

"Cool. When?"

"Next year, sweetheart. A few months after Christmas."

"Oh, wow. If Mummy's in Salzburg or somewhere, can we go and see it when it's born?"

"She'll be at home, I promise."

"That's awesome, Daddy. Can I have the day off school?"

"Wait and see, Carly. It'll be exciting, won't it?"

"Yes, Daddy, it'll be brill."

We watched Sarko and Ségolène at it for a bit longer.

"Daddy?"

"Yes."

"Does this mean Mummy loves you better than Uncle Sergei?"

"Yes, darling, I'm sure she does."

"Can I still go on his private plane?"

"Well, maybe not, sweetheart. I don't think Mummy's going to see quite as much of Uncle Sergei after we get back. So you'll have to put up with my clapped-out old Passat, like the rest of us mere mortals."

For the first week of our holiday we were in an idyll without end. Days spent rubbing factor ten all over ourselves, and dipping into the pool, were followed by evenings of quiet self-indulgence, and nights of chaste closeness.

And then came week two, and the ghastly dawning realisation that soon we were going to have to face up to the problems that awaited us in

England. Lindsey became more tense as the week wore on, as no doubt did I.

Our final evening was marked by another of our Montpellier rituals – dinner in our pavilion for Mme Dupuis and Sylvie. In the early days it had included Monsieur Dupuis, but he had long since flown the coop into the arms of an air hostess from Perpignan. Sylvie's brother had also come occasionally, but he'd never much liked it, and in any case had now left to go to College. So it was just the five of us for supper, which consisted as usual of a gastronomic miracle performed by Lindsey with the left-overs from our fridge. She was a fabulous cook, whenever her absurd schedule allowed her time to prove it, and on this occasion we had figs and *Jambon de Bayonne*, followed by a prawn *risotto* into which Lindsey had emptied nearly a bottle of white wine, and which was as delicious as anything we had eaten all fortnight, or all year come to that.

Finally there was a huge *salade de fruits*, made from everything that was left in our fruit bowl. It occasioned a lot of interest from the local wasps, which sent Carly into near-hysterics, but this was a godsend for me, as I was allowed to smoke to keep them away. The evening finished with coffee and some *petits fours* from our lady in the *boulangerie*.

Ever since boarding school, I had found the end of a holiday almost unbearably traumatic, and this one was worse than any I could remember. Mme Dupuis stood at the gate waving us off, in floods of tears. Sylvie was crying too, and so was Carly, who was complaining about being dragged away from the people she loved, and having to go back to our horrible house in horrible London.

But the worst thing was Lindsey. No histrionics at all from her, just tight-lipped outrage. And who could blame her? She was going home to face a life where all the certainties had been taken away from her. She was desperately worried about her voice – I knew this from the odd comment she had let slip during the fortnight. She was about to find out that her father had six weeks to live. She was pregnant, and although the morning sickness appeared to have stopped, she still had to face physical discomforts and worries of which I as a mere male could have no conception.

And on top of all that her former lover, and possible father of her child, was about to emerge from his self-imposed Russian purdah and inflict himself once again on all of our lives. What would Lindsey do if Sergei made a bid to become the new Mr Templeton? Because I had a nasty suspicion that had been his plan all along.

238

As we got on the plane we must have seemed to our fellow passengers a sad, depressed little family. Carly was going back to school, and Lindsey and I were off home to begin yet another bloody opera. Johann Strauss's *Die Fledermaus*, or in English *The Bat*, is suffused with a champagne spirit. Maybe this spirit would re-invigorate our lives. But I somehow doubted it.

ACT 3: DIE FLEDERMAUS

29

In a fit of irresponsibility I hadn't taken my mobile to Montpellier. Lindsey had hers, so had there been a real crisis with her Dad Evie could have contacted her on that. But I was determined to avoid communications from Angus, or Max Polgar, or Tatyana, or just about anybody, really. Being out of touch was bliss. By God, I paid for it when I got back, though.

We had had a hideous Bank Holiday Monday journey, including a fist-fight on the plane, between a drunk Englishman and an incomprehensible but very assertive Spanish air steward. Lindsey and I had closed ranks round Carly, who had been furious because our protective efforts blocked her view of what was going on.

I switched the phone on as soon as I walked into the flat. It rang instantly with a voicemail message. Well, eight voicemail messages, in fact. Five were from Angus, in various stages of inebriation and temper. Their gist was: (a) when the fuck are you ever going to switch your phone on, you tosser? And (b) do you realise the closing date for applications for the Opera London jobs is the first of September? In one of the messages I heard Gloria's voice in the background say very clearly, "Angus, you sex god, come back to bed and let me lick that gorgeous lollipop of yours," which at least confirmed that their relationship was still intact.

Then there was a message from Miep, in Amsterdam, checking that we still wanted Saskia to au pair for us, now Lindsey wasn't coming to do *Eugene Onegin*. I rang her straight back. Yes, we were very much looking forward to Saskia's arrival, I said. Miep was thrilled, and told me that

Saskia, too, was looking forward to her exciting year. I promised to pick her up from Stansted at two thirty on the Sunday afternoon.

That left two messages from Grace, who had arrived back from Tenerife on the day we left for France. The first was chatty and relaxed, but the second sounded panicky. There was a crisis, she said, and if there was any way I was picking up my messages before I got home, please could I phone her back immediately?

There was no point in ringing her now – no-one would be at the theatre on a Bank Holiday. So I tried to keep my stress level down, telling myself there was nothing I could do before the next day, and to stop worrying.

There was, let's face it, a more pressing problem. A matter of life and death, in fact. So when Lindsey had gone upstairs for a siesta I dialled Albert's number.

He answered himself, sounding perfectly normal. For an idiotic second I thought it had all been some ghastly mistake.

"Jamie, lovely to hear from you. Are you safely back in Blighty?"

"We certainly are, Albert. How are you?"

"I've been better, to be perfectly honest. But there we are, that's life, eh? There's no new news, if that's what you're asking. Now then, the thing I want to know is did the lass make you tell her, or did you manage to resist the pressure?"

"I resisted, Albert. She thinks you've got sciatica."

"Well done, Jamie lad. I'm proud of you, and enormously grateful. But it leaves us with the problem of who the hell's going to break it to her? It's the worst part, you know. Having to tell people, I mean."

"Albert, it's your call. If you want me to tell Lindsey, then it's the least I can do. But if you feel you'd rather tell her yourself, that's fine too."

Albert heaved an enormous sigh. "Frankly, Jamie, I don't think I can face it. I'm sorry to be so pathetic, but if you're offering then I'm going to accept gratefully."

"Right you are, then. No time like the present. She be up there, you know, first thing tomorrow morning."

"When does she start work again?"

"Monday of next week. She's in London, which I must say is a mercy."

"Oh, Jamie, that's wonderful news. I thought she was going to Amsterdam."

"She was. Last-minute change of plan. She's doing *Fledermaus* at Opera London. Thank God."

"Yes, Jamie, thank God as you say. So you'll tell her now?"

"Yes, I'll tell her now. And Albert…"

"Yes, Jamie?"

"I don't quite know how to say this. It's just that I'm so sorry. About you. About it all."

"I know you are, Jamie boy. It's kind of you to say so. Now off you go and do your son-in-law's duty. Good luck."

Lindsey was flat out on our bed. She looked peaceful, with her black hair spread out around her head. Her face was just beginning to fill out, as pregnant women's faces do.

I shook her shoulder gently, and said her name quietly. She opened her eyes in an instant, and said: "it's Dad, isn't it?"

How in God's name did she know? "Yes it is darling. I've just spoken to him. I'm afraid you're going to have to prepare yourself for a shock."

She just stared at me, wide-eyed.

"Linds, your Dad's terribly ill. He's got cancer."

"I knew it. I knew when I saw him at the Prom. How bad is it?"

"It couldn't be worse, darling. He's got secondary tumours in his spine and brain. The doctors don't give him longer than a couple of months."

She stared at me again. Then, very slowly, a tear began to emerge from her right eye. It trickled down her cheek. I reached out to hold her hand, but she pulled it away from me.

"When did you know, Jamie?"

Shit.

"I knew before we went away, darling."

She looked at me with a mixture of astonishment and hatred. "You BASTARD. How COULD you let me go away on holiday knowing my father was dying?"

"Linds, Albert insisted. He said the most important thing to him in the world was that you should have a decent holiday. Evie made me promise I wouldn't say anything till we got back."

Lindsey was crying properly now. I didn't know what to say. What the hell *do* you say when you've just told someone their father's got two months to live?

The best I could come up with was: "the doctor mentioned chemotherapy, but in the end they all agreed that it's too late. He should have gone to see someone months ago. I'm so sorry, Linds."

Without another word she heaved herself up from the bed. Gone was the serenity of sleep. She went downstairs, and picked up the phone. I stood beside her while she dialled, and I heard her say: "Dad, I've just heard. I'm coming now. Don't say anything else." And she put the phone down.

"Jamie, I'm getting in the car now to drive up to Dad's."

Carly was standing in the doorway. She'd been watching a DVD in the other room, and had obviously been disturbed by the commotion.

"Where are you going, Mummy?" She looked really worried.

"I'm going to see Grandad. He's very ill, I'm afraid, sweetheart."

"Is it his back?"

Lindsey shot me another look. "Oh my God, don't tell me you told her too?"

"No, darling, it's just that she noticed he had a bad back when she was staying there last month."

"Couldn't you just have TOLD me, Jamie?"

Carly looked as if she too was dangerously close to crying. "STOP SHOUTING, Mummy," she screamed.

"Yes, of course darling, I'm sorry," said Lindsey. "Listen, maybe you'd like to come with me to see Grandad? We need to go and tell him how much we love him."

"Can Daddy come, too?"

"No, Carly, he can't. Now do you want to come, or don't you?"

"Yes please, Mummy."

"In that case we'll go upstairs right now, and pack some bags. Then we'll get in the car. We'll be there in time for supper."

They disappeared upstairs, and I heard noises as they packed. Within ten minutes they were back.

"We're going, now," said Lindsey as she picked the car keys up from the hook in the hall. "I've no idea when we'll be home."

I made as if to give her a hug. She shrugged me off, then made for the door.

Carly was cowering behind her. She said: "will you be all right, Daddy?"

"Yes, darling, I'll be fine. I'll give you a ring."

It was at this moment that Carly began to cry in earnest. Whether it was the sight of her daughter weeping so piteously I don't know, but to my astonishment and huge relief Lindsey suddenly turned towards me and said:

"Jamie, I'm sorry. I'm a selfish cow. You don't deserve this. And I know you only did what you thought was best. But I'm afraid I absolutely can't cope with it. Any of it."

They disappeared through the front door, and Lindsey shut it behind her. That was it. They were gone.

Unable to think of anything useful to do, I sat and watched a bit of a one-day international on the telly. We'd won the Ashes, and as usual this afterthought competition was a complete anticlimax. I watched them all playing tip and run in their coloured pyjamas for a while, then got bored and started flicking between the channels. *Big Brother* was reaching its so-called climax, which seemed an excellent reason to turn the TV off.

I picked up the phone and dialled Angus's number.

"How sweet of you to take your mobile to France with you," he said. "I've so enjoyed getting all your news."

"Angus, I needed a break, right? I bet no-one's really missed me."

"Well I have, darling. Sergei's back in town from next Monday, having renewed his marriage vows in Mother Russia. I think we should meet and talk strategy before then."

"Good idea, Gussie. What about tonight?"

"I expect it could be arranged. Where shall we go?"

"Could you face coming round here, do you think? I'm all on my own. I'll nip out to Sainsbury's and get us a couple of steaks."

"Top hole. I've got a couple of bottles of cracking Châteauneuf du Pape. Shall I bring them?"

"You must have read my mind. Seven o'clock okay?"

"Splendid. Where's the Deev, by the way? Off on some nice little earner?"

"I wish. She's gone to her Dad's – he's very ill – and she's taken Carly with her. It's all a bit sudden. I'm rather lonely."

"Well I'll pop over and cheer you up. Make sure you buy decent steak."

Angus was relaxed after spending August at home with Gloria, whose appetite for sex had apparently reached new heights.

"She's doing splendidly, actually, Jamie. I've been faithful for all of four months. But what about you? I mean you were ridiculously well-behaved in Bregenz. I hope the Deev appreciated your sacrifice?"

"Good God, Gussie, I wouldn't dream of telling her about Ulrike, or whatever her name was. I mean I kissed her, that's bad enough."

"Oh, for Christ's sake, Jamie, this is the twenty-first century. No-one does monogamy these days. Especially not in our business. If Lindsey doesn't fancy doing the deed at the moment, go and get it elsewhere. She has, after all. What about that little Grace?"

"Get thee behind me, Gussie."

"Well, I must say it's a surprise, but I suppose if you want to do a spot of uphill gardening it's up to you. But not with me, I'm afraid. What about Jason? He seems amenable."

"Very funny. But in all seriousness, I couldn't possibly do anything with Grace. It'd be a bit disloyal, with Lindsey off ministering unto her dying father."

"Look, Jamie she's been bloody disloyal to you, hasn't she? It's time you returned the compliment."

I found myself disturbingly intrigued by the idea, and as we got deeper into the *Châteauneuf du Pape*, it got even more attractive. So in order to take my mind off it, I asked Angus what I had to do to get the official nod for the General Administrator's job. Apparently I needed something called an 'application pack.' It seemed a ludicrous charade, but Angus was insistent that everything had to be done by the book, so I wrote a letter on the computer, shoved it in an envelope, and left it on the hall table to take into work the next morning.

Next I asked him about the Scarlatti piece he and Gloria had seen in Bregenz. He was wildly enthusiastic. The production had been superb, even if the music had been a bit thin. We decided that it would be one of our first imports when it came to regime change at Opera London. This led us to an in-depth discussion about the artistic direction we planned to take.

By the time we'd finished the *Châteauneuf* and opened a rather nasty Australian shiraz I happened to have lying around, we had ambitious plans for a new *Ring* cycle and the complete works of Benjamin Britten, plus a retrospective of nineteenth-century Russian opera which we thought would keep Sergei happy.

Lindsey featured strongly in our plans. I had some qualms about the number of foreign engagements I was going to have to cancel on her behalf. I was also privately worried that her voice would never come right, although Angus didn't seem to have been informed that she'd had problems in Salzburg, and I wasn't about to let on.

At eleven o'clock Angus decided he'd had enough. He called a taxi, and after five minutes or so it arrived. On his way out he said:

"Listen, Jamie, if you and Grace fancy a joint trip with Gloria and me to a discreet little club I know in Fitzroy Square, just tip me the wink. We could have a magnificent time."

And he rolled down the path and climbed into his taxi.

When I got into work at ten the next morning, Grace was already there. She was tanned, and looked absolutely ravishing. I aimed a kiss at her lips, but she turned her face away and only let me get as far as her cheek. She was seriously cross.

"Bloody hell, Jamie, what do you think the game is? I spent the whole of Friday fielding calls from Olivier Leclerc and his agent. Why on earth didn't you have your phone switched on?"

"Oh. Sorry, Grace. Nice to see you too, Grace."

"No, but honestly, Jamie, what in hell were you thinking of?"

"It's just that I needed a complete break from everything..."

"You have to stay in touch, for God's sake. That's what mobile phones are for."

"What's Leclerc getting his knickers in a twist about, anyway?"

"He wouldn't tell me. Insisted on speaking to you personally. He's an arsehole."

"Well, that's something we can agree on, at least. You'd better give me his number. I'll ring him now."

I rang his mobile, and after a couple of bleeps which told me he was somewhere in Europe, he answered.

"Leclerc."

"Olivier, it's Jamie Barlow."

"Oh my God, where ze fuck 'ave you been? Hi needed to talk to you on Friday."

"Yes, I'm sorry, Olivier. I was on holiday."

"Weez your wife?"

Irritating little sod. "Yes, with my wife and daughter, as a matter of fact."

"Eet eez your wife 'oo eez ze problem. Last week Yvonne Umfreville tells me zat Leendzi sing Rosalinde in my *Fledermaus*. Hi 'ave never agreed. Hi sought we were 'aving Hevangeline Bolls-er. Zen I 'ear Bolls sing Tatyana een Hamsterrdamm." His accent always got worse when he was cross.

"Yes, that's right. We were having problems with Miss Bolls's work permit. Ton de Wit thought the Dutch Government would be more helpful than the British. So the two sopranos swapped roles."

"But Hi was not consulted."

"No, that was bad of me. I apologise. We were very short of time."

"You 'ave a beeg problem now, Jemms. Becozz-er Hi do not accept your wife een zees role."

"Oh, come now, Olivier. Lindsey has just had an enormous success as Fiordiligi in Salzburg. She will be perfect for Rosalinde."

"Hi know about Salzburg. Hi was zere, doeeng *Ascanio in Alba*. Hi went to see *Cosi*. Leendzi was sheet-er."

"Which performance did you see?"

"Ha. So you know some of zem were bad? Heet was near ze end-er, but not ze last one. A Sursday, Hi sink "

"Lindsey had a terrible journey back from London after the Prom performance of *Figaro*. I'm afraid it knocked her for six. The performance that night, and to some extent the subsequent shows, suffered as a result."

"Hand zis is your fault, one guesses?"

"Well, it was an unfortunate clash of dates, and she had exceptionally bad luck on the journey. But the whole thing was agreed in advance with Graf von Göstl-Saurau."

"Hi do not expect zis kind of treatment. When Miss Danieli was engaged originally, and Miss Bolls also, Hi was consulted. Not zis time."

"No, and for that I am most extremely sorry Olivier. But you cannot surely argue with Lindsey singing the role? She is one of the biggest stars in the world."

"Ze important sing 'ere eez zat you 'ave be'aved hextremmly badly. Let me assure you, Jemms, heef I succeed in getting ze job of Museec Director, Hi weel not tolerate zis kind of sing. You, for example, weel no longer 'ave any job een my organisation."

"I am sorry to hear you do not value my talents, Olivier. I would have been more worried about losing my job if Mr Knipe had not resigned. As it is, I am confident that Mr Rebroff will see to my continued employment.

He laughed, very unpleasantly. "Meester Rebroff seem to like severals member of your family very much indeed, no?"

"I'm not sure what you mean Olivier. But I think we should address the issue in hand. I am not going to sack Lindsey, and I'm afraid she is most unlikely to withdraw. Of course we are thrilled that you are applying for the job of Music Director. I am sure that in the current circumstances you are keen to help the Company in any way you can. I can only ask that in all our best interests you agree to accept her."

There was an audible intake of breath at the other end of the phone. "Ha. You are slightly more clever zan I sought. In ze circonstance Hi weel agree to Mees Templeton eef, hand onnly eef, 'er voice eez now back to eets proper sound. I promise you, 'owever, zat eef she cannot seeng, Hi will be een your office *tout de suite*, and Hi weel be very hangry." Then the line went dead. The little tosser had hung up on me.

Further confirmation that people were talking about Lindsey and Sergei. But that wasn't the problem – another hideous possibility had occurred to me.

If Lindsey was in as shaky a state mentally and vocally as I feared she might be, how likely was it that she would back out of *Fledermaus* altogether? I could see her digging her heels in about leaving Albert during his dying days, and staying at Stockencote for the duration. Leclerc would be happy, but God alone knew who we would find to sing such a crucial role at such short notice. And the opera business was a very unfriendly place when someone was perceived as having vocal problems.

It was all much too stressful. I contented myself with sending a round-robin email confirming Lindsey's engagement to sing the role, just in case there was anyone else I'd forgotten to tell about it. Then I called over to Grace, and offered to take her out to lunch. She flashed her most radiant smile, said that she was sorry to have been such a bitch, and that she'd love to.

We went to Caffe Italia. I bought us both bacon and avocado sandwiches and fruit smoothies. She looked, as I believe I may have mentioned, drop-dead gorgeous.

"So tell me about your holiday, Gracie.," I said. "You look fantastic, by the way. The break's done you good."

"Thanks, Jamie. Yes, it was great. Terrific." Very guarded.

"Are you still angry about the phone business?"

"What? Oh, no not really. I mean I was furious on Friday, but I do understand. You needed a break as much as I did. More, probably. How was it by the way? How are things with Lindsey?"

"It was fantastic, actually. We had two great weeks, and unwound completely. We avoided anything controversial, and just enjoyed the sun and the food."

"Oh, Jamie, thank God for that. You two need each other. How's the pregnancy going?"

"Much better. The morning sickness seems to have stopped." I took a bite of my sandwich. It tasted like cardboard and slime. "Look, Grace, I asked you to lunch to talk about a couple of really important things. Firstly, I need you to organise me. Since all this business with Sergei started, my brain's gone like a sieve. As you implied this morning, I can't go on doing this sort of thing if I'm going to be General Administrator. No-one will take me seriously."

She smiled. "Don't worry," she said. "I'll look after you. If you're going to the top, I'm going with you. There's something else, though, isn't there?"

"You know there is, Gracie. I've missed you like hell. I want to know if, well, if you've missed me."

She took a sip of her smoothie. "Too late, Jamie, I'm afraid. I can't say I haven't thought about it. But the thing is, I've met someone else."

"Well that, Grace, is an absolute bugger. Who's the lucky bloke, then?"

"He's a solicitor. He's thirty-two, divorced, lives in Clapham and works in Holborn. I met him in Tenerife, and he looks like Brad Pitt."

"Well, good for you, Grace. I mean really, well done. You deserve someone nice. It's just a bloody shame it's not me."

"Jamie, stick to that wife of yours. Where is she now? She starts rehearsing with us on Monday, doesn't she?

"She's up in Rutland with her Dad, who's very ill. I don't think she's speaking to me."

"But I thought you said the holiday went well."

"It did. Except that we ignored all our problems. Including the fact that her Dad was ill, which I knew but she didn't."

"That'll have made her really happy, Jamie."

"It wasn't my fault. Her Dad insisted she finish her holiday before she was told."

"In that case she'll come round. Give her time. But do not, and I repeat do not, have an affair with anyone else in the meantime."

"That's not what Angus says."

"Angus Lennox is a great conductor, Jamie. He is anything but a great human being."

We finished our smoothies, and left most of our nasty sandwiches. Just before we left the café, I said:

"You promise you won't desert me then, Grace? I mean I know you'll be with your new bloke and all that. But I'm going to need you more than ever."

"Don't you worry, Jamie. I'm in this for the duration. Just remember one thing – Lindsey is the most important thing in your life, and you have to do everything you can to keep her. For the sake of you both, and for Carly and the baby. I'm not going to get into bed with you, which is probably a very good thing for both our sakes. But I may just be able to save your marriage."

30

With Lindsey and Carly away, I was left on my own in the house to prepare for Saskia's arrival. So for the rest of the week I spent the evenings giving the house a thorough clean, and making the spare room habitable.

I hadn't spoken to Albert since the diagnosis was confirmed, and time was passing at an alarming rate, so on Friday night I took my courage in my hands and phoned Stockencote.

It was Evie who picked up the phone. Apparently things had progressed much faster than anyone had feared. Albert was allowing Evie to dress him in the mornings, and bring him downstairs for lunch, then having a siesta in front of the telly in the afternoons, before eating a bit of tea at five o'clock, and retreating back to his bedroom for the night.

Carly had distracted them, Evie said, which had been good for them all. She didn't seem to understand how ill he was, and was as busy as always helping Gordon around the farm. She was also getting on really well with Cedric, the pony, and Fliss had been organised to come in every day to teach her.

She went on: "But Jamie, I'm terribly worried about Lindsey. She keeps sneaking off to distant parts of the house to make phone calls. She's gone for hours sometimes. It's not you she's been ringing, is it?"

"I haven't spoken to her since she arrived, Evie."

"No, I was afraid of that. Jamie, I don't suppose you could come up, by any chance? We need to see a fresh face. And Albert would love it."

"I was hoping you'd say that. In any case Lindsey starts rehearsals in London on Monday, and Carly starts school on Tuesday, so I've got to think about getting them home. What about if I get there in time for lunch tomorrow? Can you cope with another mouth to feed?"

"Oh, yes, of course, that's sounds wonderful. About twelve o'clock?"

"That's fine with me. Can someone pick me up from Peterborough station at about eleven thirty?"

"I'll ask Lindsey. It'd do her good to get out."

"That's terrific, Evie, thanks. I'll text her the arrival time of the train."

"I can't tell you how pleased we'll all be to see you, Jamie."

Very possibly true, in Evie's case, and in Albert's. As for Carly, I had my doubts. And we'd find out how Lindsey felt about it in the car, wouldn't we?

When I emerged from the front of the station there was my crappy old Passat, waiting for me in the short-term parking area opposite the station. Lindsey was sitting in the driver's seat. I went over and put my bag in the boot, then opened the passenger door and climbed in.

"Hallo, darling," I said. No reply. I tried to give her a kiss. Nothing doing.

"How's your Dad?"

"Dying."

"Look, Linds, I want to help in any way I can, you know."

Her face softened, ever so slightly. "I know, Jamie. But there's not much you can do, is there? Unless you've brought a miracle cure with you from The Big City."

"Do you want me to drive back?"

"Yes," she said, "yes, please. That would be kind." We each opened our doors, and swapped sides. As we passed each other behind the boot of the car there was a tiny pause, and I thought she might be about to say something. But her eyes dropped to the floor, and she walked past me.

We spent the half-hour journey to Stockencote in total silence.

Evie was waiting for us.

"Albert's in the study. I've lit the fire because he's feeling the cold terribly. Will you forgive me, Jamie, while I go and sort out lunch?"

Albert's study was where they always sat in the evenings, when they didn't want to open up the big, formal drawing room. It was more than just a study. At one end of the room there was a Victorian desk and swivel chair. At the other were three armchairs gathered around a fire, with a television in the corner.

Albert, who was sitting in his favourite chair, was straight-backed and smiling, but had the look of a man in permanent pain. His skin, which was almost translucent, was hanging in folds from his jaw.

"Jamie, lad, how wonderful of you to make time for an old sod like me. First things first, dear boy. I hear congratulations are in order."

"What? Oh, you mean the baby." I looked at Lindsey. She was looking at the floor.

"Yes, thanks, it's fantastic news, isn't it?"

"The best. I'm over the moon."

"And what about you, Albert? How are you feeling?"

"Pretty bloody, if I'm honest. But never mind. The sun's over the yardarm. Let's lose no time in celebrating. What are you having?"

"Gin and tonic would be nice, Albert, thanks."

Lindsey looked up at me. She looked absolutely stricken.

"Lindsey, lass," said Albert, "don't look at your young man like that. He's just come all the way from the Smoke. He needs a drink." He turned to me. "You'll have to get it yourself, I'm afraid, Jamie. Gilt, it is, don't forget. G. I. L. T. Gin, Ice, Lemon, Tonic. And check the tonic's fizzy. It has to be fizzy, or you might as well be drinking meths."

I went over to the tray where the bottles and glasses were set out, along with an ice bucket and a little saucer of lemon slices.

"Anyone else fancy one?"

"Oh bugger it, why the hell not?" said Albert. "Go easy on the gin though. I don't want Evie shouting at me."

"What about you, Linds?" I said.

She was looking at the floor again. "I'll have a tonic with no gin."

I made the drinks, and handed them round. Albert was full of excitement about the baby.

"Maybe you'll have a lad this time, Jamie. A son and heir. Although we're not allowed to say that these days. Carly's the first-born, and so she's the daughter and heiress, isn't she?"

I didn't seem to be able to do bonhomie, and Lindsey wasn't any better, so it was up to Albert to keep the conversation going.

"Carly's been keeping us busy, hasn't she, lass?"

"Yes, Dad, yes she has."

"Evie tells me she's riding well."

"Yes, Fliss is very pleased with her."

"And how have you been keeping, Jamie lad? You look a bit tired."

"Oh, I'm fine, Albert." I couldn't stand it any longer. "Albert, I'm no good at this sort of thing, but I just want to say that this is an absolute bugger."

Lindsey shot me a filthy look.

"No, lass," said Albert, "don't look at him like that. You've got to give the lad a bit of help. None of us finds this easy. The worst of this bloody disease is coping with other people, and when someone I love tells me they mind about it, I really appreciate it."

"Well I mind, Dad." Lindsey was almost whispering. "You know I do."

"Course I do, sweetheart." He turned his face towards me. "The lass and I have been having long talks, Jamie, about Lottie, Lindsey's Mum. It was a terrible time when she died – I've never got over it. But the one thing it makes me realise now is how lucky I am. I've got a chance to make my peace with everyone – to say all the things I've always meant to say, and talk about all the things we never seem to have had time to talk about. That's a great privilege, and we all have to make the most of it. So let's none of us waste this God-given opportunity by being embarrassed, or fretting about what might have been."

He paused, exhausted by the effort of making this speech. I looked at Lindsey, who was staring into her tonic glass, and said to them both:

"It's wonderful that you two have the chance to talk properly to each other. You must be dreading Lindsey having to come home tomorrow."

Lindsey looked up. "I wanted to talk to you about that, Jamie. I've been thinking about the next few weeks. I can't bear the thought of not being close to Dad, so I wondered about… about staying here."

"Christ, Linds, you're not going to cancel, are you?"

"No, no, of course not. I can easily commute to London for rehearsals – it's less than an hour on the train from Peterborough. I've spoken to Evie, and she says she can manage. What do you think?"

"I can't think of any reason why not. What do you think, Albert?"

"Well it seems a bit of a rum do. Travelling all that way every day, I mean. But I must say I'd love it. Would you let me have her for a few weeks?"

"Of course I would, Albert, it goes without saying. We've got a new au pair starting tomorrow, and we'll be perfectly all right. I only hope Lindsey doesn't get too tired."

"I'll be fine. Thanks, Jamie, that makes me feel so much better."

It was the first time her face had brightened since I'd got into the car at Peterborough. I looked at her and smiled. There was just a suggestion of an answering smile, then she looked down at her glass again, and said quickly: "I'll go and see if Evie needs any help in the kitchen." Without another word she got up and left the room.

"She's taking it very hard," said Albert when she'd shut the door. "I get so worried about what's going to happen after I'm gone."

"Albert it's hardly surprising she's upset. She adores you, you know that."

"It's not just that, Jamie. She keeps getting these phone calls, and disappearing into her room for hours on end. We'd been hoping they were from you, but Evie says you told her last night you hadn't spoken to her. What's going on?"

I took a gulp of my gin and tonic.

"I don't know for certain, Albert, but my guess is that she's talking to Sergei Rebroff, the guy who's taking over Opera London. She saw quite a lot of him in Salzburg, and I think he's turned into her *confidant*, for want of a better word. And he wants her to sing with the Company as much as possible, which has to be good for all of us."

"Any funny business going on?"

"You don't have to worry about that, Albert, because all three of us have talked about it together, and I know Sergei wouldn't do anything to hurt us. He's got a wife and family in Russia, and he adores them. Lindsey needs a shoulder to cry on at the moment, and that's fine with me."

"But shouldn't she be crying on your shoulder? You're her husband, after all."

"I think she's still angry with me for not telling her you were ill. She won't talk to me about anything."

He sighed. "Jamie, I'm sorry. It wasn't fair of me to put that burden on you."

"Nonsense, Albert, you were absolutely right. And she did get a fabulous holiday – I've never seen her look so relaxed. She'll come round."

"Well, I'm glad you know all about this Russian chap, and I'm glad you're not worried. But keep an eye on him, won't you?"

"I'll do my best, Albert."

"Jamie, there's just one more thing I need to sort out. I'll have to be quick, because Evie'll probably call us into lunch any moment. I'm

256

concerned – very concerned – about this place. The thing is, it's really important to me that the land remains as a farm, and that Gordon still has a job. Of course I'm leaving it lock, stock and barrel to Lindsey, but I have to know that neither of you will try and sell it."

"Heavens, Albert, I hadn't thought about it. What about inheritance tax? We might have a bit of a problem if we had to pay the full whack."

"No need to worry about that, Jamie lad. When Lottie died there was a life assurance policy, which paid out quite a substantial sum. Then a chum of mine recommended some unit trust, and I invested the lot in that. Haven't touched it since, except to pay in a bit of a monthly contribution on top. I rang the company the other day. Apparently it's worth over seven hundred thousand. They've been sending me statements all this time, but I never take the slightest notice of that kind of thing. I don't really understand the whole tax situation, but I spoke to the same chum and he said death duties will be more than covered, so you'll get this place clear of all encumbrances."

"In that case, we won't need to sell it."

"No, you won't *need* to, but you'll be tempted. Philip Butcher – he used to farm all that land this side of Oakham, just inside the new by-pass – he sold up a few years ago for fifty-five million. The number of houses they've managed to squeeze on has practically doubled the population of the town."

"But they'd never grant planning permission here, right by Rutland Water."

"Don't you be so sure, Jamie. There are ways and means. I want you to promise you won't even *try* to get planning permission. I want you to promise Stockencote will be left as a farm, for as long as you both shall live."

"Yes, of course Albert, I promise. It would be a tragedy to see all this land built on. But what are we going to do about running the farm? Would Gordon be willing to take it on?"

"I've asked him, Jamie. He says he's too old. You'll have to get a tenant in – some young whizz-kid from agricultural college, probably. They'd give their eye-teeth to get their hands on a place like this. But you'll have to insist that they keep Gordon on. And it wouldn't be a bad idea to convert one of the barns for Evie – she's not getting any younger, and I'd like to see her settled. The thing is, Jamie, I've never concerned myself as much as I should with the business side of things, so I don't really know how all this works. But you've got to promise me it'll all be okay."

"Albert, I give you my solemn promise. I don't know how I'll do it, but I'm sure Evie and Gordon will help, and I'll organise it somehow."

He leant forward and grabbed my hand. His felt thin and dry. He squeezed surprisingly hard, then he almost fell back in his chair, exhausted once again by the effort.

"Jamie, you're a good lad, I've always said so. I can't thank you enough."

Lindsey opened the door and looked in.

"Lunch is ready. Dad, you look absolutely exhausted. Come on, lean on my arm."

The rest of the day was surreal. We had a stunning bottle of Chablis with lunch, and later on Carly roared about the house with seemingly limitless energy. I had to play tennis with her in the yard for two hours before tea. But at the back of everyone's minds lurked the awful thought that this wouldn't be many more of these wonderful days, and that Albert would soon be gone.

He went to bed straight after supper, and the rest of us settled down to an extended game of Monopoly. Carly won, which was probably the best outcome, as it kept us all busy telling her not to be such a pain in the neck about having hotels on Mayfair and Park Lane, and about being the richest person in the room. Lindsey and I managed to avoid difficult topics of conversation completely.

However, the moment we had shut the bedroom door behind us, all that changed.

"Jamie, I'm sorry, but I'm afraid I can't handle your sharing my bed."

"Linds, why not? I mean, I'm really sorry about misleading you about your Dad's illness, but he insisted. Surely you can't still be cross?"

"No, Jamie. I was, but I understand why you did it. But it's got way beyond that, I'm afraid. And I know it's not fair of me. But I can't help it."

She turned her back on me and started to take off her clothes, as if I were some poor sap who'd found himself in the girls' changing room. Things were already bad enough, so I decided that it was worth taking the plunge.

"Who have you been on the phone to all week? Albert's worried that it's upsetting you."

258

"Who do you think?"

"Well, Sergei, presumably."

"Congratulations, Jamie. You have just won a hundred million pounds."

"Is he back from Russia, then?"

"Yup. He's in London, sorting out behind-the-scenes stuff with Max Polgar and the Board. He wants to see me as soon as possible."

"And are you going to see him?"

"Yes, I bloody well am."

"For Christ's sake, Linds, why don't you just leave him alone? I thought you'd got over him."

She turned round. By this time she was demurely clothed in a full-length white satin nightie which I suspected she'd borrowed from Evie. She looked wearier than she had before we went on holiday.

"I thought I had, too, Jamie. But the moment I saw his name flashing on my phone it was like a bolt of electricity going through me. I'm sorry, I truly am, but I'm in more turmoil now than I have been at any stage in this whole saga."

"But Linds, you're not going to leave me?"

"I don't know. You should never have let him back into my life, but now you have, I've got to see this thing through."

"Oh Jesus Christ, Lindsey, that's monstrously unfair."

"SHUT UP Jamie," she whispered, urgently. "DON'T wake Dad." She began to sob.

I felt powerless. We weren't even allowed to have a row about it. So I found a couple of blankets in the wardrobe, and lay down on the floor. Soon afterwards, I heard Lindsey's breathing change to a more regular, less ragged pattern, and I knew that she was falling into a blessed, if slightly irritating sleep. I got up, quietly switched off her bedside light, and lay back down on the floor for one of the most wakeful and uncomfortable nights I had ever experienced. It wasn't helped by the almost certain knowledge that, next door, Albert was a bloody sight more uncomfortable than I was.

I had to collect Saskia from Stansted at two thirty, and then drive straight back to Queens Park, so after breakfast I took Carly upstairs with me and helped her pack her suitcase. Lindsey had gone to sit in the study with Albert – they were both reading the Sunday papers, and I didn't fancy asking her to help.

But one thing I did need to know was whether she'd turn up the next day for the first rehearsal day of *Fledermaus*. I took some coffee in at about eleven. I was struck by the cosy normality of the situation. The papers were resting on their knees or strewn around the room. They were deep in discussion about an incident from Lindsey's childhood. Albert recapped for my benefit.

"She was six, Jamie, and already mad keen on horses. She became completely hooked on the Munich Olympics – I don't suppose you remember but that was the year Richard Meade won individual gold in the Three Day Event, and the British won the team gold. Fliss was the reserve member of the team, as a matter of fact. When Dorian Williams, the commentator, shouted 'It's double gold for Great Britain' as Meade cleared the last show jump, Lindsey got up and danced round the room. So did I, actually.

"And then it was only a couple of days later that those Israeli athletes got taken hostage. They went on with the Games, but no-one had any appetite for them. And little Lindsey took on terribly, saying that it was unfair that some horrible men had started a war, and what were they going to do about the lovely horses that had won the gold medals? She thought they were all going to get killed. They'd probably been shipped back to Britain already, but there was no telling Lindsey that. She was all for me getting on a plane and taking her to Germany so we could rescue them."

Lindsey didn't seem to enjoy Albert's recitation. As soon as I had walked into the room, she had taken one look at me and slumped back into her chair. So when I brought up the subject of *Fledermaus* she wasn't best pleased.

"I'll be there tomorrow morning, Jamie. I haven't given up my sense of responsibility, you know."

"Have you had time to relearn it?"

"No, I haven't cracked open the score."

"What about the dialogue? It's a brand new translation."

"Oh for God's sake, Jamie. They'll change every word before we open. And I know Rosalinde quite well enough, thank you very much. I can look after myself, don't you worry."

Albert was looking pained, so we had to stop. I finished my coffee, then made my excuses and left the room.

Carly was highly unimpressed with leaving Stockencote, especially given that the day's remaining task was to collect a new au pair, and that she had to go back to school on Tuesday.

Albert managed to drag himself to the front door to wave us off, along with Lindsey and Evie. Lindsey and I managed a peck on the cheek, then when Carly hugged her she burst into tears. There was an awful possibility that all of us would follow suit, so without further ado I bundled Carly into the car with her little pull-along suitcase, and headed off down the drive.

We got to Stansted with time to spare, and waited for Saskia at the arrivals door. At the allotted time a staggeringly beautiful girl walked through from baggage reclaim, followed by a vast blue suitcase on wheels. I held up my hand-written sign saying SASKIA FRANSMANN, and when the beautiful girl caught sight of it, the devil made her change direction and walk towards me.

"Saskia?"

She beamed.

"Yes, of course, you must be Mister Jamie." The R burred, as in an American accent, because the Dutch appear to learn their wildly impressive English largely from American sitcoms. A set of perfect white teeth grinning at me, and a pair of massive brown eyes looking deep into my soul.

She removed a drab top she was wearing to reveal a little brown T-shirt with *FCUK FOR BRITAIN* in white writing crawling across her perfect breasts. The 'K' was particularly favoured by its position – the outline of a hard little nipple jutting out, giving it extra prominence. The T-shirt was too short, and revealed a pierced belly button with what looked like a ruby winking at me, set in the middle of flesh just tanned enough to suggest it had been kissed by the sun very recently, but not too often or too much. And a pair of skinny blue jeans with legs so long it looked as if she was on stilts. Alarm bells began to clang uncontrollably inside my head.

Carly, to my absolute astonishment, hurled herself into Saskia's arms.

"Welcome to England, Saskia. You're beautiful. I'm going to like you."

Saskia beamed even more. "I think I might like you too, Carly. And I'm sure I'm going to like your Daddy. We'll all have a wonderful time, won't we Mister Jamie?"

Saskia, it turned out, was a vegetarian, which was a bit of a blow, but she offered to cook that night's meal, and produced a stir-fry with courgettes and cashew nuts which was so delicious that I had second helpings. Carly loved it too. We had a great evening, despite the fact that I had to issue instructions for the following day's sort-out of Carly's gym kit and school uniform. The two of them seemed to regard this task as a pleasure in store, and everyone went to bed at ten thirty. Stockencote, with all its worry and sadness, seemed suddenly a million miles away.

31

The next morning I left the house before either of them was up, and went straight to Opera London's rehearsal rooms in Hammersmith. The model showing for any new production was a big occasion, and I would have attended whatever the circumstances, but today was exceptional. *Die Fledermaus* was the first new production of the Rebroff regime, so would attract a lot of interest from the press and the public.

As I walked from the Tube to the rehearsal rooms my phone rang. I pulled it out of my pocket, and there flashing on the display were the words *Lindsey calling*. For a tiny second my heart leapt.

"Jamie, I'm not coming to the model showing."

"Christ, it's not your Dad, is it?"

"No, no, don't worry. He's furious with me for not going. It's just me. I don't want to leave him. I'll come tomorrow."

"But Linds, after the talk-through you're supposed to be having a music rehearsal with Leclerc all day. What do you want me to say?"

"Oh, come on, Jamie, you know as well as I do that it's a complete lottery whether singers bother to turn up on the first day. In Salzburg we had to wait a whole week before bloody Randy Youngman deigned to come. Why shouldn't I behave badly for once?"

I had almost arrived at the rehearsal rooms. Several of the cast, and various other bods to do with the production, were standing outside the front door nattering and, in one or two cases, smoking. They looked at me, and a couple of them waved. I waved back, then walked on past. All this time I was whispering urgently to Lindsey.

"Listen, darling, are you worried about your singing? I never got a chance to ask you over the weekend."

"No, the singing's fine. Well, I haven't done much, actually. I needed a rest."

"Yes of course you did, but you need to be getting going again now, surely?"

"Jamie, stop giving me a hard time. I'm not coming today, but I'll be there tomorrow."

"If you're still at Stockencote now there's nothing I can do, is there? You wouldn't be here till half past twelve, and all the awkward questions will have been asked by then."

"What awkward questions?"

"Oh I don't know, the usual. Like whether you're away doing some other job, for instance."

"Jamie, I can't cope, all right? Please just sort it out for me."

"All right, I'll do what I can. But promise to come tomorrow."

"Don't worry, I'll be there. Goodbye."

What the hell was Olivier Leclerc going to say? I didn't have time to form a strategy. It was twenty-five past ten already.

In the far corner of the packed rehearsal room, talking to Leclerc, was Yvonne Umfreville, who, I had learned from a peremptory email the previous week, had elected to play for the main *Fledermaus* rehearsals herself. With them was Yvonne's partner Olga, who had been engaged for the trouser role of Orlofsky, the androgynous Russian millionaire who throws the party in Act Two. Olga was dressed from head to toe in skin-tight black leather, and was as glamorous as her lover was dumpy. The three of them were obviously engaged in some fearsome gossip, and gales of intimidating laughter greeted each new arrival in the room. When they saw me I saw them look first amused, then concerned. I assumed they were watching the door to relish the moment of Lindsey's arrival, and were disappointed she wasn't with me.

Chairs had been set out around the model of the set, which I could see over the far side of the room. But the cast, the chorus, and all the hangers-on like me were standing around talking and drinking coffee which they had bought from the tawdry little canteen on the way in.

The other principal singers were all there. Julian Pogson, who was singing Eisenstein, the head of the household and fall-guy of the opera, was wearing a thigh-length, pink satin jacket, and unpleasantly tight suede trousers. I suspected the whole outfit had come from some designer shop in Salzburg. He was also wearing eyeliner.

264

Falke, Eisenstein's friend, and the man who sets him up, was a young baritone who lived in Italy with his English father and Italian mother. He was extraordinarily handsome, and Pogson was already in deep conversation with him. I happened to know, however, that he was a ladies' man of no small accomplishment, which put him in something of a minority in the crowded room.

Gloria, the ladies' maid Adele, was for once unaccompanied by Angus, but had still dolled herself up in a little black dress, very low cut, and appeared to have had her hair done for the occasion. Alfred, Rosalinde's former lover and, in this case at any rate, toy-boy, was being played by none other than Jason Tang. This was his first major role since leaving the chorus, and he had marked the occasion by buying himself, as far as I could tell, a complete new wardrobe. Of course he wasn't short of a bob or two these days, and he reeked of designer chic.

Then there were the older members of the cast – Colonel Frank, the prison governor, sung by a Welsh bass with a highly distinguished career with the Company, who was now limiting himself to comedy roles; Blind, the lawyer, sung by a tenor who to my knowledge was the wrong side of eighty, and who had been specialising in character roles of this kind for the last forty years; and last but not least Frosch, the gaoler. This was a speaking role, normally cast with a well-known actor from some sitcom on the telly. However, Ursula Zimmermann had conceived the brilliant, and as far as I knew unprecedented notion of casting a woman in this role. I had already seen the costume designs, and the actress concerned, who had made her name twenty years earlier as an impressionist, was going to be dressed as Margaret Thatcher. It would either make or break the production.

Ursula Zimmermann caught my eye immediately, and screamed out "JAMIE" at the top of her voice. I made a beeline for her.

She had bottle-blond hair cut fairly short, and was dressed from head to toe in black. Her face had a few more lines on it than when I had last seen her, but her smile was as broad as ever. Her lips were painted an improbable shade of scarlet, as were her eyelids. I couldn't have been more pleased to see her if she'd been the Archangel Gabriel.

"Ursula, good to see you." She pulled me into a stifling embrace, then placed her hands either side of my face and kissed me full on the lips. Then she backed away, and made great play of wiping her lipstick off me.

"Oh wow, Jamie, this is GREAT. Lindsey's in it, too. I only knew a few days ago, but I'm thrilled. Even if I am just a TEENY bit sad not to meet Miss Balls."

"Disappointingly, she turned out to be called Bolls, Ursula. That's why I sacked her."

She hooted with laughter again. "Where is Lindsey, anyway?"

"Ah, well, that's a bit of a problem, I'm afraid."

"She's not here?"

"She's just rung me. She's staying at her father's place in the country. He's ill. She was planning to travel down this morning, but she's in the early stages of pregnancy, and she's not feeling too good, so she's coming tomorrow instead. She asked me to apologise."

She didn't look best pleased. But any earful I might have been about to get from her was as nothing compared to the hysterical scream I heard issuing from Olivier Leclerc's mouth. Somehow he seemed to have heard, or divined, what I had said. He was crossing the room at lighnting speed, and was only a few feet away.

"Leendsi eez not 'ere? Why eez she not 'ere?"

"She didn't feel too well this morning. She is pregnant, you see."

This was a mistake.

"My God, zese pregnant women are a fucking pain in my asshole," he said.

Mercifully Ursula seemed to find this very amusing. "And I expect your asshole has quite a high pain threshold, Olivier."

Olivier's face darkened, but there was no time for this to develop into a full-scale row, because one of the stage managers was calling the assembly to order. As we moved over towards the seats, I caught my breath. Walking in through a rarely-opened access door behind the model were Mutt and Jeff who had hidden their guns as discreetly as they could underneath their ill-fitting suits. They were closely followed by Tatyana. Sure enough, a couple of seconds later, in walked none other than the new Chairman of Opera London, Sergei Ivanevitch Rebroff himself. There was a buzz around the room, and then the everyone burst into spontaneous applause. I noticed one or two people glancing nervously at me.

Sergei held up his hand for silence. Although he had no notes, his speech was, even by his standards, extraordinarily fluent. I guessed he had had it professionally translated.

266

"Ladies and Gentlemen, I am Sergei Ivanevitch Rebroff, your new Chairman. This is the proudest day of my life. For the first time I stand before the people who matter in an opera company – my opera company, if I dare say it. You are the workers, the talented ones. I salute first of all Ursula Zimmermann, your director; Franzi Reinhardt, your designer and Olivier Leclerc, your conductor. These three are already, I am sure, known to all of you, as they are around the world.

I salute also the principal singers. You all possess great gifts, and a wonderful ability to communicate these gifts to other people. I eagerly await the contribution you will make to this production. Members of the chorus, I welcome you. You are the backbone of this show, as you are of so many operas. Then there are all those behind the scenes. I pay tribute to all of you, and wish you enormous success with this new production of *Die Fledermaus*, and with all your endeavours over the coming years. If I, with a few million pounds, have helped to secure your future, and to enable great art to be made, then I have fulfilled my lifetime's ambition."

The room once again erupted into a cacophony of cheering, whistling and foot-stamping.

Eventually the noise died down, and he was able to say "and now I would like to hand over to Ursula Zimmermann, to introduce this production." For the moment everyone was so taken with Sergei that they appeared to have forgotten we had no Rosalinde in the room. Either that or they had failed to notice.

Ursula got up, and invited everyone to say their names, and what their job was. The cast announced themselves with varying degrees of chutzpah, or in the case of some of the younger ones embarrassment. When it came to Jason's turn, he caught my eye and giggled. Then we had everyone else, including the entire chorus of forty. Last of all it was my turn. It was a surprisingly difficult speech to make.

"Hi, my name is Jamie Barlow, and I am casting director, and acting Lord High Everything Else. I am also husband (I nearly said 'acting husband') of Lindsey Templeton, who sings the role of Rosalinde. Unfortunately she is not well, and is unable to make it today. However, she promises to be here tomorrow.

There was a nervous titter around the room. One or two people looked at Sergei. He had taken a seat at the front, next to Tatyana and opposite Mutt and Jeff, whose eyes were scouring the room in a most disconcerting manner. Sergei himself managed to retain a serene countenance. Lindsey had probably rung him to tell him she wasn't coming before she'd told me.

The model showing and talk-through took until midday, when Ursula announced the coffee break. People in the room were excited by her ideas, especially when she got to Act Three, and revealed that Frosch was going to be Maggie Thatcher.

I was planning to leave at this point, but as soon as the break was announced Sergei made straight for me.

"Jamie, it has been too long. How was your summer?"

"Oh, terrific, thanks Sergei. Except for our awful news about Lindsey's father. Or perhaps you hadn't heard?"

As if.

"Yes, Lindsey has telephoned me to tell me. I am so sorry. He sounds wonderful man. Has he no chance of recovery?"

"None at all, so the doctors say. Lindsey is devastated."

"That is why she is not here?"

"No. Well, in a manner of speaking perhaps. She is not well today, but I am sure she will be here tomorrow."

"I hope so, Jamie. She is crucial to success of production."

"Yes, that's very true, she is, Sergei."

He'd finished with me. And he'd also, it seemed, bestowed enough of his precious time on the rehearsal, because he gathered up his entourage, and slipped out of the access door through which they'd entered. I snuck out past the coffee queue and walked back to the Tube.

Umfreville had sent me a stinker when I opened my emails on my arrival at the office. There was no '*dear Jamie*', or '*hi*'. It simply said '*will not tolerate bad behaviour by any singer, Templeton included. Make sure she is here tomorrow. We can ill afford to lose rehearsal time. Y.U.*'

I rang Stockencote. Evie answered. Albert was angry with Lindsey, she said, and they'd had a bad morning. He'd retired to his bed for an extended siesta. Lindsey had done some singing, and had come back looking depressed, and saying that she didn't know how she was ever going to persuade her voice to work properly again. But, come what may, Evie promised to push her out of the door the next morning. Albert's Merc. was sitting gleaming in the garage, and needed a trip. Lindsey was going to borrow it to get to Peterborough station. Inevitably it wasn't possible to talk to her, so I contented myself with sending my love to them all, and ringing off.

The rest of the day dragged by without much excitement, and I managed to get home by five thirty. Saskia had left a note to say she'd gone to the shops with Carly. I shoved the few dirty dishes in the dishwasher, and just as I finished the two of them arrived back.

Both of them looked radiantly happy, and Saskia looked, if possible, even sexier than the day before. Yesterday's slightly-too-short T-shirt had been replaced by a pure white garment which was half way between a crop top and a boob tube. Her nipples were jutting out fiercely, and acres of her perfect stomach were showing. This time she had a green stone in her belly button, which set off her tan to even better effect. Finally there was a denim mini-skirt which sat on her hips, and finished practically as soon as it had started.

Carly and she had clearly hit it off in a big way. I was presented with a bill for twenty-seven pounds for food for our tea, and stationery for school. I was going to have to tell Saskia to be more careful with my money. But I couldn't face it tonight, so instead I offered her a gin and tonic, which she accepted with a bat of her eyelids. Then she went into the kitchen to cook.

It was when I had finally managed to make Carly go to bed that the trouble began. Saskia asked me whether she could roll a joint. She had brought some excellent weed from home, she said. Maybe I would like to share it with her? The real trouble was that this offer was accompanied by a frank and ridiculously sexual wink.

She smiled her perfect smile at me, and very gently licked her lips. "Come on Mr Jamie. It'll be fun."

I looked deep into her powder-blue eyes, and I swear I was within I millisecond of accepting. But thank God we hadn't opened a bottle of wine, and I was only one G and T the worse for wear. This meant that the voice of conscience was just strong enough to win. I managed to make myself say that I'd rather she didn't smoke anything in the house, especially when Carly was there. I refrained from pointing out that she was bloody lucky to have got the stuff through customs without being caught.

I wondered whether she was going to utter the fateful words 'to hell with the spliff, Mr Jamie, let's go to bed and fuck like bunnies anyway,' but the moment had gone. She pouted a bit, announced that she too was going upstairs, and waited for me to kiss her demurely on the cheek before she went.

I'd got away with it. Just. The words of Ton de Wit kept repeating themselves inside my head: 'She is so drop-dead gorgeous that no heterosexual male can keep his hands off her'. I opened a bottle of Sauvignon, poured myself a very large glass, drained it, and immediately had another. Then I shoved the cork back in the bottle, put it in the fridge and did the washing up.

32

I woke up the next morning with a profound sense of disgust at my all-too-close call with Saskia. It felt like my life was spinning out of control. So I decided I would at least attempt to get a grip on things by forbidding myself the very temporary pleasure of shagging her brains out. I wrote myself a little note on a Post-It slip, saying: 'keep your dick inside your trousers'. Then I folded over the sticky edge and put it in my pocket, intending to keep this little *aide-memoire* with me at all times.

Lindsey did manage to turn up at the rehearsal at ten-thirty. I knew this because I had asked Pogson to text me when she turned up. I didn't dare communicate with her, and I didn't dare risk talking to Umfreville or Leclerc, because I didn't want to show them any sign of weakness. Zimmermann would have been more sympathetic, up to a point, but she too would get paranoid if she saw that I was really worried.

What I really needed was a spy in the rehearsal room – someone who could tell me what was happening on a day-to-day basis. Even Pogson wasn't the ideal person, because if he spotted anything he regarded as remotely juicy or gossip-worthy it would be all round the Company by the next morning. So the only serious contender was Jason Tang. He was already harbouring one huge secret, after all, so I reckoned one more wouldn't make that much difference.

I emailed him as soon as I got into the office. *Hi Jason. Please call my mobile as soon as rehearsals are finished. I need to talk privately to you.* Then I settled down to the day's work as best I could.

Grace had been as good as her word. Ever since our Caffe Italia lunch she had been beavering through all my papers and my computer files, making sure everything was organised for my move to the fourth floor.

She had already sorted me out with the 'application pack' for the top job, and had made sure I'd filled in all the forms, and signed on every dotted line.

She also had to make sure that I was seen to be taking my casting director's responsibilities seriously, so today's task was to review our plans for the next two seasons, and make plans to fill in the gaps. By the end of the day she had put a trip to Leeds into my diary for the following Tuesday. Opera North were opening a new production of *Tristan und Isolde*, and had by all accounts found a sensational new South African *heldentenor* for the title role. If he was as good as people were saying he could be the backbone of our new *Ring* cycle. I had rung Angus to see if he was free to come too, but he had recently begun rehearsals of Janáček's *Katya Kabanova* at ENO, and couldn't extricate himself in time to make the five o'clock start. So I would have to go to Leeds on my own, which would at least give me the opportunity to stay the night at Stockencote on the way back, and find out how Albert was, and whether Lindsey was coping at all.

As I walked back home from the Tube my phone rang.

"Hi Jamie, this is Jason Tang. I got your message."

"Hi Jason, thanks for ringing back. How's *Fledermaus* going?"

"Oh, great, thanks Jamie, really exciting. Ursula Zimmermann's a legend. And Olivier seems to be enjoying himself. Most of the time, that is."

"That's terrific. How was Lindsey?"

There was a bit of a pause. Then he said, a bit hesitantly: "yeah, fine. I mean she just marked her part today. She didn't sing out at all."

"Did she look okay?"

"Um, yes, I suppose so. I don't really know how much I'm supposed to say."

"Can you meet me for a drink, Jason?"

"Er, yes, I should think so. When?"

"Now would be good."

"Um, okay, that's fine. Where?"

"Could you come to my place? I need to be private. Lindsey's not here by the way – she's staying at her father's."

"Okay… Where is it??"

"Queens Park. It's five minutes from the tube. I'll tell you what, why don't you come and have supper – I'm sure Saskia, my au pair, will be

272

able to make the food stretch – and then we'll talk while Saskia puts my daughter to bed."

When he arrived an hour or so later, looking like a frightened rabbit, Saskia was in the kitchen. She and Carly had decided to cook something with chillies. This surprised me, but my daughter so adored Saskia that if Saskia liked chillies, she was damn well going to like them too.

I poured large glasses of Pinot Grigio for Jason and me, and left Carly and Saskia to finish cooking. The two of us went and sat in the living room. It occurred to me it would be no bad thing if he got a bit drunk – I'd told Saskia about his being gay, and she'd giggled in a predatory way. I hoped she'd find him a more exciting prospect than her boss.

"Jason, I need your help. Don't worry, it's nothing like last time, but I would really appreciate your keeping an eye on things at the rehearsals of *Fledermaus*, and letting me know what's going on."

"Um, yeah, sure Jamie. What sort of things do you want me to look for?"

"Well, it's a bit delicate, actually, Jason. I need to take you into my confidence."

"Don't worry, Jamie, I'm very good at keeping secrets." He giggled nervously, then took a large glug of his Pinot Grigio.

"You really do have to keep this to yourself, Jason."

"Okay, I Promise."

"I'm a bit worried about her singing. She had some trouble in Salzburg in the summer, and she hasn't sung much since. Her Dad is very ill, and I think the stress of that is getting to her. Also she's pregnant."

"Yes, I knew that, actually. Olivier told me."

"Does everyone know, do you think?"

"Yes, I think they do."

"And are they saying anything else about it?"

He looked at me for a moment. "You want me to be honest, don't you?"

"Yes, Jason, I do."

"Okay then." He took another swig of wine, and I refilled his glass. "Everyone's saying Lindsey's having an affair with Sergei Rebroff, and that no-one knows who's the father of the baby. Is that true?"

This time it was my turn to take a gulp of wine.

"Absolutely, I'm afraid. Except that Lindsey says it's mine."

"Well, she should know, surely?"

"Yes, she should, but I don't think she's being honest with me."

"Shit. You've got yourself a bit of a problem, haven't you, Jamie?"

"Yes, I'm afraid so. And because of all this, Lindsey won't talk to me, so I can't ask her what's going on. Also Olivier is looking for an opportunity to sack her. So what I need you to do is listen carefully to Lindsey's singing, and tell me if she sounds okay. Also, I'd be really grateful if you could tell me what Olivier and Yvonne Umfreville are saying about her. Would you mind doing that?"

To my astonishment, his face cracked into a huge smile. He drank some more wine and said: "no, Jamie, I wouldn't mind at all. I love this kind of thing. Are you going to pay me some more money?"

"Er, no, I don't think I can, I'm afraid. But what I can do is look seriously at what roles we can offer you in the next few years. You're very talented, after all, and I'd like you to feature a lot in our plans."

"Oh, yeah. That'd be awesome. Did you have anything in mind?"

"One thing occurs to me. Angus and I are planning to do a lot of Britten – if we get the top jobs, that is. One of the things we'd like to do is *Albert Herring*. It hasn't been done in London for years. You'd be fantastic in the title role. How does that grab you?"

He looked stunned, and still hadn't said anything when Saskia walked in. She smiled at him.

"I've cooked a Chinese dish with aubergines and chilli. Do you like hot things, Jason?"

She was staring straight at him, with the same lascivious look she'd used on me. I expected him to be embarrassed, but instead he held her gaze, and said: "I love hot things, Saskia. And I'd love to try something new."

She went on staring at him for longer than was strictly necessary. Then she turned round and walked out of the room.

He picked up his empty glass and followed her like a puppy. As he reached the door through to the hall, he turned and looked at me. "Albert Herring would be fantastic, Jamie. You've got yourself a deal." Then he pointed over his shoulder with his thumb. "She is HOT," he said, and went through into the kitchen. I felt in my pocket for my Post-It slip. Maybe I'd remain intact for another night. You lucky bastard, Jason, I thought.

Carly was beside herself at having Jason for supper. She had helped Saskia in the kitchen, and between them they had produced a delicious concoction of aubergines, spring onions, garlic, and God knows what else, which they served with noodles *and* rice, at Carly's insistence. She ate voluminous quantities, as did we all – eating vegetarian was going to be no hardship.

Carly spent the entire meal discussing some American sitcom with her two new-found friends. Saskia and Jason enjoyed talking to her almost as much as they enjoyed flirting with each other, which they managed to do simultaneously and apparently without Carly noticing.

After supper the two of them offered to do the washing up while I put Carly to bed. I sent her upstairs, and said I would follow shortly, and while Saskia nipped to the loo I managed to snatch a few private words with Jason, who by now was pretty squiffy.

"Hey, Jamie," he said. "That girl is soooo hot. I think I might be about to find out what I've been missing all these years. Do you mind?"

"Of course not. Why the hell should I mind?"

"Well, it's your house, and everything. And I bet you fancy her too. Have you been to bed with her yet?"

"No, Jason, of course I haven't."

"Maybe you should come up with us now. I love threesomes. Oh, but of course you know about that." And he produced another of his disconcerting peals of girly laughter.

Saskia appeared behind him. "Is this naughty little Chinese boy trying to persuade you to come to bed with us, Mister Jamie?"

I was speechless. Saskia deftly moved Jason out of the way, and draped herself over me. Percy nearly went mad.

"I think it's a great idea," she said. "And from what I can feel down there you do too, Mister Jamie."

"No, I really don't think so, if you don't mind. I'll go up and see Carly, then I'll watch the telly. But don't let me stop you two." I managed to extricate myself awkwardly from her embrace.

Saskia smiled the wickedest smile I'd ever seen. "Okay then, Mister Jamie. Some other time, maybe." And she reached down and gave Percy a tweak, which bloody nearly caused a serious accident. I walked bandy-legged to the kitchen door, then turned round to face them.

"Have fun," I croaked.

Carly was in her pyjamas, waiting for me.

"Have you done your teeth," I said.

"Yes, Daddy. Jason is really hot, isn't he?"

I was getting a bit fed up with everyone asking me this. "Heavens, Carly, I don't know. If you say so."

"Well I think he is. And so does Saskia."

It was on the tip of my tongue to ask her if Saskia thought I was hot, too, but I managed to restrain myself.

"You like Saskia, don't you Carly?"

"I love her, Daddy. She's my favourite nanny of all time."

"She's an au pair, not a nanny, darling."

"What does that mean?"

"It means she comes from a foreign country."

"Okay then, she's my favourite no pair of all time. And she's way better than any of our nannies. I've decided to be a vegetarian."

"That might be a bit difficult when Mummy comes back, Carly. She likes cooking meat."

"When is Mummy coming back?"

"I don't know, sweetheart. But I think Mummy will stay with Grandad for a while longer. Would you like to ring her now?"

"Yes, please. Can I talk to Grandad, too?"

"Better wait and see. I'll go and get the phone."

I went into our bedroom and picked up the portable phone from the bedside table. It had run out of battery. So I ran down the stairs to get the one from the living room. I opened the door to find Saskia, completely naked, astride Jason. She had the most perfect body I had ever seen. She was in mid-hump.

"Oh, sorry," I said. "Don't mind me. Sorry. Just getting the, um, phone."

I edged past them to where the thing was recharging on its cradle. Saskia's powder blue eyes watched me all the way.

"Sure you won't change your mind, Mister Jamie?"

"Er, no. I mean yes, I'm sure, thank you."

"Jason would like you to, wouldn't you Jason?"

No reply. It looked to me as if Jason was far too busy to care.

"I'll be off, then. Please would you turn out the lights before you come to bed?"

Saskia laughed, which occasioned a grunt of pleasure from Jason. I shut the door, and went back upstairs. I was shaking like a leaf.

"What were you talking to Saskia about?" said Carly.

"Just asking her to turn out the lights when she came to bed."

"Is Jason still here?"

"Er, yes, darling, he is."

"Oh, great. Maybe we can have breakfast together. Shall we phone Mummy now?"

"Yes, let's." I tried to dial the number, but my hands were shaking so much I couldn't manage it.

Carly groaned. "Give it to me, Daddy. Which buttons do I press?"

I told her, and she dialled as I spoke.

"Hallo, is that Auntie Evie? It's Carly here. Can I talk to Grandad, please?"

Pause.

"Oh, okay. I'm just going to bed, too."

Another pause.

"Yes, I'm fine, thanks. We're having fun here."

After a moment Carly said brightly:

"Hi Mummy. Yes, I miss you too. But we're having such fun here. Daddy brought someone called Jason to see Saskia, and she really likes him… yes, and I'm a vegetarian now. And I like chillies. When are you coming home?"

There was a long pause while she listened to Lindsey's reply. Her face gradually fell.

"Mummy, Grandad's really going to die, isn't he?"

Another pause.

"I want to come and see you at Grandad's. Please can we come? Yes, Daddy's here. I'll pass you over."

She looked terribly sad as she handed me the phone.

"Hi, darling," I said. "How's Albert?"

"Actually he's not too bad. We've been talking a lot. It's funny, I'm really enjoying being here. It's almost like being a little girl again. I just wish it could go on for ever."

"Carly's desperate to come and see him, Linds. And you, for that matter."

"I think Dad would like that. So would Evie."

"Then we have to fix something up. How about Carly's birthday, a week on Saturday."

Carly's face lit up again. She nodded frantically at me.

"Carly thinks it's a great idea," I said. "Would that would be any good? Will your Dad manage it?"

"I'll go and ask Evie," said Lindsey. "Hang on…"

There was a long pause. I took the opportunity to tell Carly I hoped it would be fine for us all to go to Grandad's for her birthday, but she really ought to go to sleep now. I kissed her goodnight, then I walked across the corridor. I could just hear Saskia making the most pornographic noises, so I checked Carly's door was firmly shut, and went into our room, again making sure I shut out the grunts and screams from downstairs. By the time Lindsey came back on the phone, all was tranquil once more.

"Evie thinks it'll be fine. We'll have to explain to Carly that he won't be like he normally is…"

Her voice tailed off. I thought I'd better change the subject.

"How was the rehearsal today?"

"Oh my God, it was grim. I didn't want to go at all this morning, but first you, then Sergei, and finally Dad told me I had to. My voice just isn't working properly. Every time I put any pressure on it I get this awful flat wobble. Olivier bloody Leclerc doesn't help. From the moment I walked in this morning he has been absolutely poisonous. Picking holes in every phrase I sing." She sighed. "What the hell's Jason Tang doing there, by the way?"

I'd had just enough time to think about this one. "Saskia asked me if there were any singers I thought she'd like to meet – not too old and boring, she said. Jason was the first one who came to mind. They seem to have hit it off nicely. Linds, listen, I have to see you soon. I know we're coming up the weekend after next, but I've got an idea when we could meet before that. I've got to go to Leeds to see *Tristan* next Tuesday. Could I stay at Stockencote on the way back?"

"You wouldn't get here till midnight. I'll be in bed."

"No, I know I wouldn't, but at least I could run you to the station in the morning. I'm sure Evie would pick you up later on."

There was a pause. Then she said, "okay, Jamie. But please can I ask you not to contact me until then?"

"It's a deal, sweetheart."

She hung up. I changed into my pyjamas, and went into the ensuite. We'd run out of loo paper, and I absolutely needed to go, so I opened the bedroom door as quietly as I could in the hope that I wouldn't disturb the lovers, who I was pretty sure had by now come up to bed. I tiptoed across the landing, went into the main bathroom, and picked up a couple of rolls. I was just about to make my way back, when in walked Jason. He was stark naked.

"Oh. Er, sorry. Not the best place to meet your boss, really." A burst of girly laughter. Jesus.

"No, I suppose not… Well then, I'll be going to bed… Sleep well. Or not, as the case may be."

"Good night, Jamie. Mind the bugs don't bite."

33

Saskia and Jason were at it hammer and tongs every night for the rest of that week. They seemed, for the time being at least, to have decided they were not going to persuade me to join them. This was a relief, even if I was almost unbearably frustrated.

I spent the Wednesday evening at the theatre at the première of the season's first revival, *The Magic Flute*. It was nice to be in a darkened theatre, and not have to face difficult conversations with anyone, or an evening of frustrated lust. Sergei had been called back on a quick trip to Russia, so was unable to attend, which was another bonus. The evening was almost wrecked when I saw Gregory Knipe wafting about in a particularly lurid green caftan that made him look like he was officiating in some high Anglican church, but to my relief he cut me dead.

Jason's reports as the week went on confirmed my fears that, although Lindsey was turning up to *Fledermaus* rehearsals each day, she was only going through the motions. Leclerc was getting increasingly tetchy about her marking her part, but couldn't really do much about sacking her until she started singing out, which would be when the world would know whether or not she could still produce the goods. My doubts grew as each day went by. I was clutching onto the hope that we might get Albert to a rehearsal to hear her for the last time, and that it would somehow make her able to sing again.

Via yet more noisy coupling between Saskia and Jason, I managed to arrive unscathed at Tuesday, the twelfth of September, and my trip to Leeds to hear *Tristan und Isolde*.

Tristan is an opera about love. Well, lust, actually. The whole piece is really one long-delayed orgasm. The climax comes at the very end when the harmony finally resolves, after five hours of the most delicious foreplay. If you can put up with its *longueurs* – the endless history lesson on Isolde's ship in Act One, and the equally protracted ravings of a wounded Tristan in Act Three – you are rewarded with some of the most deeply satisfying music ever written. True, Isolde's probably a twenty-three stone, rugby-playing Amazon, with pop-eyes and a sad inability to get up unaided from a kneeling position, but you forgive everything for the visceral pleasure bestowed by that climax. Provided it's well conducted, that is. Wilhelm Fürtwängler, the great mid-twentieth-century German conductor, understood the life-enhancing significance of that moment. He obviously needed his life enhanced, since when he was not conducting he was busy sending off his subscription to the Nazi party, or attending rallies in Nuremberg where large groups of the German *Volk* would get together and sing jolly songs about the greatness of the Third Reich. If you can get hold of a copy of his live 1943 recording of *Meistersinger* from Bayreuth, you can hear the influence of these splendid occasions on the singing of the Bayreuth Festival Chorus, which by all accounts was actually a mixture of the cream of the *Hitler Jugend* and the *Waffen SS*. Listen to them in the passage about *die heil'ge deutsche Kunst* at the end of Act Three. Thrilling stuff, but grotesque.

Opera North had imported an elderly Austrian, Gottfried Lorenz, to conduct these performances of *Tristan*. He had absorbed from his mother's womb the music of the great German romantics, and when his grizzled, lived-in face appeared in the orchestra pit of the Grand Theatre at the beginning of the show the audience went berserk. He conducted an unhurried, considered performance which allowed the magnificently-structured music to unfold in the grandest, most moving way possible.

The South African *heldentenor* I had gone to hear would be an okay choice for Opera London's Siegfried, so my trip to Leeds was justified. But I spent an absurdly high proportion of the evening in floods of tears, moved by the sheer awesome magnificence of the piece. No doubt my tearfulness was enhanced by the state of my private life.

I was desperate to get away to Stockencote after the show, but absolutely had to go to the First Night Party in the Grand Hall. Graham Butterfield was there, which was entertaining. He teased me mercilessly about the game of swapsies I had played over Lindsey and Evangeline Bolls with Ton de Wit. I also caught sight of Archie Foster across the other side of the bar. He gave me one swift wink, but otherwise we didn't communicate.

I was about to extricate myself from the proceedings and head down the A1 towards Stockencote when I saw Max Polgar bearing down on me.

"Jamie, how splendid to see you. Wasn't that wonderful? Gottfried Lorenz is just about the best Wagner conductor in the world, in my opinion."

"Electrifying, Max. I'm going to force Angus to come and hear him. Mind you, he demands three times as much rehearsal with the orchestra as anyone else. We don't want Angus getting those kind of ideas, now do we?"

"Oh come on, Jamie. We can spend what we like now, surely? That's exactly what Sergei wants – to use the extra money to enhance artistic standards."

"You have a point, I suppose. But it's a bit of a surprise hearing a senior Board member actually encouraging us to spend money." I looked around to make sure no-one was earwigging. All sorts of confidential stuff could go for a burton at first night parties. "But here I am talking as though it's a done deal. What's the latest? Who's applied?"

"All the usual suspects. The only serious contender for your job is Damien de la Chapelle, and I think we can make a case for ignoring him because he won't leave the Châtelet. Of course the two companies were going to be under one umbrella, but that's dead in the water now Gregory has resigned. Likewise Angus's only real rival is Olivier Leclerc, which is slightly more problematic, but the current thinking is that we'll play the nationality card. British conductor for a British company."

"Seems reasonable to me. Will the press swallow it?" I saw Janet Hopkirk, slightly nearer to us than I had realised.

"Better be quick," said Max, very quietly. "We're arranging interviews right now, but we've all agreed that the jobs are going to you and Angus. After all, I've interviewed you both already, and it's not as if the members of the Board don't know you. I've just spoken to Archie Foster too, and he's fine about it."

Hopkirk extricated herself from another conversation, and tried to look inconspicuous as she sidled up to us. I decided attack was the best form of defence.

"Janet, marvellous to see you. Do you know Max Polgar?"

"Only by reputation. Max Polgar, the power behind the Opera London throne."

"You flatter me, Miss Hopkirk."

"Oh no I don't think so, Mr Polgar. Unless things have changed since Sergei Rebroff took over?"

I cut in. "Mr Rebroff seems to admire Max's work even more than his predecessor did, Janet."

"Splendid. Continuity is so important, don't you think?"

"Yes, quite." Time to change the subject. "Didn't you think tonight's performance was terrific?"

"Oh, yes. Well, fairly terrific. I didn't think much of the soprano. Has Lindsey ever taken on any Wagner?"

"Not so far, Janet. We all know too many singers who've moved into Wagner before they were ready. Lindsey seems to be able to pick and choose her roles, so I don't think there's any need to rush things."

"No, quite. How very wise you are. When a singer makes a mess of something, everyone in this very small world of ours knows all about it almost before the curtain has fallen."

"Yes, that's all too true. I hope you haven't been hearing bad things about anyone at Opera London?"

"Oh, it wasn't at Opera London I was thinking of, Jamie." She took a self-satisfied sip of her nasty white wine.

"I'm sorry Janet, Max," I said. "I have a long drive ahead of me. Will you forgive me?"

Max gave me the merest trace of an imploring look.

"Oh, Max," I said, "did you say you were staying out towards the motorway? I'll drop you off."

"That would be very kind, Jamie. Miss Hopkirk, what a pleasure to see you. I shall read your review with interest."

"And I shall look forward to the new *Fledermaus* down at the other end of the M1." She looked me squarely in the eye. "The new regime. So exciting!"

As we walked down the ornate staircase towards New Briggate Max turned to me and said, under his breath: "that woman is the most poisonous bitch I have ever met. Does she think she knows you're getting the job?"

"God knows, Max. Better not to ask. Let's just get the next few weeks over with, then maybe we can all settle down to producing operas, instead of worrying about raddled old bags like Janet Hopkirk."

Max was staying at the Hilton, which meant I fell foul of Leeds's one-way system, and didn't make it to Stockencote until twelve thirty. I had rung ahead, only to find Lindsey had gone to bed.

Evie, however, had insisted on staying up. She had a glass of whisky and some cheese on toast for me. We sat at the huge table in the kitchen, in front of the Aga. While I ate Evie drank a cup of tea, and filled me in on Albert's condition.

"He's still refusing morphine, which means he's probably in mortal agony, but at least we can talk to him. His main concern, of course, is Lindsey. He's determined to stop her pulling out of *Die Fledermaus*."

"God, Evie, is she thinking of cancelling? She hasn't told me."

"Oh, Blimey, I've put my foot in it. But have no fear, Albert won't let her. Lindsey's being here while he's ill is important to him, but not as important as his daughter's career. Any sign of her flagging and he'll pack her off home. Mind you, Lindsey's as stubborn as he is, and she's determined to stay here with him to the bitter end." She had a sip of her tea. "He's opened up, you see. They're able to talk about things they'd never have dreamt of discussing before. For instance I think Lindsey feels that for the first time in her life she knows who her Mum was."

She paused for a moment, looking at me while I polished off the last of my cheese on toast. Then she said quietly:

"Jamie, I'm sure she's still talking to that Russian chap. She knows that Albert and I are worried about it, so she leaves it until after she's gone up to her room, but sometimes I hear her talking when I come up to bed. There's nothing going on, is there?"

I didn't know what to say. After a moment Evie picked up my plate and took it over to the sink.

"I don't mean to pry, Jamie. I'm sure it's nothing to do with me."

"No, no, Evie, you're not prying. It's just that I don't want to burden you with any more worries."

"Now you listen to me, Jamie Barlow. I'm not such an old fuddy-duddy as you think I am. I know what goes on in the world, and while I might not like it much, if there's anything I can do to help you and Lindsey, I'm ready and willing."

"Evie, if I tell you what's really happening, you won't tell Albert, will you? Or Lindsey, for that matter?"

"No Jamie. I promise. You kept a pretty big secret for me, after all."

"Okay then," I said. "But it's not much fun, I warn you. You know that Lindsey's pregnant?"

"Yes, dear."

"Well, she's admitted having an affair with Sergei Rebroff. She says the baby's definitely mine, but I think there's some doubt in her mind. I can see it in her eyes every time we talk about it."

She came back over to the table and sat down. "I knew there was something, Jamie dear. But I *am* glad you've decided to tell me. It's far worse not knowing, you know."

"Thanks, Evie. Anyway, while we were on holiday Sergei went back to his wife and family in Russia. Lindsey calmed down a lot, and we really did have a lovely time. But when we got back there was all the worry about Albert, which made Lindsey come straight up here. Then Rebroff arrived back in London, and then, well, it seems they started speaking to each other again."

"Who is this man, anyway?"

"Believe it or not he's the new Chairman of Opera London. So he's my new boss, and he's about to make me General Administrator. He insists I'm the guy he wants in the job. Which is a bit uncomfortable, since what I'd really like to do is beat his bloody head in."

"He must realise that Lindsey wouldn't stay with him five minutes if he didn't bring you along for the ride."

"Evie, come on, that can't possibly be true. He's trying to get her away from me, surely?"

"I told you, Jamie, I'm not such an old fool as you think. Not such a fool as you, maybe. Lindsey adores you. Always has, and unless I'm very much mistaken, always will."

"Then why in hell won't she tell him to bugger off? Sorry. Pardon my French."

"She's waiting for you to do something about it, Jamie. She wants you to take control. Tell this awful man where to go."

"But how can I, Evie? My whole career's dependent on him."

"That's where he's been so clever. But if I'm not mistaken he has no intention of leaving his wife."

"No, I think that's right. In fact he told me so himself, one night when he was drunk."

She drained the last drop from her second cup of tea, then put it back on its saucer and sighed.

"Jamie, I can't tell you what to do about this. You'll have to make your own decisions. But maybe I've planted a few seeds in your mind. Meanwhile I think you had better tell me the truth about Lindsey's singing. You're worried about it, aren't you?"

"I never meant to tell you any of this, Evie. Lindsey'll kill me if she finds out."

"She won't, Jamie. I'm not going to tell her, and I'm quite sure you're not either."

"No, quite. Well, it started the night after the Prom. I thought I'd convinced her that Albert was just exhausted, but now I'm not so sure. She had a terribly stressful journey back to Salzburg, and had to sing a taxing performance of *Cosi* before she'd had time to think. At that performance she started getting a recurrence of a technical problem she used to have in her early days at college. Over the next couple of performances the problem came and went. Then John Standish, who's her gynaecologist and a close friend, gave her some pills which seemed to sort out her brain, and she sang the last performance brilliantly.

"She didn't sing at all while we were in France, and as soon as we got back she came up here. Then she missed the first day of *Fledermaus* rehearsals, and she hasn't sung out properly in any of the sessions she has since been to. The conductor is furious, and is looking for a chance to sack her, which is as much to do with politics as it is to do with standards.

"In some ways it might appear to make sense for her to withdraw before he gets a chance to kick her out. But if the opera world thinks she has a long-term vocal problem it could be disastrous for her career. Also, I think she's worried that if she admits defeat she might never be able to sing again. This often happens to singers, you see. If they're under a lot of pressure or stress their voices pack up. Well, it's not their voices so much as their brains."

"You're right," said Evie, "we can't tell Albert. He would die a broken man if he thought there was any problem with Lindsey's singing. He wants to hear her once more, by the way."

This was what I'd been hoping for. I thought for a moment.

"Evie, you don't think he'll make it as far as opening night, do you?"

"No, I really don't. It'll have to be soon."

"Then I've got an idea. I think I could arrange for him to be allowed into the first orchestral rehearsal. It's called a *sitzprobe*, and it's where the singers sit in a room with the orchestra, and sing through the opera reading the music from their scores and not acting at all. Almost like a concert, really. It's in two and a half weeks. Do you think Albert could make it that far?"

"I'd back him to, if he knew it was coming."

"Then what we do is get John Standish to give her some more of the pills, just for that day. That'll get her through I'm sure, especially if she knows how important it is for her Dad."

"What's in them, Jamie?"

"Standish won't say, but he does say they won't do her any harm. Look, I know it's not ideal, but these are exceptional circumstances."

"Yes, they are, I'll give you that."

"I'll tell Lindsey on the way to the station tomorrow morning. Will you tell Albert?"

"I'll get the old bugger there if it's the last thing I do. Now you ought to go to bed, Jamie. Do you think you'll have any problems with Lindsey? You could always have Carly's room."

"No, no, I doubt if Lindsey will mind. Do you really think she still adores me?"

"I'm certain of it. Now get yourself to bed."

"Thanks Evie. I don't know what to say."

Lindsey never even woke when I went in. I eased myself into bed next to her, turned over onto the side facing her back, and listened to her regular, deep breathing. In no time at all I too was asleep.

We were civil to each other when we woke up the next morning. Lindsey needed to be at Peterborough station in time to catch the eight fifty train, which meant leaving Stockencote at eight. Albert had apparently been determined to get up for breakfast to see me, but Evie had left him asleep. He needed all the sleep he could muster, she said, and in any case I would be back at the weekend, bringing Carly for her birthday celebrations.

We were in the middle of an Indian summer, with the weather apparently set fair, and it was a beautiful morning. After leaving Stockencote, we turned right towards Stamford, and drove past the edge of Rutland Water, which glittered in the sunshine. Lindsey and I lapsed into silence, but I knew I had to broach the subject of her singing, and Albert's last trip to London to hear her.

"I had a word with Evie last night," I said. "We've had a thought about a rehearsal for Albert to come to."

Her reply was very quiet. "Jamie, I don't know if I can."

"I had a thought about that, too. If you're really worried you could ask John Standish for some more of his happy pills. Do you think they'd do the trick?"

"I can't do that. It's the slippery slope."

"But just this once, Linds. It's for your Dad, after all. And you wouldn't have to take them if you decided you didn't want them. You could keep them in reserve, just in case."

She sighed. "When would you bring him?"

"Evie and I thought he might be able to come to the first *sitzprobe*. Evie thinks that's about the limit."

"No, I can't talk about this, Jamie. Sorry."

"Look, Linds, I don't want to be mean, but if we're going to fix for Albert to come we've got to do it now. I'll sort it out. Will you agree to let me?"

Eventually she said in a small voice: "all right. Just don't involve me in the arrangements."

I parked in the short-term car park, and Lindsey was just about to get out of the car, when without any warning she turned to me and gave me a devastating hug, which must have lasted all of thirty seconds. Then she got out of the car without a word, and walked into the station.

34

Friday was the day of Lindsey's dating scan. She had had an n/a booked from *Fledermaus* rehearsals since the middle of August, so although Leclerc was furious there was nothing he could do to stop her going. Ursula Zimmermann hadn't made any fuss about it – she was excited about the baby, and was already threatening to knit something for it. In any case they needed a morning to rehearse the Eisenstein-Falke duet in Act One, when Rosalinde is offstage.

I met Lindsey at Kings Cross at ten to ten. It was another beautiful morning, so we walked the short distance along Euston Road to UCH. It reminded me of the day we went for Carly's first scan. Except that on that occasion we had been as excited as children going to a birthday party, whereas now we found ourselves walking in subdued silence.

When we got there, we were shown into a depressing room full of notices about AIDS and unwanted pregnancies. We passed a hideous period of twenty minutes reading old copies of *Hello* magazine.

Standish was waiting for us when we were finally called into the scanning room. He was all bedside manner and bonhomie.

"Hallo, both. Looking cracking, if I may say so, Lindsey. Pregnancy obviously suits you."

"Thanks, John. It's good to see you."

"How's the singing?"

"Oh, you know. So-so."

"Keep me posted. I'm a friend and admirer, don't forget."

Lindsey managed a wan smile.

"Now then, let's get down to the business of the day. Quick resumé of what we're trying to achieve. Basically two things: firstly we're screening for one or two potential problems the baby might have. Nothing to be alarmed about – it's routine, but it does give us a few clues which may be useful later. The most important one, particularly for a woman of your age, Lindsey – sorry my dear, but anyone over thirty-five is classed as geriatric as far as we obs and gynies are concerned – is called the nuchal fold translucency test. It's the newest and classiest screening test for Down's Syndrome. The amount of fluid between two layers of skin behind your baby's neck is greater in Down's babies than in normal ones, so we measure this fluid, then feed the measurement into UCH's magnificent computer – every bell and whistle you could wish for – along with your age, your baby's heart rate, the results of some blood tests we're also going to take today, and young Jamie's sperm count."

He looked at Lindsey and grinned, but got no response.

"Sorry, my dear, that last bit was a joke. Anyway, the machine will give you a rating which is, basically, your chance of having a baby with Down's. If your risk is shown as being high, you may wish to opt for a diagnostic test such as CVS or amniocentesis. Any questions about that bit, my dear?"

"Do I get the computer's answer straightaway?"

"No, because we have to wait a week or so for the results of the blood tests."

"And amniocentesis and the other thing, they carry a risk, don't they?"

"A slight but significant risk of miscarriage, I'm afraid. Which is why this nuchal fold thing is the cat's whiskers. Because if your rating is low you don't need to bother with Nigel the Nasty Needle." Standish gave Lindsey his most reassuring smile. "So if we've cleared that up, let's move on to the second main purpose of today's fun-packed session, which is to tell you when your baby's due. Of course you may already know the answer to this question. You just have to extrapolate forward nine months from the date of conception. On the other hand Jamie may be pointing Percy at your pudenda two or three times a night, so it may be difficult for you to be accurate. Naturally I wouldn't wish to pry, so instead I am planning to offer my own opinion as to your dates. It's a kind of game, really. Any questions about that?"

Not a flicker crossed his patrician face as he said this. I looked at the floor. Lindsey just said to him: "I'd definitely like to know when you think the due date is, John. Shall we get started?"

"It'll be my pleasure."

He set to work. First he took two blood samples from Lindsey's arm, labelled the bottles and stuck a plaster where the needle had been. Then he shook the ultrasound gel to the business end of the tube, and apologised for its coldness as it slurped onto Lindsey's belly.

He started to move the wand over her, and a trapezoid green shape appeared on the screen. Lindsey and I had been so excited when we saw first saw the little jelly bean which was to become Carly. This time it was different. You could have cut the atmosphere with a knife.

Standish, however, affected not to notice, and stuck to banalities while he was working – "there you are, you can see the heart beating", and "keep still, you little bugger". While he was doing the nuchal fold measurement he was concentrating hard, and all was quiet. But of dates he mentioned not a word until after it was all over, and Lindsey was cleaned up and fully dressed.

"Right then, you lucky parents, I would say your eagerly-anticipated new arrival will be with you sometime between the twelfth and the twentieth of March. Putting conception sometime between the nineteenth and the twenty sixth of June. Now tell your Uncle John well done, because that conclusion has only been reached after some rather tricky work measuring the distance between the crown and the rump of your gorgeous fetus, which clearly wants to go on the stage like its mother because it was practising its dance steps throughout the entire proceedings."

I sneaked a glance at Lindsey's face. She wasn't giving away a thing.

"Thank you, John," she said. "What happens next?"

"We should have the results of your blood tests within a week or so. At that point we can assess the risk of Down's. Then you can decide about your amnio, which if you need it will be done in about four weeks' time. There is another test available, which rejoices in the name Chorionic Villus Sampling, or CVS. This would have to be done immediately, but I don't recommend it, because if your rating is low you may not need a test at all, and by the time the computer makes up its mind it will be too late for CVS."

"Did you get any idea from looking at the scan whether I might need one of these tests?"

"Tough one to answer, my dear. Really you would be much better to wait for your results."

"John, you've been so kind, thank you. Oh, and by the way, thank you for those wonderful pills you gave me in Salzburg. What was in them, for heaven's sake?"

"Nothing much, my dear. Just enough to subdue your demons. I sometimes have them before doing an important op. Don't tell anyone, whatever you do. But they do one no harm, as long as one doesn't indulge in them too often."

"John," I said, "if we were to ask you for one more dose for a special occasion, how would you react?"

"For heaven's sake, dear boy, consider it done. I'll have a small packet delivered to the stage door of the theatre this afternoon. Is that all right with you, my dear?"

"Yes, oh yes I suppose so, thank you John. Listen, Jamie, I really think it's time I went. I'd like to get to the *Fledermaus* rehearsal as soon as possible."

"*Fledermaus*, of course," said Standish. "What a mouthwatering thought. I absolutely must come. I'll book for it as soon as you've left."

The phone went the moment I walked back into the office.

"Jamie? God, you're finally back. It's John Standish."

"Christ, John, nothing wrong I hope?"

"No, no, nothing at all. Baby gives every impression of being a cracker. It's just that I've never seen two happy smiling people like you and Lindsey so hideously transformed in my life. You scarcely spoke to each other. And Lindsey looked shocking."

"You said she looked great."

"Bedside manner, dear boy. Listen, what can I do to help?"

I looked round the room. Grace was at the photocopier, and everyone else seemed preoccupied with their own business. I lowered my voice anyway. "Simple answer, John. Can you be any more precise with your dates?"

"Bugger it, Jamie. I thought I did rather well."

"The dates you gave include both the ones that concern us."

"Shit."

"Can't you give me any more idea? Earlier, later, anything?"

"Nothing I'd be prepared to stick by."

"But just a clue?"

"Sorry, Jamie. No can do."

292

Grace had returned form the photocopier and was about to sit down at her desk. I made an urgent gesture telling her to go somewhere else. She pouted at me like a three-year-old, then picked up her handbag and went off to lunch.

"Sorry about that John, I was just making sure we weren't overheard. We're no nearer knowing whose this baby is. Is that right?"

"Yes, dear boy."

"Then I have to ask you if there's any chance you'll agree to do the DNA test."

He paused. "Well, I do think it likely that she'll need an amniocentesis if she wants to be sure the baby hasn't got Down's. Absolutely nothing to worry about – my guess is that her risk will come up at no more than one in two hundred. But the nuchal fold did look slightly more filled than I would ideally like."

"Then in theory, if she does have the amniocentesis, you'd be able to do a paternity test?"

"Absolutely not. Unless Lindsey agrees."

"Well, I'm not asking her."

"For God's sake, man, don't be such a bloody wuss."

"You don't understand, John. I'm certain she'll refuse."

"And what will you do if you don't get the test?"

"I suppose I'll have to wait till it's born, then study its face for Slavic features. If it turns out to be his, I can't say what I'll do. But bringing up his baby is out of the question."

"This really means everything to you, doesn't it?"

"Yup."

"Oh Christ." He paused for some considerable time. I said nothing. Eventually he said: "two tickets for the first night of *Fledermaus*. Centre stalls. No nonsense."

"Done. You're a star, John."

"Don't give me that shit. This is a venial act on my part. I've just rung the box office. No chance of anything at all. Not even if I offer the young lady my body, which I did."

"You'd probably have had more chance if it had been a young gentleman, given the average employee in the Opera London box office." I was practically jumping up and down, I was so excited. "I wish I'd known that's what it would take to make you change your mind."

"Bollocks, Jamie. I'm a bloody fool. That's all there is to it."

"You're not a fool, you're a Saint. What do I have to do?"

"Firstly, you impatient sod, you wait for the blood test results to see whether your poor wife actually needs this amnio. Then if she does, which I think is likely, you go hotfoot to some not-very-respectable chappie in Harley Street and pay him a fortune to take a buccal cell test from you. It's just a swab from inside your cheek, and it'll have your DNA on it. Make sure the place you choose is competent and discreet, which probably means expensive. They will try and send the swab to a laboratory for testing – don't let them. Make them give it to you, and rush it round to Denise, who is trained not to ask questions. I will let you know the answer as soon as possible."

"John, I don't know what to say."

"Make sure the seats are the best in the house. And I want an invitation to the after-show party."

Lindsey and I were to meet at home after we'd both finished for the day. We were picking up Carly and driving together to Stockencote – the whole *Fledermaus* cast had been given the weekend off. It seemed Ursula Zimmermann was pleased with the way the production was going.

Standish had been as good as his word, and a little package of pills was waiting for me at the stage door as I left. I put them in my briefcase, and arrived home at six. Lindsey got back ten minutes later.

It was the first time she had met Saskia. Both were scrupulously polite. They exchanged pleasantries about Jason – Lindsey told Saskia what a good singer he was, and Saskia told Lindsey she felt lucky to have found such a sensitive boyfriend so soon after arriving in England. The question of his indeterminate sexuality didn't enter the conversation.

Saskia asked Lindsey if she would mind her having a few friends round to dinner the following evening while we were away. I don't think Lindsey liked it much, but she agreed.

"Is Jason coming, Saskia?" she asked.

"Oh yes, of course. We haven't spent a night apart since we met."

Lindsey's face tightened, and she looked at me accusingly. "Oh well," she said with a false little smile, "the house looks nice, so I'm sure you're taking care of it. Have a lovely evening, then."

The two of us went upstairs to pack some clothes. Lindsey was cross.

"For heaven's sake, Jamie, do you think it's right to let those two sleep together every night in our house?"

"Oh come on, Linds. This is the twenty-first century. Since when did you turn into a prude?"

"It just seems a bit much, with Carly asleep next door."

"At least it's not me having sex with Saskia."

"You'd like to, obviously."

"No, of course not".

She gave me an old-fashioned look.

"In any case," I said, "I've kept myself scrupulously chaste. Since the day we were married, actually."

She snorted contemptuously. Women. I ask you. Is that fair?

The three of us set off at six forty-five. The rush-hour traffic had begun to die down, and we made it to Stockencote by nine. Ethel was waiting for us in the kitchen, and gave us her usual haughty greeting, then waddled back to her bed. We ate a late supper which Evie had saved for us, then took Carly upstairs and kissed her goodnight, before reconvening in the kitchen.

Evie looked drawn. Albert, who was already in bed, was losing ground, she said. He was determined, though, to make it to London for Lindsey's rehearsal.

We talked about the baby, and Lindsey quizzed Evie about amniocentesis and nuchal translucency tests. It was all new since Evie had worked as a junior nurse on a maternity unit however, and by her own admission she couldn't cast much light on it all.

We went to bed at midnight. Evie, bless her, had fixed for Fliss to come and give Carly a riding lesson in the morning, and Gordon was going to take her out on the tractor in the afternoon. This left Lindsey and me free to go shopping in Peterborough for Carly's birthday.

As soon as we climbed into bed Lindsey said quietly but firmly: "good night, Jamie". It wasn't unpleasant, and was a whole lot better than being made to sleep on the floor, but it still left me with a powerful sense of the unjustness of things. When I finally got to sleep, my dreams involved all sorts of carnal activity with Saskia. I awoke in a panic at seven o'clock, and was relieved and somewhat surprised to find that I hadn't had a wet dream.

Albert made it down to breakfast. The rictus of pain had tightened round his face, but he was having no truck with depression or any such nonsense. Over his cup of tea he quizzed Carly about her forthcoming lesson with Fliss.

"Cedric's still out, you know Carly. The weather's been so lovely, I'm not having him in eating my hay when he can be out eating grass. Fliss won't like it if he looks a scruff, so you'd better get him in and groom him. What time's she coming?"

Carly looked blankly at Evie, who smiled at her and said "ten thirty. Your Grandad's right, Carly. Can you get him in on your own?"

"Course I can. Will you come and watch my lesson, Grandad?"

"I will if Evie'll drive me up to the manège."

"Of course I will," said Evie. "We can take the barbeque up in the back of the Land Rover at the same time. They say the weather'll hold for tomorrow, so Carly's birthday lunch can be outside. Would you like that, Carly?"

"Ooh yes please, Auntie Evie. I *love* barbeques. Is Hattie coming?"

"Yes, darling. I rang the pub last week, and her Mum said she'd love to. What meat would you both like?" said Evie.

"Burgers and hot dogs. Oh, and ribs for Hattie. She likes ribs."

No more thoughts of being a vegetarian, then.

"Evie, make sure you get everything they want," said Albert. "And I'll butterfly a leg of lamb for us. I want this to be the best birthday party Carly's ever had."

Lindsey and I spent most of Saturday at the Queensgate Shopping Centre in Peterborough, spending far too much on presents for Carly. We had lunch at Macdonalds, which sat heavy on our stomachs all afternoon, and we were frazzled by the time we arrived back at Stockencote. We had a cup of tea in the study with Albert, then Lindsey took herself upstairs for a nap. And very possibly a phone call, I thought.

Albert and I were left alone. He was making a superhuman effort, and had been excellent company during tea. As soon as Lindsey had disappeared he got straight down to the subject which was clearly preoccupying him.

"Jamie, I've thought long and hard about the farm since we spoke, and I've come up with the beginnings of an idea."

"Okay, Albert, fire away."

"I've been getting the sense with the lass during the last few days that she isn't very happy about her singing. Am I right?"

"Oh. Well, no, I wouldn't really say that, Albert."

I had never heard him shout before. But this time he let me have it.

"For God's SAKE, will you all stop treating me like a bloody idiot? I'm may be dying, but I'm not stupid. She comes back every day from that place, and won't talk about the rehearsals at all. No enthusiasm, no spark, no nothing. Just a long face and a shake of the head. Now tell me what's going on, bugger you." He slumped back in his chair, exhausted by his own vehemence.

"Yes, yes of course. We didn't want to worry you, that's all. Lindsey *is* worried about her singing. She has been ever since Salzburg. Now she won't risk singing out properly."

"Have you spoken to her about it?"

"Not really, not since she started in London. Although the irony is it's part of my job – if she were anyone else I'd have had her in my office by now, for a concerned chat."

"Well get on with it, man. She needs you."

"I find it so hard to talk to her when she's angry, Albert."

"For Christ's sake, Jamie, what are you, a man or a mouse?"

"All right, Albert, I'll talk to her, of course I will." Time to change the subject. "You were saying something about the farm."

"I was coming to that, Jamie. I told you, I'm not losing my marbles. But Lindsey's singing has a huge bearing on what I was about to say. How would you react if I asked you to take over the running of the farm yourselves?"

It was like a punch in the pit of my stomach. I was about to be appointed to one of the top jobs in British opera – the summit of my career.

"Gosh, Albert, it's a grand idea, but I don't see how we can. I mean it's not just Lindsey. I'm about to start a fantastic job."

"What, working for that bloody Sergei Rebroff?"

"Well, I mean, he'll be Chairman, yes of course. But he won't want any artistic control."

"Oh for God's sake, Jamie, how naïve can you get? I don't pretend to know what's happening at that company, but I do know one thing. I don't trust that man. I don't trust him with my daughter, or any of my family. And I don't reckon those rich Russians are to be trusted with any business, let alone one as full of head-in-the-clouds idealists as an opera company."

I was angry, despite myself. "Look, Albert, this is out of the question. I'm sorry, I can't consider pulling out. And I have every confidence that

Lindsey will get back to singing well very soon. She's Britain's top opera singer. You can't want her to stop, surely?"

He heaved a huge sigh, and suddenly looked very old and sick. "No, Jamie lad. I'm sorry. You're right, of course. And an old sod like me shouldn't be interfering. I'm incredibly proud of Lindsey, you know I am. And as long as she's enjoying her career, I'm a hundred per cent behind her. Just bear in mind what I say, because more than anything I want her to be happy, and I reckon she's as happy here as anywhere in the world. Am I still coming to hear her rehearse, by the way? I wouldn't want to embarrass the lass, not if she's not on top form."

"Yes, yes, of course Albert, of course you must come. I'm convinced that having you there will be exactly what she needs to sort herself out. You think you'll be able to manage it?"

"I'll get myself there if I have to crawl, Jamie."

"What about the farm? What do you want to do?"

"You just put it in your pipe and smoke it, lad. If you and Lindsey both want it, it's there for you. And if she wants to go on singing, and you want to go on being a big cheese in the Smoke, you can go back to plan A, and get a tenant in. I'm sorry I brought it up. Now, I think the sun's over the yardarm. Get me a gin and tonic before I go mad."

The evening was one of the most heartbreakingly beautiful I could remember at Stockencote, or anywhere else for that matter. We had dinner in the dining room, because there was a nip in the air, but after Carly and Albert had gone to bed, Lindsey put on her coat, and said she was taking Ethel for a walk, and would anyone like to join her? Evie shot me an urgent glance, so I got up and said yes, I quite fancied a stroll down to Rutland Water.

There was a harvest moon – huge and bright in the sky, and lighting up the fields as if it were some ghostly version of the sun. We walked down to the reservoir, which at this point was no more than a strip of water, and looked across to Normanton Church, half submerged in its watery grave, and seeming to leak moonlight through some invisible wound in its side. The water lapped at our feet, and Lindsey stood there and wept silently, the tears catching the light as they slid unchecked down her face: white and flawless in the moonlight, like alabaster.

Was she weeping for her father, or her marriage, or even her absent lover? Maybe she was mourning the passing of her wonderful talent. We walked silently back to the house, where Evie had a kettle on the boil, and made us a cup of tea. We all three sat shrouded in melancholy, and after a while Evie and Lindsey went off to bed. I wrapped Carly's outrageous number of presents, and took them up to our bedroom, where I laid them out at the foot of our bed, then changed into my pyjamas and brushed my teeth.

Lindsey lay on her side, blessedly asleep and astonishingly beautiful. As gently as I could I lay down next to her, and surrendered myself to a sense of total despair.

Carly opened our curtains at six, wildly excited. The sun streamed in through the window, and woke us both up.

"Oh, hallo darling, happy birthday," I said, heaving myself up onto my pillows.

"Happy birthday, sweetheart," said Lindsey.

"Are these my presents?"

"They're the ones from Mummy and me. There might be some more downstairs from Grandad and Auntie Evie."

"Awesome." She tore the carefully-applied wrapping paper off each one in turn, scarcely stopping to look at what was inside. Within five minutes she was finished.

"Can I have Grandad's and Auntie Evie's now?"

"No darling, they're still asleep. Why don't you have another look at what we've got for you?"

"Oh. Okay. The iPod's really cool. Can I have some songs?"

"You'll have to wait until we get home, darling. Grandad doesn't have broadband."

She found an electronic game which she'd wanted for months, and ran back into her room to play it. I managed to get a few more minutes of half-sleep before I had to get dressed and go downstairs with Carly. By the time the others came down to breakfast we'd visited practically every animal on the farm so Carly could tell them it was her birthday.

Breakfast came and went. Carly was so excited she was in danger of being sick, which had happened the previous Christmas, so Albert decided that as a birthday treat she should be given a ride on the tractor. Gordon was working anyway, even though it was a Sunday, and he said he'd be delighted to take her.

I was relaxing over my fourth cup of tea when my phone went. I'd wanted to leave it switched off, but I'd learnt my lesson after we got back from Montpellier. It was Angus.

"Sorry to disturb your Sunday, old thing, but have you seen the *Witness*?"

"No. Trouble?"

"'Fraid so. You were spotted gossiping to Max Polgar at the party after the Opera North *Tristan*."

"Bugger. Hopkirk was there. It'll be something to do with her."

"Very possibly. It's in the *Hunter Gatherer* column, in the *Weekend* supplement. You'd better look at it on the Web."

"Can't. We're at Lindsey's Dad's place. The technology's older then God."

"Then go out and buy the newspaper."

"Okay, if I must. It's a bloody nuisance, actually."

"Just go and get it, Jamie."

I drove into Oakham in a rage, which at least made a change from the blank depression of the last couple of days. I went and bought the *Sunday Witness* from the newsagent in the High Street, and looked through the *Weekend* section while I was still in the shop. The *Hunter Gatherer* column was towards the back, and the Opera London piece was tucked into a corner.

Hunter Gatherer went to the premiere of Leeds-based Opera North's production of Wagner's epic Tristan und Isolde last Tuesday, and spotted something very interesting at the after-show party. Jamie Barlow, husband of opera star Lindsey Templeton and hot tip for the top job at Sergei Rebroff's new acquisition Opera London, was engaged in a very chummy conversation with Hungarian émigré businessman Max Polgar. Polgar, who is second in command to Rebroff on the Opera London Board, is widely seen as being kingmaker in the current battle for the vacant posts of General Administrator and Music Director. Questions have already been asked in the press about the transparency of the selection process; however Hunter Gatherer confidently expects Barlow, together with young British conductor Angus Lennox, to be confirmed shortly as the new management team. Another stitch-up with the much-maligned Arts Council of England? You heard it here first.

Angus was right, we were in trouble.

I drove back to Stockencote. As I arrived at the front gates the phone went again. It was Polgar.

"Have you seen it?" he said.

"Yes. We've got a problem, haven't we?"

"Well, the jobs are still yours, of course. But I've spoken to Sergei, and we've agreed you'll both have to come in for interview."

"When did you have in mind?"

"It's got to be Wednesday. It's the only day Sergei and all the other Board members are free. Leclerc and Chapelle are already coming in. Best time for you would be seven o'clock. Can you make it?"

"Of course I can Max."

"It's not just *Hunter Gatherer*, whoever the hell he or she is. It's Leclerc. One of my colleagues on the Board saw Gregory Knipe the other day, and apparently our friend Olivier is looking for trouble. He thinks he's not going to get the job without pulling some strings, so he's been in touch with Gregory, and he's trying to get him to orchestrate a campaign to discredit the selection process. I wouldn't be surprised if he's behind this article. And I think it's likely there'll be more."

"I take it the Board won't be swayed."

"No, no of course not. In any case it's Sergei's money, well, Sergei's and the Arts Council's, but we've got that sewn up through Archie Foster, and Sergei's determined to have you two. All we have to do is convince the Press it's free and fair."

I had been parked in the yard for a couple of minutes by now. Evie emerged through the back door and waved a coffee pot at me, then pointed into the kitchen and smiled.

"Right you are, Max. I've got to go, I'm afraid. I'll be outside the Board Room at seven on Wednesday."

"Fine. Sorry about interrupting your Sunday, Jamie."

Livid, I slammed the car door, and went inside, leaving the paper on the back seat. Lindsey and Evie were still at the breakfast table. They looked a picture of domestic bliss.

We spent the morning sorting everything out for the barbecue in the field. It was one of those lunchtimes which only September can bring – genuinely hot but with a tinge of melancholy, caused by the knowledge that there won't be many more such occasions before the winter closes in. This year, winter's chill seemed more fearsome than ever.

Albert wasn't in a fit state to stand over a barbecue, so I did the honours. Hattie from the pub was beautifully behaved, and kept complimenting me on the quality of the food. I'd brought a padded chair from the house for Albert, and Evie had driven him out to the field.

He had two or three glasses of claret, and for a few minutes tiny splodges of colour appeared in his cheeks. He laughed, and ate a bit, and slept in his chair with Ethel on his knee. Lindsey relaxed, Evie smiled, and the sun shone. If we hadn't known it was the last party of Albert's life, it would have been a perfect afternoon.

At about five we started to clear up, and I took Hattie home, while Evie got Albert back down to the house. By seven, everything was put away, and I had packed our things into the Passat. Carly appeared from the stables, where she had been saying goodbye to Cedric.

"Thank you for my party, Auntie Evie, and thank you, Grandad. I've had the best birthday ever."

Albert's eyes filled with tears. "That's all right, my lovely. You make sure you come back and see me soon."

Carly started to cry, too. "Please don't die, Grandad. I love you."

"Don't you worry, my little bunny rabbit." He hadn't called her that since she was four years old. "It'll be all right. You'll see. I love you too, poppet."

Without warning, Lindsey turned on her heel and fled back into the house.

"Don't chase her, Jamie lad. Just think about what I said."

"Thanks, Albert, I will. See you a week on Friday, at the rehearsal. Look after him, Evie. I'll ring you to make the arrangements. And thank you for a wonderful weekend."

Without saying a word, Evie put her arms round me, and hugged me. Then she hugged Carly, and said, very quietly, "goodbye darling." We got into the car, and drove off, waving. Carly cried silently all the way home.

35

Everyone at work had seen the *Witness* article by the time I got in the following day. There were plenty of comments, mostly good-natured. I was expecting some contact from the press, but either the Press Office was fielding the calls, or there weren't any.

My phone did ring at half past three, but it was just Carly. Emma had asked her for the night, she said, and her Mum had said it was fine as long as I didn't mind. I thought it would take her mind off things, so agreed enthusiastically.

Jason turned up at home, as usual, at about seven. We had a gin and tonic together while Saskia finished cooking the tea. He looked tired and, I thought, rather fed up.

"You were doing Act Three today, weren't you?" I said.

"Yes, that's right. This morning we did all my stuff with Frosch, or Frau Osch, as she's now called. And this afternoon we started staging the trio with me, Julian and Lindsey."

"And how was that?"

"Difficult, actually. Lindsey still hasn't sung a note. Everyone's getting angry about it, and it's making the atmosphere pretty toxic. I'm not enjoying it – no-one seems to have any time for me. Except Olivier, that is. He's being fantastic."

That was the first time I had ever heard anyone call Olivier Leclerc fantastic.

"How does he feel about Lindsey not singing?"

"Ursula Zimmermann's asked him not to talk about it in rehearsals. But he's been talking to me. He and Yvonne Umfreville keep having meetings about it."

"Sounds serious. They haven't said anything to me."

"They've decided not to. Olivier says you're too closely involved. Sorry, Jamie."

"No, no, don't be sorry. You're doing exactly what I asked you to do. How much does Lindsey know about what's going on?"

"I don't know. She just comes in and does the job – without singing out, of course. She's on her own during all the breaks, then goes home as soon as we finish. At least she usually goes home. Today she was picked up in a huge black Mercedes."

The contents of my bowels did their familiar trick of heading rapidly for the floor. "Is that the first time that's happened?"

"Well, it's the first time I've seen it. I happened to be walking out of the door when the car pulled up. I heard her say: 'yes, please, the Savoy', then the car pulled away. I must have been staring, because the driver winked at me. He was gorgeous. Don't tell Saskia." He produced one of his irritating high-pitched giggles.

"Um, no, of course I won't. That's really helpful, thanks Jason. We'd better go and see if supper's ready."

I opened a bottle of Chablis, because I felt like getting drunk. I didn't eat much tea, even though Saskia had cooked a wonderful fish curry – she liked fish, she said, because she didn't think fish had very big brains, so they couldn't have feelings.

I was both furious and upset. Lindsey couldn't bring herself to talk to me about Albert, or about anything else, for that matter. But she was talking every day to Sergei, or so it seemed. And now she'd taken herself off to his suite at the bloody Savoy, where no doubt he was comforting her with caviar and Krug champagne. For all I knew she'd be staying the night.

My mood wasn't helped by a lovers' tiff which developed during the meal. Jason seemed determined to upset Saskia. I opened a second bottle of Chablis, hoping it might jolly things along a bit, but it only made it worse. He started to talk in glowing terms about Olivier, and then about the driver of Lindsey's car. Then he started on me.

"I need to have a man." He was slurring his words badly. "Why don't you come to bed with Saskia and me tonight, Jamie?"

"No, Jason, I really don't want to do that. I've told you that already."

"Oh, come on. Saskia wouldn't mind, would you Saskia?"

Her eyes flared. "Jason, you are obviously completely homosexual. Of course this I already knew, but I thought maybe I could change you. I was wrong. You are a horrible, horrible person." She began to cry.

"Well, I don't need to be insulted by YOU, thank you very much Saskia. I think maybe I had better go home."

"Yes, that would be a good idea," she said. "Why don't you go to a gay club on the way? This I think you would much prefer."

Unbelievably, Jason did yet another of his girly laughs. He rose unsteadily to his feet and turned to me.

"Jamie, I am sorry to be rude. This creature has suggested I go to a club, and I think I might. You wouldn't like to come with me, by any chance?"

"No, Jason, I wouldn't."

"Then I'll go. He tried to kiss me. I ducked out of the way. "Thank you for all the nice wine, darling. And gin. Bye."

He stumbled out of the room and slammed the front door behind him.

"Leave him," said Saskia.

"He'll regret it in the morning. If he remembers it."

"Mister Jamie, don't worry about him, please. He isn't worth it."

I handed her a hanky – I happened to have a clean one in my pocket – and she dried her tears and blew her nose. Then without warning she got up and sat on my knee.

"Mister Jamie, you're really kind to me, do you know that?"

"Saskia, please. I really don't want to do this."

I was half-heartedly trying to get her off my lap, but succeeded only in rubbing Percy against her. Her face suddenly lit up with the most lascivious smile.

"Oh, I think you do, Mister Jamie." She placed her full, wet, lips softly over mine, and started to explore my mouth with her tongue. I was too drunk to resist. I felt in my pocket for my Post-It note, scrunched it up, and flicked it across the room.

After a while she pulled her mouth away from mine, and made a sign for me to wait. Then she ran upstairs, and reappeared moments later clutching what I believe is known as a spliff, and an orange plastic lighter.

"Don't say nothing, Mister Jamie. No-one will know."

She lit the spliff, and presented it to me. I took it between the thumb and forefinger of my right hand and took a tentative pull. Nothing happened. Except that she took it back and had a lungful herself, then put in down on a saucer and locked her mouth over mine again, straddling me on my chair as she did so. Sod Lindsey, I thought. She and Sergei were probably doing exactly the same thing on one of those black velvet sofas in the Savoy.

My hand was creeping inside Saskia's T-shirt and lifting it off. No bra, as usual. I began to caress her left breast. Her skin was like silk, soft and slippy. Her tongue was feeling mine, probing, licking. My own tongue found its way along her row of perfect teeth. Just like Lindsey's. Another little shock of guilt, followed immediately by one of anger. Both instantly overwhelmed by lust.

We broke off for another tug on the spliff, then Saskia got off my lap, and led me to her room. We took another drag, then suddenly both of her hands were undoing my belt. There was a clink of metal. She unbuttoned my jeans, and took hold of my Calvin Kleins and a handful of what was inside.

She was completely naked. My finger slipped quietly around her, massaging her, slipping inside her. Then she pulled me towards her, kissing me all the while. She smelt of dope and of sex.

Then she pulled me down on the bed, and guided Percy right inside her. She was tight, young, unbelievable. She moaned quietly – little low noises with each breath, getting gradually higher. Then her body convulsed, and so did mine - shatteringly. She screamed, and I grunted, like one of Albert's stud boars.

I rolled off her, and she re-lit the spliff, and offered it to me. But I wasn't interested. The guilt had already taken over.

We didn't sleep together. I made some excuse about needing to be right by the phone in case Lindsey rang, and tottered uncertainly back to our room. After a couple of hours of soul-searching I made up my mind to tell Lindsey what had happened. Then, after a couple of minutes of fitful sleep, I woke up in a muck sweat, and changed my mind. This process repeated itself about thirty times during the course of that ghastly night. At seven, when I'd already been in to wake Carly, only to remember she wasn't there, I finally decided to keep my mouth shut, and make sure Saskia did too. It wasn't that I couldn't face telling Lindsey. It was just that I judged, rightly or wrongly, that our marriage had slightly more chance of surviving if I shut up.

I was downstairs finishing my breakfast when Saskia walked in, wearing nothing but a short T-shirt and a very skimpy pair of knickers. I was ready to be embarrassed and tongue-tied but she didn't give me the chance.

"Hi, Mister Jamie. Lovely day. It's a treat not to have to take Carly to school, isn't it?"

And with that she removed the piece of toast from my hand and put it down on my plate. Then she smiled. She gently took hold of the back of my head, and lowered her mouth onto mine. I made a half-hearted effort to protest, but between the toast still left in my mouth and Saskia's determined lips I didn't get much chance. She lifted me quietly up from my chair, still locked onto me, and started to undo my belt. Pausing only to sweep my plate and half-full coffee cup onto the floor, she pulled me down on top of her, and we did it again, this time on the kitchen table. God help me.

I managed to get myself out of the house and off to work by dint of a lot of Hugh Grant apologising. I was horrified, not only by what I had done, but by the knowledge that it was going to be almost impossible to resist doing it again and again. I'd been paranoid about having a one-night stand. Now I was having a full-blown affair.

Work, however, was blessedly free of controversy. Whatever follow-up I'd been expecting to the *Witness* article had, so far at least, failed to materialise, and I was able to concentrate on sorting out my plans for the future of the Company. For all Max Polgar had said about the next day's interview being a formality, I was determined to make a good impression.

I found a moment during the afternoon to ring Stockencote, ostensibly to see how Albert was getting on. What I really wanted to establish was whether Lindsey had gone back there last night.

Evie answered. She sounded frazzled.

"Hallo Jamie, how lovely to hear from you."

"Hi, Evie. I just wondered how Albert was bearing up. And you for that matter."

"Don't worry about me, Jamie. I can handle this. But Albert's being awfully stubborn. Yesterday he was on a high after the weekend, so he wasn't too bad. But today he's in a lot of pain, and he's being pretty short with me. Dr Storey came this morning and told him he ought to be allowing himself some proper pain relief. But he won't hear of it. He says he's going to get himself through to the end of next week, so he can hear Lindsey's rehearsal, then he doesn't care what we do with him."

"Well, you have to admire him for that. How's he been with Lindsey?"

"She's hardly seen him. She didn't get back till one o'clock last night – she was out gallivanting with the cast, apparently. This morning she looked terrible – really tired. She looked in on Albert before she left, and apparently all he said to her was 'for God's sake get yourself to bed at a reasonable hour, lass. You look shocking.' Jamie, she's got to start looking after herself for the sake of the baby."

"Tricky. You're a stubborn lot, you Templetons."

"Don't I know it, Jamie."

"Is Albert awake now?"

"No, he's having his nap. I'll tell him you were asking after him."

"Yes, please do, Evie. And give him my love."

I might have added 'and tell him I shagged the au pair last night and this morning – he'll like that'. But even though I could think of almost nothing else, it didn't seem quite the right thing to say.

Carly was back home when I walked in about six thirty. She was wrestling with some hideous maths homework given her by Mrs Bodley. I sat down with her and tried to concentrate on it, but was distracted by the little smiles Saskia kept giving me every time she found an excuse to walk into the living room.

"Daddy, why is Saskia smiling at you so much?"

"Because we had a private joke this morning, darling. Something in the newspaper."

"But you aren't smiling back at her."

"I'm trying to do your homework, Carly."

"Saskia's *my* friend, Daddy, not yours. You're supposed to be her boss."

"And you're supposed to be working. Now do you understand that fraction? You have to turn it upside down when you move it to the other side of the equation."

"What's an equation?"

We went on like this until tea was ready. We had something delicious with monkfish and Carly had second helpings. After tea we took ages to finish her maths, and it was her bed-time by the time her books were packed up in her school-bag ready for the following morning. We had shouted a lot, but at least we'd got it done.

She was so cross, however, that she demanded to be put to bed by Saskia. I stayed downstairs to do the washing-up. While I was doing it I made up my mind that no matter what the provocation Percy was staying locked up inside my trousers.

This would have been substantially easier to achieve if Saskia hadn't removed her top by the time she got back into the kitchen. Her breasts were bouncing softly up and down as she walked. There was no way I could resist giving them the tiniest of kisses.

And then we were at it again, in the living room this time. I had to run to the window wearing only my jeans, and close the curtains, so no-one could see in. Half way through I got a sudden, unwelcome vision of Albert's gaunt face staring disapprovingly at me from across the ether. But it didn't stop me having another overwhelming orgasm.

Once again, for the sake of discretion, we slept apart. There was no real argument about this with Carly in the house. I slept the sleep of the truly knackered, and only just got myself out of bed in time to get Carly to school, before travelling on to work.

I walked into the Board Room on the dot of seven that evening. Sergei was all smarmy charm.

"Ah, Jamie. Good to see you."

"Good to see you too, Sergei."

"You know everyone?"

"Not quite."

So Max Polgar introduced us all. They looked a bit cowed in the presence of their new Russian chairman. The one unexpected guest was Archie Foster, who extended an affable hand.

"Jamie, splendid to see you. My Lords and Masters have sent me along to ensure fair play. Hope you don't mind."

"Heavens no, of course not Archie. Good to see a friendly face."

Polgar shot me the briefest of warning looks. But Sergei appeared not to notice.

"Jamie, we all know why we are here", he said. "I have made no secret that I would like you do become General Administrator. Now it is up to you to convince everyone in this room that you would be right man for job. I have asked Max to conduct the interview."

"Right you are, Sergei. Of course."

Max put the tips of his fingers together. "Jamie, we've all been impressed with the job you have done as casting director over the last few years. Your artistic judgement seems to be excellent, and the product has been almost universally of top quality. But you have never had to make strategic decisions. Please be so good as to outline your vision for the Company."

Grace had been coaching me in this for days. "With Sergei's incredibly generous gift," I began, "and with the continued backing of the Arts Council, we have a unique opportunity to concentrate on artistic merit. This doesn't mean taking our eye off the balance sheet – for too long successive bosses have run the Company as they feel an international opera company should be run, without worrying about who was going to bale them out next time there was a financial crisis."

There was a general murmur of assent.

"I feel that we must exploit the skills so readily available within the Company – many of the nuts and bolts staff have been here for years, and have built up great expertise in mounting productions in this rather difficult space. It may surprise you to know that years of budgetary restraint have fostered a culture of economy within the Company – unlike many foreign houses, where they seem to be only too eager to throw money at a problem first, and ask questions afterwards. This seems in my experience to be particularly true in France."

I couldn't resist slipping that one in, knowing that Chapelle was my main rival for the job.

"Artistically my first priority is the musical standard. When productions are sung in English, the words must be audible throughout, ensemble must be immaculate, and the playing of the orchestra must be beyond reproach. I have made no secret that Angus Lennox would be my favoured choice of Music Director, and would trust him absolutely with this side of things.

"That leaves the production side. For at least twenty-five years the pioneering work of directors has been the backbone of the Company's reputation. Sometimes their work has courted controversy – we can all think of shows where the setting has worked against the music, as opposed to enhancing it."

There was another general grunt of agreement.

"However, in my opinion it has been the policy of allowing directors their head which has produced the most memorable work the Company has done. No-one complains when updating an opera's setting works triumphantly well. We must all accept that with experimentation comes an element of risk, and there will be some failures to put alongside the successes. I would, however, be inclined to limit the most controversial directors to non-standard repertoire, which in practice mostly means works of the twentieth century. This has two advantages – more modern pieces can often, because of their dramatic content, stand up more robustly to unconventional treatment. And secondly it means that when we do produce a new *Traviata* or *Boheme*, say, these shows will tend to have a longer shelf-life, thus saving too many expensive mistakes.

"From a management point of view I am prepared to acknowledge my relative inexperience, so would suggest promoting Anna-Gre Tapp to be Chief Executive, with responsibility for the workforce. She does an excellent job – I think she should be rewarded and encouraged."

I paused for breath. Max Polgar looked round the table.

"Does anyone have any questions for Jamie?"

A voice immediately said "yes, I do." It belonged to Avril Bishop, a Labour MP, and the Board's self-appointed Voice of Political Correctness. She went on: "Mr Barlow, what is your view on the importance of education and outreach in the Company's work?"

"I believe these two things are of vital importance, second only to the actual business of putting on high-quality performances of opera. The Company's existing initiatives seem excellent, and entirely fit for purpose. I would give them my wholehearted support."

There was silence for ten seconds or so. Then Sergei spoke.

"Jamie, I, too have question to put to you. It concerns your ability to manage singers, well, one singer in particular. We are all aware that you are husband of Lindsey Templeton, who will I am sure be central to your plans?"

"Of course she will, Sergei."

"Very well. Do you feel that you are able to make unbiased decisions about her abilities, and which operas she should sing?"

"Is there a particular reason why you ask, Sergei?"

"Yes. I have spoken yesterday to her. She is concerned that her father's poor health is affecting her singing, and has suggested she may withdraw from production of *Fledermaus*. Are you aware of this?"

There was a sudden chorus of outraged comments from round the table. "Oh , that would be a terrible shame." "She *must* sing in Sergei's first new production." "Surely a professional singer should be able to deal with that sort of pressure?"

"Yes, Sergei, I am aware that Lindsey is worried."

"She must sing in *Fledermaus*, Jamie. I insist on it."

I was determined to control my temper. I said, in as measured a voice as I could manage: "I have often known singers suffer from stress-related impairment to their voices. I suspect Lindsey will be able to deal with the pressure, although she herself may have doubts. I would not encourage her to cancel at this stage."

"She suspects that Maestro Leclerc, whom by coincidence we have already interviewed today for the job of Music Director, may want her out."

"Olivier Leclerc will, I'm sure, do what he is told. He is very keen to make a good impression on you all."

"Then you are prepared to tell both Lindsey and Leclerc that she must sing?"

"I think we should give it until the end of next week. That is the day of the first *sitzprobe*. If she has not regained her confidence by then, I think we may be forced to consider Lindsey's position."

Sergei sighed. "We must now discuss amongst ourselves what you have said. You are last of our interviewees for General Administrator. We have only Angus Lennox left to see. We will be in touch soon."

He rubbed his face with his hands. Max Polgar said "thank you so much for coming in, Jamie."

Angus was sitting in the ante-room.

"How did it go?" he said. Have you got your feet under the table?"

"Not yet, Gussie, not officially anyway. They're worried about whether I can manage Lindsey."

"God, old boy, I should think there's no-one in the world better at managing the Deev than you are. If that's the best excuse they can muster you'd better start ordering wallpaper."

There was a bit more half-hearted banter, then the secretary emerged from the room and said:

"Mr Lennox, would you be so kind as to come in now?"

As he got up, I said "impress them, Gussie. You're my family's meal ticket." I got up and walked out of the office, and down the stairs to the street. Then, mindful that Saskia would probably be waiting for me with lips parted and libido cocked, I decided to walk home. I didn't get back till half past eight.

Carly and Saskia had eaten earlier, and were watching telly. Gales of laughter were emerging from the living room. There was a bit of food left over for me, which I ate, washed down with the end of a bottle of nasty Australian Chardonnay left over from the previous night. I finally joined the other two at about nine.

"Carly, you ought to be in bed."

"And hallo to you too, Daddy. Did you have a good day?"

"Sorry darling, I'm a bit frazzled."

"That's no reason to take it out on us, Daddy."

"Maybe not. But you ought to be in bed."

"I want Saskia to put me to bed."

Saskia looked at me and yawned. "I can if you want, Mister Jamie."

"Then will you come back downstairs?"

"No, I don't think so. Not tonight. I'm tired."

"Okay then. Carly, come and give me a kiss."

"Eeeuuu. Do I have to?"

"Not if you don't want to. Night night, darling."

"Night, night, DAHling."

They hooted with laughter, and went upstairs. I decided to risk ringing Lindsey. She might be at the Savoy, of course, but then again she might not. I rang the landline at Stockencote.

Evie answered.

"Hi Evie. How's things?"

"Much the same. He's hanging on pretty well, really."

"Still on for a week on Friday?"

"Yes. I reckon he'll make it."

"Great. Is Lindsey there?"

"Yes, she is, Jamie. She's relaxing in front of the television for once. I'll get her."

The line went quiet for a minute, then Lindsey said: "Hi Jamie." Her voice sent a shock of guilt right through me.

"Hi darling. How was today?"

"Same as all the other days. I'm still marking everything. I daren't sing out, even though Olivier wants me to. Yvonne Umfreville's beside herself."

"Ignore them, sweetheart. I saw Sergei today. He's determined you should sing."

"I know, Jamie. I saw him the other day."

"And?"

"And nothing. I went to the Savoy for dinner. It was lovely. Then I came back to Stockencote."

"Don't you think it would be better if you didn't see him at the moment?"

There was a pause, then a sigh.

"I'm sorry, Jamie, but I can't deal with this. Can I just talk to Carly?"

"She's gone up to bed. I'll get her. Hang on…"

Taking the phone with me, I legged it two at a time up the stairs and into Carly's room. Saskia was bending over the bed to give her a kiss. She was wearing a mini-skirt, and at the fork of her nut-brown legs I could see a stripe of white knicker.

I must have been staring, because when Carly stopped kissing Saskia she gave me a very funny look. Acutely aware that Lindsey was listening on the other end of the phone, I said as quickly as I could:

"Carly, it's Mummy. She wants to talk to you."

I handed over the phone, and Carly began an animated conversation with her mother. Saskia blew her a kiss, as did I, and I turned off the light. We extricated ourselves from the room together, and shut the door.

She made as if to go into her bedroom, but before I knew what I was doing my hand had found its way to the spot I'd just been gazing at.

Saskia took no second bidding. She said "I was hoping you were going to do that, Mister Jamie," and kissed me. Then she led me into her bedroom. Within two minutes she was impaled on top of me, screaming her head off. I hoped to God we weren't interrupting Carly's conversation with my wife.

This time I stayed in her bed when we'd finished. I couldn't tear myself away from the dishevelled, amoral creature lying beside me. We both lit cigarettes, and I pulled the smoke deep down inside me. It felt fantastic. Afterwards she nestled down onto my shoulder, and we both fell asleep.

A little while later I woke needing the loo and a drink, so got up and went downstairs, realising that I still had to lock up and turn out the lights. On the way back up the stairs I saw Carly coming out of the bathroom. I was bollock naked.

"Oh, Daddy, hi." She was trying to act natural, but not quite managing it. "You're in the nude."

"Yes, darling. I was hot."

"I've just been into Saskia's room, but she's asleep…"

Jesus Christ, that was a close one.

Carly was looking distinctly uncomfortable. "Um, Daddy, please can you change my bed?"

"Why?"

"Because I need clean sheets."

"But why? You haven't had an accident, have you?"

"Um, well, sort of. Sorry, Daddy."

She hadn't wet the bed since she was five years old.

"Hang on then sweetheart," I said. "I'll get a dressing gown."

I went into our bedroom, shut the door and quickly pulled the duvet off the bed, so it looked as if it had been slept in. Then I grabbed my dressing gown and emerged, tying my belt as I went.

Carly's bed was absolutely sodden. She stood over me hopelessly while I took off the sheet and duvet, and stuffed them into her enormous washing basket. Saskia would have to deal with them.

"Daddy…"

She hesitated again.

"Daddy, I don't suppose I could sleep in your bed tonight?"

"Yes, darling, of course you can. Do you need a wash?"

"Just had one, while you were downstairs."

I opened our bedroom door and told her to get into bed while I went into our ensuite. I went to the loo, then washed myself all over, as quickly as I could. Then I put on a clean pair of pyjamas from the pile in the airing cupboard, mercifully located right there in our bathroom, and went back to the bed. I'd hoped Carly might have gone to sleep, but her little face was peering at me, cocooned in duvet and pillows.

I climbed in next to her, and said: "You've decided to go on Mummy's side, sweetheart."

"Yes. I miss Mummy. Don't you?"

"Yes, of course I do."

"I don't think Saskia does though, do you?"

"Saskia hardly knows Mummy, darling."

"When's she coming back?"

"I don't know. It depends on Grandad."

She sighed. I put my arm round her, and she snuggled in next to me.

"I love you, Daddy," she said.

"I love you too, sweetheart."

I felt like the world's biggest shit.

36

Max Polgar rang the following morning to confirm that the job was mine, saying that the Board had been impressed with my interview. He also said that the press could be difficult to handle when the announcement was made. There were some people who had strong objections to the new regime, he said, and he was almost certain they would kick up a fuss. Strictly off the record, he was sure the campaign was being headed by Leclerc and Chapelle, who were convinced that they weren't getting the jobs. But he hadn't confirmed this to them, and was hoping they would hold their fire until they knew for sure.

He was going to delay the announcement for a few days, and wait for some big item of national news to occur, so he could slip the information out unnoticed. Once the announcement had been made, I was to move upstairs to Dunwich's old office. Anna-Gre Tapp, whose appointment as Chief Executive would be announced after a couple of weeks, would eventually have an office next door.

I was curiously underwhelmed by it all, obsessed as I was by Saskia, Lindsey, and poor Albert. For the next few days I indulged in successive bouts of sex and guilt. The lust was too strong for me. I did make a point of sleeping in my own bed, but Carly had no more accidents, thank God, and I slept alone.

The press office emailed on Friday to ask for a quote to include on the press release. I rang Angus to check he wasn't going to say precisely what I was, then did a potted version of my Board interview, and sent it off with a curious mixture of indifference and apprehension.

The eight o'clock news on the following Monday morning was dominated by some whacking great scandal involving a cabinet minister and a rent boy, and Max Polgar called me at eight thirty to say he was seizing his opportunity and sneaking out a press release.

I opened my emails the instant I walked into my office. There it was, waiting for me:

OPERA LONDON ANNOUNCES NEW GENERAL ADMINISTRATOR AND MUSIC DIRECTOR

Opera London is delighted to announce that Jamie Barlow has been appointed with immediate effect as the Company's new General Administrator, and Angus Lennox has been appointed its new Music Director. Mr Lennox's tenure will begin in April next year, when he will conduct the Company's new production of Richard Strauss's Der Rosenkavalier.

Both men already have a close association with the Company. Mr Barlow has been Casting Director for the last five years, and Mr Lennox, one of the most exciting of the current generation of young British conductors, has conducted many productions for Opera London, making his debut in 1998 with Rigoletto. Most recently he conducted the hugely successful new production of The Marriage of Figaro, including a sellout performance in this summer's Henry Wood Promenade Concerts.

Sergei Rebroff, Chairman of Opera London, said:

I am delighted at the appointments of Jamie Barlow and Angus Lennox, after a rigorous interview process. Both men bring with them a passion and flair which I have no doubt will, together with the Company's new-found financial stability, ensure a new golden age for opera in London.

Jamie Barlow expressed this passion in the following comment:

The extraordinary generosity of Sergei Rebroff heralds a magnificent opportunity for Opera London. The Company will be free to pursue an artistic policy unfettered by the crippling financial constraints of yesteryear. Together with Angus Lennox, who will I have no doubt ensure the most rigorous musical standards, I am confident we can return to the cutting-edge excitement which has always characterised our work, bringing to Opera London the very best of British and international singers, directors and conductors. I am thrilled to be given this extraordinary opportunity to lead the Company I love.

Angus Lennox said:

I have always wanted to be Music Director at Opera London. To be appointed at this time in the Company's history, under the generous and inspired chairmanship of Sergei Rebroff, and in tandem with my distinguished friend Jamie Barlow, is indeed a rare honour.

All enquiries to Opera London Press Office… etc.

I instantly picked up the phone, and dialled Angus's number. He was about to go into a rehearsal at ENO, but we managed a quick conversation.

"Gussie, congrats, old boy. It's all official."

"Well, congrats to you, old thing. I've just seen the press release on my Blackberry."

"What happens next, Gus? I've never been the boss before."

"Well, the world and its wife will want to talk to us both for the next month or so, then we can settle down to turning the Company into London's operatic flagship. For the moment you can content yourself with moving into your new office and looking grand. Enjoy it. Tomorrow morning the nation's press will be baying for your blood. Mine too, I dare say…"

I heard a woman's voice say 'Angus, I've just heard. Fantastic news.' Angus said 'thanks Deborah. See you in a moment…', then came back on.

"Sorry old thing, I've got to go. See you in the corridors of power."

Three bleeps announced that he'd rung off. I looked up, and realised that everyone in the room was looking at me and smiling. Led by Grace, they sang a chorus of *for he's a jolly good fellow*. Then everyone came up to my desk and started offering their congratulations.

I decided not to move offices until eight the next morning. Grace agreed to come in early and help me transfer everything. In the meantime I suddenly had a thousand emails and calls of congratulation to deal with.

Amongst the cheery messages of goodwill there was one stinker, from the lovely Yvonne Umfreville. It read as follows: 'Maestro Leclerc very unhappy about continuing situation with Templeton. Either she sings out today, or we meet to discuss whether she should be replaced. Y.U.' Maestro Leclerc, for God's sake. Poncy bitch.

I dashed off a reply which said: 'She is under extreme stress at the moment. She needs more time. Get off her back'.

I thought I'd better establish contact with Lindsey to let her know they were really after her. Worried she might not answer my call, I texted the following to her:

Hi sweetheart, I think we should speak about Leclerc, Umfrevville etc. Sergei concerned that you are not feeling on top form – best if you and I discuss before others poke their noses in. Luv J x

She rang me at lunchtime. She sounded weary beyond belief.

"Do they want to sack me?"

"They can't sack you, darling; Sergei and I won't let them."

"Oh, it's 'Sergei and I' now, is it? Congratulations, by the way. I hear it's all official."

"All thanks to you, sweetheart. Is your voice feeling any better?"

"I don't know. I've got to the stage where I daren't try it, in case I can't sing at all. All I can think about is I've got to do it for Dad on Friday. It's keeping me going, but it's frightening the life out of me at the same time."

I lowered my voice. "I'm sure Friday will be fine. I've got Standish's pills safely stashed away – I'll get them to you in plenty of time. Why don't I tell Umfreville and Leclerc that you guarantee to sing out at the *sitz*? They can bloody well wait till then. And look what happened last time you took those things. You sang the performance of your life."

"All right then, I suppose I'll have to go along with it. I've got to start singing sometime, that's for sure."

"Absolutely. I'll talk to those two, then."

"Okay, Jamie. By the way, what's going on with Jason? He says he's stopped seeing Saskia."

Ding dong went the alarm bells.

"They had a lovers' tiff," I said. "I think he's decided he's better friends with Dorothy than he is with Saskia."

"What the hell are you talking about?"

"Friend of Dorothy, darling. It means gay."

"Oh God, this is all too much for me. We'll have to talk about the arrangements for Dad and Evie on Friday. And you have to get those pills to me."

"Of course, darling."

There was a pause.

"Jamie, I wanted to say …?"

319

Another pause.

"What, darling?" I said.

"… I just wanted to say… well, that I'm lucky to have you. That's all."

And without another word she rang off.

Standish phoned at two thirty.

"Jamie, I've got Lindsey's blood test results. She's going to need an amnio."

"Fantastic, John. Then you'll do the DNA test?"

"It's really not fantastic, Jamie. It carries a small risk to the baby, you know."

"Yes, I know. Sorry. Of course it's not fantastic. There's nothing to worry about, is there? I mean the baby's not really likely to be Down's, is it?"

"No, the odds are still low – one in two hundred. And the risk from the amnio is low too."

"But you will do the paternity test?"

"Yes, dear boy. I've promised. Thanks for the *Fledermaus* tickets by the way. All arrived safely. An invite to Sergei Rebroff's after party, too. Terrific."

"Yes, I thought you'd like that. I'm dreading it."

"You'll be on show, I imagine. Well done, by the way. Little bit in today's Herald. They've taken their time announcing it, haven't they?"

"There were lots of hoops to jump through, John. I'm expecting the shit to hit the fan tomorrow."

"Could be. Anyway, listen. We'll write to Lindsey, of course, to tell her the result of the blood tests, and get her to book an appointment for the amnio. But do you want me to ring her now? It'd be courteous, not to mention ethical. Her body, after all."

"If you could, John." I gave him her number. "You'll probably just catch her before she goes back in to rehearsals. You'll make it sound routine, won't you? She doesn't need any more stress."

"Course I will. Bring your buccal cell swab in with you to Lindsey's amnio, by the way. All right about that?"

Buccal cell swab. Jesus. I logged onto the Internet, expecting to find a list of Harley Street cowboys who would do the test for me. Instead, to my amazement, I found someone who for £250 would send me a self-testing kit, which I was supposed to send off so they could profile my

DNA. Ideal, I thought. All I had to do was test myself, then forget the rest of the procedure and take the swabs round to Denise in Standish's office.

Lindsey's call wasn't long coming.

"Jamie, I haven't gone into the afternoon session. I can't. John Standish has just rung saying I should have an amniocentesis. He thinks the baby might have Down's syndrome." She burst into a flood of tears.

"Sweetheart, I've spoken to him too. That's not what he's saying. The test is a precaution – the chances of you having a Down's baby are one in two hundred. But you'd rather know, wouldn't you?"

"Well, whatever, I'm not going back in there this afternoon. I can't stand that bloody Yvonne Umfreville any longer. Every time she opens her mouth it's to make some snide comment about me. Or you, of course."

"Never mind about Yvonne, darling. Do you want me to book the appointment for the amnio?"

"I'm only going to have it if John Standish is doing it himself."

"Leave it to me."

Denise was very solicitous.

"They say the test's very straightforward. I don't see all that many of them, what with Mr Standish being a gynae, not an obs."

"He won't mind doing it himself, will he, Denise?"

"No, no, of course not. Not for Lindsey. He'd do anything for Lindsey."

"We're both very grateful, Denise. When should we come in for the test?"

"Well, now, let me see. Mr Standish has left me a message. He suggests the fifth of October, at eleven o'clock. Any good for you?"

The timing was terrible – right in the middle of the stage rehearsals. Zimmermann and Leclerc would be incandescent. Sod them.

"Absolutely," I said. Lindsey might have to be at the theatre later on that day, but I'm sure if she doesn't feel up to it she could pull out of one day's rehearsals."

"Oh, yes, Mr Barlow. She mustn't be put under extra strain."

"No, of course not, Denise. I'll make sure no-one expects too much of her. I'm really grateful, thank you. Next Thursday at eleven, then. Bye."

"Bye Mr Barlow. And wish her luck from me. Poor love."

When I arrived home that evening Saskia informed me with some enthusiasm that she had PMT, and that I wasn't to mess with her. So while she stomped about the kitchen making supper I went to help Carly with her homework. It was a project, and Mrs Bodley had given them *carte blanche* to choose whatever subject interested them. Carly had chosen Opera London, bless her. Trying to find interesting and upbeat things to say about the place helped concentrate my mind on my response to the nation's press the next day.

After supper, while Saskia took Carly upstairs to bed, I rang Jason, to get an update on the *Fledermaus* rehearsals. He took a little while to answer, and when he did I wished I hadn't rung. In the background was a monumental din of rock music and loud voices. He was obviously very drunk.

"Well done angel. You're the Big White Chief. Miss Whiplash herself."

"Thanks Jason. Where the hell are you?"

"I'm in the *Wessex*. It's a gay pub in Shepherd Market. I've been here since five o'clock. It's lovely. Why don't you come down and join me?"

"Not quite my scene, Jason, thanks all the same. Listen, can you go somewhere a bit quieter? I can't hear myself think?"

"Yes, dear, just a minute." There were a few muffled thuds, then I heard him say to someone: "wait here, gorgeous. Shan't be a moment. Got to talk to the boss." He did one of his high-pitched giggles, then there was a long pause. Eventually things went a bit quieter, and he said:

"Sorry about that Jamie. I've come into the loo. No-one here, thank goodness, so we can talk."

"I shan't keep you long, Jason. I just wondered how things were going in Hammersmith?"

"Oh, sweetie, it's been a bit of a trial, to be honest. I couldn't resist telling Olivier that I'd been having an affair with a girl. He was livid."

"I'm sorry about that. He'll come round, I'm sure."

"Don't be so certain, dear. She can be a bit nasty when she wants to be."

"Who can?"

"Olivier."

"Oh I see. Listen, sorry to be an old fuddy-duddy, but could you say 'he' if you're talking about a bloke? I find it less confusing."

"Darling, you're so old. Very well, if that's what you want."

"Is he being difficult with Lindsey?"

"Is who being difficult with Lindsey?"

"Olivier. Is Olivier being difficult with Lindsey?"

"Oh. No. Well, yes, a bit. He was *very* upset when she didn't come in to the afternoon session."

"What about Yvonne Umfreville?"

"She was cross too. But then she's always cross. Yesterday she told me I sounded like Charles Danvers. She's a bull-dyke bitch."

"What about everyone else? Is Ursula Zimmerman happy?"

"Not really. She threw a hissy fit when Lindsey didn't show up, although she calmed down a bit when stage management explained why. And she told Olivier to fuck off yesterday."

"What had he done?"

"He'd told Julian Pogson he was the only person in the cast who was taking it seriously. He likes Julian. Well, a bit *more* than likes, actually." Giggle.

"What do you mean?"

"You must have heard. Ever since I told that bitch Olivier about Saskia, she, sorry, he, has been looking for someone else to fuck. Julian Pogson, as more or less *everyone* knows from personal experience, likes fucking a lot. So Olivier and Julian have been fucking. A lot." Giggle. "Julian's such an arse-licker. Figuratively *and* literally." Shriek.

"Listen, Jason, you've been a terrific help, thanks. I can rely on you to be discreet, can't I?"

"Darling, I'd do anything for you. Whoopsee, there's someone coming in. Two people. Oh, get a room, you two. No I don't want to join in."

37

The next morning, Tuesday, I bought the *Statesman* at the Tube station. There was a small piece on the front page, which struck the fear of God into me.

Opera London yesterday announced, as widely predicted, that Jamie Barlow will take over immediately as its new General Administrator, and that Angus Lennox will become Music Director, taking up his appointment in March next year. Former Chairman, Tory MP Gregory Knipe has today written to the Daily Statesman questioning the wisdom of these appointments, and criticising his successor, billionaire Russian businessman Sergei Rebroff, who recently made a donation of £100 million to bail out the struggling Company.
      See letters page 31.

Fumbling with the unwieldy broadsheet, I turned to the letters page. Knipe was on vintage form:

Sir,
While sour grapes are not an attractive dish, I fear that for the sake of the artistic health of one of the nation's most beloved institutions I must risk being accused of consuming them. The current shambles at Opera London, which I so recently left as Chairman, beggars belief. Mr Sergei Rebroff, whose ill-gotten gains have featherbedded the Company to the absurd tune of one hundred million pounds, has, as every opera lover feared he would, decided that his money is safe only in the hands of a most improbable management team. The new General Administrator is to be Mr Jamie Barlow, whose previous experience consists solely of being a rather ineffectual casting director at the Company, and whose chief claim to fame is his marriage to

Lindsey Templeton, a British soprano and 'close friend' of Rebroff. In a ménage à trois unpleasantly reminiscent of the Hamiltons and Lord Nelson, these three now appear to have the future of the Company exclusively in their hands. Miss Templeton's name has suddenly started to appear far more regularly on Opera London cast lists, despite the widely-held view that she is not the singer she once was. Mr Barlow's close friend, Angus Lennox, who is named today as the new Music Director, is similarly inexperienced, and appears to be qualified only by his close friendship with Barlow. Huge quantities of taxpayers' money are being squandered on this shameless display of nepotism. The whole affair reeks of corruption, and should be closely investigated by The Arts Council of England, an organisation scarcely worthy of the name.

I am, sir, yours sincerely,

Gregory Knipe

Terrific. Knipe was accusing us of having a *ménage à trois*. I supposed he must have the bloody things on the brain.

When I arrived at work, Grace had already carted two drawers full of files upstairs to my new office. A copy of the *Statesman* was lying on my desk. I must have looked pretty crestfallen because as soon as she saw me, she put down her armful of papers and hugged me.

"I'm sorry, Jamie, really I am. But I suppose we should have known that hideous creep wouldn't go quietly. Anyway, if this is the opening shot in a big campaign, which is what it looks like to me, then your great advantage is that it's being led by Greg the Dreg, who's only a little more popular in this Company than Attila the Hun."

"Grace, you're the best. Thanks. Come on then, let's get cracking."

We finished the removal job by nine, then whizzed downstairs to *Caffè Italia* and ordered two large cappuccinos.

"You have to get hold of Lindsey," said Grace. "She'll be pretty vulnerable. You'd better speak to her now, before she walks into the rehearsal room."

I pressed Lindsey's speed dial on my phone. Nothing doing. No signal downstairs. So I left Grace drinking her coffee. When I got outside, I lit a cigarette, then tried Lindsey again.

"I'm in the quiet coach, Jamie," she whispered. "What do you want?"

"I've got to tell you something, sweetheart. It's not very pleasant."

"It's not Carly, is it?"

"No, no. It's just Gregory Knipe's written a letter to the *Statesman* this morning, implying that you and Sergei have had an affair."

"Jesus. Just a minute, I'll go to the end of the carriage."

There was rustling on the other end of the phone, and I heard her say 'I'm so sorry.' After a moment or two she came back on.

"Right then, Jamie, you'd better tell me what that toe-rag has got to say."

"He calls you a 'close friend', in inverted commas, of Sergei's, and says the three of us are having a *ménage à trois* reminiscent of Lord Nelson and Emma Hamilton and her husband."

"Christ. I can't cope, Jamie."

"Where are you now?"

"On the train."

"Where? Have you gone through Stevenage?"

"Ages ago."

"Then you must be between tunnels. Get yourself to Hammersmith Tube. I'll meet you there, by Tesco's. We'll go in to the rehearsal together."

The phone went dead. I stubbed out my cigarette, then whizzed back downstairs.

"Spoken to her, Grace," I said, a bit breathlessly. "I've told her to meet me at Hammersmith Tube. We're going into the rehearsal together."

"Good boy, Jamie. You'd better get going."

Maybe Tesco's at Hammersmith Tube wasn't such a bright idea. I had to wait fifteen minutes for Lindsey, during which I made seven separate inspections of the wine section. It was the only bit of the shop where I could be reasonably certain none of the *Fledermaus* cast would go at that time in the morning. Umfreville and Olga came in to buy their lunch, followed by Jason, Pogson, Gloria, and three members of the chorus.

Eventually I saw Lindsey walk towards the shop, and look around uncertainly. I extricated myself, almost forgetting to put back a nice-looking bottle of Gigondas. She looked ill. Before I knew where I was, I was hugging her in front of the hurrying commuters, one of whom tutted in annoyance at our being in the way.

She sank into my arms, and burst into tears. It was ten twenty-two.

"Linds, we've got to get into that rehearsal by ten thirty, otherwise they'll know Knipe's got to us. Can you make it?"

"Yes I fucking well can, Jamie. Bugger the lot of them. They *won't* get me down."

We started walking towards the rehearsal studios. I still had my arm around her.

"I'm sure Leclerc is behind all this," I said. "He's been spoiling for a fight ever since Knipe resigned. You mustn't give him any more ammunition."

"Does that mean I have to sing out this morning? Because I don't think I can."

"No, no, better if you don't. They know you're not singing out until the *sitzprobe*."

"Have you got the pills?"

"Safely tucked away."

We walked on in silence. After a minute or two, she said:

"Jamie, what are you going to say when we walk in?"

"That there's a letter from Knipe in the *Statesman*, and that we're asking everyone in the Company not to comment on it."

"Aren't you going to deny the rumours?"

"Best left alone. People will draw their own conclusions anyway."

"Have you spoken to Sergei?"

"No. But I guarantee he'll have some plan to shut Knipe up. He's frighteningly clever at this sort of thing."

By this time we'd arrived at the front door. We stood outside the room for a moment while Lindsey collected herself, then we both went in. It was ten twenty-nine.

The buzz of conversation died down instantly we appeared. Everyone looked at us. Time for my first speech as General Administrator.

"Ursula, sorry to butt in, but could I steal just two minutes of your rehearsal to talk to everyone?"

"Why sure, Jamie. Go ahead."

"Thanks, I'm really grateful. Ladies and gents, no doubt you'll have seen the delightful letter written to the *Statesman* by our recently departed Chairman. I just wanted to say that I'm not surprised by it. Mr Knipe's nose is out of joint because Sergei Rebroff's generous gift forced him to resign."

I managed not to catch Jason's eye as I said this.

"Please disregard anything of this kind you read in the papers in the next few days. And most importantly, please do not in any circumstances speak to the press about this or any other matter to do with the Company. Thank you; that's all I wanted to say."

Ursula Zimmermann sprang to her feet. "Hey, we're totally with you on this, Jamie. That guy Knipe is the pits."

There was just a little less than total assent round the room. Leclerc and Pogson looked at the floor. Umfreville and Olga looked cross. But Jason and Gloria, and most of the chorus, plus the stage management, music staff, and directors, burst into a round of applause. It was Bill Buckley, a baritone who was the chorus's Equity rep and had been with the Company nearly thirty years, who had the last word.

"Jamie, I hope you don't mind me putting my oar in on behalf of the chorus, but we haven't had the chance to congratulate you on your appointment. It's been a strange few weeks, but I know I speak on behalf of us all when I say that what's happened to the Company since last season is fantastic news. Mr Rebroff's gift, and the appointment of you and Angus Lennox, well, we couldn't be more delighted."

The applause began again, and a lot of people came up and patted me on the back, obscuring my view of the scowling Leclerc. I would have enjoyed it far more if Lindsey hadn't been sitting in the corner, looking as if she was about to burst into tears.

After a moment or two I shouted "thanks everyone, I'm really touched. Now I must go, because we've all got work to get on with."

There was a groan around the room. Lindsey caught my eye and I smiled at her. There was a glimmer of a smile back, then she got out her dialogue script.

As soon as I was out of there, I texted her the following message.

Darling, I love you more than anything in the world. We'll get through this. Xxx

My phone rang as soon as I had finished. Not Lindsey, as I'd hoped, but Tatyana.

"Misterr Barlow, Sergei would like to have a word with you. Is now good time?"

"Yes, fine."

There was a click, then an unpleasantly familiar voice said:

"Jamie, good to talk to you. Congratulations on your appointment. I couldn't be more pleased."

Well, I couldn't really say fuck off, could I? So I said:

"Thank you, Sergei. I'm thrilled too."

"But we have problem. You've read Knipe's letter?"

"Yes."

328

"And Lindsey also?"

"Yes, I've just left her at the rehearsal room."

"She is upset, no doubt?"

"Of course. But determined to face up to it."

"Good. This is good. I would like to see you. Are you free for lunch?"

"Well, I expect when I get into the office all hell will have broken loose, but there won't be much I can do about it today, so yes, I'm fine for lunch. Could we make it early?"

"Twelve o'clock at Savoy."

"Is Angus free?"

"I don't want to see Angus. Just you."

"Oh. Fine. Twelve o'clock at the Savoy, then. Will Tatyana meet me downstairs as usual?"

"Of course."

And he hung up.

The same rigmarole with Tatyana, and the lift, and Mutt and Jeff. Then the same embarrassed entrance into the inner sanctum.

Sergei sprang up from his chair when Tatyana showed me in. There were some sandwiches on the coffee table, plus bottles of chilled Chablis and Badoit.

"Jamie, thank you for coming. Please sit down and help yourself to lunch. I hope sandwiches are all right?"

"Of course, Sergei. I might pass on the wine, though. I'll need a clear head when I get back to work."

"Yes, absolutely. Mr Knipe's charming letter."

"What are we going to do, Sergei?"

"Nothing. Leave Knipe to me. He will not say anything further, I can assure you. He still has reputation to preserve, and career to manage."

"But what shall I say to the Press?"

"My own people will liaise with Opera London Press Office. You, Lindsey and I have forged friendship through our work. This has in no way affected decisions involving Company. That is all we need to say."

"What if this is the beginning of a campaign?"

"Who would be likely to join campaign? I thought Mr Knipe was very unpopular."

"He is, but he has some powerful allies, the most obvious of whom is Olivier Leclerc."

"I don't think we should worry too much about Leclerc. He is conductor. He is not politician."

"He is also a nasty little bastard, Sergei." I took a bite of a sandwich which had chicken and some wonderful unidentifiable goo in it. Sergei was not eating anything at all.

"Will he go ahead and conduct *Fledermaus?*" he said. "Now he's not getting job of Music Director?"

"He would be seen as very unreliable if he didn't."

"Then let us wait until première and go on press offensive once it has opened. I assume it will be success?"

"I gather it's going very well, apart from the uncertainty about Lindsey's singing."

"She will be all right, yes? You said in your interview that we should give her till end of week to improve."

"She has agreed to sing out at the *sitzprobe* on Friday. We shall see then whether she has recovered."

"I will come to this rehearsal."

That's all I needed – Albert and Sergei in the same room. Albert would probably kill him. He'd probably kill himself in the process.

"Um, oh, fine, I'm sure that will be fine."

"Of course it will be fine, Jamie. I am Chairman now."

"Yes, of course. But er…, well, protocol dictates that anyone who wishes to visit a rehearsal should first clear it with the director, or in this case the conductor."

"Tatyana will ring Mr Leclerc. I am sure he will not refuse permission." He laughed unpleasantly.

At one fifteen Lindsey phoned. She was in a terrible state.

"Jamie, thank God I've got you. I've just had the most horrible time with Julian Pogson."

"Julian? What happened?"

"We were doing the watch duet in Act Two – the last bit, where the two of us sing together. Leclerc asked me to sing out so that Julian could listen to me for the timing, and I apologised, as I have done a thousand times before, and said I couldn't sing out, because I was still ill. Leclerc just shook his head and tutted, and was about to carry on, but then Julian said 'oh for fuck's sake, there's more than one person in this show, Lindsey. Why don't you just cancel so we can get on and do it with someone else?' I don't know what came over me. I screamed 'don't you speak to me like that you fucking queen,' and I slapped him, really hard."

"Christ, Linds, what happened then?"

"He looked stunned for a minute, then he laughed, really nastily. The whole chorus was watching. I said sorry, and I didn't know what had come over me, and he said 'you fucking well will be sorry, you filthy whore.' Then Ursula sent us all out for an early lunch. It only happened three minutes ago. What should I do?"

"I think you'd better go back to Stockencote. I'll ring Ursula, and tell her to get on without you this afternoon."

"Then what?"

"God, I don't know. Go to King's Cross. I'll ring you back."

Ursula was full of sympathy.

"I'm not surprised she snapped. That poor girl's under so much pressure it hurts."

"Ursula, can you manage without her for a few days? It would give her cover a chance to learn it, just in case things do go pear-shaped."

She groaned. "It's a fucking pain in the ass, but I suppose so. Lindsey doesn't want to cancel altogether, does she?"

"No, no, she really doesn't. She's going to sing out at the *sitzprobe* on Friday. If you can manage, let's wait until then. Hopefully we can put all this behind us next week."

I got hold of Lindsey as she was boarding the train at King's Cross.

"Darling, I've spoken to Ursula. She says don't come in until Friday – they'll use your cover in the meantime."

"She's not going to sack me, is she?"

"Not a thought of it, darling. She's on your side. She says to go home and make sure you get plenty of rest."

"What about you, Jamie. Are you mad with me?"

"Course I'm not, sweetheart. I hope you hit Julian bloody Pogson really hard. Just go home and look after yourself. And your Dad, of course. I'll be in touch to make sure you get Standish's pills in time for Friday's rehearsal."

38

Friday, September the twenty-ninth dawned hot and sunny. We were promised blazing sunshine and soaring temperatures right into the following week.

The DNA testing kit had arrived on the Wednesday morning. I'd checked that it contained everything Standish needed, then packed it up again and hidden it in our bedroom. I would leave the actual swab-taking to the day of the amniocentesis.

That night I'd rung Jason to see how things were in the rehearsals. Lindsey's cover was in, he'd said, and she was doing fine. Pogson had pronounced himself relieved that Lindsey wasn't there, but had otherwise confined himself to looking grumpy, conversing only with Leclerc and occasionally Umfreville. Jason had described him as 'a pain in my cute little ass', but that was a road I didn't particularly want to go down, so I'd thanked him, and asked him to ring if there were any more developments.

Saskia, meanwhile, was still in a mood, and I was sleeping alone. Carly was being charming for once, which made me feel doubly guilty about my brief affair, and I was beginning to think I must put an official end to it soon. But not right now. It could wait until after the *sitzprobe*.

Evie was driving from Stockencote to Victoria with both Lindsey and Albert in the car, and they were leaving at seven am. I had suggested they might prefer to stay the night at ours, or even in a London hotel, but Evie had rejected the idea, saying the only way she was going to get Albert there was if he had slept in his own bed. He was holding himself together for this occasion by sheer force of will.

I set out for the office at eight thirty, having made bacon and egg for Carly, who was furious that Mummy, Grandad and Auntie Evie were all coming to London and she wasn't going to see them. I checked all the newspapers at the station, but there was nothing. So far, there had been no reaction at all to Knipe's letter. Maybe Sergei had *kompromat* on the editors.

When I got into the office I dealt with my emails. There were further messages of congratulation (they had been coming in all week), plus a foul one from Umfreville saying she hoped that today we were finally going to find out whether Templeton could still sing at all.

At five to ten I went down the stairs, through the pass door which led backstage, and made my way to the dressing rooms to wait for Lindsey. The place was empty – no wardrobe or wigs people came in on *sitzprobe* days, and the chorus wasn't coming either.

Lindsey arrived, alone, about five minutes later, looking tired but still gorgeous, in a summer dress which showed off what was left of her Montpellier tan. She hugged me.

"Gosh, Jamie, I'm really pleased to see you."

An unwelcome image of Saskia's breasts swam into my mind.

"Isn't your Dad with you?" I said.

"Yes, Evie's waiting with him at the stage door. He says he's feeling fine, but he's obviously in agony. A couple of times on the motorway he actually cried out with the pain. He kept apologising, and saying he promised to be as quiet as a mouse in the theatre. Evie's finally forced a couple of Nurofen on him – not that they'll touch the sides, I wouldn't think, but he won't take anything the doctor's given him. He insists he has to be *compos mentis* for the rehearsal. Speaking of which, have you got my pills?"

"Yup, here they are." I handed her the little packet I had been keeping so carefully. She immediately took a couple, washing them down with a glass of water from the tap.

"There are loads of these pills here," she said. "John Standish must think my singing's really terrible." She sighed. "Leave me alone now, please, Jamie. I'm going to warm up."

I got up and left, closing the door behind me. Almost immediately I heard her begin singing from within the room. I paused to listen. Tentative at first, she completed one scale, then started again a semitone higher. Within a minute or so she was climbing towards the top of her voice. And to my astonishment, her voice began to sound as lush and beautiful as ever. A massive shiver went down my spine. I walked off down the corridor towards the stage door, to meet Evie and Albert, and to take them into one of the boxes.

Albert looked like a wraith. His back was bent into a stoop, and his eyes – watery, but with an unnatural brightness – were sunk deep into their sockets. His lips were pulled back into a grimace, as if he were trying to hold back the pain. His old man's hands emerged from his sleeves on the end of stick-thin arms, and he clutched onto Evie for his very life.

But he managed a wry smile when he saw me. "Don't say a word, Jamie lad. I know I look like Quasimodo's corpse. But I'm here, and that's what matters."

I smiled back as best I could. "Albert, I can't tell you how glad I am that you've made it. And Evie too."

"I wouldn't have missed it for anything, " said Evie. "Nor would Albert. He's spoken about nothing else for the past week."

"Absolutely true, Jamie lad. Just as well, eh? Poor Evie doesn't want an old sod like me boring on about his ailments."

"We must go through to the auditorium," I said. "We've got fifteen minutes."

Evie looked worried. "Just one thing, Jamie. Would you mind paying this blessed Congestion Charge for me? I've managed to park the car, but I keep seeing notices about it, and I'm terrified of what will happen if I get something wrong."

"Of course I will, Evie. You've brought the Merc?"

"Yes we have. Will it cost a lot? It's such a big car."

"No, no. I just needed to know for the registration number. You two follow me. Can you walk okay, Albert?"

"'Course I bloody can. Evie wanted me to bring the wheelchair, but I was buggered if I would."

Once I'd got them installed in their box, I whizzed out to the newsagent and paid the Congestion Charge. At the same time I checked to make sure today's *Herald* hadn't arrived, but apparently it wasn't due for another hour.

When I got back to the auditorium it was ten twenty-nine, and I sat down in the stalls, close to Albert and Evie's box. The last members of the orchestra were rushing into their seats in the pit. Leclerc was fussing about like a mother hen. He was deep in conversation with Umfreville, who was seated in the front row of the stalls, immediately behind his podium.

The singers were sitting in a row at the front of the stage, with the safety curtain in place behind them. Lindsey was in the middle. There was a buzz of excitement around the stalls, with quite a number of staff members – the ones who could find an excuse to leave their desks – taking their seats discreetly. I noticed a commotion at the back of one of the boxes on the opposite side of the auditorium, and in walked Mutt, followed by Tatyana and Sergei. I guessed Jeff was stationed none-too-discreetly in the corridor outside.

Once the members of the orchestra had tuned up, Leclerc called them to order, and introduced the singers to them. This was a time-honoured ritual, which conductors forgot at their peril. When he got to Lindsey there was a murmur of approbation, and the string players tapped their bows on their stands. It wasn't a demonstrative show of affection, but it was enough to prove they were glad to have her back. She smiled, looking every inch the Diva.

The formalities completed, the band struck up the overture. There are few openings in all music as exciting as the first bars of *Fledermaus*, and I felt another frisson run down my spine. I was as nervous as I had ever been, even in the days when I was performing myself.

But I needn't have worried. When it came to Lindsey's turn to sing, after Gloria had done Adele's first twiddly number, all nerves were instantly quelled. I swear I have never heard her sing so beautifully. Her voice seemed to have acquired an extra dimension – honey-sweet at the bottom and gleaming like steel at the top. Of the much-discussed wobble there was not a trace.

After she had sung the first little duet with Gloria there was a breathless silence. I waited for Leclerc to produce some nasty comment, but instead he too paused, as if unable to believe what he had just heard.

"Ledeez zat wass hextrimly beauteeful. Hi 'ave nossing to say."

Julian Pogson, sitting on the far right-hand side of the row of singers, scowled at his chum in the pit. Whether Leclerc caught his eye or not was difficult to say. All he said was:

"We do plizz ze next number. Trio."

Gloria sat down, and the ancient tenor singing the lawyer, Blind, rose to his feet, as did Pogson. He looked irritated, almost fearful.

But Lindsey was suffering no such affliction. Her joy in her own rediscovered ability was written all over her face, while every corner of the theatre was filled by her mesmerising voice, whose soft radiance was allied to a reserve of strength often untapped, but always evident. And every word was crystal clear, making her singing involving and meaningful, as well as gut-wrenchingly beautiful.

The trio progressed – Pogson blustered away as Eisenstein, the errant husband, and Blind squeaked away hilariously. But every bar of Lindsey's contribution was a revelation. I looked round at Albert and Evie. Both were struggling to hold back the tears.

Overall the sense of joy in the auditorium was palpable. When at around midday Leclerc announced the break, the spectators burst into spontaneous, and as far as I knew unprecedented applause. The band members put down their instruments and joined in, as did the other singers. Except Pogson, of course. Lindsey stood in the middle of the stage and beamed. I looked over my left shoulder, and saw Sergei and Tatyana standing at the front of their box applauding enthusiastically. Even Yvonne Umfreville had the suspicion of a smile playing around the corners of her mouth.

The ovation didn't last long – the clarion call of the canteen was too strong. But as the auditorium emptied, the memory of that astonishing display of affection hung in the air like a cloud.

I made a sign to Albert and Evie that I would come round the back into their box, and headed for the exit. On the way I was clapped on the back by everyone I met. Sergei actually vaulted over the front of his box and came over to me, trailing a panicky Mutt in his wake.

"Jamie, please stop one second. This was wonderful. Crisis is over, I think."

"I am over the moon, Sergei. But please forgive me – I must go and see Lindsey's father and aunt, who are in that box."

"Of course. I must leave now. I have business to attend to. Please convey my congratulations to Lindsey."

I made my way via more enthusiastic comments to Albert and Evie's box, and let myself in. They were both sitting there, stunned by what they had just heard.

"Oh, Jamie," said Albert. "I've never heard her sing like it. I don't know what to say."

"To be honest, Albert, I'm speechless too."

At that moment there was a tentative knock on the door. I opened it, and there was Lindsey.

"God, Linds, you sound fantastic," I said.

"Thanks, Jamie. It feels heaps better. Dad, how are you getting on?"

"Just fine, my darling girl. I don't think I've ever been as happy in my life."

Lindsey bent down and put her arms round the frail shoulders of her father. They remained in that rather awkward hug for a good minute, during which Evie and I looked at each other, afraid to speak. Eventually they pulled apart.

"Can I get you a cup of tea or anything?" said Lindsey.

"Don't you trouble yourself lass. We're perfectly happy just as we are, aren't we Evie?"

"Of course we are, Albert. And I don't want any of that peely-wally southern tea anyway. You go off and have a cup of something, Lindsey. We'll be fine."

"Okay, I'll run down to the canteen. I'll come back when the rehearsal's over. You stay put till I get here."

She gave her Dad one more hug, and disappeared through the door.

I stayed in the box for the second half of the session. Lindsey was as superb after the break as she had been before, and finished the rehearsal with a quite staggering rendition of the *Czardas* – Rosalinde's showpiece aria, in which she pretends to be a Hungarian countess. I had heard no end of starry divas come a cropper on this number, with its tricky *coloratura* and scorching high notes, but Lindsey made it sound as if it had been written for her. The morning finished with another ovation from everyone in the theatre, which by now was half full of staff members who should have been working. Word had obviously spread round the building.

I asked Albert and Evie to wait for a few moments, then I too leapt over the front of the box and into the stalls. I headed straight for the seat immediately behind the conductor's podium. Umfreville, who was sitting in the next-door seat, was deep in conversation with Leclerc.

"Excuse me for interrupting, *maestro*," I said. "Many congratulations. This morning's rehearsal was a revelation."

He turned to me. The look on his pasty face was distinctly peevish. "Yes, yes, zat is true. Leendsi was surprisingly good."

"She was satisfactory, thank goodness," said Umfreville. "I don't think we have anything else to worry about."

"I agree. I am grateful to you both for your patience. I am sure the production is going to be something very special."

Leclerc smirked at me. "Eet eez a very special day for all of us, Jemms. 'Ave you seen ze *Hevening 'Erald?*"

"No, no I haven't."

"Mebbee you should go 'ave a look."

When I got back to the box, Lindsey had arrived, and the three of them were deep in conversation about the morning's events. Albert looked exhausted, but had clearly had precisely the experience he had hoped for. If it was to be the last time he heard Lindsey sing he couldn't have wished for a better occasion.

But if there was something vile in the *Herald*, I knew that above all I didn't want Albert to see it, and in an ideal world it would pass Lindsey by as well, at least while she was still with her Dad. They were planning to leave London together – Lindsey had finished rehearsing for the day – and drive straight back to Stockencote. At all costs I had to get them to the car without them seeing any lurid headlines.

"I'll tell you what," I said, "why don't I get the car and bring it to the front door of the theatre?"

To my relief Lindsey said: "Jamie, that would be brilliant. It would mean Dad hasn't got far to walk."

Evie handed over the keys and told me where the car was parked. I went to the stage door, taking the steps two at a time, then emerged onto the pavement, looking in trepidation at the newsstand on the opposite side of the road. The banner headline said: "**INTEREST RATES: BANK'S DECISION**", but there was nothing about us. I ran across the road, narrowly avoiding being knocked down by a screaming taxi driver, and bought a paper. Nothing about us on the front page either, so I walked quickly to the car park, leafing through the pages as I went.

It was on pages six and seven. There was a massive headline across the two pages, screaming:

Divorce For Sergei Rebroff?

The page was filled with pictures. There one of Lindsey's old publicity shots, and another of Sergei and some woman on a yacht, both wearing swimming costumes. Then there was Opera London's theatre, and a ridiculously blurred picture taken outside some nightclub. Hiding their unidentifiable faces from the camera were a man and a woman who purported to be Lindsey and Sergei.

I couldn't face reading the text, not until I'd sent the three of them back to Rutland. So I threw the paper in the nearest waste bin, and ran all the way to the car park. I handed over the twenty pound note which Evie had insisted on giving me, and drove the car at high speed down the ramp and out into Eccleston Street. By the time I had worked my way round the one-way system Lindsey, Evie and Albert were waiting for me outside the front of the theatre. Thank God the headline wasn't about us. They were staring straight at it.

I stopped the car and jumped out. Between the three of us we got Albert painfully into the passenger seat. I leant into the car to say goodbye. To my embarrassment, Albert tried to embrace me. We ended up in an awkward clinch, which had me grabbing at the door-frame to stop myself falling into his lap.

"Jamie lad, I can't thank you enough. Best day of my life."

"Pleasure's all mine, Albert. I'll ring tonight, to make sure you got home okay."

He patted me on the back a couple of times, then I gently extricated myself, gave Evie a brief hug, then looked at Lindsey. I felt paralysed in front of her.

Eventually I said: "you were just fantastic, Linds. I'm so proud of you. Look after your Dad. And yourself."

She looked at me for a second longer, then climbed into the back seat. Evie waved briefly, then drove off.

As soon as they were out of sight, I crossed the road, bought a second copy of the *Herald*, and opened it at page six. The pictures on the right-hand page were in hideous technicolor. There was my wife staring into the camera with her perfect red lips slightly parted. I remembered the session when this picture had been taken. It was only a few months after Carly was born, and it had been a celebration of Lindsey regaining her perfect figure after a rigorous and closely-observed diet. We'd been thrilled with the photo – it made her look like an international star, I'd said. But what had seemed glamorous then now looked tawdry and cheap.

The text was grotesque – light on facts, but heavy on carefully-worded speculation. It went as follows:

Sergei Rebroff, billionaire Russian businessman and Chairman of Opera London, may be facing a costly divorce following speculation about his close friendship with opera star Lindsey Templeton. An Opera London insider yesterday suggested that

Rebroff, who only last month made a donation of £100 million to save London's ailing third Opera Company, may be the father of Miss Templeton's unborn child.

The rumours of a relationship between the oligarch and the singer were fuelled on Tuesday by a letter to The Daily Statesman from Rebroff's predecessor as Chairman, Gregory Knipe. Tory MP Knipe, who is hotly tipped to become Arts Minister in a future Tory Government, hinted at a sinister side to the close friendship between the two of them and Miss Templeton's husband, the new General Administrator of Opera London, Jamie Barlow. Mr Barlow was Rebroff's personal choice for the job, and was appointed despite widely-expressed doubts about his qualifications and experience.

Rebroff's wife Nadezhda, who lives in the couple's Black Sea dacha with their two children, is seldom seen with the tycoon, and was today unavailable for comment. However, sources say she is 'devastated', and may already have consulted divorce lawyers in Russia. If proceedings are initiated, she may be in for one of the biggest divorce payouts ever. Some estimates put the figure as high as two billion pounds.

The source claimed that the scandal was creating a bad atmosphere within the Company, and that the forthcoming production of Johann Strauss's Die Fledermaus, the first new offering of the Rebroff/Barlow regime, was likely to be badly affected.

Who the hell the 'Opera London Insider' was, God only knew. I felt physically sick. I was really angry, but it wasn't with Lindsey. It was with Sergei Ivanevitch Rebroff. How dare he fuck up the lives of our family? We'd been just fine before he came along – a bit fed up with being apart, maybe, but chugging along okay. I wanted to kneecap him.

So when I got back to work, trying to avoid the embarrassed glances of the people in the office whom until five minutes ago I had thought of as my friends and supporters, I decided to ignore the message on my desk to ring Tatyana as a matter of the utmost urgency. I had other things to deal with. Messages from Angus, Polgar, the Press Office, and Saskia, for a start, all telling me to ring them as soon as possible. Grace was at lunch, so I was on my own.

Before I had a chance to start calling them back, my phone rang. Voicemails from all the same people, saying the same thing. Ring now.

But I couldn't, because, God help me, the bloody thing rang again. The display told me it was Jason.

"Hi, Jamie, I've just seen the *Herald*. I'm really sorry."

"Oh, thanks Jason. I appreciate that."

"How's Lindsey taken it?"

"She hasn't seen it yet. She went straight home with her Dad after the *sitz*."

"Shit. You know who it was, don't you?"

"No I don't."

"It was that arsehole Julian Pogson. I heard him telling Olivier he was going to do it."

"Jesus, the absolute wanker. I thought he was supposed to be her friend. Doesn't he realise the pressure she's under?"

"Julian doesn't think about anything except Julian, Jamie. And then of course he's fucking Olivier. They're both bastards." He started crying.

"Listen, Jason, I can't talk now. Why don't you come round for supper?"

"I don't think Saskia will speak to me," he wailed. "No-one's speaking to me."

"Bollocks, Jason. She'll be fine. Anyway, Carly's there, so Saskia can't behave all that badly."

"Oh. Okay then. What time shall I come?"

"About seven thirty."

"Seven thirty at yours, then." He sniffled. "Thanks, Jamie."

"It's me who should be thanking you, Jason. That's quite a piece of news you've just given me."

The Press Office told me Sergei had expressly forbidden any reaction. Period. They were tearing their hair out, they said. He seemed to think he could manage the whole thing single-handed.

Max Polgar ranted and raved at me as well. He told me the scales had fallen from his eyes, and he now realised we'd taken on a control freak whose only redeeming feature was his wealth. He urged me to stand up to him, while accepting that I was in an absurdly difficult position to do so. The rest of the Board would stand behind me, he said.

"But whatever you do, Jamie, don't make him so mad that he pulls the donation."

"But surely the money's already in place?"

"Oh no, Jamie, he's not that daft. Dribs and drabs over the next ten years. He can't take back what he's already given, but he can make things impossible for us very quickly if he chooses."

When he'd rung off I looked at my watch – two twenty-five. I should catch Angus before he went in for his afternoon session.

"Jamie, what the hell have you been doing?" he said. "I've had a call from Sergei. He's in a filthy bate. Says no-one's to say a word to our friends from the newspapers. Or the telly or the radio, or anyone. And he's jumping up and down because he can't get hold of you. Have you spoken to him?"

"Can't. I'm too bloody angry."

"Bit late to start playing the cuckolded husband, isn't it?"

"Angus, may I just remind you whose idea this all was?"

"Okay, Jamie. You have a point. But don't blow everything. Got to go."

"Probably just as well."

Sod him. Sod the bloody lot of them.

That left Saskia. She said it was important, so I had to ring. For all I knew, Carly might be under a bus.

"Saskia, hi, it's Jamie. Is everything okay?"

"Yes, fine, Mister Jamie. It's just that Mrs Anstruther-Fawcett rang this morning to ask if Carly could stay the night. I said I had to ask you."

"Oh, right. Yes, well of course it's fine. Is that all?"

"Yes. Well no, one more little thing. If Carly's out, we can have a nice evening on our own, can't we?"

"Ah, well no, not exactly, Saskia. Jason's coming for supper."

"Oh, I see Mister Jamie. A threesome." She did a sexy little giggle which caused a brief stir in the Calvin Kleins, followed by guilt so overwhelming it almost made me sick.

"Yes, Saskia, as you say, a threesome." I tried to laugh too.

"What time would you like to eat, Mister Jamie?"

"About eight would be great, thanks. Jason's coming at seven thirty."

"Already I am looking forward to it."

I bloody wasn't. I nipped down the stairs and had a quick cigarette, to bolster me up for the afternoon.

I meant to ring Lindsey. I really did. But I kept finding excuses to put it off.

At four thirty, she rang me. She was incandescent with rage.

"So it takes my lover to ring me and tell me about that piece of filth in the *Herald*? My husband can't manage it."

"Oh Jesus. Hang on a second while I shut the door."

That was one perk of high office. When I wanted to have a private conversation, I didn't have to hang around whispering in the stairwell. Grace gave me a thumbs-up through the glass screen.

"That's better," I said, "now we can be private. You can't be overheard, can you Linds?"

"Of course not. I'm hardly likely to include my Dad in this, am I?"

"Has he seen the article?"

"No, thank God. He's gone to bed."

"Oh. I see. Anyway, listen Linds. I was going to ring and tell you, it's just that I haven't had time."

"That's your trouble, Jamie. You're always *going* to do things, but you never actually do them."

"Oh come on darling, that's not fair."

"It's not bloody fair that some bastard's accused Sergei of being my baby's father. Who the hell was it? Sergei wants to know too."

"It was Julian Pogson."

There was a pause. Then: "Christ, that dirty little gossipy fucking queen. CHRIST! How do you know?"

"Jason told me. He overheard him talking to Leclerc after you'd had your row. Jason doesn't want anyone to know it was him who told me."

"I thought Julian fucking Pogson was my friend."

"Some friend. How did he know so much about it?"

"I told him during that awful journey to Salzburg. I thought I could trust him."

"Did you tell him Sergei might be the baby's father?"

There was a long pause. Very long.

Eventually she said, very quietly: "yes, Jamie, I did."

"You said it was definitely mine."

"I know I did."

She started crying.

"Linds," I said, as gently as I could manage, "whose is it? Do you know?"

"No. You know my dates better than I do. You know perfectly well it could be yours. What you don't know is that the first time Sergei and I made love the condom broke…"

More crying.

"Linds, I knew you were uncertain. I saw it in your face when you first told me you were pregnant."

"Well why the hell didn't you say so?"

"I kept trying, in a roundabout sort of way. I kept asking you if you were in any doubt."

"I couldn't admit it, Jamie. I was frightened that if it turned out to be Sergei's you'd insist on me having an abortion."

"How would *you* feel if it were Sergei's?"

"I don't know, Jamie. The only thing I'm absolutely certain of is that I *need* this baby. I'm keeping it, whoever the father is. No-one can stop me. Not you, not Sergei, not anyone."

I was reeling by the time I got home. I had had no visitors since about three o'clock, and as I left the building I noticed several people avert their eyes. On an impulse I hailed a taxi.

Saskia was waiting for me at seven when I walked through the front door. She was wearing the skimpiest pair of shorts I had ever seen. Her legs were so sexy they were shocking. She waited for me to put down my briefcase, then walked slowly up to me and kissed me full on the lips.

"Oh Mister Jamie, it's a long time since I did that. Why have you been avoiding me?"

"Um, sorry Saskia. It's just been a bit difficult, what with Carly and everything."

"Well, she's not here now."

She kissed me again, this time working her tongue gently between my lips. I pulled away as politely as I could, but not before a familiar stirring in the Calvin Kleins had given me away.

"Ah, Mister Jamie, you have missed me too. Also I wanted to say I am sorry about what I read in the newspaper this evening. You must be upset."

She kissed me a third time, giving Percy a gentle stroke. "Maybe I can do something to make you feel better."

"Er, well no, thanks all the same, Saskia, I'll be fine." I pulled away again. "I'll tell you what, let's have a gin and tonic."

"Oh, yes, that would be very nice." She gave me another little tweak as I went off to get the drinks.

G.I.L.T. Or was it G.U.I.L.T? I finished making the drinks, and handed one to Saskia.

"Cheers, Mister Jamie."

"Cheers. Look, Saskia, I ought to make a phone call before Jason comes. Will you forgive me a moment? I'm sure you can get on with making the tea…"

"Sure I can, Jamie. You go and make your call." She smiled as she turned and went into the kitchen. "Jason is coming, yes. Pretty little Jason. My other fuck buddy…"

Thank God Jason turned up early, so I didn't have to hide for too long, pretending to phone. I went to the door to intercept him.

"Hi, Jason," I whispered. Listen, very quick warning. Saskia is on the rampage – I think she wants sex. Are you up for it?"

He wailed like a banshee. "No I'm NOT, Jamie. I'm far too upset."

We managed to get through to the brandy (I didn't have any Grand Marnier in, thank God) before the crisis really hit. Saskia swigged hers back in one, then pushed her chair back, scraping the floor loudly. She was pretty far gone.

She moved to behind Jason's seat, and draped her arms over his shoulders, and down his front, not stopping till she got to his dick. Then she licked the back of his neck, and started kissing his cheek.

Jason was fairly pissed too. But sadly he hadn't changed his mind about taking Saskia off my hands for the night.

"Saskia, I'm sorry, but I'm not in the mood."

She stood up, slightly too abruptly, and swayed on her feet.

"Well go and kiss Mister Jamie, then. You prefer men, after all."

"No, darling, I couldn't do that. I think I'd better go home."

"Actually no, Jason, I don't want you to go home. I want to make love."

"Look sweetie, for a girl you're very sexy, but I'm not in the mood, okay?"

"Jason's right Saskia. I think he should go home."

"Then you make love to me, Mister Jamie."

"I'm afraid I'm not going to either, Saskia."

"Fuck you. I want to have sex."

Jason looked terrified. "Jamie, I'm going, okay?"

"I WANT TO HAVE SEX."

"Look, Saskia," I said, "I think maybe you've had a bit too much to drink. Shall I take you upstairs?"

"Not unless it's to fuck me."

"No-one's going to fuck you, Saskia. Jason, it's fine, you go home."

"No it's NOT fine," screamed Saskia. "And if you won't fuck me, either of you, I think I'm going to go running off to the papers to tell them another little story about you both."

I'd been in the process of lifting her bodily off the floor to take her to her bed. I froze.

"What in particular were you going to tell them?"

"What Jason told me, one night after we'd made love." I looked at Jason. He'd gone white as a sheet.

"A story all about someone called Mr Knight or something. A very important man, who had sex with naughty little Jason and another boy, I think he said. Another important person. And how he got paid lots of money for doing it. By someone Russian, wasn't it, Jason? AnOTHer important man. There are so many, aren't there?"

She looked at each of us in turn, with a look so petulant I wanted to kill her.

"They'd pay me lots and lots of money, wouldn't they, for telling them that?"

Jason looked at me, panic stricken.

"Saskia," I said, "calm down."

"I am very calm, Mister Jamie."

"What do we have to do to stop you going to the newspapers?"

"Fuck me. Actually, maybe not. Maybe I will go to the newspapers anyway. I would like to have all this money. I can buy myself some diamonds when I get back to Amsterdam."

"Listen, Saskia, please don't do this. If the money is an issue, I'm sure we can sort something out instead. Wait till tomorrow morning, then I will ring a friend and ask him if he will give you money not to do this."

"Your friend is Russian, I expect?"

"Got it in one, Saskia. Why don't you go up to bed, and I'll get this sorted out tomorrow."

She smiled at me – a gross, lascivious smile – and put her hand squarely on Percy, giving him a rub as she did so. Then she kissed me softly on the lips, and tottered upstairs.

When she'd gone Jason reached out and gave me a great big hug, like a little boy. Then he gathered up his things, and let himself out of the front door.

39

I had no idea what time oligarchs got up on a Saturday morning, but I guessed it wasn't late. When it got to eight o'clock I couldn't stand it any longer, so I dialled Tatyana's number. Her phone rang four or five times before she answered it, and she did sound unusually sleepy.

"Ah, Misterr Barlow, I am glad to hear from you. No, no, it is not too early. Sergei is always up at this time. He is looking at morning papers. He wishes to talk to you urgently."

"Thank you, Tatyana."

There was a click, and the phone went silent for a moment. Then His Imperial Highness spoke.

"Jamie, I have asked you to phone me yesterday. I am not accustomed to waiting."

"Erm, yes, sorry Sergei. I was rather busy yesterday afternoon."

"I am your top priority. Not your second or third."

"Yes, of course. Sorry."

"It is about article in *Herald*. I do not mind for myself – I am accustomed to people writing bad things about me. But I feel very bad for Lindsey."

"Yes, so do I. Thank you for telling her, by the way."

"You were too busy to talk also to your wife?"

"Not too busy, no Sergei. I was hoping that since she was not in London she would not see it. Also I didn't want her father to know."

"It is good thing I was able to speak with her. I wish to say to you same thing I have said to Lindsey. Please do not speak to Press. If you are approached, you offer no comment. I will deal with whole thing.

But I would like to know from you who is Opera London insider who has given story to paper?"

"I gather it was Julian Pogson."

"Baritone who is singing Eisenstein?"

"Absolutely. He had a row with Lindsey during the rehearsal the other day, and realised he had some ammunition to use against her. She told him her story while they were travelling to Salzburg together."

"I will finish him."

"I admire you for the sentiment, Sergei, but I would ask you to be careful. With rehearsals at such a late stage, it might upset the balance of the show if you were to insist on his being replaced."

"But Lindsey cannot work with him after what he has done."

"I may be mistaken, but I suspect the instincts of a good colleague will motivate her more than revenge."

"I find your defence of him unbelievable. However, I will respect your judgement. I will speak to Lindsey before making decision about Pogson. You are aware, I expect, that your delightful English Press will make life very difficult for you? There are probably journalists and photographers outside your door now."

I was still in bed, so I got up and had a look out of the window. The street outside was heaving with people and cameras.

"Oh my God. You are absolutely right, Sergei. What shall I do?"

"Do not speak to them unless you must. Do you have to leave house this morning?"

"I don't know."

"Well, if you do, offer no comment. This also applies to anyone else in your house."

"Ah. Funny you should say that. I have something to tell you about the other person living in our house."

"What are you talking about?"

"She is our au pair. Her name is Saskia Fransmann, and she is eighteen years old, from Holland. Can I speak freely on this telephone line?"

"Use discretion please, Jamie."

"She has been sleeping with Jason Tang, and has certain information which she wishes to use to blackmail us. He was rather indiscreet, I'm afraid."

Sergei uttered something incomprehensible, which I guessed was a Russian expletive.

"What does she want?" he said. "Money?"

"She is motivated by both money and revenge."

"Revenge for what?"

"She resents Jason for no longer sleeping with her. She also resents me."

"For same reason, presumably?"

I did not reply. To my amazement and intense irritation he suddenly roared with laughter.

"I do not blame you, Jamie," he snorted. "Fidelity is clearly difficult also for you." He chortled for a moment longer, then said: "I wish simply to know whether this girl can be bought off?"

"Yes, Sergei, I believe she can."

"Then please offer her hundred thousand Euros to keep her mouth shut, and send her immediately back to Netherlands."

"What shall I do about Carly? She loves Saskia, and needs someone to look after her."

"Yes, your poor daughter. She suffers because of actions of adults. As do my own sons, I'm afraid. But for all of our sakes it is imperative that Saskia leave now. If you need help in finding someone for care of Carly ,Tatyana will help. But I am also concerned about Jason Tang. We must ensure that he says nothing to anyone else."

"Judging by the look on his face when Saskia threatened to tell the papers I don't think he'll make that mistake again."

"Perhaps he should be removed from production of *Fledermaus*?"

"Sergei I beg you to accept my advice on this. You cannot remove Jason, any more than you can remove Julian Pogson. The relationships between the characters will by now be firmly established. They have been working on them for weeks. The team must be left unchanged, or you risk wrecking the show."

He sighed, a long, world-weary sigh. "Running oil company is far simpler than this. I will accept your advice, Jamie. Meanwhile, please arrange for Saskia to go home. And ring Tatyana if you need help sorting things out."

"Thank you, Sergei."

"Goodbye, Jamie."

I went into Saskia's room with a cup of tea. A cup of tea, for fuck's sake.

"Saskia, I need to talk to you."

"Oh, Mister Jamie, what time is it? Do I have to get out of bed? Or would you like to get into bed with me?"

"No, I won't be getting into bed with you, Saskia. Here's a cup of tea."

"This is the first time you have ever brought me tea. There must be something wrong." She took the cup from my hand, gazing into my eyes as she did so.

"Yes, I'm afraid there is, Saskia. Do you remember what you said last night?"

"Oh, yes, Mister Jamie, I remember very well."

"My friend has offered you one hundred thousand Euros not to tell your story to the papers."

If it hadn't been my job to do the washing, it would have been very gratifying to watch her dropping the tea all over the duvet.

"Shit. That is a lot of money." She peeled off her T-shirt, and started trying to mop up the mess. Her tits wobbled up and down.

"Saskia, he only agrees to pay you if you leave London. You must go home today."

"Oh. He is obviously worried about what I have threatened to do."

"Yes, Saskia, he is."

"Then maybe I will demand two hundred thousand Euros. And I will stay here. I am happy here."

"Saskia, let me give you one piece of advice. Sergei is a very frightening man. Do what he says. We all have to do what Sergei says."

"Why do you not stand up for yourself, Mister Jamie? This man has fucked your wife."

"Saskia, believe me, if I could stand up to Sergei I would. It is not possible. Now please pack your things. I will find you a flight, then I will ring your mother to say you are coming home.

I was still talking to Miep when the doorbell rang. I looked out of the window, and saw the photographers crowding round the front door. I was going to ignore them completely, when I suddenly recognised the Anstruther-Fawcetts' bright blue car parked on the road.

"Miep, Carly's just got back from a friend's. I'll have to ring off while I let them in. I'll sort out the ticket. Got to go, sorry."

I ran down the stairs in my dressing gown, and opened the front door a crack without looking out. Immediately Carly, Emma, and Emma's Mum, Carolyn, ran into the house, accompanied by a cacophony of

350

questions. "Is that Mr Barlow's daughter?" I heard, and "are you a friend of Mr Barlow?" Carolyn slammed the door behind her.

"Are you all right?" I said to her. She was as white as a sheet.

"My God. I suppose so. It's a terrific way to start a Saturday morning."

"Yes, it's vile. I'm sorry."

"Is Mummy going to leave you now, Daddy?" said Carly.

"No, Carly. Whatever gave you that idea?"

"That's what one of those men outside said when we were getting out of the car."

A surge of impotent rage rose in my chest.

"Carly, you mustn't take any notice of those men out there. They are real baddies."

"It's okay, Daddy. You only get paparazzi if you're a celebrity. Emma said."

I looked at Emma. A more gormless child it would be difficult to imagine. I doubted whether she was capable of uttering any of the comments attributed to her.

"Do you want a coffee?" I said to Carolyn.

"No, thanks. We've got lots to do, haven't we Emma?"

Emma grunted.

Carolyn smiled inanely. "So we'd better be off. I hope this mess sorts itself out soon. Don't worry about seeing us out. You don't want to see a picture of you in your dressing gown in tomorrow's *Daily Mail*."

Emma snorted. It was a laugh, I realised. They left in almost as much of a hurry as when they'd arrived.

Carly, for all her bravado, looked upset.

"Have you had breakfast, darling?" I said.

"Only corn flakes."

"The let's have some bacon and egg. That'll make us feel better."

While I was cooking Saskia appeared from upstairs. She was furious.

"So, Carly, we have to say goodbye now."

"What? Why?"

"Because your weak father says so. I have to go away for ever."

Carly looked stunned. "But I don't want you to go. I love you."

"I'm sorry, darling," I said. "There's nothing I can do about it."

"Who's going to look after me?"

Good question.

"Don't worry about it, Carly. We'll sort something out."

I cracked an egg into the frying pan, and it broke. "Shit," I said. I got a spatula out of the drawer, and fished the egg out so I could throw it away.

Saskia laughed nastily. "Yes, indeed shit." She turned to Carly. "I do not want to go. Your Daddy is making me."

My eleven-year-old daughter looked at me, incredulous. I could see her little, outraged face, out of the corner of my eye. Suddenly she got up so violently that she knocked her chair over. It made a clatter that threatened to split my head open.

"I HATE you Daddy, you fucking wanker."

She ran out of the room and up the stairs into her bedroom, slamming the door behind her.

"Well done, Mister Jamie. I hope you are proud."

I'd picked up a second egg to replace the broken one. At this point I hurled it, shell and all, into the pan, and it shattered, splashing my face and hands with scalding hot fat. "Fuck, fuck and fuck. Get OUT!"

Saskia screamed, and followed Carly upstairs, leaving me frantically sluicing myself down with cold water from the tap. After a moment I stopped to turn off the gas under the frying pan. Almost immediately my face and hands started to hurt like hell.

It seemed so utterly fitting that I should have scalded myself that I didn't feel justified in trying to stem the pain, so I sat down at the kitchen table and revelled in it. Waves of self-pity washed over me. I buried my burning face in my burning hands, and burst into tears.

It was two hours later by the time I had pulled myself together. I'd cleaned up the grease-spattered kitchen and gone upstairs to dress, and to shave my painful face as best I could. There were two livid blotches on my right cheek.

After shaving I went downstairs, and booted up the computer. I booked Saskia a ticket from Stansted to Amsterdam for four o'clock that afternoon, and rang Miep to say when she'd be arriving.

During all this time neither Carly nor Saskia had emerged. Indeed there had been no noise at all from upstairs. Eventually I went and knocked gently on Carly's door. There was no reply. I walked in, to find the two of them cuddled up in bed together, fast asleep.

I shook Carly gently on the shoulder. Her eyes opened wide, and she looked startled for a moment. Then she said:

"Daddy, your FACE. What's happened?"

"I splashed myself with fat while I was making breakfast, sweetheart. Don't worry. It doesn't hurt any more."

She looked incredulously at me. "It's sick."

"Never mind, darling. You both have to get up now."

Saskia was looking at me, contempt written all over her face. "I suppose I have to pack my bags now. We leave soon, yes?"

"Yup, I'm afraid so. Your flight is in four hours' time. Your mother will pick you up from Schiphol."

She got out of bed, and slouched off to her room. That left Carly still staring at me. She looked like a frightened mouse.

"Daddy, what are we going to do?"

"I'll tell you what, sweetheart. When we've dropped Saskia at the airport, let's go to Grandad's for the night. We'll feel better in the morning, and then we can decide what to do. Would you like that?"

"Is Grandad dead?"

"No, darling."

"Can I see him?"

"It depends how well he is. But I expect so."

"Then I'd like to go. There's something I want to give him. Daddy?"

"Yes, sweetheart?"

"Does Saskia really have to leave?"

"Yes, darling, I'm afraid she does."

The trip to Stansted was vile. I picked up Carly and carried her out of the house, because I thought the army of Press people were less likely to be aggressive if I had a child in my arms. One wag shouted "whose is *that* child, Jamie?" We had to fight our way to the car, and the assembled throng were furious when all I came up with was 'no comment'. Carly insisted on sitting next to Saskia in the back seat. "I'm not sitting next to you, you pig," she said to me, which caused some hilarity.

Neither of the girls spoke much on the journey. When we arrived at the airport, they hugged for at least two minutes, and both of them wept buckets. Eventually, without saying a single word to me, Saskia took the emailed confirmation slip out of my hand and stumped off to the terminal building, dragging her enormous suitcase behind her.

Things didn't improve when we arrived at Stockencote. I'd spoken briefly to Evie before we left, to check they could do with us. She'd said 'yes of course, Jamie, how lovely,' but she'd obviously been distracted. Lindsey was waiting for us in the kitchen.

"Thank God you've come. Dad's taken a turn for the worse. He finally agreed to have morphine this morning, because the pain was so terrible. Within half an hour of taking it he was delirious. The doctor's been, and doesn't give him more than a few days."

"What for?" said Carly.

A look of the utmost tenderness settled on Lindsey's face.

"Darling," she said, "Grandad's going to die soon. You knew that, didn't you?"

Carly dissolved in a flood of tears. "Of course I know Grandad's going to die, Mummy. But I don't want him to."

"Nor do any of us, darling."

"Maybe Grandad will be a bit better in the morning," I said. "Then perhaps we can go and see him. What do you think, Linds?"

She heaved a long, deep sigh. "I don't know, Jamie. Let's have a drink. Evie's upstairs with Dad, but she's got supper sorted, so there's nothing much we can do to help. What have you done to your face, by the way?"

"Oh, I splashed myself with fat while I was cooking. It's nothing much."

I left her consoling Carly while I went off to get G and T's for us, and a Coke for Carly. As I was cutting the three slices of lemon I had a sudden and powerful vision of Albert, telling us with a huge grin on his face that the sun was well and truly over the yardarm, and that you always had to make sure the tonic was fizzy.

And make sure that daughter of mine knows who's boss, Jamie lad, otherwise it'll be a rod for your own back, and flat tonic for you from here to eternity.

After a chaste night of half-sleep, Lindsey and I woke early. The previous evening I'd managed to avoid the subject of Saskia's departure, but now, lying in bed next to her, I thought I'd better break the news. Saskia had found it very difficult, I said, when Jason dumped her, and she was missing home.

All bollocks, of course, but Lindsey swallowed it. She was pleased Saskia had gone. Her worry was Carly. I suggested she stay with my Mum and Dad for a while, but Lindsey wasn't enthusiastic.

I walked over to the bedroom window, which overlooked the front drive, to check that no paparazzi had followed us to Rutland. The drive was empty, and as peaceful as ever. I felt foolish for thinking we could be famous enough to excite such interest.

When the three of us got down to breakfast, Evie had been up for hours. She looked pale and drawn, but fairly cheerful.

"He's reasonably *compos mentis* this morning. I reduced the dose a bit last night because I wanted him to see you. I've told him you're here. Perhaps you can all pop up after breakfast?"

Carly put down her cereal spoon. "Mummy, can I come and see Grandad too?"

"Of course you can, sweetheart."

"I've got something to give him. But I've got to do something first."

"What is it, Carly?"

"I'm not telling *you* Mummy. It's for Grandad."

She wolfed down the rest of her cornflakes and creamy milk, and tore out of the room and up the stairs like one possessed.

Half an hour and three cups of tea later she reappeared. She was clutching a bright orange envelope.

"I've written it."

"What, darling," said Lindsey.

"My CARD. Emma's Mummy told me you always have to have a card for ill people. So we went and bought one on the way to Emma's on Friday. I chose it myself. Can I give it to him now, Mummy?"

Albert was lying flat on his back. The change during the last forty-eight hours beggared belief. He looked barely human, but his eyes were open, and there was just a suggestion of the old light in them.

"Don't say anything," he drawled. "I know I look like Henry Cooper after twelve rounds. Have you brought my little Carly?"

Carly didn't say a word, but thrust out her hand with its bright orange envelope in it.

"What's that?"

"It's a card for you Grandad. I've written something in it."

"Oh, thank you. Thank you darling." He made a pathetic effort to heave himself up into a sitting position, and almost immediately collapsed back with a yelp of pain.

"Sorry. Sorry all of you. Sorry."

"Dad, for heaven's sake. Do you want me to read it to you?"

"Yes please, lass." It was scarcely more than a whisper.

Lindsey opened the envelope.

"*Dear Grandad*," she read. "*I would like you not to die, but I know you are going to. I will be very sad without you, and so will Mummy and Daddy, and Auntie Evie, and everyone. But I just want you to be happy. I love you so much. Love from Carly.*"

Lindsey paused for a moment.

"It finishes with lots of kisses," she said, with a bit of a struggle.

"How many?" There was a smile on Albert's face. Only just, but it was definitely there.

"Sixteen 'x's, I think, plus eight 'o's."

Albert's two claw-like hands emerged from underneath the sheets, and reached out for Carly. He pulled her to him with a look which was half bloody-minded determination, half love, and they embraced for a long time. Carly looked amazed at the effect her words had produced.

"I'm a bit knackered now," Albert whispered eventually. "Better have a snooze."

We looked at each other uncertainly for a moment, then Lindsey stroked her Dad's forehead, and we all left the room.

Half an hour later Evie announced that he needed more pills, and that she was going to take him a cup of tea. Lindsey said she'd come with her, and I asked if I could come too. Carly, who was still a bit nonplussed by what had happened half an hour before, said she'd go and watch telly in the study.

Lindsey opened the door for Evie, who took her tray straight over to Lottie's old dressing table. By the time she looked round at Albert, Lindsey and I already knew. He was lying on his back. His face was contorted. There was no question in any of our minds. He was dead.

Lindsey had gone white as a sheet.

"He's gone, isn't he Evie?"

"Yes, darling, I'm afraid he is."

"How can that happen so quickly? He was fine half an hour ago."

"The poor boy probably had an aneurism. Cerebral, I expect."

"What, a stroke?"

"It can happen so easily. One sudden pain in his head. It'd be quite enough to take him off, in his weakened state. He's lucky, really. He's missed out those awful last few days of cancer."

"And he was so happy after Carly's card. It's almost as if he chose when to die."

"I've heard of stranger things, Lindsey, believe me."

Lindsey bent down and kissed him softly, as did Evie. Then Evie picked up the tray, and we all left the room. Lindsey was last out. As she reached the door she turned round, and said so quietly that I only just caught it: "goodbye Dad". Then she shut the door gently behind her.

They don't make it easy when someone dies. You feel you've a right to expect armies of helpers to swarm through the front door, bringing tea and sympathy, and ready to make all necessary arrangements.

Instead, all you have is people staring blankly at each other, exchanging ill-informed opinions about who you have to ring to take the body away, register the death, and check to make sure the poor bastard wasn't murdered. That's how we spent the rest of the day at Stockencote. A locum doctor came, as did the Police. They advised us to wait until the next day to contact an undertaker. Of course they did. What self-respecting undertaker is going to work on a Sunday?

And in amongst it all we had to work out what we were going to do. For a start, Carly still had no-one to look after her. Pretty swiftly we all decided that she could have a week off school – she was only eleven, for God's sake, and it wasn't going to do her much harm. She could stay at Stockencote – even if it was melancholy it had the virtue of familiarity, and it also happened to be Carly's favourite place in the whole world. I would contact the school to get them to send her some work, and if instead of doing it she spent the week helping Gordon on the farm so bloody what?

I would go home and work pretty much as normal. I fondly hoped that the paparazzi would have found something else to interest them over the weekend. Of course there could have been some new ghastly thing about us already – we'd all switched our phones off, and no-one had bothered to buy a newspaper. But in any case, surely they'd lay off when the news broke that Lindsey's father had just died?

By supper time everything was sorted, with one glaring exception. Lindsey knew perfectly well that she couldn't face rehearsing for the next few days, but the question remained whether she should go the whole hog and pull out of *Fledermaus* altogether. As we sat toying with the cold meat and salad Evie had produced, it was the main topic of conversation.

"What really worries me," said Lindsey, "is Sergei's reaction." Evie and I exchanged the briefest of glances. "He's made my appearance in the show such an important part of his first few weeks as Chairman that I don't feel I can let him down."

"Linds, you know I'd take care of that if you couldn't face it. He'd have to understand. It's not every day your father dies."

We talked on and on. Repeatedly I tried to persuade her to cancel, but all the time I was competing with the absent spectre of my boss and rival in love.

It was over coffee that Evie suddenly sat up straight in her chair.

"Heavens, I've just remembered something rather important. Albert made a tape, of all things, which he wanted me to play to you both when he was... when he was gone. He did it just after your last visit. He was going to write something to you, but then I found an old Dictaphone of mine, so Albert decided to speak it instead. I've no idea what's on it."

She rushed out of the kitchen and up the stairs. A couple of minutes later she was back, clutching an ancient-looking machine.

"There was a tape already in it. He did the whole thing himself, and said he was sure it had come out fine."

When she was ready she looked up at us both. "He said it was for you two to listen to together. I'll switch it on, then Carly and I will have to go out of the room."

"Nonsense, Evie," I said.

"I want to listen to the machine," said Carly.

Lindsey said softly: "If it's something Dad wanted you and me to hear on our own, we should respect his wishes. Carly, you must go out with Auntie Evie."

Carly looked miffed. "Please, Mummy."

"No darling. That's my final word. How long is it, Evie?"

"Not very long, I don't think. If it doesn't work you'll have to call me back in."

She pressed the button, then took Carly quickly out of the room. The machine worked fine.

"Lindsey, Jamie, I'm sorry to do this to you. A voice from beyond the grave is probably not much fun to listen to. But I have something I want to say which I don't think I'll manage if I try to do it face to face, and anyway, I'd better get it done while I'm still making sense, and before the quacks get at me with their terrible drugs."

358

Lindsey reached out for my hand.

"I haven't been down to your rehearsal yet, Lindsey love, but I'm sure you'll do fine, like you always have. If I've died before the show opens, and I'm pretty sure I will, I want you to go through with it for me. Something Jamie said to me the other day really struck a chord – apparently having your old Dad with you might be the thing you need to get over your worries. And I do know you're worried, Lindsey love, however much you've tried to protect me. But you pull yourself together for me, my lovely girl, because I want the audience to love you one last time."

A sharp intake of breath and a squeeze of my hand were all that Lindsey dared risk.

"Because you see, I might be dying but I'm no fool. I know my little girl better than anyone – better even than you, Jamie. You're not happy with this singing lark, Lindsey love, and I'm frightened that it's wrecking your lives – you two and my precious Carly. I've watched you for a few years now, getting more and more tense, and being tetchier and tetchier with each other. I've watched Carly get hooked on coming here – the one place where she has real stability. So now you're about to get it right between the eyes – on old man's dying wish. Bit cheesy I know, but you'll have to put up with that. I want you to give it up, Lindsey, and I want you, Jamie lad, to give up that Opera Company, and I want you both to give up that bloody Russian sod who's ruining everything I hold dear. I'm leaving you the farm – that's no great surprise, I'm sure – but what you won't be expecting my girl, unless Jamie's told you what I said, is that I want you to come here and farm the land, and save it from the developers who've had their greedy eyes on it for years. Then Carly and the baby can have a proper, country childhood, living in the nearest thing to paradise you'll find this side of the Pearly Gates. Which is where I'm going right now, unless I lie down. I'm knackered. I love you both with all my heart.

There was a click, followed by a disturbing little bit of Evie's voice which must have been left on the tape. I got up to switch off the machine. Then, without warning, another click was followed by Albert's voice speaking again, this time far weaker and less distinct.

"I've just got back from London, from your rehearsal, Lindsey my love. You were unbelievable. Was it me being there that made you sing so well? I don't know, although I'd like to think so. But you have to do this one final run of performances for me, Lindsey, and you have to sing like a goddess, like you did this morning. I know

you will. Then tell the lot of them to sod off, and come home to Stockencote where you belong. Where you all belong. Oh, hallo Evie. Have you come to send this old bugger to his grave?"

More clicks, and a sort of whooshing noise which suggested to me he was trying to turn off the machine. Then Evie's voice:

"Come on Al, take your medicine like a good boy. I'll turn it off…"

Then, like a bad sitcom, Evie's voice from years before saying something about Mrs Henderson's Preparation H having run out, and her not being very comfy at the dinner table. I got up and switched the Dictaphone off.

Lindsey looked at me. A single tear was rolling down her cheek. I went to hold her, but she pulled away from my embrace.

"I can give up the singing, Jamie, that's no problem. And I'd love Dad to be right about all of it. But I just don't know if I can give up Sergei. Sorry."

It was like a blow in the pit of my stomach. I was nearly sick.

"Oh. Right then. What am I to do?"

"Give me time, Jamie. Give me till *Fledermaus* is on, and Dad's buried. I might need much longer – till the baby's born, maybe. I don't know what to do…"

Now her tears started in earnest. I stood up, uncertain how to react. Eventually I excused myself rather awkwardly, and went into the study to tell Carly and Evie that Albert had had some wonderful things to say, but that Mummy had been a bit shocked by hearing his voice, and she might need a cuddle. Carly rushed into the kitchen, followed by Evie and me. She flung her arms around Lindsey, and they both wept, while Evie and I pottered around stupidly, doing the washing up.

When there was nothing else to be said, or done, or cried, Lindsey said:

"Jamie, you'd better get back. Don't worry about anything. We'll all be fine, won't we, Evie?"

"Of course we will. Thank God I've still got you two here to look after. Jamie, Lindsey's right, you'd better go."

I kissed them all in turn – all three on the cheek. Lindsey didn't look at me. I walked towards the back door, and picked up my bag from the side. Just as I was walking out of the door, Lindsey called after me.

"Jamie, drive carefully. And ring when you get there — I want to know you're safely home."

The first job I had to do on leaving Stockencote was to switch on my phone, which I did as I drove through Hambleton towards the Stamford road. My voicemail rang instantly.

But instead of the five or six apoplectic messages I'd expected from Sergei, or Angus, or some vile tabloid journalist, I only had two. The first was from John Standish, and was as sympathetic as I could have wished.

"Jamie, dear boy, I'm so sorry about that piece of filth in the *Herald*. It makes me glad I'm about to do the little favour for you, as nothing would give me greater pleasure than to be the one who scotched these hideous rumours. Don't forget to bring Denise my present on Thursday. I'll be there of course, but magnificently discreet as always. Let me know if there's anything else I can do. Oh Christ, I hope Lindsey doesn't pick up your messages. If that's you, Lindsey, ignore everything I've just said. Toodle-pip."

The second message was from Mum, saying how awful the thing in the paper had been, and how dare they print something like that when they knew it wasn't true. With the usual pang of guilt I realised I hadn't spoken to her for ages, so I rang her and told her about Albert. She was shocked he'd faded away so soon, and sent her love to Lindsey. She didn't mention the *Herald* article.

Standish's message didn't seem to require a reply, so I switched the phone off again, put my foot a little nearer the floor and got home in record time. To my relief the paparazzi had gone.

I dialled Lindsey's mobile as soon as I'd opened the front door. She answered straight away.

"Oh, I'm so glad you're there safely, Jamie."

"Was there anything special you wanted, sweetheart?"

"No, no, just to make sure you were safe. I'm sorry about everything. You know that, don't you?"

"Yes, my love, I think I do. Listen, you've just gone through the worst experience anyone can have in their life. You need to rest, so you should be going to bed. I'll make sure all the *Fledermaus* people know you won't be there until the stage rehearsals on Thursday. Okay?"

"I've counted John Standish's pills, Jamie. I'm going to take them before every rehearsal, and every performance. I've got enough to get me through to the first night – that's if I start back on Thursday – so yes, that's okay. But I'm going to need more for the other performances. He'll give them to me, won't he?"

"If he knows you're giving up afterwards, I'm sure he will, sweetheart. We'll ask him on Thursday morning, at the amnio."

"I suppose that's the next time I'll see you?"

"I guess so. Go to bed. I love you."

There was a pause, then she said, so quietly that I only just caught her words: "I know you do, Jamie."

40

What Sergei had done, and to whom, was anyone's guess. But there was nothing in any of the papers on Monday morning, or, to my astonishment, on Tuesday, Wednesday or Thursday either. Maybe he'd given the benevolent funds of every news organisation in the country some fantastic sum of money. Maybe he had indeed obtained *kompromat* on all their editors.

Mrs Billington had been very understanding about Carly. She agreed that she shouldn't come into school, and sent her love. She promised to get a package with some homework sent up to Rutland, and told me not to worry. She was sure a week off wouldn't do her too much damage.

Everyone at work was full of sympathy, and passed on their best wishes to Lindsey. Even Umfreville briefly showed her human side when I told her the news about Albert. She agreed that Lindsey would miss the rehearsal room run on Tuesday the third, and the second *sitzprobe*, which in any case was mostly chorus, on Wednesday the fourth, and would reappear for the first stage rehearsal on the fifth.

I spoke to Lindsey regularly but our conversations were confined to the subject of Albert. Dr Storey had seen the body, and confirmed that it had been a stroke which had killed him, weakened as he was by the ravages of cancer. They could go ahead and fix the funeral, he said.

There was to be a service at the Church of St Andrew in Hambleton, followed by cremation at Peterborough Crematorium, after which everyone would troop back up to Stockencote for tea, cake and something alcoholic. Albert had been quite specific about that.

Finding a day for the funeral had been hellish. There were *Fledermaus* rehearsals for the whole of the following week, and unless we were to keep poor Albert waiting till the cows came home, I had to fix it for Lindsey to miss yet more. Eventually we agreed on Thursday the twelfth of October – the day of the piano dress. Lindsey's cover would do this one, and everyone agreed that, in order to give this long-suffering girl a fair crack of the whip, she should also do the orchestral pre-dress rehearsal on the Friday. This would give Lindsey an extra day to recover from the trauma of the funeral.

Thursday the fifth was the day of Lindsey's much-heralded amniocentesis. So I got up at sparrowfart, rescued from the drawer in our bedroom the little package containing the DNA testing kit, and ceremoniously took it downstairs with me to the kitchen. It sat on the table looking at me while I had my lonely breakfast and while I did the washing up. Eventually I braced myself and opened it up, preparing myself for some hideous and possibly painful ritual. It turned out all I had to do was brush a thing like a toothbrush up against the inside of my cheek, making sure it was nice and wet with my saliva. Then I had to repeat the process with a second toothbrush, and leave both to dry completely.

Once I was sure everything was done I wrapped them both carefully in plastic bags and stuck on little labels. There was a jiffy bag thoughtfully provided to send them back in, so I took this and its precious contents upstairs and shoved it in the breast pocket of my jacket.

The whole process made me feel grubby and degraded, so I had a shower and a shave in an attempt to restore my equilibrium. I finally left the house for King's Cross at nine thirty.

I met Lindsey there just as I had for the scan. She was terribly nervous, and not much inclined to talk, so we walked to UCH in near-silence.

We arrived ten minutes early, but Standish was already there and Denise was with him. As we walked through to the consulting room where he was going to take the sample of amniotic fluid I hung back for a moment, and slipped the jiffy bag containing the DNA samples into her hand. She uttered not one word, but for a fraction of a second pressed my forearm with her stubby fingers.

Standish was his usual urbane self. "Now then, Miss Templeton, you appear to be rather nervous. May I ask one question?"

"Yes, John, of course."

"How on earth do you manage to get yourself on stage to sing Fiordiligi at the Salzburg Festival if a little thing like an amniocentesis gets you into such a flap? Before you answer, I'd like to add that in all my thirty years of sticking my hands and needles into various parts of women's anatomies I've never lost a single baby. Mislaid a couple, but that's because I'm a victim of CRAFT. It's an elderly person's disease. Short for Can't Remember A Fucking Thing."

Lindsey giggled politely, but didn't reply.

"Okay, it's all systems go go go. Please pull down your skirt and knick-knicks to reveal your splendidly fertile womb. Well, its outer covering, anyway."

She demurely did as she was told. I knew she hated Standish's hit or miss humour, but she trusted him completely. Poor Lindsey. Little did she know the trick we were about to pull.

Standish began by doing an ultrasound scan.

"I need to establish the exact position of the baby, so I know where to insert the needle".

Lindsey gave an involuntary shudder. Standish put gel on her stomach and moved the wand over her as before. The familiar green shape appeared on the screen. "Looks a healthy little bugger. Or buggeress, of course. Do you want to know the sex?"

"No thank you," said Lindsey. "I just want to know it hasn't got Down's Syndrome."

"Of course, my dear, of course. I'm going to clean the skin with this antiseptic, then insert this needle into your womb to collect a sample of amniotic fluid. It shouldn't be too uncomfortable."

The needle was attached to a syringe, which filled with brownish fluid as he pulled the plunger out. Then he painstakingly extracted the needle from Lindsey's abdomen, and held the syringe aloft in triumph.

"There we are, all over," he beamed. "That wasn't too bad, was it?"

"Is that all there is to it?"

"Absolutely. There may be a little discomfort for a few hours – somewhat akin to period pain, I gather, but having never had either I can't comment authoritatively. Paracetamol will help with this, should you feel inclined. We should have preliminary results for you within seventy-two hours, with confirmation to follow after about two weeks."

He lowered his arm and busied himself with the syringe, a sample bottle and some labels, very similar to the ones I'd used for my buccal cell test earlier that morning. With his back to Lindsey, he continued: "can you go home and put your feet up for the rest of today?"

Lindsey chuckled mirthlessly. "Hardly, John. I've got a stage and piano of *Fledermaus* this evening."

"Oh well, I shouldn't worry unduly." He turned back to face her. "If I recall you used to give whole concerts with those awful endometriosis pains. A little sing through of a piece of froth like *Fledermaus* should present no problems. Of course if you get any serious discomfort you must stop, but it's most unlikely."

"Can I take some of your magic pills?"

"Ah. Well, I don't see why not. Have you been using them much?"

"Just the once, for a rehearsal a week ago. They worked a treat."

He smiled an enigmatic smile.

Lindsey swung her legs off the bed, and began to get dressed. "John, if I promise never to take them again after this run of eight performances, will you allow me enough to get me through them all?"

"But how will you manage for your next outing?"

"There's not going to be a next outing. I'm giving up."

He frowned, and his bottom jaw fell slightly. He stood for a moment in this position, looking like a fish whose mouth had stuck open, then placed his index finger underneath his chin and pushed it closed again.

"That, if I may say so my dear, is a tragedy of epic proportions. Why, if one may make so bold?"

"Because I can't stand the pressure any longer, John. And because my father wanted it. He died on Sunday, by the way."

"Oh my dear, I'm so sorry."

"Thank you, John. Anyway, how do you feel about supplying me with some more pills?"

"Yes, yes of course. It goes without saying. Oh dear, I'm afraid this is something of a shock, my dear. A bit like Mrs Thatcher resigning. Except that the old trout's departure, of course, was an unalloyed pleasure, while yours is a disaster. The world of opera will be devastated."

"It's kind of you to say so, John, but there are plenty more where I came from."

"Not true, my dear. Even in one's wildest flights of fantasy one cannot expect to encounter more than one Lindsey Templeton in a lifetime. I shall come to every single performance of *Fledermaus*. I shall cancel everything to be there. And I would like if at all possible to attend all the remaining rehearsals as well. Any chance, Jamie?"

"Yes, John, yes of course. Lindsey's personal physician, why not? Starting tonight?"

"Absolutely. And you may have all the pills you like, my dear. They'll do you no harm, as long as you stick to your instructions, and they'll make an old gynaecologist very happy. Just let me know when you need them."

Lindsey gave me strict instructions to leave her alone before the rehearsal, so I was able to meet Standish at the stage door at six twenty-five. He looked buoyant.

"It's yours, dear boy. Managed to get down to the lab myself this afternoon."

A wave of relief swept over me. It was so strong it almost took my breath away. I must have looked poleaxed.

"Gratifying reaction, dear boy. We must celebrate. But not until we've heard the Diva. Has she taken the pills?"

"I haven't seen her, but she said she was going to."

"Splendid. Let's go down."

We marched through the wings to the auditorium. Well, Standish walked, I floated. On the way we passed Jason, waiting to sing his first offstage number. I nearly picked him up and kissed him.

We installed ourselves in the same box I had shared with Albert and Evie at the *sitzprobe* less than a week before. Before Umfreville started playing Jason's introductory music I had time to spot Sergei, also sitting in the same place as last week. Tatyana and the goons were there too. I had an urge to yell: "it's mine, you impotent piece of Russian shit." But instead I smiled politely. He flashed me an insincere version of his famous grin, then almost immediately the music began. I did my best to transfer my attention to the stage.

The rehearsal was mostly taken up with matters technical – entrances and exits, problems with props and costumes, timings of various bits of the action now they were finally on the stage. But they sang through each of the numbers. Gloria and Jason sang out full voice throughout the evening, and both did really well. Pogson marked – he looked out of sorts, and complained about everything from his costume to the noises backstage. I glanced across at Sergei during one particularly hysterical outburst. He had his chin in his hands, and an expression of glum resignation on his face.

But there was no doubt who was the star of the evening. People in opera will forgive almost anything if someone produces the goods, even if it's at the eleventh hour. Lindsey was cheered and applauded by everyone in the theatre the moment she walked on for the first time – everyone had by now heard about Albert, not to mention the *Herald* article and Knipe's letter in the *Statesman*, and that applause was filled with support and sympathy. At the end of her first duet with Gloria, which both of them had sung divinely, there was more applause, and one of the covers, who were huddled together in the dress circle, produced a deafening whistle. Even though the auditorium was sparsely filled, the action stopped completely for several minutes, and eventually the stage manager had to walk onto the stage to remind everyone they had work to do.

By the time we had got to the tea break, it was an accepted fact that Lindsey was back on form. Better than that – just as at the *sitzprobe*, her voice had a new depth and richness, while the top was as gleaming and brilliant as ever. I took Standish down into the canteen for a cup of tea – alcohol was banned from the premises – and I was clapped on the back by almost everyone I saw. When we'd bought our tea, we went up to Lindsey's dressing room. Her Amazonian dresser Hilda was sitting outside the door. She was full of it.

"Oh, Jamie, it's so lovely to see you. I haven't congratulated you on your appointment – we're all absolutely thrilled. No more of that awful Mr Knipe. And isn't it wonderful about Lindsey's singing? And her poor father not yet cold in his grave. Oh dear, that sounds awful. What I'm trying to say is she's amazing to be able to sing like that when she's had such tragic news."

"Thanks Hilda. I'm as excited about Lindsey's singing as you are. This is her private physician John Standish, and I must take him in to see her before the break finishes."

"Oh, yes of course. You don't want to listen to me burbling on. There's nothing wrong, I hope?"

"Not at all," said Standish. "I just want to congratulate her."

"Well, in you go. There's that gorgeous Mr Rebroff in there as well, with one of those great big bodyguards he always has with him. What a lot of sexy men there are around here tonight."

I looked briefly at John, who nodded at me, then I knocked on the door. Mutt opened it a crack, and when he saw it was me he let us both in. Sergei was standing behind my wife, with his hands on her shoulders. He was giving her a massage, and showed no sign of stopping when he caught sight of me. It was all I could do not to pull him off her and punch his lights out.

She at least had the good grace to look embarrassed. She looked at Sergei in her mirror and lifted one of his hands gently off her shoulder, then he let go of her, clearly irritated.

Standish was brilliant. "Ah, Lindsey, forgive me for intruding. Your husband was all for keeping me out, but I told him your personal physician urgently needed to see you. Of course it was just to tell you how magnificent you are. That medicine you've been taking is working wonders. Jamie, I'm quite incoherent at being in the presence of the Diva, and she doesn't want to have to bother with me in the middle of a rehearsal. Introduce me to this impressive-looking gentleman who must be very important if he needs his own bodyguard."

"Yes, of course, John. Sergei, this is John Standish, Lindsey's gynaecologist and one of our oldest friends. John, this is Sergei Rebroff, Chairman and saviour of Opera London."

"Mr Rebroff, I am honoured to make your acquaintance. As a devoted operagoer, may I take this opportunity of thanking you for transforming my life with your generosity."

"You are very kind." Sergei still looked cross. "Lindsey is jewel in my crown. You should really be thanking her."

"Oh, Sergei," said Lindsey, "you are ridiculous. Listen, Jamie, I hope you don't mind, but please don't come back afterwards. Sergei is taking me out."

Standish was gobsmacked, judging by the look on his face. So was I.

"Um, no, of course not, Linds. Will you be all right to get the eleven thirty from King's Cross?"

There was a sticky pause. It was Sergei who spoke up.

"Jamie, I have told Lindsey she must not travel tonight – she has rehearsal at ten thirty tomorrow morning. I have arranged for her to stay at Savoy."

Lindsey picked up a make-up sponge and started dabbing her face with it. I tried to catch her eye in the mirror, but she was studiously avoiding my gaze.

Standish needed all his social dexterity to break the tension. After looking intently at me, he took a deep breath and said: "Lindsey, my dear, Jamie and I must leave you to your art. My advice is that you should be entirely alone, in order to prepare yourself for the rest of the evening's work." He looked squarely at Sergei for a moment. "I am glad that Lindsey is not doing that ridiculous journey twice in the next twelve hours. But the doctor says she is not to be too late to bed. The baby needs a lengthy night of unbroken rest."

Sergei looked at the floor. I would cheerfully have kneed him in the balls, but Mutt was looking agitated, and I didn't fancy my brains being spattered all over the dressing room, so I opened the door, and ushered Standish out. I did finally manage to catch Lindsey's eye as I left. There was an apology implied in that look, but I swear there was also fear.

We sat through the rest of the rehearsal, but the joy had gone out of it. Afterwards Standish offered to take me out for a bite to eat, but I couldn't face it, so we parted company. I gave him a pass to get in and out of the theatre so he could attend rehearsals without me. I'd had enough of Sergei and the whole bloody lot of them.

This feeling was compounded the next day, when all anyone could talk about was how wonderful Lindsey was. I had always loved being a part of her success, but this time it made me angry. I wandered around work for the whole of the Friday trying to control my temper.

I escaped from the office at the first available opportunity, and jumped in the car as soon as I got home. Stockencote was the only place I had any desire to be, even though my dirty stop-out of a wife would be going back there. I found myself in the Hatfield tunnel on the A1 at six o'clock, bang in the middle of a perfectly foul rush-hour.

I didn't arrive until nine, by which time I was frazzled to the point of distraction, but as I walked into the kitchen, I was cheered up by the fabulous sight of Evie ladling steaming hot stew and mashed potatoes onto a plate for me. She and Carly had had their supper earlier, and Carly had already gone up to bed.

Ethel the pug was sitting by Evie's feet. She looked balefully at me and snorted.

"Jamie, you've done well to make it," said Evie. She offered me a pink cheek to kiss. "Lindsey won't be back till late, but I assume you know that."

"Yup, she's rehearsing till nine thirty. Has she got the car at Peterborough station?"

"Yes, dear. She left it there yesterday morning. She stayed in Town last night. I gather she was staying at the Savoy." She put my supper in front of me, and sat down, looking at me quizzically.

"Wow, Evie, this looks fantastic." I picked up my knife and fork, and tucked in. The question mark on her face was still there.

"Jamie, you'd better tell me what's going on."

"Well, I gather Rebroff arranged for her to stay there. He has a suite which seems to occupy the whole of the top floor, so there would have been plenty of room for her." I paused, and crammed some more stew into my mouth. "What I don't know is what the sleeping arrangements were."

"Jamie, what on earth are you going to do about this? She's not thinking of leaving you for him, is she?"

"Evie, the ghastly thing is that I don't know, and I don't think Lindsey does either. And it's not exactly the best time to tackle the subject, is it?"

"When is the best time, Jamie?"

Another pause. Another forkful of food.

"I'm going to have to do it this weekend, aren't I?"

"As soon as possible, Jamie. You owe it to Carly. And to the baby."

"That is the one piece of good news, by the way. I'm definitely the father."

"Good God, Jamie, how on earth do you know?"

"I've had my DNA tested against the results of the amnio."

"Lindsey knows, presumably?"

"Not yet, Evie, no."

"You mean you did the test without her permission? How did you manage that?"

"Lindsey's gynaecologist, John Standish, is a personal friend. You might remember him, he came to our wedding. I'm afraid he agreed to do it without her knowing."

She looked truly shocked. I finished off the last of my stew, unable to think of what to say next.

"Jamie," she said, eventually, "do you realise how serious this is? That man could be struck off."

"I know that, Evie, but I don't see why anyone should find out. Obviously I'll have to tell Lindsey, but I'm sure when she knows the result she'll forgive him. And me, hopefully."

371

"When did he tell you?"

"Last night."

"Then you absolutely must tell Lindsey this weekend. She'll be furious, of course, but I suppose it might make her come to her senses. Dear God, this is just awful."

She got up from the table, and took my plate to the sink. Then she did the little bit of washing up, refusing my offer of help. She didn't speak again until she had opened the kitchen door to go up to bed.

"Jamie, I'm very fond of you. So was Albert, as you know. But the time for being nice is over. Get this ridiculous business with Lindsey sorted out now, or get out of this house for good."

She closed the door softly behind her, and I heard her padding up the stairs. Ethel rolled over onto her back, legs akimbo, with her bottom pointing towards me. She farted softly.

I got up, found a bottle of Albert's brandy and a glass, and sat myself back down at the kitchen table to await Lindsey's return.

She turned up at eleven forty-five, dog-tired. "Jamie. I wasn't expecting to see you here. Is everything all right?"

"Just dandy, thank you my dear. How was the rehearsal?"

"Oh, fine. More technical stuff. But we've got through the show. Nothing till Monday afternoon now, when we get the orchestra."

"Oh goodee. Are we going to have a roaring success on our hands, then?"

"You're drunk. Yes, I think we are going to have a massive success, actually. Ursula's done a wonderful job. The thing of Frosch, sorry, Frau Osch, being Mrs Thatcher is fantastic. That woman is so funny."

"Splendid. And how was last night."

All the enthusiasm disappeared from Lindsey's face. "Fine, thank you Jamie. He didn't jump on me, if that's what you're wondering."

"Just as well. Wouldn't have been very good for my baby to have thirteen stone of horny Russian oligarch landing on top of him. Or her." I giggled.

"What do you mean, your baby? I told you, it might be Sergei's. Our condom broke."

"Well it's not, actually. It's mine, you'll be disappointed to hear."

"How the fuck do you know?"

"A little bird told me."

"Jamie, for God's SAKE! Will you stop being such an arsehole and talk to me properly?"

"Okay then, here's the story. And don't go blaming anyone. I did what I had to."

"What, precisely?"

"I persuaded Standish to test the amnio results against my DNA."

"Jesus Christ." It was no more than a whisper.

"Yup. Sorry, old girl. But I had to know, y'see. Anyway, joking apart, I'm jolly glad it worked out the way it did. I'd have hated our baby to have had Slavic features and a propensity to swindle the State out of billions of roubles."

Lindsey made a really odd noise, half way between a grunt and a scream. Then she slapped me, really hard. On my fat-spattered cheek, too, which was just beginning to recover. It hurt like buggery.

"Get out, Jamie."

"Can't. Pissed."

"I don't care how drunk you are. Get out. Now."

She turned and made for the door.

"And one more thing, Jamie. You can tell John Standish not to bother coming to any more fucking rehearsals. I'll do without his bloody pills. I never want to see him again. Or you, as a matter of fact."

She went through the door into the hall, and shut it gently behind her. I was still sitting at the kitchen table, a half-empty brandy bottle open in front of me. I carefully screwed the top back on, then washed up my glass, and left it on the draining board. Then I scrawled a note, which said *Dear Evie, thanks for the stew. It was delicious. Dear Albert, thanks for the brandy. I'm pissed. Dear Lindsey, thanks for wrecking my life. Love to all, Jamie.*

I propped it up against the brandy bottle and tottered out to the car.

I drove with extreme care all the way to Queens Park. I concentrated like hell, determined not to kill anyone (although I wouldn't have been remotely concerned about killing myself), and in order not to arouse the suspicions of the Police, I kept the car at about three miles per hour above the speed limit. This was a theory of mine which had been developed over many years of dinner parties and pub crawls, and it had always proved effective.

In the event I encountered almost no traffic, and only one Police Car, which I overtook on the fifty mile-an-hour section of the A1 in Sandy.

He was doing forty-eight, so I risked fifty-one. It took me an age to get past, but I did so without him apprehending me.

I must have aged twenty years during that journey. I will have been at about twice the legal limit. But I made it intact, and at two fifteen I slumped onto my bed. I was lonely, drunk, miserable, and pathetic.

41

The weekend was ghastly. I couldn't face shopping, so stayed in and ate crap. At no stage on either day did I bother to shave, or even get dressed. I flicked through all nine hundred channels on Sky about a thousand times, and found precisely nothing which gave me the remotest pleasure or satisfaction. I did at least manage to phone Mum and Dad. They would be coming to the funeral, they said.

My head pounded with the awful events of the past week, not to mention a great deal of Hungarian Pinot Grigio, which I'd found on offer weeks earlier at Sainsbury's. Despite applying myself to my problems with relentless, if somewhat confused zeal, I came up with no solutions. My only option, I decided, was to wait and see what happened next.

Monday dawned with a most un-General-Administrator-like hangover, which was particularly unwise as I had a meeting with Angus and Anna-Gre Tapp at ten. I ran into the office at two minutes past. The other two were already hard at it.

"Jamie, old thing, what a huge, if somewhat tardy pleasure," said Angus.

"Ah, Jamie," said Anna-Gre. "I am glad you have arrived – we have much to discuss."

Actually, I'm sorry to report that we didn't have much to discuss at all. Angus and I went over the planning outline for the next two seasons with Anna-Gre, but he and I had already drafted that before we were appointed, and in any case Anna-Gre kept pointing out that Sergei had his own amendments to suggest. Apparently they'd already had a meeting, at which Sergei had mumbled something about not being able to get hold of me because of *Fledermaus* rehearsals. I was pretty certain he hadn't tried.

Angus was scathing. "Jamie, he clearly wants to do the planning himself. You're being frozen out. For Christ's sake get back to him today – you can't let this happen."

"It's all very well for you to say, Angus. He's the boss, after all, and has all the money. If he wants Yekaterina Bogova in five times next season to sing a cycle of Moussorgsky operas in Russian, that's what he'll have to have."

"Jamie is right, Angus," said Anna-Gre. "Sergei calls the shots here, I'm afraid."

Angus looked at me with an expression I'd never seen before. "I'm beginning to see the philosophy behind all this, Jamie. He's appointed us, the promising youngsters, because he thinks he can get away with running the shop himself. We're being shafted."

"But what in God's name can I do?" I said.

"Talk to Archie Foster," said Angus. "If the Arts Council get wind of this, they could get very shirty with Sergei, which seems to me to be exactly what we want."

"That's not a bad idea, Jamie," said Anna-Gre. "Archie may just be your only hope of establishing yourself. He's booked for the first night of *Fledermaus* next Monday. You'd better find a moment then. But whatever you do, sort Sergei Rebroff out now."

"Anna-Gre is quite right, Jamie," said Angus. "Sort the bastard out. Before it's too late, ideally."

Standish rang a few minutes after the meeting.

"Just got preliminary results of the amnio, dear boy. Baby's in the clear. We get confirmation in about a week, but I'm as sure as I can be that everything'll be okay. I know the sex, too. Do you want to know?"

"I'll have to talk to Lindsey about that."

"Never a bad idea, dear boy. How is the Diva? Not suffering from any unwanted after-effects of the test?"

"I'm afraid I wouldn't know. Haven't spoken to her since Friday. But I suppose if she had anything really serious she might have rung."

"Oh bugger, Jamie, are things bad again?"

"'Fraid so. I told her about being the Daddy."

"And she cut up rough?"

"You could say that. Kicked me out of her father's house. I had to drive home at midnight, pissed out of my brain."

"And presumably she's not talking to me either."

"No. Hates your guts, John. Sorry. My fault."

"For God's sake, Jamie. This self-pity is pathetic."

I walked over to the door, to shut out prying ears. Grace was beavering away at something, but I knew damn well she was listening.

"That's easy for you to say. Your wife isn't fucking your boss, is she? I thought I might be getting somewhere when Albert died, because I thought she needed me, but then she announces that she can't give that Russian tosser up. I follow that up with an announcement that I've gone behind her back, and persuaded her favourite gynaecologist to do the dirty on her. Between us we've tricked her into giving us a sample of the baby's DNA, and found out without her permission who the father is. It's not the best thing to have done if I'm trying to impress her, is it?"

Standish paused for a moment. "On reflection, dear boy, I incline to the view that it's the first grown-up thing you've done in this whole sad business. I'm sorry to hear that Lindsey's upset with you, and even sorrier that she's upset with me, but overall I would be prepared to bet a considerable sum of money that she'll come round. By the way, I suppose I'm no longer welcome at the rehearsals?"

"You can come if you're prepared to hide at the back of the dress circle. She won't see you there."

"I'm not hiding anywhere, if you don't mind. This is not a situation I relish. Do me a favour. Sort out that frightful Russian boundah, will you? And soon."

"You're the third person to say that in the space of an hour, John."

"Then you know what to do, don't you, Jamie?"

No. No, no, no. I did *not* know what to do. But I did know that I would have to find Lindsey when she came in for her rehearsal at two, and tell her about the result of the amnio.

I was outside her dressing room at one o'clock. The thrilling, flawless, unbearable sound of her voice told me she'd already arrived. I knocked tentatively on the door.

The voice stopped, and the door opened. She looked terrible.

"Oh, it's you. I'd like to tell you to fuck off, but you're my boss, so I suppose you'd better come in."

"How are you feeling, Linds? No problems after the amnio?"

"No, I've been fine. As if you care."

"Of course I care. Listen, John Standish phoned this morning."

She groaned. "Oh God, he's not coming again is he? I don't want to see him."

"He just phoned to say the preliminary result of the amnio is through. The baby's fine."

She sat down in her make-up chair. "Thank God for that, Jamie. You can't possibly know how worried I was."

"I was worried too, Linds."

I touched her shoulder. Or rather I tried to touch it, and she pulled it away. Then she picked up a tiny little make-up brush, and pretended to do something to her eyes, but her hand was shaking too much. I looked at her for a long moment, but she wouldn't catch my eye, so I said "toi-toi for this afternoon", and left the room.

I tried Archie Foster, but his mobile went straight onto an answering machine, which told me he was in the States all week, and please *not* to leave a message because it would cost him a fortune to pick up. Then I toyed with the idea of ringing Tatyana, and trying to get through to God Almighty himself, but I couldn't imagine what I would say to him, so I chickened out.

There seemed to be nothing useful I could do, so I snuck down to the auditorium. The rehearsal was going badly. Leclerc was being tetchy with the orchestra, and they were acting up. At one point he said to the leader, or principal violinist of the orchestra, "is eet better if Hi beat zese bars in two or four?"

The leader was quick in his response. "It would be better if you could maintain a steady *tempo* rather than getting slower."

"But Hi am doeeng an *allargando*."

"But Strauss didn't say he wanted an *allargando*, did he?"

This kind of exchange with the leader did not bode well for the performances. I knew the players loathed him, but I'd thought he could at least keep them in order.

Lindsey, however, was once again singing wonderfully. I sat back in my seat and listened to her, and tried to forget my problems. Some hope.

I vacillated my way through Tuesday and Wednesday, pretending to take responsibility for everything, and achieving nothing. Lindsey was coldly polite, no more. I went into her room on the Wednesday morning, which was the last rehearsal she was scheduled to do before the Dress on Saturday, and offered to drive her up to Stockencote when she'd finished, but she refused, saying she needed to sleep on the train back, and anyway she was sure I shouldn't be leaving work that early. I didn't argue. I just frittered away another day, then took myself home, packed my dark suit and black tie, and got in the car alone for the drive to Rutland, and Albert's funeral. What a treat that promised to be.

The following morning dawned grey and sinister, as all funeral days must. I got up at seven, to find Evie and Carly already downstairs. Carly was in a state of unnatural excitement, a kind of wild energy glittering in her eyes, and she was charging about the kitchen like a mad thing, pretending to be one of the Harriers from nearby RAF Cottesmore. I heard myself saying "you should have more respect for your dead Grandad, Carly", which was mean, but it did succeed in shutting her up.

Evie had decided the previous night that such a special occasion required bacon and egg for breakfast, to give us strength for the day, and she was busy cooking over the Aga.

Lindsey didn't appear until ten minutes later. She refused her bacon and egg, and her breakfast consisted of four cups of tea, which she sipped her way through, silent and immovable, apart from the regular activity of lifting the cup to her mouth and putting it down again on its saucer. Evie kept refilling it, but Lindsey didn't seem to notice.

Eventually Carly could no longer stand the stultifying atmosphere in the kitchen, and roared off into the living room to resume her game of buzz the village. I had to chase after her and send her upstairs, away from the crockery and glasses which Evie had laid out for the afternoon's wake.

When I got back to the kitchen Evie had gone upstairs to dress, leaving the empty shell of Lindsey's inert body sitting at the table. I shut the door as gently as I could, and sat down next to her.

"Linds, you must eat something. You'll have no strength for the day."

No response.

"Darling, have your bacon and egg, for goodness' sake."

"It'll be congealed and horrible by now." The lips tight, the voice scarcely more than a whisper.

"Then I'll make you some more. The eggs are fantastic."

379

"Jamie, you can't make this better, all right? He's dead, and I wish he weren't. It's going to be a bugger of a day, and there's nothing you can do about it."

The uncompromising blackness of everything – the cars, the weather, the clothes – wasn't the problem. It matched the mood, and made me feel, for once in my life, deadly serious. But the expressions of condolence stitched onto the faces of the undertakers really were too much to take. Carly took one look at them and fled into her mother's arms.

The four of us – Evie, Lindsey, Carly and I – got into the car and sat in silence as we made the short, familiar journey to the church. Rutland Water was grey and still, the surface disturbed only by the persistent rain, and the occasional feeble gust of wind. The sailing boats bobbing in the water at Edith Weston looked inert and mournful, only just visible through the mizzle. The only colour was provided by Lindsey's huge spray of crimson roses on top of the hearse in front of us, making its sedate way up the hill towards Hambleton.

We pulled up in front of the church, and climbed out of the car. Two of the undertakers produced shroud-like umbrellas. Evie took Carly's hand, and waited for Lindsey and me to go first. To my astonishment Lindsey slipped her arm through mine. We waited for the morning-suited men in the hearse to sort out the coffin.

Lindsey's roses were placed on top, and then it was hoisted onto the undertakers' shoulders. Or rather five of the undertakers, plus a shattered-looking Gordon, who had insisted on being one of the pall-bearers. Our little family group followed the coffin into the church.

As we walked up the aisle I looked around at the friends and strangers who had gathered to pay Albert their last respects. So many people whom I'd met over the years at parties or in the pub. And there, right at the back, for once unaccompanied by any of his entourage, was Sergei Rebroff. Lindsey saw him at the same time as I did, and let out a tiny, almost inaudible gasp. Then she gently withdrew her hand from the crook of my elbow.

The service was taken by Matthew Roberts, vicar of the Benefice of Oakham, Hambleton, Egleton, Braunston and Brooke. Albert had not been an especially religious man, but Reverend Roberts had been a family friend ever since Lottie's death, and there was never any question that Albert would have a church funeral. Evie gave a short and moving eulogy, and we had Albert's favourite hymns, including *Lord of all hopefulness.* When we got to the words: *Be there at our sleeping and give us, we pray, Your peace in our hearts, Lord, at the end of the day,* Lindsey began to shake uncontrollably, and had to sit down. I remained standing, and somehow steered my clapped-out voice through to the end of the hymn, but by the time we'd finished I too had tears falling down my cheeks.

The service ended, and we processed out again. The rain had stopped for the time being, and we had to face the assembled friends and relatives.

When Sergei emerged from the church, doing his best to look inconspicuous, I was all for leaving him to bugger off home ungreeted. But Lindsey couldn't wait to get away from me and some cousins of Albert's, who were at that moment expressing their sympathy. Rather sooner than she decently should have done, she ran over to him – it was the fastest I'd seen anyone move during the entire ceremony. They retreated round the corner of the church and disappeared from view.

I made some excuse to the cousins, and extricated myself, quickly and no doubt rather rudely, from their little group. Then I hurried through the crowd, trying to look distracted enough to justify ignoring the faces I recognised.

As I approached the place where I had last seen the two of them, I heard them talking just around the corner. I realised with a guilty thrill that if I stood in the shadow of the buttress I could hear what they were saying to one another. I buried my head in my hands, and tried to look grief-stricken. Then I strained my ears for all they were worth.

"Sergei, you shouldn't have come. I'm very touched, of course, but it's going to be difficult to explain you away."

"I had to come. You have suffered so much with death of this great man. How can I expect to be part of your life if I cannot share such grief?"

"Sergei, please, not now. I have told you it is too soon to make a decision about leaving Jamie. And there's something I must tell you."

"What, Lindsey?"

"Jamie… Jamie had a test done. It was against my wishes, but he didn't tell me until after it was done. Sergei… the baby's not yours. Jamie is the father."

There was a pause. For one frightful moment I thought they were going to walk round the corner and bump right into me. Then Sergei spoke again.

"My darling, listen to me. I would like to finish your bastard of a husband. You have only to say. Then I will leave Nadezhda, and you and Carly can come to live with me."

"But… don't you mind that the baby is not yours?"

"Of course I mind. But if it means I can have you, I will love it because it is yours, just as I will love Carly. And later we can have baby of our own."

"Sergei, this is not the time or the place for this. I must go back to the guests. When can I see you?"

"Come to stay with me in London, my darling. I will cancel my trip to Russia."

"I'll try. I have Evie and Carly to think of. And Jamie, of course."

"Lindsey, you are too good to that weak man."

And then, God help me, I heard the hideous sucking noise of two people kissing. If poor Albert hadn't been waiting in the hearse not fifty feet away, I swear I would have gone and smashed Sergei's head in. As it was I could take no more. I lifted my head, and walked back into the crowd, meeting Evie and Carly, who were talking to the cousins I had left a few minutes before.

"Jamie, are you all right?"

"I'm just upset, Evie. Albert would be ashamed of me."

"Nonsense, Jamie, that's what funerals are for. Come on, we'd better get off to the Crem. We'll miss our slot. Do you know where Lindsey is?"

Carly piped up: "she went round behind the church with Uncle Sergei."

At that moment the two of them appeared round the corner. Lindsey looked flustered. Sergei, God rot him, looked immaculate and self-possessed. He made a sign towards the road, and I caught sight of Jeff, who had presumably been there from the outset, protecting his lordship from some unexpected but wholly understandable act of violence.

I had never seen Evie looking so furious. "Ah, there you are, Lindsey. And who, may I ask, is this young man?"

"Um, Evie, this is Sergei Ivanevitch Rebroff, Chairman of Opera London."

"How good of you to come, Mr Rebroff. Or should that be Mr Ivanevitch-Rebroff? I am so poor in my use of the Russian patronymic."

"It is not necessary, Mrs…?"

"It's Miss. Miss Evie Templeton, sister of the deceased. I am surprised to see someone so important gracing my brother's funeral. Albert was not a grand man, Mr Rebroff. But he did hold his family very close. Especially Lindsey, of course, and Jamie and Carly. Didn't he, Lindsey?"

Lindsey was almost in tears. For one ridiculous moment I felt sorry for her. "Yes, Auntie Evie, he did."

"Good heavens, that's the first time you've called me Auntie Evie in years. She must be very upset, mustn't she, Mr Rebroff?"

Sergei was a model of urbane charm. "Of course, Miss Templeton. I must leave now, but please allow me first to convey deepest sympathy to you and your family. Lindsey, rest well. I need you next week for my opening night."

"Yes, Sergei, yes of course. Thank you for coming. Have a good trip back."

Then bugger me if he didn't bow to us before he left. I'll tell you what. He'd have fucking well bowed if I'd kicked him in the balls.

The conversation in the car on the way to the crematorium consisted of the following exchange:

"How odd of Mr Rebroff to come all this way for the funeral of a man he never met."

"I think it was nice of him to come. I'm sure Dad would have been delighted."

"Well there, Lindsey my dear, we shall have to agree to differ."

And that was it.

All feeling had left me by the time those few of us who had made it to the Crematorium took our seats. The dirge-like organ music coming from the 1970's speakers at the front of the chapel only added to my numbness. When the coffin came in, now bereft of its crimson garnish, it perfectly reflected my mood.

There was an apology for a ceremony, and one more hymn – *Dear Lord and Father of Mankind* – before Albert's earthly remains made their last journey along the conveyor belt towards temperatures of 1000 degrees centigrade, and oblivion. The John Lewis curtains swung shut, and we were left there, gazing at an image of nothingness. Nobody cried. I sneaked a surreptitious glance to my right, where Evie was standing. Her face was set in an expression of grim determination.

The flowers outside were dominated by Lindsey's spray of roses, which no longer looked magnificent, but blowsy and over the top. We all managed the required politenesses, then for the last time we climbed back into the undertakers' car for the journey back to Stockencote. Carly started the only conversation.

"Where's Grandad gone now?"

"Heaven, darling," said Evie.

"Oh. I thought he'd gone to be burned to a crisp."

God forgive me, I laughed. Lindsey shot me a filthy look, but I wasn't really in the mood.

I didn't get a chance to talk to her until after everyone had gone home. I'd stayed sober, as I'd already decided to get myself home that night. No decision had been taken about Carly, but I didn't think it would do her any harm to miss the last school week before half-term. So since Lindsey was staying the night at Stockencote I could travel back alone, which suited me just fine.

I waited for her to approach me. I was determined not to give away the fact that I'd earwigged on their lovers' exchange.

"Jamie…"

"Yup."

"Er, Jamie, I'm going to need to see Sergei this weekend. We have to talk."

"Oh."

"So is it okay if I go and stay with him at the Savoy?"

"Which night?"

"Saturday and Sunday."

"Will you be knobbing?"

"For God's sake, Jamie, this is difficult enough."

"Well, will you?"

"No, we will not be knobbing. There you are. Are you satisfied?"

"Haven't been satisfied for months. Not by you, anyway. Yes, okay then, fuck off to the Savoy for the weekend. Although why the hell you need my permission is anyone's guess."

"Thanks, Jamie."

"Don't mention it. Any idea what's happening to Carly?"

"Um, no, not really. What do you think she should do?"

"Keep Evie company here for another week. Then it's half term, and we'll have time to think."

"Fine. Good idea. And anyway, I'll be here tomorrow. I'll go down to London on Saturday morning. It's the *Fledermaus* Dress on Saturday afternoon."

"I know it is, Lindsey. I'm General Administrator, in case you'd forgotten."

When I got home the numbness hadn't gone. I cracked open two bottles of Frascati, which tasted like raw lemons and quite suited my mood. I rolled into bed, paralytic, at eleven o'clock.

I had a dream, in which Albert was the star. Grotesquely, he was making passionate love to Saskia, who in turn was giving Sergei a blow job. But Albert was not giving the task his full attention. While taking her from behind, he was engaged in a deep and very serious conversation with me.

"See what I'm doing, Jamie lad? Fucking the opposition. And doesn't she love it. Are you loving it, Saskia?"

No reply.

"She can't answer me, you see. Too busy sucking on Mr Ivanevitch's patronymic. Bite it off, would you lass? He's got plenty more where that came from."

Saskia obligingly bit hard on what I'd thought was Sergei's dick, but she opened her mouth, and spat out a what appeared to be a bat, complete with leathery wings. On closer inspection, this animal turned out to have Lindsey's face. It looked up and spoke to me."

"Jamie, please do something. I love you so much. I don't want to lose everything. I just want to be with you and our children. Is it too much to ask, you shambles of a man?"

Saskia had disappeared, and so had Sergei. Only Albert was left, looking at the bat with Lindsey's face.

"I told you so, Jamie lad. Now get a move on, before the sun's well and truly over the yardarm."

42

At work the following day I stomped about the theatre in a rage. Everything conspired to remind me about Lindsey and Sergei – even the piano dress rehearsal of *Fledermaus* which was on stage during the morning. It went fabulously – the atmosphere was lighter without Lindsey, and the whole cast, scrupulously rehearsed by the skillful Ursula Zimmermann, acted up a storm. But all I could think of was listening to the two lovers kissing behind the Church wall the previous day.

Then there was the extraordinary silence maintained by the Press. For a day or so they'd doorstepped me, then everything had gone quiet. I hadn't had a single request from the Press Office to do an interview. Since I was the new boss of a highly controversial National Institution which had just been the recipient of the largest donation ever made to an Arts organisation in Britain, this was extraordinary.

I rang the Press Office. No, they said, they'd heard nothing from the papers. They'd put out the usual press releases, and had expected an overwhelming response, but nothing seemed to be normal since Sergei had taken over. They spent half the time twiddling their thumbs, they said. They were beginning to wonder whether their jobs were still safe. Perhaps I could have a word with him to find out what was going on.

Well, why not? Trying not to feel nervous, and determined to assert myself over Sergei Rebroff, I dialled Tatyana's number. She was very chatty.

"Misterr Barlow, I am very glad to hear from you. Firstly please allow me to say how sad I am about Lindsey's father. Please convey condolence to her."

"Thank you, Tatyana. Lindsey will be glad to know you are thinking of her."

"I am looking forward to opening night, Misterr Barlow. Will Lindsey still sing?"

"Yes, I'm sure she will be fine. Tatyana, I'm sorry to change the subject, but I haven't seen any recent press reaction to the situation at Opera London. I wondered if Sergei had said anything to you about it?"

She laughed. "Yes indeed, Misterr Barlow. He is very pleased with himself. He has spoken to, how shall I say? influential people. He has made bargain with them. They may print anything they wish, as long as they wait for first night. I think he wants to protect Lindsey from attentions of Press. And you, Misterr Barlow, of course."

"How extremely kind of him, Tatyana." Then I heard myself saying: "is he available to talk to, by any chance? Or perhaps he is out of the country, on business, or visiting his wife?"

"He is here, Misterr Barlow. He has decided to buy house in London. With quarters for me, perhaps in something called 'granny annexe'. I am very excited. I love London."

"How splendid, Tatyana. Would it be possible to speak to him, then?"

"Yes of course. Please wait…"

There was a click, followed by a pause which was rather longer than I expected. Then Tatyana came back on, sounding slightly chastened.

"He is exceptionally busy, Misterr Barlow. But he can spare you one minute."

Another click, then that oily voice. It made me want to vomit.

"Jamie, I am glad to hear from you. Please allow me to say how sorry I am about Lindsey's father."

"Thank you, Sergei. It was good of you to come to the funeral."

"I felt I must come. What can I do for you, Jamie? Forgive me, I am pressed for time."

"Um, I just wondered if you knew why the Press have been so silent, er, recently."

"They will not publish anything else about us until after the première. Is that all?"

"Er, yes, thanks. Great. Er… bye then."

"Goodbye Jamie. And thank you for taking the trouble to ring me."

I gave up on the Friday. What the bloody hell was the point of even going in? I'd no idea what I would do when I got there. I didn't want to hear yet another rehearsal of *Fledermaus*. I didn't think I could face Grace, or the Press Office, or anyone much. So I threw a sickie (me, the boss!) and lay on the sofa in front of the box all day, watching a tedious one-day international between South Africa and Sri Lanka. Kallis got five wickets and made fifty. So bloody what?

The Saturday was a different matter. The Dress Rehearsal, or General, to use OperaSpeak, of *Fledermaus*. It was the most anticipated opera production in London for the past ten years at least. It had everything going for it – excellent, mostly British cast, including Lindsey Templeton, National Treasure. Wacky, trendy German director, with enough off-the-wall ideas to make the show look cutting-edge, without there being so many that the more traditional punters would be put off. Young, thrusting conductor. Even a B-list celeb doing the acting role. Add to that a brand-new management team, and an exciting new Chairman with more money than sense, and you had the ingredients for something sensational.

Just one small problem. Leclerc had had another queeny fit after the previous day's rehearsal, and insisted on closing the General to anyone except those immediately concerned with the production. The orchestra had mucked him about again, and he had roared up to Anna-Gre Tapp's office, saying he couldn't possibly allow the public in when "ze fucking band eez takeeng ze peess."

It was, to a large extent, an act of revenge on Leclerc's part, since the General was traditionally the occasion when friends and family of the band came to watch the show. A Saturday General was a rarity indeed, and all the children of the players had been looking forward to it hugely.

Ursula Zimmermann was incandescent. She needed an audience, she said, so the singers could have a shot at timing the dialogue. But Olivier was not to be swayed, and Tapp had eventually caved in. She hadn't bothered to ring me to consult, I noticed in passing.

So there we had it. The curtain-raiser to the most exciting night in British Opera for a decade, and no-one to see it. Stupid French pillock. I went to Lindsey's dressing room to see how she was feeling, but she had a *DO NOT DISTURB – THIS MEANS YOU* notice on the door. I hoped it applied to Sergei as well as to me.

By the time I made it into my usual box Sergei was installed, chaperoned by Tatyana and one of the goons, in the box on the opposite side of the stalls. He looked as if he hadn't shaved. What in God's name was this paragon of elegance doing, going out in public like that?

Angus had come in to see the show in his dual capacities as Music Director Designate and knobber-in-chief of Gloria Forrest. He chose to sit next to me, which was rather reassuring.

Sergei stared at me stony-faced. Battle is joined, he seemed to be saying. And what did my cheery smile seem to be replying? Yes of course Sergei, absolutely anything you choose to say or do is fine with me.

Very shortly afterwards, thank the Lord, the lights dimmed and the dazzling overture began. Or rather it should have been dazzling. The playing was sloppy and ill-disciplined, and Leclerc grew visibly tetchier with each ragged piece of ensemble, and each fluffed horn note. The orchestra was getting its own back.

By the time we'd reached the interval, things had gone from bad to worse. Lindsey had begun okay, but her wobble made a couple of brief but disturbing appearances, and before Act One was over she had started to mark, to Leclerc's obvious fury. Umfreville uttered the loudest 'tut' I'd ever heard, and sat back in her seat with her arms folded, petulantly unwilling to take any further notes.

What I hadn't contended with was that this disaster would turn out to be my fault. Before I'd had time to get up from my seat and disappear to Caffe Italia for a coffee Umfreville had arrived at my box.

"She can't walk in at this stage and wreck everything. You'll have to talk to her."

"I presume, Yvonne, you are talking about Lindsey?"

"No, I'm talking about the Queen Mother."

"If you are indeed talking about my good lady wife then I suggest you talk to her. She's excellent at taking notes."

"You cast her, Barlow. You sort out the problem."

"I think you'll find that today the real problem is not Lindsey, but the orchestra. They are throwing their toys out of the pram because they couldn't bring their chums to this afternoon's rehearsal."

"So this is all Olivier's fault, is that it?"

"Far be it from me to criticise such an eminent *maestro* as Olivier, Yvonne."

"God you're a tosser, Barlow. Go and sort out that bloody wife of yours, now."

"She has *do not disturb* on her door."

"Oh diddums. Will she shout at you, Jamie-Wamie."

"Yvonne, fuck off and leave me alone. If you value your job, that is."

She snorted, and stalked off to the front row of the stalls, behind the conductor's podium. Leclerc was still there, studying his score. Umfreville said something to him, and they both looked back at me, smirking.

Much as it pained me to act on the rancid cow's instructions, I supposed I did have a responsibility to enquire after the Diva's wellbeing. I went to her dressing room, which was still sporting its notice. Ignoring it, I knocked gently.

"Go away."

"Linds, it's me. I need to come in for a moment."

"All right then, come in if you must."

She was sitting down, staring into her mirror. The brightly-burning light bulbs around the outside did her no favours. She had obviously been crying, and her mascara had run.

"Christ, Linds, are you all right?"

"Stupid bloody question, Jamie."

"Have you run out of Standish's pills?"

"I've got one more dose left. I didn't want to use them today. I wanted to see if I could cope without them. I can't."

"I'll ring him to get some more."

"Oh no, Jamie. I'm not accepting anything from him."

"Darling, I don't think you really have any choice. Not if it's the only way you're going to get through the shows."

"Do you know how it feels to have both you and Sergei bullying me to sing, when we all know full well that my career's over? I feel like a prostitute."

"Linds, after these performances are over, we'll have more time to decide what to do. But for all our sakes – mine, Sergei's, the Company's, and especially yours, you have to see them through. If the only way is with John's pills, then so be it."

She buried her messed-up face in her hands. Then, so quietly I could hardly hear it, she whispered: "okay then. Leave me alone, and I'll take the last dose now. For God's sake make sure I get some more by Monday."

"Linds?"

"What?"

"I love you."

390

Was there the briefest movement of her head in acknowledgement? I wasn't sure.

The orchestra were still playing like amateurs at the beginning of the second half, but Lindsey was miraculously transformed. The Watch Duet with Eisenstein was, to Julian Pogson's evident annoyance, a *tour-de-force* from Lindsey. By the time she started the *Czardas* the band had woken up a bit, and when she finished it what audience there was burst into spontaneous applause. The end of Orlofsky's party acquired the pizzazz the first half had lacked, and Act Three was superb. Frau Osch was hilarious, and by the time they arrived at the final chorus everything sounded wonderful again.

As soon as the lights went up, I looked across at Sergei. He still looked daft with his mucky face and piss-elegant suit, but instead of scowling he was beaming at me. He made a sign for me to wait while he made his way behind the auditorium to the back of my box.

But Umfreville was the first to arrive "God, Jamie, I don't know what you said, but I take my hat off to you. She was awesome."

"You should take your hat off to Lindsey, Yvonne, not me."

"Will she be okay for Monday?"

"Yes."

"Definitely?"

"Yes."

"Then that's all I need to say. You'll have to tell me your secret some day." And bugger me if she didn't wink at me. She waddled off, a broad grin on her face.

The door at the back of the box opened, and there was Mutt, looking suspicious. He grunted at me, then stepped back and Sergei walked in. He was still smiling.

"We must congratulate ourselves, Jamie. And especially we must congratulate Lindsey. To give such a performance three days after her father's funeral is stunning achievement." The unshaven face was an attempt at a beard. No doubt he was trying to look arty. Stupid tosser.

"Yes, I agree. You will no doubt be able to discuss it with her over the weekend."

"Ah." The smile became just a shade thinner. Yes, you are quite right, she has agreed to stay at Savoy tonight and tomorrow night. I felt she must rest before première."

"Oh goody. She will be in expert hands, I am sure."

A flash of irritation crossed his hirsute face. Then he turned on his heel and left.

I texted Lindsey the following brief message:
"Well done, darling. Everyone thrilled with you. Will see you Monday with your present. Rest well over the weekend. You deserve it."
I'd rewritten it five times, determined not to make it sound judgmental. If she had to go and work things out with Sergei, I didn't want to interfere. Let them play their game on a level playing field.
So I went home. There didn't seem to be much else to do.

The Sunday was shit. I didn't get out of bed, except to go to the lav. I didn't eat. I didn't even open a bottle of wine. I just lay there, thinking about my pregnant wife fucking the opposition.

Jamie Barlow, you pathetic useless lump of shite, you are, in name at least, General Administrator of one of London's three International Opera Companies, and today is the day of the première of the most eagerly anticipated operatic event of the last ten years. And you, at nine thirty in the morning, are still lying in bed, feeling sorry for yourself. So get up, have a shower, put on your best Hugo Boss suit, pack your dinner jacket in its plastic carrier, and get yourself down to that theatre for a bit of troop-rallying and image-enhancing. And if your Chairman *is* in bed with your Missus, get over it.

It was on the way to the Tube that I suddenly remembered I hadn't rung Standish to replenish Lindsey's supply of happy pills. With my heart in my mouth I rang Denise, who to my relief answered immediately.
"Hallo there, Mr Barlow."
"Denise, I wonder if you could help me?"
"Oh, gladly, Mr Barlow. Anything for you."
"Is John there?"
"No, I'm afraid not, Mr Barlow. He's operating. But don't despair, all is not lost. I think I know what you might want."
"Heavens, Denise, do you really?"
"I may sound a bit scatty, Mr Barlow, but I know *all* John's secrets. I keep telling him I'm going to write a book one day."
"You will promise to leave me out, won't you Denise? And Lindsey?"

"Oh yes, of course, you funny thing. Now, would it be a little packet of pills you were looking for?"

"Got it in one."

"John said it would probably be you who rang. He said it would be a good sign if it was you. If it was Lindsey he'd be worried. Apparently she's not speaking to him."

"Well, no, not for the time being. But I'm sure she'll come round."

"That's what John says. Anyway, I'm being terribly indiscreet. What would you like me to do with this little package?"

"I'll be there in half an hour."

So I changed direction, and instead of going straight to the theatre, I went via UCH, where Denise couldn't have been nicer. She gave me a concerned look when I arrived, and told me I was too thin, and ought to be looking after myself. At one point I thought she was going to get up from her seat and give me a hug, which given the threadbare state of my emotions would undoubtedly have made me cry, so I smiled as cheerily as I could, and asked her to forgive me because I was already late for work.

"Ah yes, Mr Barlow, the General Administrator himself. I don't believe I've congratulated you on your appointment."

"That's sweet of you, Denise, thank you. Watch this space, though. I wouldn't be surprised if before long you're commiserating with me on my premature departure from the very same job."

"Stuff and nonsense, Mr Barlow. British opera needs you. And don't look at me like that – I know what I'm talking about. Mr Standish told me so himself."

I stuffed the packet of pills into my pocket, and made my way down to Victoria. I went in via the foyer, as Sergei was having the place specially decorated for the première. He was paying for it himself, as he was for the sumptuous after-show dinner in the Telenorth bar.

The place was a hive of activity. There was a *Fledermaus* theme to the decorations which were beginning to take shape – in one corner was a vast pyramid of champagne saucers, and bats were peeking out from behind bits of furniture. Lying on the floor waiting to be hung were a couple of huge floral bats, and enormous quantities of the most fabulous orchids.

Mincing about the foyer issuing waspish instructions was a tiny, shaven-headed chap in his twenties. He was wearing a purple silk shirt and ball-crushingly tight black leather trousers, and he was obviously in charge of proceedings.

With some trepidation I approached this vision of loveliness. "I'm so sorry to interrupt – you're obviously very busy."

He looked me up and down, disapprovingly. "Yes."

"This is going to be marvellous. I've never seen anything so spectacular in this theatre."

"Well, that's hardly surprising, dear, in an opera house. I mean there's never normally any *money* in an opera house, is there? Not in this country anyway."

"So where do you usually work?"

"Oh, Buckingham Palace, Beckingham Palace, you know. Society weddings, that kind of thing. Places where they have the dosh not to impose too many limits. And to pay my fees."

"So, if you don't mind my asking, how much is all this going to cost?"

He looked me up and down again, as if deciding whether it was acceptable for him to be speaking to someone wearing a suit like mine. "I do mind, as a matter of fact."

"But I'm the General Administrator of Opera London."

He laughed, in the same girly way as Jason. It was not at all pleasant. "In *that* case, dear, you should know how much it's costing and if you don't, then I'm not about to start spilling the beans. Go and talk to that gorgeous Mr Rebroff. Now *there's* a man with class."

He spun round and walked away. His leather trousers had become stuck up the crack of his arse.

The offices were buzzing with what was about to happen. Just like the floral designer had said, opera companies – in Britain, anyway – simply weren't used to money being thrown about like water, and almost everyone in the building had by now seen what was happening out front.

I'd texted Lindsey, more in hope than expectation, to ask if she'd like one of our pre-performance late lunches, but all she'd said in reply was: *No. When can I have my pills?* I'd replied that I'd bring them down to her room at seven.

I watched the clock creeping round – four, five, six, six thirty. I had to go to the loo five times during the afternoon, knocked sideways despite myself by the electric atmosphere all around me. When, after what seemed to be an age, the clock crept round to six forty-five, I went to the gents to change into my dinner jacket. I hung up the Hugo Boss suit in my office, then ran two at a time down the stairs, nearly falling arse over tip at the bottom.

As usual Lindsey was concentrating on her make-up. I waved the little packet between her eyes and the mirror, and she put her brush down and turned to face me. "Thank you, Jamie," she said. "I don't know how I'd have managed without them."

Hilda the dresser had told me some of the other singers were being sick they were so nervous. So I stitched my most reassuring smile to my face, and did the rounds, telling them they were all wonderful and that they were about to take part in a historic production. Then I took myself off to the stalls bar, bought two bottles of champagne, and took them to my box, where Angus was waiting for me. With twenty minutes to curtain up, we set about attempting to enjoy the evening.

43

The champagne made me feel much better. Angus had just had a sheaf of wonderful reviews for his ENO first night, all of which had said what a breath of fresh air he would be at stuffy old Opera London. His tetchiness and worry of the past few weeks were forgotten, and he was back to the old Gussie. Add to that the fact that I had managed to avoid Sergei thus far and my mood was much improved. We were two thirds of the way down the second bottle by the time the overture started, and since we were in the privacy of our box I saw no reason not to carry on drinking into the beginning of Act One.

The band were on top form, thank Christ. The terrifying piccolo passagework in the overture was flawlessly played, and the violins were going at it as if their lives depended on it. Leclerc, who had walked in with a look of grim determination on his face, quickly relaxed as he realised that the professionalism of the orchestra had won over their fit of ill-temper. The music took on a real Viennese swing.

And the singing was superb. When Gloria came on to sing the first number her voice was freer and more radiant than I'd ever heard it – the top spinning effortlessly, the *coloratura* sparkling like jewels, and every word as clear as a bell.

"Bloody hell, Guthie," I whispered, lisping so as not to disturb anyone, "what'th she on?"

"My dick, half an hour ago, ath a matter of fact."

"Ah. That ekthplainth it."

And when Lindsey came on, something truly extraordinary began to happen. There are no superlatives adequate to describe the liquid perfection of her singing, or the total commitment of her acting. She was beautiful, heart-wrenching and hilarious by turns. I hoped she hadn't had the same preparation for the show as Gloria.

Everyone sang brilliantly, even Pogson. Olga, Umfreville's girlfriend, made a convincing and sexy Russian Prince. Jason's beautifully placed voice pinged out across the auditorium – I was expecting that – but what I wasn't expecting was his talent for comedy, which seemed, appropriately enough given his origins, to have taken a Great Leap Forward over the weekend since the General. The applause at the end of the first half nearly brought the House down.

Angus and I risked emerging from the safety of our box, and were instantly mobbed. By the time we made it the few yards to the bar we had each had a glass of champagne thrust into our hands, and during the next twenty minutes we were each given at least three more.

Max Polgar was very much to the fore in this crowd of well-wishers, as was Archie Foster. Max was the worse for several glasses of something, but was clearly enjoying himself hugely.

"Jamie, Angus, I can't say how thrilled I am. The Theatre looks quite exceptional. And this production – it is very funny and brilliantly designed. I am overwhelmed. So is Archie – aren't you, Archie?"

"Certainly. It's a triumph. And whatever teething troubles the new regime's having, when the show is this good all is forgiven. Well, it is by my lot of Venerable Old Tossers, anyway."

"And that's what counts," said Max, "eh, Jamie?"

"Yes. Quite. Asslutely. And her indoors is doing triffically, don't you think?"

"Fantastic," said Archie. "Breathtaking. How is she, by the way?"

"As you can hear, in cracking form."

"And all is well back at the ranch?"

"What was it Max just said? Few teething troubles. Nemmind."

I tried to take a slurp of champagne but missed my mouth.

"Oh shit. Best suit. Anyway, what I was saying was don't believe everything you read in the papers. Just some of it."

"Glad to hear it, Jamie. Probably shouldn't have asked. It's just that the Venerable Old Tossers and I would much rather everything in the garden was rosy. With Mr Money, I mean."

"Oh I shouldn't worry about lovely Sergei, Archie. Doing a triffic job. I've got this feeling, by the way, that there was something I was s'posed to dishcuss with you. Can't just rember, at the mo…"

At that moment I caught sight of Standish across the other side of the bar.

"JOHN!" I yelled. Max and Archie looked round to see who I was shouting at. So did most of the people in the bar. There were a few embarrassed titters.

Angus whispered: "careful, old thing. Bit squiffy. Don't let the side down." Standish looked up, and for the briefest moment a worried frown crossed his brow. It was swiftly replaced by his usual cheery grin. He made his way as quickly as he could towards me.

"Jamie! Superb, dear boy. Wonderful. The Diva's singing divinely. Which is only to be expected, of course. And the rest of the show is electric. Full marks to the new regime. Now, introduce me to your chums."

"What? Oh, I see. Yup. Well, this is Angus, you know him, and this is Max Polgar, who's the power behind our revered Chairman, and this is Archie Foster, who's the most important man in British opera bar none. Gentlemen, this is John Standish, opera buff and gynaecologist to the stars."

"Splendid," said Standish. Then, thank God, the gong rang for the end of the interval, and I was off the hook.

"'Slovely to see you all, chaps. Gussie and I've got to go back to our box. Haven't we, old thing? Via the lav, in my case."

Max and Archie excused themselves, which left me with Standish and Angus. Gussie and I were just about to walk off when Standish grabbed me by the arm.

"Jamie, I imagine I can talk freely in front of Angus here?"

"'Shlong as you do it quietly, Johnny boy."

"I've been in, you know, to all the rehearsals. I've been hiding upstairs in the Dress Circle. Presumably she ran out of the stuff on Saturday? Thank God she let you get her some more."

"Oh, quite, John. Asslutely. And thanks a million." A second gong rang.

"*Ladies and gentlemen,*" said the public address system, "*please take your seats. The performance will resume in two minutes.*"

John ignored the interruption. "But is she still planning to pack it in?"

"As far as I know, John, at the end of the run." I was bursting for the loo, and going to be in serious trouble if I didn't find one quick.

"Bloody tragic, Jamie. We'll have to see if we can't find some way of sorting out her problem."

"Easier said than done, I'm afraid. Listen, shorry, need the loo. Shee you at the party."

I practically ran into the gents, with Angus following close behind – it seemed he was in similar straits. Another gong rang. Then:

"Ladies and gentlemen please take your seats. The performance will resume in one minute."

"'Sno good, Gussie. Got to go."

"So have I, old boy."

When we were the only ones left at the urinals, Angus said: "What's all this about Lindsey?"

"SSshh." I pointed at the closed door of one of the cubicles. This caused me to miss. Drips began to dribble down the wall.

"Whoops," said Angus, and we both burst into hysterics. It began to dawn on me that we were not going to make it back in time for the start.

"Got to get a move on, Gussie."

"Shit." We both tried to concentrate. There was a flushing noise from behind the cubicle door, and we waited with bated breath to see who emerged. After an agonisingly long wait, during which we both managed to finish and zip ourselves up, an elderly gentleman appeared. I doubted he would have picked up on our brief exchange. We all three washed our hands, and the gentleman said:

"Oh dear. I think we're going to be late." He shook the water off his hands, and left the loo with as much haste as he could muster. I was just about to follow when Angus put a wet hand on my sleeve, and indicated for me to wait.

As soon as we were alone, he said: "doesn't actually matter a bugger if we miss the start. We can slip into the back of the box once you've spilled the beans. Tell me what's going on."

So for the next five minutes I filled him in on everything that had been happening – Albert's death, Lindsey's vocal problems, the pills, the DNA test result, the lot. I wondered if he was so drunk that he wouldn't take it in, but he seemed *compos mentis*.

"Fuck, Jamie. What are you going to do?"

"Tell you th'truth, Gussie, haven't the firsht idea. Wait and see, I s'pose."

"I think I need a serious word with the Deev."

"Hang fire, Gussie, there's a good chap. I really think thish one's down to me."

We snuck back into the box after squaring the usher – a lady of a considerable age who had been with the Company as long as anyone could remember, and who had a soft spot for me. They were just starting the dialogue before Lindsey and Pogson's Watch Duet. We installed ourselves, and waited for the vocal fireworks at the end of the number.

Whether Angus actually heard them, or Lindsey's *Czardas*, or anything which followed I have no idea. Within two minutes of sitting down the champagne had caught up with me, and I was sound asleep, with my head resting on the velvet ledge at the front of the box.

I was woken by Angus nudging me urgently.

"Jamie, you plonker, you've missed the whole bloody thing."

The audience was going berserk, with deafening applause and shouts of *bravo* from all over the auditorium.

"Wake up for God's sake. How the hell can you sleep through all this racket?"

"Always been able to. Shit. They seem to've enjoyed it."

"It's a Grade A hit, old thing. Fantastic. We're made."

"Triffic. Better go back and see the Deev then, eh?"

We let ourselves out of the back of the box, and managed to get backstage before anyone else. We stood at the side and waited for the cast, plus Leclerc and the production team, to finish their curtain calls.

The applause must have lasted a full ten minutes more. The stage manager kept bringing in the curtain but it had no effect. After a while he brought up the house lights, but even that made no difference. The cast had to walk through the curtain six more times to acknowledge the rapture of the audience. Eventually, by dint of bringing the curtain up one final time, then bringing it back in slowly, the applause died down, causing a new burst of whooping and clapping on stage as the cast congratulated each other. Angus and I walked on, and over the next five minutes I hugged everyone, even Leclerc and Pogson. Only Lindsey was lukewarm in her embrace, which I realised was because our lord and master Sergei Ivanevitch Rebroff, plus entourage, had found his way onto the stage, and was standing behind me patiently waiting for his turn.

While Lindsey was in dressing room number one's private shower, I went off to the evil-smelling gents backstage, where I relieved myself, then slooshed water over my face in an attempt to sober up. This made me feel a lot less groggy, and I wandered back to her dressing room ready to tackle the next big hurdle: the after-show party.

It took her a good twenty minutes to doll herself up. She looked unbelievable, in a dark green silk Valentino dress which had been lent to her for the occasion. It disguised her nascent bump beautifully. At last she was ready, and we made our way through the pass door and the stalls bar towards the foyer.

"Jamie, I'm more nervous about this bloody dinner than I was for the show." After a moment's hesitation she slipped her arm into mine. We walked up the stairs looking for all the world like a happily-married couple.

There was a crush of people on the landing, all waiting to go into the Telenorth bar for a sit-down dinner. When we were spotted climbing the stairs there was a ripple of applause for Lindsey, which grew as more people realised that she had finally arrived. We headed for the seating plan – a huge poster on a wooden board, resting precariously on a Props Department easel.

There we were on the top table – the General Administrator, accompanied by his wife the Diva, otherwise known as Lindsey Templeton, Sergei's prize. The woman he had bought with his hundred million was installed on Sergei's right. Lord Dunwich, now designated patron of the Company, was next to her. Then came Gloria Forrest, me, Tatyana and Angus, and finally Lady Dunwich, sitting on Sergei's left. I found myself wondering where Mutt and Jeff were sitting. They seemed to have disappeared for the night.

I think it was at that point that I started shaking. I reached out for the nearest tray of champagne and knocked two glasses back as quickly as the bubbles would go down. Half way through glass number three, with Lindsey giving me Class A evils from the other side of the champagne tray, I heard his voice.

"Jamie. How fantastic." Sergei was smarming over towards us. He still hadn't shaved. "And Lindsey. My God, Lindsey. All my life I have dreamed of this moment. My own opera company, with world's greatest singer in starring role. You were absolutely wonderful, radiant. Words fail me."

Lindsey blushed irritatingly, but held his gaze. There was a moment of communion between them which I found nauseating. She'd never been able to countenance the idea of me growing facial hair. Why the hell hadn't she made Sergei shave off that mess?

401

"Sergei," I heard myself saying in a loud voice. "New beard. Nice. Do you get food caught in it? Or snot?"

For a moment he had difficulty maintaining his smile, but recovered his poise almost instantaneously. "No Jamie, I am keeping it carefully trimmed. Maybe you should have glass of olive oil. Very good for lining stomach before alcohol. They are giving out olive oil at bar. Please help yourself."

"Olive oil. Gosh, thanks, Sergei. Is it, by any chance, extra virgin?"

"Of course, first cold pressing. From my own olive groves in Spain."

Lindsey, who looked as if she wanted to kill me, reached across and took my arm, then turned me round and led me away.

"Pull yourself together, Jamie. You're drunk."

"You're pregnant, but I'll be sober in the morning."

She tightened her grip, and sped me over to the bar. "Drink this," she said, and handed me a rather beautiful glass of green gloop.

I downed it in one. It tasted like mucus.

"Christ that's foul. What a bloody stupid idea."

"You're supposed to have it before you drink anything, Jamie. The problem is it's too late."

But it did seem to settle my stomach a bit. Everyone was trooping into the bar, so Lindsey manhandled me after them.

The bar looked breathtaking. From a specially-erected metal grid on the ceiling about a thousand bats were hanging upside down, their beady eyes staring at the guests. There were champagne bottles everywhere, and every nook and cranny was filled with orchids. You could probably have paid for a new production of Wagner's *Ring* with what Sergei had spent prettifying the place. People were milling around trying to find their seats. All the singers in that season's roster had been invited, as had the directors and conductors. Everyone who was anyone in international opera appeared to be there, and my God it was a glittering affair. It made Salzburg's *Cosi* party look like amateur night.

We took our seats. To my horror I realised that Gregory Knipe was taking his seat at the next table, the vast expanse of his back facing mine. He'd been put with Leclerc and Pogson.

An enormous seafood platter was placed on each table – lobsters, langoustines, crabs, and huge oysters on the half shell, all on a bed of seaweed and crushed ice – and white plates, each with a little pot of mayonnaise perched on it, were pre-set for each guest. There were enormous bowls of salad leaves, and glass oil and vinegar sets, presumably containing more of Sergei's wretched first cold pressing.

"I see we've got extra virgin on the table," I said. I was desperately trying not to slur my words. "Good show. I'm all for extra virginity."

Lady Dunwich roared with laughter – a deeply resonant smoker's laugh. Sergei appeared not to have heard. He reached for half a lobster, and gestured for us all to do likewise.

With varying degrees of success we all began to attack the creatures in front of us. The Dunwiches handled their crustaceans with practised ease, as did the Russians, but poor Gloria was having the devil of a job with a langoustine. She was trying to hoick the tiny bit of meat out of one of its claws, and there seemed to be more langoustine on her cheeks than in her mouth.

Lindsey was doing better, although I doubted that she was actually eating very much. I concentrated on my own plate, only bothering with the tails of the langoustines and lobsters to make the task easier.

There was an animated discussion between Dunwich and Sergei about Russian opera, and specifically about which of Tchaikovsky's operas was his finest. I was dimly aware that I should be contributing, but I was too busy making sure my glass was always empty whenever the waitresses came round with refills. I noticed that Dorothy Dunwich was doing the same – she was deep in conversation with Angus, and kept fluttering her eyelids at him.

"But of course we must do *Onegin* next season," said Sergei. He put a proprietorial arm around my wife's shoulders. "Tatyana would be fine role for Lindsey. She would be very great in final scene, when Onegin asks her to leave her husband." He smiled at everyone, then removed his arm and went on eating.

Lindsey caught my eye. There was a touch of defiance in her which I didn't much care for. Angus shifted slightly in his seat. It was Dunwich who broke the silence.

"Well, I think that's a terrific idea, Sergei Ivanevitch. Lindsey does an excellent line in scarlet women."

"Scarlet women means what?" said Sergei.

I gazed full into his black eyes. "Women who cheat on their husbands," I said. It came out a bit louder than I'd intended, and one or two people from the next table looked round at me.

Angus cut in quickly. "Does anyone want the last lobster claw?"

"Let's halve it," said Gloria.

She lifted the claw up with her fork and dropped it with a clatter onto her plate. More people from around the room looked up. Then she started to attack it with her claw-cracker. It pinged out from between the cracker's arms, and shot straight past Dunwich, landing on Lindsey's plate and sweeping her untouched pot of mayonnaise onto her knee. Sergei's hand disappeared towards her crotch and emerged a moment later clutching her napkin, in which were imprisoned the claw and the china pot. I wasn't sure whether he was amused or irritated.

"Gloria, you are excellent shot." He opened up the napkin, and threw the claw back to Gloria. Unfortunately Dunwich had chosen that precise moment to reach for his glass, and the claw hit the sleeve of his dinner jacket, spattering it with mayonnaise. His face went purple, whether with rage or embarrassment I couldn't tell. Lady Dunwich cackled loudly.

"Henry, you look like you're about to explode," she drawled. "Don't worry Hennikins, we'll get the suit dry-cleaned tomorrow." Dunwich grunted crossly, and handed the claw back to Gloria, who took it and gamely started attacking it again, this time with a little more circumspection.

Lindsey, on the other hand, was getting up from the table. The Valentino dress had a gob of mayonnaise right in the crotch area. She flashed me a look and said in a slightly curdled voice: "please excuse me, everyone. I'm just going to clean up. Jamie, would you please help me?"

She took my arm, and we negotiated our way between the tables, squeezing with some difficulty past Gregory Knipe's back. We made as quickly as we could for the calm of the orchid-bedecked landing. Lindsey sat on a banquette, and started to lift the mayonnaise carefully off the dark green silk of the dress. She had brought a clean knife with her for the purpose.

"Jamie, if you're going to cause a scene then we have to leave now. It will be ghastly and deeply embarrassing, but I am only staying if you pull yourself together."

"I don't really think any of this is my fault. But if you insist, I'll try my best."

"Just stop drinking. There's plenty of water on the table. If Gloria hasn't targeted it with her bloody lobster claw, that is." She got up. There was a grease mark left on the dress. "What the hell am I going to do about this? She must have done five thousand quid's worth of damage.

I did a bit of aimless wiping with my napkin.

"Get your hand off my crotch. You're as bad as each other, you and Sergei."

She seized my napkin and held it in front of the skirt, then we went back in. The room went quiet. Lindsey smiled brightly, and sailed back to our table. Left to my own devices, I had to concentrate on walking in a straight line as I tried to follow her.

The seafood platters were removed, and a pretty little redhead offered me more wine. I put my hand over my glass, and reached instead for my water, which I glugged back. Exquisite little chocolate tarts appeared, and were eventually replaced by cups of coffee and *petit fours*. Angus and Sergei began a lively discussion about Janáček, telling Lindsey how magnificent she would be in the great roles of *Jenůfa*, *Káťa Kabanová*, and Emilia Marty in *The Makropoulos Case*. She began to relax, enjoying attention of a more welcome kind.

Eventually Sergei got to his feet, and tapped his glass with his knife. The assembled company, still on tenterhooks after the excitement, came quickly to order. He had managed to remain immaculate through the whole lobster-eating debacle – aside from the ridiculous beard, that is. He cast a self-satisfied look around the room.

"Ladies and gentlemen, I am deeply happy man. Always since I was boy, music has been my life. Today, my ambition is realised. This great Company has done me honour of accepting my donation, and making me Chairman.

"I would like to pay tribute to three women, who are foundation of my life and of my happiness. I will not detain you long. You have given or seen a fabulous performance, and you do not want me boring pants off you." He looked very pleased with his idiomatic use of English, and there were some polite titters around the room.

"The first of these women is my mother – great singer with most beautiful voice, who sadly never performed in professional opera. But she sang to me, her little Sergei, always arias from great Russian operas of Moussorgsky and Tchaikovsky. She died when I was twelve years old, and hole in my heart only now begins to be filled with happiness. I dedicate my work and work of Company to her beloved memory. For her we will make greatest Opera Company in world."

Applause rang out around the room for his eloquent tribute to the first of his three women. Who the bloody hell were the other two going to be?

"But I am sad today because my wife Nadezhda cannot come from Russia. I love her deeply, and I wish to pay tribute also to her. She has baby next month," (that was a new one) "and she must not travel. After today I return to her, and I hope we come together soon to London, also with my other children Aleksandr and Mikhail."

I glanced at Lindsey. She was looking up at him with her listening-to-speeches smile on her face, and it was hard to tell what she was thinking.

"But I am today most happy because of my third woman. Despite terrible unhappiness of her father's recent death, Lindsey Templeton is here tonight, and has sung for us all. She is greatest diva of modern world."

He was interrupted by whoops of delight and the odd wolf-whistle. The cheers went on for at least half a minute. He looked down at her, and she looked down at the table, clearly embarrassed. I was dreading what he was about to say and I had a feeling she was dreading it too.

"It is for Lindsey that I have decided to bring my money to England and to Opera London. She has extraordinary talent as singer, and as woman. And she has great good fortune to be married to my new General Administrator, Jamie Barlow."

To my horror he walked round the table towards me and put his hand on my shoulder. "Lindsey too has baby coming. She and Jamie will soon have new brother or sister to go with lovely little Carly."

I don't know why it was this that lit the blue touch paper. All I know is that I suddenly heard myself shouting:

"Why don't you just fuck off out of all of our lives, you smug Russian arsehole?"

And I stood up, knocking my chair over, collected a handful of his shirt and tie in my left fist, and thumped his nose with my right. It hurt like buggery, but to my overwhelming satisfaction he yelped and staggered backwards, falling into the next door table and knocking coffee and *petit fours* all over Gregory Knipe's caftan.

All hell broke loose. From nowhere, Mutt and Jeff materialised. Mutt grabbed my shoulders, and manhandled me painfully back into my seat, while Jeff threw himself headlong over Sergei's prostrate body. The table collapsed noisily under his weight, and Knipe, Leclerc and Pogson leapt out of the way, as did the other diners at that table. Gloria was screaming, and Angus was on his feet trying to comfort her.

Then, still held down in my chair by Mutt, I caught sight of Lindsey. She hadn't moved from her seat, and was white as a sheet. And it was at that moment that I was absolutely certain that I'd screwed everything up for ever.

406

But she stood up, and said in a very clear and calm voice: "Mr Lebedev, please release my husband. He will not attack Sergei again." Then she announced to the room: "Jamie and I are going home. I am sorry everyone for the upset. Thank you for dinner".

Sergei had managed to extricate himself from Jeff's untidy embrace, and was on his feet. He was holding his nose, which to my joy looked as if I might have broken it.

"Lindsey, your idiot husband makes pathetic attempt to hurt me. Now you stay here with me. Tatyana, order car for Jamie."

"No, Sergei," said Lindsey. "I will take him home. Please forgive him for what he has done. We are leaving."

And she took me by the arm and walked me, in as dignified a way as she could manage, to the door. Gregory and Angela Knipe were outside on the landing. She was cleaning his caftan and trying to repair his shattered dignity. As I passed them, he said:

"Oh bravo James, bravo. About bloody time someone did that to him. Almost knocked the bugger senseless. You'll be handing in your resignation tomorrow, I assume?"

"Um, dunno. 'Spose so."

"Oh, I think you will. Welcome to the scrap heap."

Lindsey was extraordinary. Not only did she not shout at me, she got hold of the fireman from backstage, and persuaded him to let her have the first aid kit, with which she bandaged up my throbbing hand. Then she led me outside to the road.

There was a car waiting for us, and its driver leapt out of his seat as soon as he saw us, to open the back door and usher us in. Lindsey was polite but firm:

"Thank you, Vassily, but we will not be needing Mr Rebroff's car tonight."

She walked me a little way up the street and hailed an empty taxi which was on its way towards Victoria.

"Queens Park, please."

We sat down in the back, and she put her arm round me. Then, to my absolute astonishment, she began to laugh.

"I've got to hand it to you, Jamie. You made him look a complete plonker, didn't you?"

"Er, well, I suppose so. I'm sorry, darling, I don't know what came over me. Aren't you angry?"

It wasn't until we'd arrived home and let ourselves into the house that she replied.

"To my amazement, Jamie, I'm not angry at all, just relieved. Let's go to bed."

And she draped her arms around my shoulders, and kissed me as passionately as I could ever remember being kissed in my life.

After a while I pulled gently away from her. "Are you coming back to me then? If so, there's a few things I ought to tell you."

"There's just about nothing I don't know already, Jamie."

"Did he tell you about Saskia?"

"Yes."

"And you don't mind?"

"I was terribly hurt, Jamie. But then I thought, why the hell shouldn't you? I started it, after all."

"Well yes, Linds, but…"

"Jamie, it's me who should be saying sorry to you. You are a wonderful man – far better than I deserve. Now take me to bed, before I go mad."

So I took her right hand with my left, which was the only one still functioning, and led her upstairs.

POSTLUDE

44

The alarm clock is just as hideous whether it rings in London, Salzburg or Rutland. Especially when it goes off two and a half hours after you've finally climbed into bed, and the previous night has been one you'll remember for the rest of your life.

It's seven o'clock on Monday March the fifth, and John Albert Barlow was born five hours ago. He and Lindsey are, I sincerely hope, sound asleep in our bedroom. I've been banished across the corridor so they can both get some sorely-needed rest.

And it's my job to tell Carly she has a brand new baby brother, before taking her off to school. He was in such a hurry to get out that no-one had time to wake his sister, who went to bed at nine in blissful ignorance of what was about to happen, and slept through the whole thing.

I scarcely had time even to alert Evie. She arrived just as Lindsey was getting the urge to push, and was the only trained medical person there – the midwife from Stamford had problems on the A606, which was still closed for weekend repairs. She had to drive all the way round through Cottesmore, and by the time she made it Lindsey's forty minute labour was over, and Auntie Evie had delivered her first baby for thirty years.

Not a trace of Slav in his squashed little features, I'm delighted to report. I did have a bit of a wobble five minutes before he emerged. I mean how could I be *sure* Standish was right about the test? But there he was, with a distinct look of yours truly, if Evie the biased temporary midwife was to be believed.

It was Lindsey who came up with the name. We both agreed that no matter how sainted the memory of her wonderful Dad, we couldn't call a twenty-first century kid Albert. Not as his first name, anyway. So we've named him after John Standish, now fully rehabilitated as a friend of the family. He's been appointed to the Opera London Board, too. I'd like to be a fly on the wall at one of their meetings.

As for my wife the ex-Diva, Grace was right all along. What Lindsey needed was for me to assert myself with that Russian pillock. So what if I lost my job in the process? And there was Archie Foster, waiting in the wings to take over as boss. The Press, finally released from their Sergei-imposed silence (I still don't know how he did it), shouted and screamed a bit. But then Archie wrote an article in the *Statesman* swearing he would stand up to the Chairman, and not allow him to take over all aspects of the running of the Company. After that the hullabaloo died down pretty quickly. Archie is by all accounts shaping up rather well – he and Angus have just announced the details of the new season, and they've managed to keep the Russian content down to one opera – Sergei's beloved *Boris Godunov* – and a couple of guest appearances by great Russian singers. Things have been made substantially easier for them by Yvonne Umfreville's abrupt departure for Paris, where Damien de la Chapelle has taken her on as Head of Music at the Châtelet, under instructions from his new Music Director, Olivier Leclerc.

Archie's taken Grace as his PA. And so far he's making a lovely job of keeping the Arts Council on board, and holding at bay the threat of Opera London being trashed by the Government, and its entire annual grant bring given to the 2012 Olympics.

I asked John Standish what was in his magic medicine. So did Lindsey. In fact when he came to Stockencote for the weekend three months ago, we pushed him so hard he nearly got in the car and left, no matter that he was the worse for two bottles of Burgundy. In the end, he grudgingly told us: "there's nothing in them you can't get hold of in any decent pharmacy. Or at any rate on any street corner. A bit of up to get you going, and a bit of down to calm your nerves. Their undoubted efficacy is principally based on the placebo effect."

Whatever the contents, they continued to work for Lindsey. She triumphed in all the *Fledermaus* performances, which were received with universal rapture by everyone except Janet Hopkirk. This bitter woman carped not only at the placing of the interval in the middle of Orlofsky's party, but also at the whole idea of Frosch the gaoler becoming Frau Osch, a Margaret Thatcher clone. But Hopkirk's splendid isolation caused her criticisms to be ignored, and in any case even she couldn't manage to find fault with my wife's god-like singing.

411

Lindsey's withdrawal from the lyric stage, on the other hand, was big news. It even made the front page of one of the broadsheets. To our immense satisfaction, her sudden departure was blamed on the behaviour of the Press, and caused yet another debate on the issue of privacy for celebs. But the fuss soon died down, and the new flavour of the month at Opera London is none other than Evangeline Bolls, much to the delight of Graham Butterfield. Sergei's been persuaded that she is, if not a match for Lindsey, certainly a reasonable substitute, and he solved her work permit problems with one phone call.

Unsurprisingly, given how much money was at stake, Lindsey's Swiss agent went berserk and threatened legal action, as did Ton de Wit in Amsterdam. However, a lengthy and carefully-worded medical assessment from John Standish, explaining the psychological consequences of her stressful pregnancy, put paid to that nonsense.

Whether she will ever sing again is a matter for regular late-night discussion at Stockencote. Evie, for whom one of the barns is being converted into a bungalow, often comes over for dinner, and has very firm views on the subject. She says Lindsey's had a wonderful career, but now she's happier than Evie's ever seen her, and in any case Albert was perfectly clear on the subject, so there's no debate. Being a farmer's wife suits her a whole lot better than gallivanting madly round the world, Evie says, so why go back to it?

Lindsey mostly agrees with her, although sometimes she hankers after the sheer physical excitement of singing with a great orchestra. Also, it has to be said, chewing the fat with the other stay-at-home mothers in the school car park occasionally gets her down. But the joy of her rediscovered relationship with an ecstatic Carly makes up for everything. Newly-enrolled in the junior department of Oakham School, our daughter is growing up fast, although as I write she's still young enough to think Cedric the pony is the most important thing in her life. To date she hasn't wet the bed again, thank God. It appears to be a thing of the past, along with crowded tube trains, airport terminals and Emma Anstruther-Fawcett.

But none of us has much time to dwell on our old lives. Lindsey's taken on the farm's paperwork, as well as having the house and garden to run. How she's going to cope with a young baby is anyone's guess.

And I'm busy as well – the amount of work involved in farming a huge estate like Stockencote has been one of the bigger revelations of my post-opera life. I did suggest that I should go to agricultural college, but

Gordon pooh-poohed the idea, saying he could teach me everything I needed to know. He promised Albert that once he'd got me he wouldn't let me go, or so he says. So the boss spends the days being told what to do by his employee. Reminds me of Grace, who's probably the only thing about Opera London that I actually miss. News of her quiet marriage at Christmas to her Tenerife lover caused me a brief pang of regret.

As for the evenings – I spend them with my head buried in books, or searching the Internet to see what new kit I can buy. Gordon's not up to speed on state-of-the-art agricultural machinery. I think he would use a horse-drawn plough given half a chance. Albert's will has left him a wealthy man, but you'd never know it.

In fact the old man's done right by us all, which is just as well, as Sergei wrought his revenge on Lindsey and me by handing out a staggeringly ungenerous redundancy package. Angus suggested, during a drunken weekend visit, that I take the bastard to an industrial tribunal, but neither Lindsey nor I has the stomach for another fight.

Mum and Dad haven't made much fuss about being stuck in London on their own. They've visited a couple of times, and Mum says it's good for them to have to entertain themselves, now she doesn't have little Charlotte to look after. They're thinking of a round-the-world cruise to mark their retirement from being full-time grandparents.

Mind you, now little Johnny's actually arrived, I'm expecting Mum to turn up with two weeks' change of underwear and lots of invaluable advice. When Carly was born she took up practically permanent residence, and unless I'm much mistaken she'll be even more enthusiastic about a grandson. Lindsey'll be tearing her hair out.

Lindsey. My gorgeous, wonderful, saintly wife. Well, she's saintly now, and I reckon there's a sporting chance we might both go on being pretty saintly till death us do part. No more private jets or nights at the Savoy. And no more sex with exciting foreigners, either. But there'll be some bloody good and extremely well-hung ribs of beef on the Stockencote dining table for Sunday lunch, and anyway who wants sex with anyone else when you've got the most beautiful woman in the world?

Do we deserve happiness? That's a hard one. But I'm certain we're a bloody sight more likely to get it when we're not leaping on and off Freshair flight 232 to Salzburg every other morning.

"Carly, it's five past seven. Time to get up."

"Oh, Daddy…"

"You'll want to get out of bed, I promise. I've got some exciting news."

"What?"

"You've got a new baby brother."

"What? Why didn't you wake me?"

"There wasn't time, darling. And afterwards Mummy and little Johnny – that's his name – were knackered and needed to be left to sleep it off."

"Can I go and see him now?"

"As long as you're very quiet."

So I let Carly into our room as quietly as I can, and she peeks round the door at the tiny baby in his tiny crib.

"Wow," she whispers. "He's so *small*."

And that's enough to wake Lindsey, who's completely dishevelled, and not at all like one of those pictures of a new Mum, with white linen everywhere, and a spotless, happy baby at her breast. But that doesn't stop her being the most gorgeous sight you could wish to see.

"Carly darling, come and say hello to Johnny."

Carly tiptoes across to the bed, and looks down in puzzlement.

"Eeeuuuu. He's all wrinkled."

"You were like that when you were four hours old," I say.

"Anyway, I don't *care* if he looks like a prune. I'm going to look after him while you get well, Mummy."

"Thank you sweetheart, but I'm not ill, just a bit tired. I'll be fine with him. And you need to go to school."

"Oh, *Mummy!*"

"Yes, go on, off you go and get dressed. He'll still be here when you get back."

So Carly stumps off to her room, and I shave and dress as quickly as I can. We both arrive downstairs at the same time.

"Come on darling, you're going to be late for school."

"What about my breakfast?"

"You've just about got time for a bit of toast."

"Daddy, you're *mean*. Mrs Armitage won't mind if I'm a bit late today. She'll be all excited about my new brother."

"Well, I suppose you've got a point. What do you want then?"

"Bacon and egg, please, Daddy."

414

THE END

Printed in Great Britain
by Amazon